MEGAN HART

Tempted

Spice

Spice

TEMPTED

ISBN-13: 978-0-7394-9499-8

Copyright © 2008 by Megan Hart.

Printed in U.S.A.

To those who've touched my life and made me who
I am today, I say this: A different person could have told
this story, but only the woman I am because of knowing you
could have written this book.

Chapter 01

*L*ight and shadow painted him. On little cat feet, like the fog, I crept toward the bed. Tug-tugging, I slid the covers off to reveal his body.

I liked to watch him sleep, despite the way it sometimes made me want to pinch myself to prove I wasn't dreaming. That this was my husband, my house, my life. Our perfect life. That there were good things to be had in the world, and I had them.

James stirred without waking. I crept closer to stand over him. The sight of him, all long, muscled limbs and smooth, sun-burnished skin, curled my fingers in anticipation of touching him. I held off, not wanting to wake him. I wanted to watch him for a while.

Awake, James was rarely still. Only dreaming did he loosen, soften, melt. If it was harder to believe he belonged to me when he was sleeping, it was also easier to remember how much I loved him.

Oh, I played a good game of confidence. I wore the ring and answered to the name Mrs. James Kinney. I even had the driver's license and credit cards to prove I had the right to the name. Most of the time, our marriage was so matter-of-fact I couldn't have disbelieved it if I'd wanted to, not when it came time to do the laundry and buy groceries, or clean the toilets, when I packed his lunches or folded his socks before putting them away. Then our marriage was solid and substantial. Granite. But sometimes, like when I watched him sleeping, the rock turned out to be limestone, easily dissolved by the slow-dripping water of my doubts.

Sunshine filtered through the tree outside our window and dappled him in all the spots I wanted to kiss. The twin dark circles of his nipples, the ridges of his ribs made sharper as he flung a hand over his head, the soft patch of hair furring his belly and meshing with the thatch between his legs. Everything about him was long and lean. Hidden strength. James looked thin, sometimes even breakable, but underneath he was all muscle. He had large, callus-fingered hands, used to working but perfectly suited for playing, too.

I was more interested in the playing as I bent over him to blow a puff of breath across his lips. Fast as sin, he grabbed me. He could pin both my wrists with one hand, and he did, pulling me onto the bed and rolling on top of me. James settled between my thighs, the only thing between us the thin fabric of my summer-weight night-gown. He was already getting hard.

"What were you doing?"

"Watching you sleep."

James pushed my hands above my head, stretching me.

then that's what makes the pleasure s

s free hand inched up the hem of my

und my bare thigh.

fingertips grazed the curls between my legs as he spoke. "Why were you watching me sleep?"

"Because I like to," I told him just before his questing fingers made me inhale sharply.

"Do I want to know why you like to watch me sleep?" His grin tipped the corners of his mouth. Smug. His fingertip settled against me, but he didn't move it yet. "Anne?"

I laughed. "No. Probably not."

"I didn't think so."

He lowered his mouth to mine but didn't kiss me. I craned my neck, seeking to meet his lips, but James kept them a breath apart. His finger began the slow circling he knew well would drive me crazy. I felt heat and hardness on my hip, but with my hands still held fast in his grip, I could only wiggle in protest.

"Tell me what you want me to do to you."

"Kiss me."

James had eyes of summer-sky blue, ringed with deep navy. The contrast could be startling. The dark fringe of his lashes swept down as his eyes narrowed. He licked his lips.

"Where?"

"Everywhere…." My reply trailed off into a sigh and then a startled gasp when he stroked me again.

"Here?"

"Yes."

"Say it."

I wouldn't, not at first, though I knew sooner or late ne'd have me doing what he wanted. He always did. It helped that I usually wanted what he wanted me to want. We were well matched in that way.

James bit down into the sensitive spot where my neck met my shoulder. "Say it."

Instead, I writhed under his touch. His finger dipped inside me, then out, swirling gently when I wanted him to press harder. Teasing me.

"Anne," James said seriously. "Tell me you want me to lick your cunt."

I used to hate that word until I learned its power. It's what men call women who have bested them. It's what women call each other when we want to wound. Bitch has become something of a badge of pride, but *cunt* still sounds dirty and harsh, and it always will.

Unless we take it back.

I said what he wanted me to say. My voice was hoarse but not weak. I looked into my husband's eyes, gone dark with lust. "I want you to put your face between my legs and make me come."

For one moment, he didn't move. Against my hip, his heat and hardness shifted and grew. I saw the pulse beat in his throat. Then he blinked slowly, and the smug smile spread across his mouth. "I love it when you say that."

"I love it when you do it," I murmured.

Then there was no more talking, because he moved down my body and lifted my nightgown to put his mouth exactly where I told him I wanted it. He licked me for a long time, until I shuddered and cried out, and then he slid up again to fill me and fucked me until we both came with shouts that sounded like prayers.

The telephone's jangling interrupted the postcoital laziness to which we'd succumbed. The Sunday edition of the *Sandusky Register,* spread out on the bed, crinkled and rustled as James leaned over me to grab the phone from its cradle. I took the chance to lick his skin as he did, sneaking a nibble that made him jump and laugh as he answered.

"This better be good," he said into the phone.

A pause. I gave him a curious look over the lifestyles section. He was grinning.

"You son of a bitch!" James settled back against the headboard, his naked knees pulled up. "What are you doing? Where the hell are you?"

I tried catching his eye but the conversation had immersed him. James is an intense butterfly, flitting from focus to focus and giving each his undivided attention. It's flattering when it's you. Not so charming when it isn't.

"You lucky son of a bitch." James sounded almost envious, and my curiosity was piqued even more. Generally, James was the object of admiration among his peers, the one with the newest toys. "I thought you were in Singapore."

I knew, then, who had disrupted our Sunday afternoon lassitude. It had to be Alex Kennedy. I looked back to my paper, listening while James talked. There wasn't anything particularly interesting in the newspaper. I didn't really care about the latest summer fashion or what cars were trendy this year. I cared even less about burglaries and politics, however, so I scanned the columns of text and discovered I'd been ahead of my time in painting my bedroom pale melon the year before. Apparently it was the season's hot new color.

Listening to only one side of a conversation is like putting together a puzzle without looking at the picture on the box. I listened to James talking to his best friend from junior high school with only the barest comprehension and frame of reference to help me assemble the pieces. I knew my husband as well and intimately as any one person can know another, but I didn't know Alex at all.

"Yeah, yeah. Of course you did. You always do."

The keen admiration was back, along with an eagerness new to me. I glanced at James. His face was alight with glee and something else. Something almost poignant. Despite having what could be a somewhat narrow focus on his own priorities, James was unafraid to be happy for someone else's fortune. He was, however, rarely impressed. Or intimidated. Now he looked a bit of both, and I forgot about the vapidity of pale melon altogether to listen to him speak.

"Ah, get out, man, you'd rule the fucking world if you wanted."

I blinked. The sincere, almost puppyish tone was as new to me as the look on his face. This was startling. A bit disturbing. It was the way a boy speaks to a woman he's convinced he loves, even though he knows she'll never give him a second look.

"Yeah, same here." Laughter, low and somewhat secret, crept out of him. Not his usual guffaw. "Fucking-A man, that's great. I'm glad to hear it."

Another pause while he listened. I watched him rub the curving white scar just above his heart, his fingers tracing the line of it, over and over, absently. I'd seen him do that before, rubbing that scar like a talisman when he was tired or upset or excited. Sometimes it was brief, a passing touch like he was flicking a crumb from his shirt. Other times, like this, the stroke-stroke of his fingers took on an almost hypnotic pace. I could be mesmerized watching James run his fingers along that scar, which sometimes looks like a half-moon, or a bite, or a frown or a rainbow.

James's brow creased. "No. Really? What were they thinking? That sucks, Alex. Really fucking sucks. Fuck, man, I'm sorry."

From elation to sorrow in half a second. This too was unusual from my husband, who might move easily from focus to focus but always managed to maintain his emotional stability. His syntax had changed during his conversation, reverting a little. I'm no prude about bad language, but he was saying *fuck* an awful lot.

In the next instant his face brightened. He sat up, bent knees going straight. The sunshine of his smile burst from behind the storm clouds of a moment before.

"Yeah? Right on! Fucking-A! You got it, man! That's fan-fucking-tastic!"

At this I could no longer hide my expression of surprise, but James didn't notice. He was bouncing a little, shaking the bed so the papers rattled and the sadly neglected classifieds fluttered to the floor.

"When? Great! That's…yeah, yeah…of course. It'll be fine. It'll be great. Of course I'm sure!" His glance flicked toward me, but I was certain he didn't actually see me. His mind was too taken up with whatever was happening in Singapore. "Can't wait! Yeah. Just let me know. Bye, man. See you."

With that, he thumbed the disconnect button and settled back against the headboard with a grin so broad and vibrant it looked a bit maniacal. I waited for him to speak, to share with me the piece of brilliant news that had so excited him. I waited quite a bit longer than I expected to.

Just as I was about to ask, James turned to me. He kissed me hard, his fingers tangling in my hair. His mouth bruised mine a little, and I winced.

"Guess what?" He answered before I had time to reply. "Alex's company just got bought out by a much larger corporation. He's like a fucking millionaire now."

What I knew of Alex Kennedy could fit on one side of a sheet of notebook paper. I knew he worked overseas in the Asian market and had since before I'd met James. He'd been unable to attend our wedding but had sent an elegant gift that must have been exorbitantly expensive. I knew he'd been James's best friend since the eighth grade, and that they'd had a falling-out when they were both twenty-one. I'd always had the feeling the rift had never fully been repaired, but then, men's relationships are so different from women's. If James barely spoke to his friend, that didn't mean they hadn't forgiven each other for whatever it was that had driven them apart.

"Wow. Really? A millionaire?"

James shrugged, fingers tightening again in my hair

before he sat back against the headboard. "The guy's a fucking genius, Anne. You don't even know."

I didn't know. "That's good news, then. For him."

He frowned, running a hand through dark hair already tipped blond, though the summer had barely begun. "Yeah, but the bastards who bought him out have decided they don't want him part of the company any longer. He's out of a job."

"Does a millionaire need to work?"

James gave me a look that said I clearly didn't get it. "Just because you don't have to do something doesn't mean you don't want to. Anyway, Alex is done with Singapore. He's coming home."

His voice trailed off at the last, sounding almost wistful for the barest second before he looked at me with another grin. "I invited him for a visit. He said he'll probably stay for a few weeks while he puts together his next business."

"A few weeks? Here?" I didn't mean to sound unwelcoming, but...

"Yeah." James's grin was small and secret, for himself. "It'll be great. You'll love Alex, babe. I know you will."

He looked at me and was, for an instant, a man I didn't know. He reached for my hand, linking our fingers before he took them to his lips and kissed the back of my hand. His mouth caressed my skin, and he looked up at me over the top of his kiss, his blue eyes dark with excitement.

But not for me.

I was Evelyn and Frank Kinney's only daughter-in-law. Though my reception into the family had been chilly when

James and I were dating and through our engagement, once I became a Kinney, I was treated like a Kinney. Evelyn and Frank had taken me into the bosom of the Kinney clan, and like quicksand, once I was so enfolded there was little I could do to escape.

We all got along well enough, for the most part. James's sisters Margaret and Molly were several years older than us, both married with children. I didn't have much in common with them aside from our gender, and though they were careful to include me in every "girls' night" party they had with their mother, we weren't close. It didn't seem to matter.

Typically, James didn't notice the superficiality of my relationship with his mother and sisters, and that was fine with me. It was all fine with me, that veneer. The shiny reflection that kept anyone from seeing what was underneath, the eddies and currents and depths of the truth. It was, after all, what I was used to.

It wouldn't have been so bad, except that Mrs. Kinney had…expectations.

Where we were going. What we were doing. How we were doing it and how much it cost. She wanted to know it all and was not contented with the knowing. She always had to know more.

It took me a few months of frigid phone calls to figure out that if James wasn't going to divulge the details, I would have to. Since she was the one who'd raised him to believe the world revolved around him, I thought she'd have figured out it was her own fault he didn't realize it revolved around her. James didn't seem to mind displeasing his mother, but I did. James shrugged off his mother's frequent fits of martyrdom, but I couldn't stand the forced silences or the thinly veiled comments about respect or the comparisons to Molly and Margaret, who didn't sneeze without holding out the tissue for Mrs. Kinney to see the color of the snot. James didn't care, but I did, so meeting Mrs. Kinney's expectations became one more peace for me to keep.

"I wish your mother would stop asking me when I'm going to give 'the gang' someone new to play with." I said this in a perfectly calm voice that could have shattered glass.

James glanced at me before fixing his attention back at the road, where late spring rain had made the roads slick. "When did she say that?"

Of course he hadn't noticed. James had long ago perfected the art of tuning out his mother. She talked, he nodded. She was satisfied. He was oblivious.

"When *doesn't* she say it?" I crossed my arms over my chest, staring ahead through the rivulets of water turning the windshield into a piece of abstract art.

He was silent as we drove, an admirable talent of his. Knowing when to be silent. It was something his mother could have learned, I thought vehemently. Tears pricked the back of my throat, but I swallowed them down.

"She doesn't mean anything by it," he said finally as he pulled into our drive. The wind had gotten stronger as we neared the lake, and the pine trees in our yard whipped angry branches.

"She does mean something by it, that's the problem. She knows exactly what she's saying and she plays it off with that little simpering laugh, like she's making a joke, but she's not."

"Anne…" James sighed and turned to me as he keyed off the ignition. The headlights went dark and I blinked, eyes adjusting. The patter of rain on the roof seemed much louder with darkness surrounding it. "Don't get so upset."

I turned in my seat to face him. "She always asks, James. Every time we're together. It's getting a little old, that's all."

His hand caressed my shoulder and tugged down the length of my braid. "She wants us to have kids—what's wrong with that?"

I said nothing. James took his hand back. I could see him now, a faint silhouette, the flash of his eyes in the hint of light from across the water. Cedar Point Amusement Park still glimmered despite the rain and the line of cars streaming off the causeway.

"Chill, Anne. Don't make such a big deal—"

I cut him off by opening my door. The cold rain felt good on my heated cheeks. I tipped my face to the sky, closing my eyes, pretending the wetness on my cheeks was only rain. James got out of the car. His heat embraced me before his arm went around my shoulder.

"Come inside. You're getting soaked."

I let him lead me inside, but I didn't talk to him. I went straight to our bathroom and turned on the hot water of the shower. I left my clothes in a pile and when the room had filled with steam I stepped into the tub and beneath the water that substituted for the rain outside.

That's where he found me, my head bent to let the hot water stream over my neck and back, working on the tension. I'd untied the braid, and my hair hung down over my breasts in kinked strands.

My eyes were closed, but the brief chill as he opened the glass door told me he was there seconds before I felt his arms around me. James held me against his chest. It took seconds for his skin to heat beneath the water. I pressed my face to his skin, hot and wet, and let him hold me.

We said nothing for a while as the shower caressed us both. His fingers traced my spine, up and down, the way he sometimes traced his scar. Water pooled in the space between my cheek and his chest, burning my eye. I had to move away to let it drain.

"Hey." James waited until I'd looked up. "Don't be upset. I can't stand it when you get so upset."

I wanted to explain to him that being upset once in a while wasn't such a bad thing, but I didn't. That a smile could be as painful as a scream. "She makes me so angry."

"I know."

His hand stroked my hair. He didn't know, not really. I'm not sure a man can ever understand the complicated matter of feminine relationships. He didn't want to understand it. James preferred the surface, too.

"She never asks you." I tilted my face to look at him. Water splashed, making me blink.

"That's because she knows I won't have an answer." He traced my eyebrow with one fingertip. "She knows you're the one in charge."

"Why am I the one in charge?" I demanded, but I already knew the answer.

It was easy for him, being blameless. "Because you're so good at it."

I frowned and pushed away from him to reach for the shampoo. "I just wish she'd lay off."

"So tell her."

I sighed and turned. "Yeah. Right. That goes over so well with your mother, James. She's so open to suggestion."

He shrugged and held out his hand for a handful of shampoo, too. "So she'll get a little pissy."

What I wanted was him to be the one to tell his mother to back off, but I knew that wouldn't happen. He, the son who could do no wrong, didn't care if he made his parents angry. It wasn't his issue. So, impotent and knowing it was my own fault, I swallowed my anger and concentrated on washing my hair. "We're going to run out of hot water."

The stream was already becoming tepid. We washed quickly, sharing the body sponge and the shower gel, our fingers tickling and doing more than just cleaning. James reached to pull the lever, shutting off the water, and I grabbed two thick towels from the stack in the closet next to the shower. I handed him one, but before I could use my own, he'd grabbed my wrist and tugged me toward him.

"C'mere, baby. Don't be upset."

It was hard to stay mad at him. James might be perfectly content in the knowledge he could do no wrong, but that allowed him to be all the more generous with his affections. He dried me carefully, squeezing the extra wetness from the length of my hair and patting my body. His towel-covered hands stroked my back, my sides, behind my knees. Between my legs. On his knees in front of me, he lifted each foot and dried it. When he set the towel aside, my heart was already thumping faster. I expected my skin, already flushed from the shower's heat, to give off steam of its own. James put his hands on my hips and drew me gently closer.

When he kissed the small patch of curls between my thighs, I stuttered a sigh. He pulled me still closer, hands drifting around to cup my buttocks and hold me in place while his tongue crept out to flick my clitoris. One, two light licks and I bit my lip against a louder groan.

I looked down at his dark head. His strong thighs, covered with coarse dark hair, bunched with muscle as he knelt. The thick mass of hair surrounding his thickening penis was in stark contrast to the smooth hairlessness of his ass and chest, only the slightest hint of hair on his lower belly. He leaned in again to kiss me tenderly. His tongue stroked, lips caressed, breath tantalized.

Any woman who doesn't feel the power she wields when a man kneels in front of her to worship her pussy must be lying to herself. I put my hand on the back of James's head. His mouth worked my flesh with eager finesse, urging me to rock my hips forward. Tension coiled low in my belly. His hands moved on my ass, drawing circles I echoed in the shift of my pelvis.

When my thighs started to shake, he used his hands to move me one half turn, until I could lean against the edge of the claw-foot tub. The cold metal should have sizzled when my flesh met it. The curved lip bit with slight discomfort into my rear, but as James, still kneeling, spread my legs wider and dove into my pussy with his mouth and fingers, I didn't care about anything else.

He moaned under his breath when he slid a finger inside me. I groaned when he added a second. James was a lover with a slow hand, just like the song. An easy touch.

I hadn't always known how to respond to him. His slow and easy caress failed me in the beginning. I hadn't expected anything else. I'd gone to bed with James because we'd been dating for a couple months and because he expected it, and because I didn't want to disappoint him. I didn't go to bed with him because I thought he could make me come.

Now he licked me slowly as he moved inside me, fingers curved just slightly to stroke the spongy bump of my G-spot. I gripped the bathtub, my back arched, thighs spread wide. In pain. Not caring. Later my fingers would be stiff and aching from holding on so tight, and my ass would be bisected with a red indentation from the tub's metal lip, but now, with James between my legs, the pleasure overtook everything else.

The first time we went to bed together, he didn't ask me if I'd come. Nor the second, not the third. Two months after we started, this time in the bed of a hotel room we'd taken for the weekend without telling anyone where we were going, he paused in kissing me to put his hand over my center.

"What do you want me to do?" His question was spoken low, but matter-of-factly, without boasting.

I'd been with boys who assumed a few moments of fingering were enough to send me into ecstasy. Going to bed with them had meant nothing, left no effect on me. Faking pleasure had become the shiny surface of sex with them, and I preferred it that way. It made it easier to find ways to break up with them by making them think it had been their idea all along.

James asked sincerely, clearly understanding that what he'd been doing so far didn't work for me, though I'd never said so. He stroked my clit and labia gently, tickling. He looked down into my eyes.

"What do I do to make you come?"

I could have smiled and cooed, told him he was perfect in bed, the best lover I'd ever had. I could have lied to him, and a month later I'd have found a way to make him believe he didn't want to see me any longer. I think I even meant to. I've never been sure why I didn't, why looking up into James's distinctive eyes made me say instead, "I don't know."

It was also a lie, but a more honest dishonesty than telling him he was doing everything right would have been. I'd opened my mouth to his kiss, but James didn't kiss me. He looked thoughtful, his hand moving in slow circles over my thighs and belly, dipping down every so often to caress my clitoris.

"I love you, Anne," he said then. It was the first time he'd ever said it, though he was not the first boy to ever tell me. "I want to make you happy. Let me."

I wasn't convinced I could do any such thing, but I smiled. He smiled. He bent to kiss me, his lips whisper-soft on mine. His hand moved, slow and easy.

James had spent an hour licking and kissing and stroking. I hadn't resisted or protested, content to let him do what he wanted. Until, at last, unable to resist, my body had surprised me and pleasure overtook everything else.

I wept the first time he made me come. Not in sorrow. With utter release. Relief. James had given me an orgasm, but I hadn't lost myself in him. I still knew who I was. I could say I loved him and mean it, and it didn't consume me. I didn't have to be afraid of drowning in him.

Now James shifted in front of me, his mouth leaving my flesh for a moment. The respite made me gasp and moan, the pleasure made more intense when he returned his tongue to me. His fingers stretched me. I wanted more. His hand closed around his cock and pumped it.

"I can feel how close you are." His voice was hoarse and a bit muffled against me. "I want you to come."

I could have, with a moment or two more of him licking me, but I was greedy. "I want you inside me."

"Stand up. Turn around."

I did. It had taken me a while to learn how to respond to James, but since then he'd learned more about me, too. His hands grabbed my hips as I gripped the side of the tub. I bent forward, offering myself to him.

James slid inside me all the way. A cry leaked from my throat. He moved, thrusting with slow and easy precision. My cunt felt swollen, embracing his erection, taking him all the way into my body. Sparks of pleasure radiated from my clitoris and ran up and down my belly and thighs, down to my toes curling in the bathroom rug.

My orgasm hovered, waiting for just the right moment to crash over me. I held my breath. I pushed back against him, and the wet slap of my ass against his belly made me groan. My hair hung down on either side of my face. I closed my eyes against the distracting sight of the spider that had committed hara-kiri on the bottom of the tub.

James's hands clutched my hips harder. His fingertips pushed the solidness of bone. His thumbs dimpled soft flesh. His cock filled me. I slid a hand down to roll a finger against my swollen clit and couldn't stop the low moans from sputtering out of me.

The phone rang.

My eyes flew open and our rhythm faltered momentarily. His penis banged the rim of my womb with a sudden pain that made me inhale sharply before we recovered. The phone rang again, a jangling distraction that had undone my concentration.

"Almost there, baby," James muttered, regaining the pace.

Another ring. I tensed but James brought me back to him with a hand on my shoulder. His fingers gripped and tugged, close to my throat. They pressed the beat of my pulse. His other hand slid in front of me to replace mine, and he rubbed my clit without mercy. Taking me closer.

The answering machine clicked on. I didn't want to listen. I stuttered on the brink. I closed my eyes again. Put my head down. Gripped the sides of the tub and pushed my ass back toward him, opening myself.

"Jamie," said a voice like slow, dripping caramel. "Sorry to call so late, man, but I lost my watch. Dunno what time it is."

I let out the breath I'd been holding. James grunted, thrusting harder. I drew in another breath and fought light-headedness. My clit pulsed under his fingertip.

"Anyway, jus' wanted to give you a call, let you know when I'd be getting in." Laughter like a secret curled out of the phone speaker. Its owner sounded drunk or high or maybe just exhausted. His voice was deep and rich and languid. He sounded like sex. "I'm heading out now, man, gonna hit a few more clubs before I leave. Call me on the cell, brother. You know the number."

Behind me, James let out a low, breathy moan. His fingers raked my back and sent me tumbling into a climax fierce enough to make bright colors flash behind my closed lids.

"And Jamie," said the voice, dipping even lower, a secret-sharing voice. "It'll be great to see you, man. Love you, brother. I'm out."

James shouted. I shuddered. We came together, saying nothing, listening to Alex Kennedy speaking from the other side of the world.

Chapter 02

"*S*he'll be late." My sister Patricia sniffed as she looked over the menu. "Let's not wait for her."

My other sister Mary looked up from the text message she was busy answering from her cell phone. "Pats, she's not late yet. Relax."

Patricia and I shared a look. We're the closest in age. Sometimes it feels like our family has two sets of daughters, separated by a decade instead of the four years between Patricia and Mary. There are an additional two years between Mary and our youngest sister, Claire. I'm not old enough to be Claire's mother, but there are times I definitely feel like I am.

"Give her a few more minutes," I told Patricia. "Yeah, she'll be late but we can wait a few minutes, can't we?"

Patricia gave me a stony look and looked back to the menu. I didn't care for Claire's lackadaisical attitude any more than my sister did, but Patricia's attitude surprised me. She could be opinionated and bossy, but she wasn't usually nasty.

Mary closed her phone with a click and reached for the pitcher of orange juice. "Whose idea was it to meet for breakfast, anyway? I mean, c'mon…you know she doesn't get up before noon if she can help it."

"Yes, well," said Patricia as she snapped her menu closed. "The world doesn't revolve around Claire, does it? I have things to do today. I can't be hanging around all day long just because she was out late partying."

This time Mary and I exchanged a look. Sisterhood is complicated business. Mary raised a brow, passing the responsibility of soothing Patricia to me.

"I'm sure she'll be here in a few minutes," I said. "And if she's not, we'll go ahead and order. Okay?"

Patricia didn't look mollified. She snapped up her menu again, hiding behind it. Mary mouthed "What's with her?" To which my only answer was a shrug.

Claire was, indeed, late, but only by a few minutes, and thus, by her standards, considered herself on time. She breezed into the restaurant like she owned the world, her black hair spiked out around her head like a sunburst. Thick black liner rimmed her eyes, making them stand out against her purposefully pale skin and crimson lips. She slid into the seat next to Mary and reached at once for the glass of juice Mary had poured for herself. Claire's bangle bracelets jangled as she tipped the glass to her mouth and ignored Mary's protest.

"Mmm, good," she said when she set the glass down. She grinned, looking around the table. "You all thought I'd be late."

"You *are* late." Patricia glared.

Claire didn't look fazed. "Not really. You guys didn't even order yet."

As if by magic the waiter appeared. Claire's sultry stare seemed to fluster him, but he managed to take our orders and leave the table with no more than a glance over his shoulder. Claire winked at him. Patricia sighed in disgust.

"What?" Claire said. "He's cute."

"Whatever." Patricia poured juice and drank it.

Chickens have a pecking order; sisters do, too. Past experience has led my sisters to believe I can be counted on to dispense advice and mediate arguments. They rely on me to keep the surface of our sisterhood polished and shiny, the way we trust Claire to shake us up and Patricia to put us all in order and Mary to make us feel better. We all have our place, usually, but today something seemed off.

"I told them expecting you to be here before noon was ridiculous." Mary reached for the basket of warm croissants. "What time did you go to sleep last night?"

Claire laughed, taking a croissant for herself. Forgoing butter, she pulled apart the flaky crust with her black-painted nails and stuffed the pastry into her mouth. "Didn't."

"You didn't go to bed last night?" Patricia's lip curled.

"Didn't go to sleep," Claire corrected. She washed down her croissant with a mouthful of juice. "I went to bed, all right."

Mary laughed. Patricia made a face. I did neither. I studied my youngest sister, spotting a telltale suck mark on her throat. She didn't have a boyfriend, or at least not one she'd ever bothered to bring around to meet the family. Considering our family, I wasn't necessarily surprised.

"Can we just get started? I've got stuff to do," Patricia said.

"Fine with me," Claire replied nonchalantly. "Let's go."

She couldn't have irritated Patricia more with her blasé response. The disregard for her anger made Patricia even more snappish. Though she and Claire had butted heads in the past, this seemed excessive. I set out to defuse the inevitable blowup by pulling out my notebook and pen.

"Okay. First thing we need to decide is where to have it." I tapped the pen to the paper. My parents' anniversary was in August. Thirty years. Patricia had come up with the idea for a party. "At their house? At my house, or Patricia's? Maybe at a restaurant."

"How 'bout the VFW?" Claire smirked. "Or the bowling alley?"

"Very funny." Patricia tore apart her croissant but ate none of it.

"Your house, Anne. We could have a pit beef barbecue, or something, on the beach." Mary's phone beeped again, but she ignored it.

"Yeah…we could." I didn't hide my lack of enthusiasm for that idea.

"Well, we can't have it at my house." Patricia sounded firm. "I don't have the space."

"And I do?" My house was nice, and by the water, true, but it was far from spacious.

Claire scoffed, waving at the waiter, who came over at once. "How many people do you really think are going to come? Hey, hon, bring me a mimosa, will you?"

"Jesus, Claire," said Patricia. "Do you have to?"

For a second Claire's insouciance slipped. "Yeah, Pats. I do."

"We could have it at Caesar's Crystal Palace," I suggested quickly to fend off an argument. "They have lots of receptions and stuff there."

"Oh, c'mon," Mary said. "The food there's super pricey, and honestly, you guys, I just don't have the cash to put toward this party like some of you do."

She gave me a significant look, then one to Patricia. Claire laughed. Mary looked at her, too, with a wiggle of brows.

"Yeah, me and Mary are poor." Claire looked up at the waiter who brought her drink. "Thanks, sugar."

He actually blushed when she winked. I shook my head and rolled my eyes. Claire had no shame.

"I think keeping the cost down is a good idea, too." Patricia said this stiffly, looking at her plate and its desiccated croissant. "Let's have it at Anne's. We can buy the paper goods at the wholesale club and make a bunch of desserts. The pit beef barbecue would be the most expensive thing, but they include the corn on the cob and rolls and stuff."

"Don't forget the booze," Claire said.

Silence ringed the table. Mary's phone beeped and she flipped it open, her face blank. Patricia said nothing. I didn't, either. Claire looked around at each of us.

"You can't seriously be thinking of not having booze," Claire said. "At the very least, you have to have beer."

"That's up to Anne," Patricia said after a moment. "It's her house."

I looked at her, but she wouldn't meet my eyes. I

looked at Mary, also ignoring me. Claire, however, met my gaze head-on.

"We can have whatever we want," I said, finally.

"It's an anniversary party for Mom and Dad," Claire said. "Now, you tell me you're going to throw them a party and not have booze."

We were saved from an uncomfortable silence by the arrival of our food. It took a few minutes to distribute and get started on consuming, but that brief time was enough. Mary sighed, stabbing a fried potato.

"We could have beer." She shrugged. "Get a keg."

"A couple bottles of wine," said Patricia grudgingly. "And we'd have to have champagne, I guess. To toast. It's been thirty years. I guess they deserve a toast. Don't they?"

They were all looking at me to decide. My fork hovered over the omelet my stomach was deciding it no longer wanted. They wanted me to say yes or no, to make the choice for them. I didn't want to do it. I didn't want that responsibility.

"Anne," said Claire at last. "We'll all be there. It'll be okay."

I nodded once firmly, the sharp action hurting my neck. "Fine. Sure. Of course. Beer, wine, champagne. James can set up a bar outside and make mixed drinks. He likes that."

We all said nothing for another long moment. I imagined I felt relief from my sisters at not having to be the ones to make the choice, but perhaps it was only my imagination.

"Now. What about the guest list?" I said, my voice firm as I took charge.

Keeping the surface polished.

* * *

I wanted James to refuse to have the party at our house, but, of course, he thought it was a great idea. He was at the grill with a beer in one hand and the tongs in the other when I broached the subject. His apron had a picture of a decapitated, bikini-clad woman imprinted on the front. Her breasts bulged every time he lifted his arms.

"Sounds great. We could rent a tent in case the weather's bad. It'll give some shade, too."

The scent of sizzling steaks should have made my mouth water, but my stomach was too twisted for me to appreciate it. "It will be a lot of work."

"We'll hire help. Don't worry about it." James flipped the steaks expertly and lifted the lid on the bubbling pot of corn.

Watching him, the master in front of his superfab-andgroovy grill, I let a small smile tug my mouth. James needed step-by-step instructions to make microwave oatmeal, but he fancied himself the Iron Chef of outdoor cooking.

"It will still be a lot of work."

He looked at me then, finally getting it. "Anne, if you don't want to have it here, why didn't you say so?"

"My sisters outvoted me. They all want a pit beef barbecue, and this is the only place to have it. Besides," I conceded, "even if we rent a tent and hire people to serve and clean up, it will still be cheaper than having it at a catering hall. And…we do have a nice place."

I looked around. Our house and property were more than nice. A lakefront home with its own stretch of beach, privacy and seclusion, surrounded by pine trees. One of the first homes built along the shore road, the house itself had belonged to James's grandparents. Others on the road were selling in the high nine hundreds and above, but we'd paid nothing. They'd left it to James in their will. It was small and worn, but clean and bright and most importantly, ours. My husband might build luxury half mansions for everyone else, but I preferred our little bungalow with the personal touches.

James slid the steaks onto a platter and brought them to the table. "Only if you want to, babe. I don't care, one way or another."

It would have been so much easier if he had. If he'd put his foot down and demanded we host my parents' party someplace else. If he'd taken the choice from me, I could've blamed him for making what I wanted come true.

"No." I sighed as he slapped an immense portion of beef onto my plate. "We'll have it here."

The steak was good, the corn crisp and sweet. I'd made a salad with in-season strawberries and vinaigrette dressing, and crusty French bread rolls. We ate like kings as James told me about the new work site, the problems he was having with some of the guys on his crew, about his parents' plans for a family vacation.

"When do they think that's going to happen?" I paused in cutting my steak.

James shrugged, pouring himself another glass of red wine. He didn't ask me if I wanted any; he'd stopped asking long ago. "I don't know. Sometime this summer, I guess."

"You guess? Well, did they think to ask any of us when we might like to go? Or if we want to go?"

Another shrug. He wouldn't have thought of it. "I don't know, Anne. It's just something my mom mentioned. Maybe sometime over the fourth."

"Well," I said, buttering a roll to give my hands a reason not to clench. "We can't go away with them this summer. You know we can't. I wish you'd just told her that up front."

James sighed. "Anne—"

I looked up. "You didn't tell her we'd go, did you?"

"I didn't tell her we'd go."

"But you didn't tell her we wouldn't." I frowned. It was typical and unsurprising, and right now, immeasurably more irritating.

James chewed in silence and washed down his food with wine. He cut more steak. He poured steak sauce.

I, too, said nothing. It wasn't as easy for me but had come about from long practice. It became a waiting game.

"What do you want me to tell her?" he asked, finally.

"The truth, James. The same thing you told me. That we couldn't take a vacation this summer because you've got that new development going in and you need to be on-site. That we're planning on using your vacation time to go skiing this winter, instead. That we can't go. That we don't want to go!"

"I'm not saying that." He wiped his mouth and crumpled his napkin, then threw it on his plate where it soaked up steak sauce like blood.

"You'd better tell her something," I said sourly. "Before she books the trip."

He sighed again and leaned back in his chair. He ran a hand over his head. "Yeah. I know."

I didn't want to be fighting with him about this. Especially since I wasn't really tense about his mother, but about hosting my parents' anniversary party. It all cycled around, though, a snake eating its own tail. Feeling pressured into doing something I didn't want to do for people I didn't want to please.

James reached across the table and grabbed my hand. His thumb passed over the back of it. "I'll tell her."

Three words and such a simple sentiment, but some of the weight dropped from my shoulders. I squeezed his hand. We shared a smile. He tugged me gently, pulling me closer, and we kissed over the remains of our dinner.

"Mmm. Steak sauce." He licked his lips. "Wonder what else that would taste good on."

"Don't even think about it," I warned.

James laughed and kissed me again, lingering though the position was awkward. "I'd have to lick it all off...."

"That sounds like a very good way to get an infection," I said crisply, and he let me go.

Together, we tossed the paper plates and put away leftovers. James found many excuses to rub and bump against me, always with a falsely innocent "Pardon me, excuse me," that made me laugh and punch his arm. Finally he backed me against the sink and pinned me. His hands closed around my wrists, pressing my hands down to the countertop. His pelvis anchored mine.

"Hi," he said.

"Hello."

"Fancy meeting you here." He nudged me with his erection.

"We have to stop meeting like this. It's really too shocking."

He pressed closer to me, knowing I couldn't move away. His breath, redolent of garlic and onion but in a delicious and not repugnant way, gusted over my face. He tilted his head to align our mouths, but he didn't kiss me.

"Are you shocked?"

I gave my head the slightest shake. "Not yet."

"Good."

Sometimes it was like that with us. Fast and hot and hard, swift and frantic fucking without bothering to do more than slide aside panties and unzip a fly. He was inside me in a heartbeat, and I was wet for him. Slick. My body gave him no resistance as he filled me, and we both cried out.

My arms went around his neck, his hand beneath one thigh to shift the angle. We rattled the cupboards. I wasn't sure I'd come but something in the way his body hit my pelvis, over and over, tipped me into a short, sharp climax. James followed just after my body tightened around him. His face dropped to my shoulder, both of us breathing hard. The position quickly became painful and awkward, and we untangled ourselves with stiff motions. He put his arms around me, and we stood together as our breathing slowed and the sweat on our faces cooled in the breeze coming in the window.

"When's your next appointment with the doctor?" James's question made me blink.

"I haven't made one."

I pushed away from him to rearrange my clothes and wash the grill utensils. The dish soap made my fingers slippery, and I dropped the tongs into the steel sink with a clatter that sounded like an accusation. James, however, did not accuse.

"Are you going to?"

I looked at him. "I've just been busy."

He could've pointed out that since the local counseling center I'd worked for had lost its funding and closed, I'd been anything but busy. He didn't. He shrugged and accepted my answer like it made sense, even though it didn't.

"Why?" I asked. "Are you in a hurry?"

James smiled. "I thought you wanted to get started. Hey, who knows, maybe we just made a baby. Just now."

That was utterly unlikely. "How lucky would that be?"

He reached for me again. "Pretty lucky?"

I snorted delicately. "To have conceived our child standing up in the kitchen?"

"Maybe she'd be a good cook."

"Or he. Boys can be good cooks, too." I tossed a handful of suds his way.

James buffed his nails on his shirtfront. "Yeah, just like his old man."

I rolled my eyes. "Oh…yeah."

Before we could disintegrate into teasing about James's lack of culinary skills, the phone rang. I reached for it automatically. James took the opportunity of my distraction to knuckle my sides.

I was laughing, breathless, when I answered. "Hello?"

The crackle of static and silence greeted me. Then, "Anne?"

I fended off my husband's wandering hands. "Yes?"

"Hello, Anne." The voice was low, deep, thick. Unfamiliar yet something made me think I knew it.

"Yes?" I said, uncertain, glancing at the clock. It seemed rather late for a telemarketer.

"This is Alex. How are you?"

"Oh. Alex. Hello." My laugh sounded embarrassed this time. James raised an eyebrow. I'd never spoken to Alex. "You must want to speak to James."

"No," said Alex. "I'd like to talk to you."

I'd already been planning to hand off the phone to James, but now I stopped. "You would?"

James, who'd been reaching for the phone, took back his hand. His other brow raised, the pair of them arching like birds' wings. I shrugged and raised a brow myself, using the subtle nonverbal signals we'd forged as our private marital communication.

"Sure." Alex had a laugh like syrup. "How are you?"

"I'm…fine."

James stepped back, palms up, grinning. I cradled the phone against my shoulder and turned back to the sink to rinse off the dishes, but James nudged me aside and took over the task. He waved a little, shooing me.

"That's good. How's the bastard you married?"

"He's fine, too." I went to the living room. I'm not much of a phone conversationalist. I always need something else to do while I'm talking, but now I had no laundry to fold, no floor to mop. No dishes, even, to wash. I paced, instead.

"He's not giving you any trouble, is he?"

I wasn't sure how to answer that, so I opted to assume Alex was teasing. "Nothing the whips and chains can't take care of."

His low chuckle tickled my eardrum. "That's right. You keep him in line."

"So…James tells me you're coming for a visit?"

The hiss of static made me think we'd lost the connection for a second, but then he was back. "Yeah, that's the plan. Unless you object?"

"Of course not. We're looking forward to it." A slight lie. I was sure James was looking forward to it. Never having met Alex, I wasn't so sure about having him as a houseguest. It was an intimate proposal, and I wasn't so good at intimacy on short notice.

"Liar."

"Beg pardon?" I stopped short.

Alex laughed. "You're a liar, Anne."

At first, I didn't know how to respond. "I—"

He laughed again. "I'd be the same way. Some rascal calls out of the blue wanting to be put up for a few weeks? I'd be a little concerned. Especially if half the things I'm sure Jamie's told you about me are true. He has told you stories, hasn't he?"

"A few."

"And you're still letting me come to visit? You're a brave, brave woman."

I'd heard stories about Alex Kennedy but assumed most of them were exaggerations. The mythology of boyhood friendship, the past filtered through time. "So, if only half of what he's told me is true, what about the rest?"

"Some of that might be true, too," Alex said. "Tell me something, Anne. Do you really want me in your house?"

"Are you really a rascal?"

"A ragged one. Running round and round that rugged rock."

He surprised me into a laugh. I was aware of an undercurrent there, a slight flirtation he was offering and to which I was responding. I looked into the kitchen, where James was finishing up the dishes. He wasn't even paying any attention, uncaring about my conversation with his friend. I'd have been eavesdropping.

"Any friend of James," I said.

"Is that so? But I bet Jamie doesn't have any friends like me."

"Rascals? No. You're probably right. A few scoundrels and a moron or two. But no other rascals."

I liked his laugh. It was warm and gooey and unpretentious. The connection hissed and crackled again. I heard a flare of music and the murmur of conversation, but couldn't tell if it was in the background or breaking through on the line.

"Where are you, Alex?"

"Germany. I'm visiting some friends for a day or so before I go to Amsterdam, then to London. I'll be leaving for the States from there."

"Very cosmopolitan," I said, only a bit envious. I'd never been out of North America.

Alex's laugh rasped. "I'm living out of a suitcase and I'm jet-lagged all to shit. I'd kill someone just for a bologna sandwich on white bread with mayonnaise."

"Are you trying to win my sympathy?"

"Shamelessly."

"I'll make sure to stock up on white bread and bologna," I said, the prospect of Alex staying in our house suddenly not as daunting as it had been before.

"Anne," Alex said after a pause, "you are a goddess among women."

"So I'm told."

"Seriously. Tell me what you want me to bring you from Europe."

The shift in conversation surprised me. "I don't want anything!"

"Chocolate? Sausage? Treacle? What? I might have a hard time smuggling heroin or pot or prostitutes from Amsterdam, though. You'd better keep it legal."

"Really, Alex, you don't have to bring me anything."

"Of course I do. If you don't tell me what you want, I'll just ask Jamie."

"I'd say treacle," I told him. "But I'm not sure what it is...does it come from a well?"

He chuckled. "It's molasses. It comes in a jar."

"Bring me that."

"Ah, a woman who likes to live on the wild side. No wonder Jamie married you."

"There's more than one reason," I said.

I realized I'd been standing still, chatting, for several minutes. Alex had so engaged me I hadn't felt the need to multitask. I looked again to the kitchen, but James had disappeared. I heard the mumble of television from the den.

"I was sorry I couldn't make the wedding. I heard it was a blast."

"Did you? From James?"

A silly question. From who else would he have heard it? Except James had never mentioned he'd been in touch with Alex. James had spoken frequently about his best friend from junior high school, though on the subject of their falling-out he'd been rather more vague. He had other friends…but we were getting married, and I have a habit of trying to make things better. I'd been the one to add Alex's name to the guest list, uncertain even if the address I found in James's outdated address book was the right one. I figured whatever had happened between them might be repaired with a little outreach. When he'd sent regrets, I wasn't surprised, but at least we'd made the attempt. Apparently it had worked better than I'd known.

"Yeah."

"It was a very nice wedding," I said. "It was too bad you couldn't make it, but now you'll get to come for a long visit, instead."

"He sent me pictures. You both look very happy."

"He sent you…pictures? Of our wedding?" I looked at the fireplace mantel, where a framed photo of us still rested even after six years. I always wondered how long it was acceptable to display wedding photos. I guessed at least until baby photos came along to replace them.

"Yeah."

That surprised me, too. I'd sent photos to a few of my friends who hadn't been able to attend, but…well, we were women. Chicks did stuff like that, giggled over pictures and sent chatty e-mails.

"Well…." I trailed off, awkward. "When are you coming in?"

"I have a few details to work out with the airline. I'll let Jamie know."

"Sure. Do you want me to get him for you?"

"I'll e-mail him."

"Okay. I'll tell him."

"Well, Anne, it's almost two in the morning here. I'm going to go to bed. I'll talk to you soon."

"Goodbye, Alex—" He'd already disconnected, leaving me to stare at the phone, a bit taken aback.

There was nothing odd, not really, about his being in touch with James. Men's friendships were different from women's. My husband never told me about talking to Alex, but that didn't mean he was keeping it a secret. It just meant he hadn't thought enough of it to share. In fact, I should be happy they'd resolved their differences. It would be nice to meet James's dear friend, Alex, the rascal. The ragged one who ran round and round the rugged rock. The one who promised me treats from Wonderland. The one who called my husband, Jamie, not James.

The one James had only ever spoken of in past tense.

Mary's phone beeped for the fourth time in half an hour, but this time she only glanced at it before shoving it deep into her purse. "So how long is he staying?"

"I don't know." I lifted a crystal picture frame from a shelf laden with them. "How about this one?"

My sister made a face. "No."

I put it back and looked around the store. "They're all like that in here. We're not going to find anything."

"Whose bright idea was it to get a fancy picture frame, anyway? Oh, right," Mary said sarcastically. "Patricia's. So why are we suckered into trying to find one?"

"Because Patricia can't come to places like this with the kids." I scanned the shelves but all the frames were similar. Overpriced and glittering with ugliness.

"Right. And I don't suppose Sean can watch the rugrats in the evening?"

I shrugged, but something in Mary's tone made me look up. "I don't know. Why? Did she say something about it?"

Sisters also share a nonverbal language. Mary's posture and expression said it all, but in case I missed what she was trying to say, she said it anyway. "He's a jerk."

"Oh, c'mon, Mare."

"Haven't you noticed how she doesn't talk about him anymore? And it used to be all, Sean this, Sean that, Sean says, Sean thinks. Tell me you haven't noticed we've been spared the Gospel of Sean lately. And she's been an even bigger priss than usual. Something's going on."

"Like what?" We abandoned the frou-frou shop and headed out into the bright June sunshine.

"Well, I don't know." Mary rolled her eyes.

"Maybe you should ask her."

My sister gave me another look. "You could ask her."

The sight of a familiar shock of black hair and a wardrobe that had dangerously malfunctioned made us both pause.

"Oh, brother," Mary said under her breath. "Goth vomited all over her."

I laughed. "Is that what that is?"

"I think you used to call it punk back in the day. Holy cow. She never quits. I thought she was seeing that guy who worked at the record store." Mary sounded awed. "Who's *that* guy?"

Claire was grinning and flirting with a very tall, very lanky young man with enough metal in his face to set off an airport security alarm. She wore a set of black-and-white striped stockings, a black lace skirt with a jagged hem and a T-shirt emblazoned with the name of a punk rock band that had swirled down the drain of drug overdoses before she'd been born.

"She definitely marches to the beat of her own drum," I said.

"Yeah, that and an electric guitar, two French horns and a synthesizer."

Claire looked up and waved from across the parking lot, said her adieu to her new suitor and headed toward us. "Ladies. Good morning."

"It's afternoon," Mary pointed out.

"Depends on what time you got up," countered Claire with an unashamed grin. "So what's the happs?"

"Anne can't decide on a frame."

"Hey!" I protested. Without Patricia here to balance on my side, I could quickly be overtaken by my two younger sisters. "It's not up to me. We should all decide."

Claire waved a hand clad in a fingerless lace glove. "Whatevs. Get whatever you want. It's not like they'll really care."

"Hey, Madonna," I said, annoyed, "1983 called. It wants its wardrobe back."

Mary snerked. Claire made a face. I felt a small, useless moment of triumph.

"I'm starving," Claire declared. "Can't we go find someplace to chow?"

"Not all of us have the munchies," Mary put in.

"Not all of us have to watch our weight," Claire retorted sweetly.

"Girls, girls," I interjected. "Grade school's over. Can we please grow up?"

Claire slung an arm around Mary's shoulders and gave me an innocent look. "Wha? Whyfor you so uptight, my sistah?"

I did love them, all of them, and couldn't have imagined my life without them. Mary grinned and shoved Claire's arm off her. Claire shrugged and leered at me.

"C'mon, princess," she cooed. "Treat your li'l sissies to a burger and fries."

"Are you going to come clean my house?" I asked. "That's worth the price of lunch, isn't it?"

"Oh, right, before James's boyfriend comes for a visit. I almost forgot." She stuck out her tongue. "You don't want him to find all your sex toys lying around."

"You never did say when he was coming," Mary said.

The three of us started toward the diner on the other side of the parking lot. The food was decent and not generally a draw to the summertime tourist crowd inundating Sandusky to visit Cedar Point. Better still, it was close, and my stomach was rumbling.

"I don't know when he's coming."

"What's his name? Alex?" This came from Claire, who held the door open for Mary and me.

"Yeah." The waitress seated us in a comfortable booth near the back and handed us menus none of us needed. We'd been coming here forever. "Alex Kennedy."

"And he didn't come to your wedding?" Mary shook sugar into her iced tea and squeezed the lemon wedge. She passed me a few packets without my having to ask.

"No, he was overseas. But his company got bought out, and he's coming back to the States. I don't know that much about it."

"What are you going to do with him while James is working?" This practical question astoundingly came from Claire, sipping water through a straw.

"He is an adult, Claire. I'm assuming he can find something to do."

Mary snorted. "Yeah, but he's a guy."

"Good point," Claire said. "You'd better lay in supplies of nachos and spare socks."

I rolled my eyes at both of them. "He's James's friend, not mine. I'm not going to be doing his laundry."

Claire made a derisive noise. "We'll see."

"Oh, listen to you," Mary said. "When's the last time you ever did anyone's laundry, including your own?"

"You're insane," replied Claire, unconcerned. "Of course I do my own laundry at school."

Mary frowned. "You should do it at home, too."

"Why? It gives Mom such pleasure," said Claire, and I was pretty sure she was being serious.

"I'm not worried about the laundry," I told both of

them. "Or about entertaining him. I'm sure he'll be able to entertain himself just fine."

"Ha. He's been in Hong Kong, right?" Claire put her hands together and pasted on a silly grin. "He'll expect a geisha, you watch."

"Geishas are Japanese, you idiot." Mary shook her head.

"What. Evs." Claire blew upward, puffing her bangs out of her eyes.

Listening to them declare disaster actually made me feel better about Alex's visit. "Singapore. And it will be fine, you guys."

"No walking around in your panties," said Claire with a doleful sigh, like that was the worst thing of all. "How will you stand it?"

"As if I do that anyway?"

"Dude," my youngest sister declared, "that shit's the best part of living on your own."

We all laughed. Mary's phone beeped again, and she dug it out. She read the message, tapped the keys and tucked it away again.

"Hey, hot stuff, you act like you're married to that thing. You holding out on us or what?" Claire craned her neck to catch a glimpse of Mary's phone.

"It's just Betts." Mary shrugged and drank tea.

Claire leaned forward. "Are you and Betts a couple?"

Mary's mouth dropped open. So did mine. Claire looked unconcerned. "Well? She keeps texting you like she can't bear to be parted from you. And we all know you're not that into dudes."

"What?" Mary, who generally gave Claire as good as she got, seemed unable to speak.

I was finding it hard to speak, myself. "Claire, good lord."

Claire shrugged. "It's a legitimate question."

"What ever gave you the idea I don't like guys?" Mary blinked rapidly, her cheeks staining bright red.

"Umm...the fact you've never had sex with one?"

"That doesn't mean anything," I told Claire.

"No," said Mary, "it doesn't, especially since, hello! I so have!"

Claire and I both did a double take. One of the delightful things about having sisters is the Three Stooges-esque quality of so many of our conversations.

"Get out! What? When? Who?" Claire squealed.

Mary looked around the diner before she answered. "I did it, okay? I lost my virginity. What's the big deal? You all did it, too."

"Yeah, but none of us waited until we were shriveled up old maids," Claire said.

"I'm not an old maid, Claire." Mary's face still gleamed from blushing. "And not all of us are rampant sluts."

Claire frowned. "Hey."

"You didn't tell me you had a boyfriend," I said to defuse them.

Both turned to look at me with almost identical expressions of disdain.

"I don't," said Mary while at the same time Claire chimed in, "Who says she's got to have a boyfriend?"

"I just thought...never mind."

Mary shook her head as the waitress brought us our platters, but waited until we were alone again before speaking. "It was just some guy."

"Some random guy?" I wouldn't have expected that from Mary, who used to dress up as a nun...and not for Halloween. "You lost your virginity to some stranger?"

Mary blushed again. Claire hooted, reaching for the ketchup. "Rock it, sister. Way to go."

"I figured it was time," Mary said. "So I went out and I found someone."

"Weren't you worried about...disease?" I shuddered a little. "Or...anything?"

"She made him wear a condom." Claire waved a fry. "Bet you ten bucks."

"Of course I made him wear a condom," Mary muttered. "I'm not an idiot."

"Well, I'm just surprised, that's all." I didn't mean to sound disapproving. I wasn't, not really. Losing her virginity to a stranger was probably no worse than my giving it up to the high school boy I mistakenly thought loved me. At least Mary had gone into it without romantic expectations.

"Spill it. Was it good?"

Mary shrugged, looking down. Her phone begged for attention again, but she ignored it. "Sure. Yeah."

"You're not convincing me." Claire nudged her.

Mary laughed. "Yeah. It was good. He was pretty hot. And I guess...he was good."

"What, you guess? You don't know? If you don't know for sure, Mare, it can't have been that good."

"Why are we getting sex advice from you, I want to know." I pressed down the top bun of my overstuffed burger, and juice puddled on the plate. I was going to eat the whole thing, I just knew it, even if I'd regret it the next time I got on the scale.

Claire shrugged and dug into her coleslaw. "Because I've had the most sex. Duh."

"Duh." Mary laughed. "I wouldn't brag about that, if I were you."

"I'm not bragging, just being honest. Geez. What I want to know is, how come you all have such a puritanical attitude toward fucking and I don't. How'd that happen?"

I laughed. "I don't have a puritanical attitude toward fucking, Claire."

She gave me a look. "Oh, really? What's the kinkiest thing you ever did?"

Silence.

"I thought so."

A triumphant, smug younger sister is quite annoying. I threw a fry at her. She ate it with aplomb and licked her fingers.

"It's not about the kink," Mary said. "Gosh, just because we haven't let anyone tie us up or spank us doesn't make us prudes."

Claire laughed, tipping back her head. "Oh, please. These days, spanking's almost vanilla."

"What's the freakiest thing you've ever done, then?" I asked calmly, turning the tables.

Claire shrugged. "Cutting."

Mary and I both recoiled. "Claire, gross!"

She laughed. "Gotcha."

"Gross," Mary repeated, looking sickened. "People do that?"

"People do everything," Claire said matter of factly.

"I'd never let anyone cut me," said Mary.

Claire pointed with a fry. "You never know what you'll do for the right person, Mare. Never say never."

Mary scoffed. "I can't imagine there could possibly be a right person who'd get me to agree to cutting."

"Maybe not cutting, but sure as hell it would be something," Claire said. "Love is some messed up shit."

"I thought you didn't believe in love," said Mary.

"Goes to show what you know," answered Claire. "I do."

"Me, too," I said. We raised our glasses and clinked. "To love. All kinds."

"Oooh," said Claire. "Anne is kinky, after all."

Chapter 03

"So. Tell me about him." I said this to James as we lay in bed, the covers thrown off us in deference to the heat wave that was too fierce for early June. The overhead fan whirred, stirring air brought in from the lake, but I was still hot.

"Who?" James sounded sleepy. He had to get up early to hit the job site.

"Alex."

James made a muffled, snorting sort of noise into his pillow. "What do you want to know?"

I stared upward, into darkness, and imagined stars. "What's he like?"

James was silent for so long I was certain he'd fallen asleep. At last, he rolled onto his back. I couldn't see his face, but I pictured it as he spoke.

"He's a good guy."

What did that mean? I rolled onto my side, facing him. Between us, heat stirred. Reaching out, I could have touched him, but I tucked my hand beneath my pillow instead and found a cool spot on the sheets.

"He's smart. He's…"

I waited but couldn't stand the hesitation. "Funny? Nice?"

"Yeah, I guess so."

I sighed. "You've been friends since what, the eighth grade?"

"Yeah." He no longer sounded sleepy. He sounded like he wanted to be sleepy.

"So…you have to have more to say about him than he's smart and a good guy. C'mon, James. What's Alex like?"

"He's like the lake."

"Tell me."

James shifted, the bed dipping as he moved and tugged the covers with his feet. "Alex is…he's deep, Anne. But he's shallow in places, too, when you don't expect it. I guess that's the only way to put it."

I pondered this for a moment. "That's a very interesting description."

James didn't say anything. I heard him breathing. I felt his breath on my face. I felt the heat from his skin, inches from mine. We weren't touching but I felt him all over me, just the same.

"Okay, how about this? Alex seems easy to know."

"But he's not?"

James drew in a breath. Let it out. Took another, a slow, easy pattern that nevertheless didn't sound relaxed. "No. I'd say not."

"But you know him? I mean, you were best buddies for a long time, right?"

He laughed, then, and the twinges of unease his answers had stirred in my gut fled. "Yeah. I guess we were."

I reached for him then, to run a hand through his hair. He moved closer to me. His hand found just the right spot on my hip, nestled into my body's curve. I lined myself up along him.

We were silent for a while. I let myself melt against him, breast to chest. He wore a pair of boxers. I had on a tank-top and a pair of panties. There was a lot of skin contact. I wasn't about to complain, even though the night hadn't yet begun to cool, and we stuck to each other.

He got hard, which made me smile. I waited, and after a moment his hand began its slow, easy path up and down my side. The thump of his heart quickened, but so did mine.

I tilted my head. His mouth found mine without effort. Our kiss was sweet and slow, without urgency.

"Don't you have to be up early tomorrow?"

James pressed my hand to his thickening cock. "I'm up now."

"I feel that." I gave him an experimental squeeze. "Whatever shall I do with this?"

"I have a few ideas." He pushed his groin against my hand, his fingers sliding between the edges of my tank top and panties. "Why not suck it?"

"Oh, that's subtle." My voice sounded dry, but I was grinning.

"Never claimed to be subtle," James murmured. He dipped his head to taste my throat.

I hitched in a breath. My hand bore down. James groaned. I smiled. I pushed him back, just a little, just enough for me to slide down his body and take his penis out of the boxers. I didn't have to see it to know every ripple and curve. I closed my fingers around the shaft and bent closer to lip the sensitive flesh around the rim.

James made a happy sigh and rolled onto his back. He put a hand on my head, not pushing me down or hurrying me along, just stroking my hair a little. His fingers snagged and tangled. A discomfort so slight it didn't qualify as pain sparked against my scalp.

I licked him, savoring the salt-musk flavor. Even fresh from the shower, this part of him always smelled and tasted different from, say, an elbow or a chin. His cock, lower belly and inner thighs all maintained a deliciousness I could only describe as male. And unique. Blindfolded I might have faltered at identifying him by the slope of his nose or bulge of muscles, but that smell and taste would prove him to be mine every time.

"If I were in a dark room full of naked men and had to find you, I could," I murmured before sliding my mouth over his erection.

"Do you often fantasize about being in a room full of naked men, Anne?" James lifted his hips to push inside my mouth. I curled my fingers tighter around the base of his prick to keep him from surging too far.

"No."

His laugh was brief, breathless. "No? Never? That's not your fantasy?"

"What would I do with a room full of naked men?"

He sighed as I sucked him. I cupped his balls, soft, and stroked my thumb along the tender seam in his flesh. "They could…do things…to you…."

I used my mouth and hand in tandem until he groaned

aloud, then stroked him up and down and gave my jaw a rest. "No. I'm a maximum two-input girl, James. All those men would just go to waste."

I put my mouth back on him, taking him in as far as I could go. His cock throbbed against my tongue. Silky precome mixed with my saliva and made him slippery. Easy to stroke. Easy to suck.

James put a hand to my hip and tugged me gently, until I spun without taking my mouth off him so I straddled his face. It was my turn to moan when he gripped my ass and pulled my clit onto his tongue. He flicked me lightly with the tip. In this position I could control how close or far my body got to his. I could hover over his lips and tongue, move my pelvis, stroke myself along his mouth.

I loved it.

My orgasm rose fast. It became difficult to concentrate on sucking him while he licked me. We got a little sloppy. I don't think either of us cared. We both came within seconds of each other, our cries mingling in the dark. After, when I'd turned around and lolled in sated content on my pillow, I noticed the air had grown cool enough I wanted to be under the blankets.

I pulled them up over both of us, though James was breathing in the just-about-to-snore way I found alternatingly endearing and excruciating, depending on how tired I was. He snorted into his pillow. I lay back, tired but not quite ready to sleep.

"What did you fight about?" I whispered into the darkness hanging between us.

The sound of his breathing changed. An indrawn

breath. Silence. James didn't answer and after a few moments, I forgot to ask again, so taken up was I in dreams.

Things changed, as they are apt to do, without warning. I'd spent the morning running errands, and I was playing reluctant hostess that evening to James's family, all of them. Parents, spouses, nieces and nephews. I planned something simple, grilled chicken and salad, fresh rolls. Watermelon and brownies for dessert.

The brownies were ruining my life.

The recipe seemed simple enough. Good quality chocolate, flour, eggs, sugar, butter. I had all the right tools for the job, as James would have said with utter seriousness. I even had the skill, though perhaps not the talent. Yet for some reason, I was thwarted at every turn. My microwave refused to melt the chocolate without scorching it. The butter splattered and burned me when, forewarned by the chocolate disaster, I tried melting it on the stovetop. One egg had a blood spot, the other the bonus of a double yolk that would have been a lovely surprise in an omelet but messed up this recipe.

A glance at the clock showed the hour I'd set aside for this project had already stretched longer than that. This made me tense. I don't like being late. I don't like being unprepared. I don't like being less than perfect.

I'd opened all the windows and turned on the ceiling fans, because I preferred a breeze to the noise and sterile chill of our stuttering air conditioner. The kitchen smelled good, like marinade and melted fat and baking bread, but it was hot. Chocolate stained my white shirt and the front of my denim skirt. My hair, unruly on its best days, had gone berserk and hung in tangled corkscrews past my shoulders. Sweat trickled down my back, tickling.

I'd forgotten to buy salad dressing, but no time for that now. I'd have to whip up something from scratch. No time, either, for the soak in the tub I'd planned as advance reward for serving dinner to the horde. I didn't care if that meant my knees would stay stubbled, but I'd been looking forward to the scent of lavender and half an hour of silence. Now if I was lucky I might squeeze in a quick scrub in the shower before changing my clothes. The way things were going, I'd have to just give myself a wipe down with a washcloth and hope for the best.

Right. Brownies. I had only one package left of the gourmet chocolate chips. If I messed up again, we'd be eating stale sandwich cookies for dessert. I set the package on the counter and poured the butter from the double boiler into the mixing bowl. One step at a time.

I stirred carefully. I re-read the instructions. I lifted the bowl to swirl the melted butter and eggs together, just like the book said.

"Hello, Anne."

Warm butter sloshed and the mixing spoon clattered to the kitchen floor. My heart stopped, my breath stopped, my mind, for one terrified moment, stopped. Like a movie put on Pause, then clicked to Fast-Forward, I jerked back to life.

I'd screamed. How embarrassing. Turning, I released my death clutch on the bowl and set it on the counter with a small clang.

The first time I saw Alex Kennedy, it was with the *thud-thud* of my fast-beating heart still pounding in my ears and throat. He stood in the kitchen doorway, one hand on the doorjamb at a point high enough to stretch his lean body. He leaned slightly forward, one foot balancing his entire weight while the other leg bent as if I'd caught him in the act of taking a step. I saw faded jeans, low-slung but with a black leather belt holding them snug on his hips. A white T-shirt. Very James Dean, though instead of a red cloth jacket he had a black leather coat tucked into the hook made by his hand shoved into his front pocket. He wore sunglasses, and the big dark lenses covered most of his face.

It was a picture-perfect moment, like something out of a movie, and for a moment we merely stood and stared at each other like we were waiting for an unseen director to shout "Action!" Alex moved first. The hand came off the doorjamb, the other eased itself from his pocket and grabbed the coat before it could fall. He finished his step, entering my kitchen like he'd always been there.

"Hi." He said this looking around the room over the top of his dark glasses before he looked back at me. "Anne."

He didn't make it a question. James had said he was smart. Who else would I be? He didn't introduce himself, either, a fact that could be taken as arrogance or nonchalance, or simple understanding that though he didn't know me well enough to know it, I was smart, too.

"Alex." I moved around the kitchen's center island, toward him. Streaks and mess coated my hands, so I didn't offer one. "Wow. I'm sorry, I wasn't expecting you."

He smiled. It's a cliché to say it took my breath away, but all clichés began as truth, or else nobody would be able to relate to them. His mouth, full soft lips, quirked on one side. He took off his glasses. The eyes beneath were dark and could only be described as languid—lazy, rich, slow. Deep. Alex had eyes that meant something important, if only I could figure out what it was.

"Yeah, sorry about that. I rang Jamie's cell and he said to head on over. He said he'd call you. I guess he didn't." His voice, too, was slow and deep. Bemused.

I laughed, rueful. "He didn't."

"Bastard." Alex slung his jacket over the back of one of the high-backed chairs at the breakfast table and hooked both thumbs in his pockets. "Something smells good."

"Oh…I'm baking bread." I grabbed a dishtowel and wiped my hands quickly and began the dishevelment dance. Hair smoothed, shirt tucked, a quick pass of face and body to make sure I was put together.

He watched me, mouth still quirked. "And making something with chocolate, I see."

"Brownies." I blushed, and blushed harder at the heat rising along my throat. I had no reason to be embarrassed. Well, aside from the disaster that was my kitchen and personal appearance.

Alex made a low purring noise of approval. "My favorite. How'd you know?"

"I didn't—" He was teasing. "Who doesn't like brownies?"

"Good point." He laughed. He looked around the kitchen again, as if taking in every detail. I found myself following his gaze with mine, cataloging the framed prints on the walls, the wallpaper, slightly peeling in the corner. The scrapes in the linoleum where the chairs had worn the pattern to whiteness.

"We're fixing it up," I said, like I had to apologize for the kitchen's imperfections.

His gaze swiveled back to me. It was disconcerting, in a way, yet also familiar. Alex had the same focus as James, though on my husband it was offset by a somehow greater sense of impermanence. James could be intense on whatever had currently grabbed his attention. He was the blackbird with a beady eye, focused on the shiny. Alex reminded me of a lion waiting in the grass, seemingly sated until his prey got close enough to capture his notice.

"It's nice. You've done some nice things."

"Oh, you've been here before?" I shook my head at my own question. "Of course you have."

"Back when Jamie's grandparents lived here, yeah. Long time ago. It's nicer now." His mouth stretched into another slow grin. "Smells better, too."

There was no reason for me to be intimidated by him. He wasn't doing anything. He was, in fact, being quite pleasant. I wanted to return his smile, and I did…but it was with a sort of hitching, confused reluctance. It was the kind of smile you give to someone who's just offered you a mint on the subway. Wondering if they're being kind, or if your breath's offending. Was he just being polite, or did he mean it?

I didn't know.

"I hope they taste good, at least. I'm not having much

luck with them so far," I admitted with a glance at the bowl.

He tilted his head to look at the mess on the center island. "How come?"

"Oh…" I shrugged with a small, self-conscious laugh. "I thought I'd be fancy and make them from scratch instead of the box. I should've stuck with the prepackaged mix."

"Nah. Things made fresh are always better." Alex moved closer to the island, and therefore, closer to me. He looked into the bowl. Without his gaze pinning me, I could watch him. "So you put the butter in with the eggs? What's next?"

He came all the way around, and we ended up shoulder to shoulder. He hadn't looked so tall from across the room. My head would reach the bottom of his chin. On James, I could reach his mouth without standing on my toes. Alex turned his head and gave me a look I couldn't interpret.

"Anne?"

"Oh…oh, I guess it's right there." I leaned over to stab the cookbook with my finger. Several grease splotches marked the pages. "Melt the chocolate. Melt the butter. Mix together. Add the sugar and vanilla…."

I stopped when I saw him staring at me. I returned his smile with a tentative one. It seemed to please him. He leaned forward, the tiniest amount. His voice dipped low, sharing a secret.

"Want to know the trick?"

"Of making brownies?"

His grin got broader. I expected him to say no. That he had another trick to reveal, something sweeter even than chocolate. I leaned forward, too, just a little.

"Hot butter will melt chocolate. You need a low flame."

"Will it?" I looked at the cookbook so I didn't have to look at him. More heat rose, burning the tips of my ears. I thought I must look ridiculous and tried to pretend it didn't matter.

"Want me to show you?" At my hesitation he straightened. His smile changed, gave us a bit of distance. Still friendly, but less intense. "I can't promise you they'll win any awards, but—"

"Sure. Yes, sure," I said decisively. "James's family will be here pretty soon and I don't want to be worrying about dessert once they start arriving."

"Yeah. Because they'll take up all your attention. I know what you mean." Alex reached for the bowl and turned toward the stove, where I'd left the double boiler I'd been using earlier.

He would know just what I meant, I thought, watching him dump the cooling butter-and-egg mixture back into the pot. He twisted the knob on the stove, bending to get his face at the level of the flame and setting it with a delicate touch. He grabbed up a spoon from the tool caddy on the counter and stirred the mixture.

"Bring me the chocolate." He spoke like he was used to being obeyed, and I didn't hesitate. I tore open the bag and gave it to him. Without looking at me, he shook the package gently, dropping chip after chip into the butter as he stirred it. "Anne. Come and see."

I moved to peer over his shoulder. The butter now had dark brown swirls that got larger and larger as Alex added more chocolate chips. After a few more moments the mix was a gooey, velvety liquid.

"Beautiful," I murmured, not really meaning to speak, and he looked up at me.

This time I didn't feel like he'd snared me with his gaze. I wasn't prey. He assessed me, then turned back to the thickening batter.

"Is everything else ready?"

"Yes."

I gathered the rest of the ingredients. Together we mixed and poured and scraped the bowl with my serviceable white spatula that was guaranteed not to crack or stain. The brownie mix smelled liked heaven and filled the baking pan exactly the way it was supposed to.

"Perfect," I said, and slid it into the oven. "Thank you."

"And of course it has to be perfect, right?" Alex leaned against the island, hands gripping the edge so his elbows bent akimbo.

I wiped my hands on the dishcloth and started putting utensils into the sink. "It's nice if it is, isn't it?"

"Even a flawed brownie still tastes damn good." He watched me clean without offering to help.

I paused, mixing bowl in my hand. "Depends on the flaw. I mean, if it's too dry or crumbly, it might not look right but will taste good. Or if the ingredients are wrong it can look perfect on the outside and taste terrible."

"Exactly."

I wondered if he'd been baiting me to say something

he'd been thinking. "Well. They looked perfect. Unless they burn."

"They won't burn."

"But they might not taste good, either?" I laughed at him. "Is that what you're saying?"

"You never know, do you?" He shrugged and gave me an upward, sideways, roundabout glance.

Teasing. He was teasing me, judging me. Trying to draw me out. Trying to feel me out. Figure me out.

"I guess we'd better taste it then." I held out the bowl. "You go first."

Alex raised a brow and pursed his lips, but pushed himself off the island and held out a hand. "In case they're vile?"

"A good hostess always allows her guests to have the first portion," I said sweetly.

"A perfect hostess makes sure everything's grand before she serves it," Alex countered, but he scooped a finger along the bowl's side. It came away smeared with chocolate.

He raised his finger, showing me. Being theatrical. He opened his mouth, tongue showing intimately pink. He put his finger in his mouth and closed his lips over it, sucking hard enough to hollow his cheeks before his finger popped out with an audible noise.

He said nothing.

"Well?" I asked, after a moment.

He grinned. "Perfect."

That was enough incentive for me. I slid my finger along the small amount of batter left in the bowl and licked it with the tip of my tongue.

"Coward."

"Fine." I stuck the whole thing in my mouth and sucked as hard as he had, making a show of it. "Mmmm, that's good!"

"Brownies fit for a queen."

"Or James's mother," I said and immediately covered my mouth to pretend I hadn't said anything so remotely derogatory.

"Even her."

We smiled at each other again, drawn together by our mutual understanding about what sort of person James's mother was.

"Well…" I cleared my throat. "I should go change my clothes and take a shower. And show you to your room. It's clean and ready, I just have to bring you some towels."

"I don't want you to go to a lot of trouble."

"It's not any trouble, Alex."

"Perfect," he said, not quite a whisper and not really a sigh, either.

Neither of us moved.

I realized my fingers were numb from clutching the bowl too hard. I loosened my grip at once and put it in the sink. I had chocolate on my fingers from the bowl's edges and I laughed, gesturing.

"What a mess." I licked them, the pointer, middle, thumb. "I'm chocolate all over."

"You have some just…there."

Alex's thumb traced the outer edge of my mouth's corner. I tasted chocolate. I tasted him.

That was how James found us, touching. An innocent

gesture that meant nothing, yet I backed away at once. Alex did not.

"Jamie," he said, instead. "How the fuck've you been?"

They collapsed into a flurry of backslapping and insults. Two grown men reverted to the behavior of fourteen-year-old boys in front of my eyes, both of them rumbling and posturing. Alex grabbed James around the neck and knuckled his hair until James stood up, face flushed and eyes bright with laughter.

I left them like that, to their greeting. I crept away down the hall and into the shower, where I ran the water cold as ice and stood beneath the spray, mouth open, to wash away the taste of my husband's long-lost best friend.

Mrs. Kinney often looks as though she's smelling something bad but is too polite to say so. I'm used to it being directed at me, that carefully curled lip, those delicately flaring nostrils. I assumed it was meant for me this time, too, until I saw how her eyes had focused over my shoulder.

I had intended to nod and smile but not really listen to her commentary on the dinner, how it was being prepared, how much to serve, where everyone should sit. So when she stopped, stuttered, actually, like a wind-up doll whose key has rusted, I turned to follow her gaze with mine.

"Hi, Mrs. Kinney." Alex had showered, too, and changed into a pair of black trousers and a silk shirt that should have looked too dressy but didn't. Smiling, he came forward for the sort of hug and kiss to the cheek she insisted on giving me every time we saw each other, though I hate casual embraces.

"Alex." Her reply was as stiff as her back, but she inclined her head to accept the peck he put on it. "We haven't seen you in a while."

Her tone clearly said he hadn't been missed. Alex didn't seem offended. He merely shook Frank's hand and waved at Margaret and Molly.

"James didn't tell me you were back," continued Mrs. Kinney, as though if James hadn't told her it simply couldn't be true.

"Yeah, for a while. I sold my business and needed a place to crash. So I'm here for a few weeks."

Oh, he knew how to play her in a way I envied. An answer, delivered in a manner casual enough to belie the fact he knew exactly what she was fishing for but not as much information as she wanted. My estimation of him went up a notch.

She looked over at James, who was busy swinging one of his nieces in the air. "You're staying here? With James and Anne?"

"Yep." He grinned, all teeth. Hands in his pockets, he rocked on his heels.

She looked at me. "My, how…nice."

"I think it will be very nice," I answered warmly. "It will be very nice for James and Alex to have some time together. And for me to get to know Alex, of course. Since he is James's best friend."

I smiled brightly and said no more. She digested that. The answer appeared to be enough, if not satisfactory, and she gave him a nod that looked like it hurt her neck. She lifted the casserole dish in her hands.

"I'll just go put this inside."

"Sure. Anywhere you like." I gestured, knowing she'd put it anywhere she liked no matter what I suggested. When she'd gone inside and Alex and I were alone for the moment, I turned. "What'd you do to piss off Evelyn?"

He smirked. "Aww, and here I thought she adored me."

"Oh, you must be right. That was clearly a look of adoration on her face. If adoration looks like she just stepped in dog crap."

Alex laughed. "Some things don't change."

"Everything changes," I told him. "Eventually."

Not Mrs. Kinney's feelings about him, apparently. She avoided conversation with him for the rest of the evening, though she didn't skimp on the "crap, I stepped in crap" looks.

For his part, Alex was cordial, polite, slightly distant. Considering how long he'd known James and how "welcoming" they were to everyone, the fact Evelyn was giving him the cold shoulder was very telling.

"Well, well, well, Alex Kennedy," said Molly as she brought me a handful of plates for the ancient, cranky dishwasher I only used when we had company. Dinner had ended and everyone stayed out on the deck. The dishes could have waited, but I was looking for tasks to occupy me so I didn't have to make small talk. "You know what they say about bad pennies."

I slotted the dishes into the washer and filled the soap dispenser. "You think Alex is a bad penny?"

I liked Molly well enough, in that I didn't dislike her. She was older than I by seven years, and we didn't have much in common other than her brother, but she wasn't as overbearing as her mother or an opinionated drama queen like her sister.

She shrugged and grabbed up the lids to the open containers of deli salad on the counter. "You know the boy your mother warned you about? That's Alex."

"Was," I said, helping her close up the plastic tubs of macaroni salad and coleslaw. "In high school."

She looked out the window toward the deck, where James and Alex were laughing quite loudly.

"I don't know," Molly said. "What do you think?"

"He's James's friend, not mine, and he's only staying for a few weeks. If James likes him—"

Her sharp burst of laughter stopped me. "Alex Kennedy led my brother down a lot of bad roads, Anne. Do you really think someone like that can change?"

"Oh, c'mon, Molly. We're grownups, now. So what if they got into trouble a few times as kids? They didn't kill anyone. Did they?"

"Well…no. I don't think so." She sounded like she wouldn't have been surprised if Alex, at least, had committed murder.

I knew she'd never think such a thing of James, the beloved baby of the family. Just like I knew that no matter how much James had been a part of whatever hijinks he and Alex had got into as kids, it would always be Alex's fault and never James's. The Kinneys hadn't done their son and brother any favors by setting him on such a high perch, in my opinion. James had a lot of self-confidence, which was good. He wasn't so great about taking blame, which wasn't.

"So tell me what they did that was so bad, then."

Molly rinsed and wrung one of the dishcloths and proceeded to wipe down the center island, though I'd already done it. This annoyed me much less from her than it would have from her mother, who'd have been doing it deliberately. Molly simply had been conditioned to following after someone else's efforts and straightening the edges—even if they weren't untidy.

"Alex doesn't come from a very good family."

I didn't comment. If you want to know how someone really feels, you almost never have to ask. Molly swiped at invisible spots with her cloth.

"They're white trash, to be perfectly honest. His sisters were sluts. One or two of them got pregnant in high school. His mom and dad are drunks. They're all low-class."

I don't think I flinched at her judgment of Alex's family. She wasn't talking about my sisters, or my parents. Or about me.

I wanted to tell her that she was lucky nobody judged her based upon how her parents acted, but I kept that opinion to myself, too. "There must have been something good about him for James to be his friend, Molly. And we aren't always what our parents are."

She shrugged. There was more she wanted to tell. I saw it in her eyes. "He smoked and drank, and more than cigarettes, if you know what I mean."

"Lots of kids do that, Molly, even the so-called good ones."

"He wore eyeliner."

My eyebrows rose, both at once. There it was. The worst of it. Worse, somehow, than the drinking or the weed smoking, or even the fact his family was white trash. This was the real reason they hadn't liked Alex Kennedy, and didn't like him now.

"...eyeliner." I couldn't help saying it like it was ridiculous, because...well...it was.

"Yes," she hissed, glancing again to the deck. "Black eyeliner. And...sometimes..."

I waited while she struggled with whether or not she could possibly bring herself to continue.

"Lip gloss," she said. "And he dyed his hair black and wore it spiked out all over, and he wore high-collared shirts with pins at the throat and suit jackets...."

I could picture him, a Robert Smith wannabe, or like Ducky from *Pretty in Pink*. "Oh, Molly. So did lots of people. It was the 80s."

She shrugged again. Nothing I could say would change her mind. "James didn't. Not until he started hanging out with Alex."

I'd seen pictures of James from that time. He'd been scrawny and gangly, a hodgepodge of stripes and plaids and battered Converse sneakers. I hadn't noticed any liner or gloss but could easily imagine him wearing it. It would have set off his vivid blue eyes quite nicely, I thought.

"Anyway," Molly said. "He doesn't seem to have changed much."

"I'll keep an eye on my makeup bag."

This time, she didn't miss the veiled sarcasm. "I'm just telling you, Anne, Alex was bad news then, and he's probably no better now. That's all. Do with it what you want."

"Thanks." I didn't want to do anything with it. The more they all hated Alex, the better I felt I wanted to like him. "I'll keep that in mind."

"We were all really glad when James didn't hang out with him anymore," she added, unprompted, and I looked up at her again.

"I know they had a fight."

If you want someone to tell you something they really want to say, all you have to do is let them.

But however much Molly might want to say about it, she couldn't. "Yes. I know. James never said what it was about. Just that Alex had come to visit him in college—Alex didn't go to college, you know."

It hadn't seemed to hurt him at all. I didn't comment on that, either.

"Anyway, he went to Ohio State to visit James and something happened, and they had a big fight. James came home for a week. A week! And then he went back to school and we never found out what had happened."

I couldn't stop the smug smile wanting to creep over my mouth, so I hid it by loading some containers into the re-frigerator. That was even worse than the eyeliner. That James had dared not to share every intimate detail of his life with them. That he had something they didn't know.

A secret.

Of course, he had it from me, too.

Chapter 04

I went to bed before the men did, and James woke me when he slid in beside me. He gave me a nudge or two, but I feigned sleep and soon his snoring buzzed over me. I'd been sleeping more peacefully before he came to bed, but now I lay awake listening to the noises all houses make in the night. The same creaks and groans, the ticking of an extra-loud clock. But tonight, something unfamiliar. The shuffle of feet in the hall, the flush of a toilet and thud of a door closing. Then the sound of sleeping again, the air heavy with it, and I let James pull me closer, until I fell back to sleep in his arms.

He was up and gone in the morning before I woke. I lay in bed for a while, stretching and thinking, until the need for the bathroom forced me up and about. Alex was out on the deck already, a mug of coffee in one hand. His eyes swept the lake and back as a morning breeze ruffled the fringes of hair falling too long over his forehead. I painted an image of mid-80s high fashion on him with my mind, and it made me smile.

"Good morning. I thought you might still be asleep." I

joined him as I sipped my own coffee. It was good. Better than I made it.

I was getting used to his languid looks. I was getting used to him. His mouth tilted.

"I'm all messed up from traveling. Time zones, jet lag. Besides, early bird and all that."

He gave me a grin so easy I had no choice but to return it. Side by side we leaned on the railing and looked out over the water. I didn't feel like he expected me to say anything, and he didn't, either. It was nice.

When he'd finished his coffee, he lifted the empty mug. "So. It's just you and me today."

I nodded. I wasn't as worried about it as I'd have been the day before. Funny how being warned away from him made me feel that much more comfortable. "Yep."

He looked back out over the water. "Do you guys still have the Skeeter?"

The Skeeter was the little sailboat belonging to James's grandparents. "Sure."

"Want to take her out? We could sail across to the marina, hit the park, grab some lunch at Bay Harbor—be tourists for a day. My treat. What do you say? I haven't been on a roller coaster in about a hundred years."

"I don't know how to sail."

"Anne." The look dipped down, one brow raised, his smile half a leer. "I do."

"I don't really like sailing…." His look, that seductive, pleading, half-pouting look, stopped me.

"You don't like sailing?" He looked over the water again. "You live on a lake, and you don't like sailing."

It did sound dumb. "No."

"You get seasick?"

"No."

"You can't swim?"

"I can swim."

We studied each other. I think he was waiting for me to tell him what I really wanted to say, but there wasn't anything I wanted to share. After a minute, he smiled again.

"I'll take care of you. Don't worry."

"You're an expert sailor?"

He laughed. "They don't call me Captain Alex for nothing."

That made me laugh. "Who calls you Captain Alex?"

"The mermaids," he said.

I snorted. "Uh-huh."

"Anne," Alex said seriously. "We'll be fine."

I hesitated again and looked at the water, then the sky. It was a beautiful day, the only clouds white and fluffy sky-sheep. Storms could flare up fast, but it was only a twenty-minute sail across the lake to the Cedar Point Marina.

"Sure, okay."

"Perfect," Alex said.

We docked at the marina. Alex had, indeed, proven himself a capable sailor. I hadn't been to the Point since last year. As always with each season, fresh paint and rides made even the familiar new again.

We were lucky. The crowds were thin that day, mostly busloads of kids on school trips who arrived early, but hung in herds leaving vast areas uncrowded.

"I had some good times here," Alex said as we picked

a direction and meandered down one of the tree-covered paths toward the back of the park. "This was my first real job. First real money. This was the first place I realized I could actually get out of Sandusky for good."

"Was it?" We stepped aside to let a fast-moving swarm of kids pass us. "Why?"

"Because I knew there were other places to work than here or the automotive parts factory," he said. "The Point hires a lot of college kids. Hearing them talk about where they were going and what they were going to do made college seem like something I could really do."

I already knew he hadn't gone.

He looked at me. "I didn't go, though."

"And now you're back here." I wasn't trying to be a smart-ass, just pointing out something interesting. A circle.

He laughed. "Yeah. But I still know there's more to the world than this place. Sometimes it's good to remember there's home, though, too."

"You still think of here as home?" We were heading toward what once had been the tallest, fastest and steepest roller coaster in the park, The Magnum XL-200. It was still an impressive structure. I liked to ride in the front.

"Someplace has to be, right?"

The queue wasn't as long as it sometimes got in the height of summer, when wait times could be hours long. Still, we did have to wait, and the line moved along slowly enough to give us ample time for conversation.

"I got the feeling you weren't a big fan, that's all." Without discussing it, we both moved toward the row of cattle chutes that would lead us to the front seat of the coaster.

"I have some good memories." He shrugged. "Who said home's the place where you go and they have to take you in?"

"Robert Frost?"

He laughed. "I guess that's why Sandusky is still home. I came back and someone took me in."

Someone had, but not his family.

The attendant waved us into the front car, where we sat knee against knee and buckled ourselves in tight. The Magnum might not be the fastest or the tallest anymore, and it might not have any loops, but it's an impressive coaster just the same. Two hundred and five feet high with a one hundred-and-ninety-five-foot drop, it's the most thrilling two minutes you'll ever spend.

The ride to the top of the first hill takes forever, but once there, the view of the park is amazing. The breeze ruffled Alex's hair, and the sun was bright enough to make me squint; I'd taken off my sunglasses in preparation for the plunge. We looked at each other, and when I saw the grin on his face I felt one on my own.

"Hands up," he said.

We raised our hands.

Poised at the top of a roller coaster, I always have time to think, "why am I doing this?" I love them, the twists and drops, the stomach-sinking feeling and adrenaline rush. But at the top, with the world spread out below me, I always pause to wonder why I'm subjecting myself to the fear.

We seemed to hang over the edge for a long time before finally beginning the downward swoop. I was already bracing myself, already opening my mouth to scream.

Alex grabbed my hand.

We fell.

We flew.

I screamed, but with laughter and without breath. It was like being shot into space, twisting, turning and dropping. Soaring. And in two minutes it was all over, and the train pulled into the station with its passengers shaking and windblown. My teeth felt dry. Alex let go of my hand.

On vaguely trembling legs I got out of the car and followed him down the steps to the exit. He held open the small gate for me at the end and turned to walk backward, facing me, his face alight.

"The Magnum is the perfect fucking coaster," he said. "They can make 'em taller, but they don't make 'em sweeter."

"James doesn't like roller coasters." It was true, but it suddenly sounded disloyal, and I wasn't quite sure why. "He says he overdosed on them as a kid."

"Nah. He never liked them." Alex shook his head and made a circle in the air with a finger. "He'll ride the Puke-a-Tron or the Barf-o-Rama twenty times in a row, but he won't ride a coaster."

"He's got equilibrium." James could go on those spinning rides without getting sick. "He's good at turning in place."

"But not so good at going up and down." Alex's hands swooped, following the curve of a coaster. "How about you, Anne?"

"I like both, I guess." We were following another winding path, past food stands and games whose vendors implored us to take a chance on winning a stuffed toy. The scents of popcorn and fries tickled my nose, and my stomach rumbled.

He slanted me a look. "But you like coasters better."

I gave him an equally sideways glance. "Sometimes."

He laughed. "Me, too."

Ahead of us was the sign for Paddlewheel Excursions, a ride the park designated Tranquil and which was in essence a staged boat ride through quirky, animated scenes and narrated by the boat's "captains." The last time I'd ridden it, the operators wore uniforms designed to look like old riverboat captains, complete with maroon vests and ruffled armbands. Now they wore regular park uniforms. I was disappointed.

"Wow. Paddlewheel Excursions. I haven't been on this ride in forever." I paused at the entrance.

"So, c'mon. Let's go."

"We don't have to. There are plenty of other rides to go on."

"So?" Alex held out a hand. "We have time."

The ride was as hokey and charming as I remembered. The jokes were silly but made us laugh, anyway, and the ride itself was serene. We sat in the back, thigh to thigh on the narrow bench. The water in the canal was a murky green.

"I always thought they ran on a track," I murmured as the captain of our boat revved the engine to avoid a sandbar.

"When I worked here, one of the guys almost sank one."

"Did he?" I turned to look at Alex. "How could you do that?"

"Hit the dock hard enough, I guess you can put a hole in anything." Alex nodded toward the dock where two other captains awaited to tie the boat in place so we could disembark.

I looked at Alex closely. "Was it you?"

For a moment he looked stunned, then started to laugh. "No. I cleaned toilets."

My surprise must have shown on my face. "I always thought—"

America's not a place comfortable with a class system. We're all equal, even when we aren't. Nobody would ever have admitted aloud that the restroom attendants tended to be not as…socially presentable…as the people they hired to operate the rides and serve the food.

"See what a bad attitude will get you?" He shrugged.

We got off the boat. I thanked the young captain, who still looked embarrassed about his close call with the sandbar. I heard his friends ribbing him as we left.

"So. You cleaned toilets. For how long?"

"Two seasons. Then I moved into full-time maintenance."

"You worked here a long time," I said.

"Until I was twenty-one. I met a guy at a club who was hiring people in his factory overseas. He put me into transportation and distribution. Two years later I had my own business."

"And now," I teased, "you're a bazillionaire."

"From cleaning crappers to self-made man," Alex said, not boasting but not downplaying his success, either. "From shit to shine."

I needed a drink and stopped to buy two large fresh-squeezed lemonades. The drink was tart and cold and puckered my mouth. It was delicious. It was liquid summer.

James had told me the big fight with Alex was during his senior year of college, when they were both twenty-one. I'd always assumed alcohol was somehow involved. Booze has made and broken many relationships.

"And you've never been back until now?" I asked.

Alex shook the ice in his cup before sipping. "No."

He'd left the country when he was twenty-one upon the invitation of a guy he met at a club and after a fight with his best friend so catastrophic neither of them would discuss the cause. Or maybe I was extrapolating and the fight had been of such minor consequence, the rest of it coincidence, that neither felt the need to comment.

I poised on the edge of asking for details but then backed off. Asking him to elaborate would mean I'd have to admit I didn't know, and what sort of wife wouldn't know something like that about her husband? I didn't know Alex Kennedy well enough not to care what he thought about my marriage.

"Well, we're glad to have you now." It was the right sort of thing to say, I thought, but he only gave me another of his slow glances and a smirk.

"I said I'd treat you to lunch at a fancy place," he said. "But I'm starving for a good burger and some nachos."

That sounded better to me than something hoity-toity, anyway. Even in the casual resort atmosphere, I felt underdressed for a place nicer than a burger stand. We grabbed food and found a table, where we ate and talked.

He was better at listening than he was at sharing, with a knack for drawing answers out of me I'd have withheld from someone else. He was both subtle and forthright, asking questions that might have sounded rude from someone who wasn't at the same time so disarming. It's easy to be interesting for someone who's interested, and I found myself waxing poetic on subjects I hadn't touched in a long time.

"I just wanted to help people," I said, when he asked me why I hadn't gone back to work after the funding for the shelter failed. "I don't want to work at Kroger, bagging groceries. Or in a factory, putting lids on jars. And besides, if we have kids…"

He was leaning back in his chair, but his body weight shifted when I said that. "Do you want kids?"

"James and I have been talking about it."

"That's not what I asked you."

The breeze had picked up and gotten colder. I looked at the sky. It had grown darker while we talked. The rumble of the roller coasters masked faraway thunder.

"It's going to storm."

"Yeah. It might." He looked back at me. I must've looked disturbed. "You want to go."

He didn't ask. He just knew. I thought about shrugging it off, protesting I was fine, but I didn't.

"Yes," I said. "I don't like being on the water in a storm."

We made our way back to the marina. The water had turned choppy and gray. The sky wasn't black, not yet, but the clouds were no longer fluffy white sheep.

Alex moved fast without rushing. Steady. He unrigged, we pushed off and he pointed us toward home. I gripped the Skeeter's sides. I didn't have a life vest on. I wouldn't let go long enough to grab one.

The wind fought us, and though we made progress toward home, it was slow and rough. Spray whipped our faces every so often. I tipped my face to the sky, no longer needing my sunglasses to protect my eyes from the glare. Was the rain coming? The lightning and thunder?

I saw the blue-white flash of it from far away and heard the hint of a rumble. My stomach lurched. We were halfway between the Point and home.

I could swim. If the boat sank, I could swim. I knew I could. But people drowned all the time in sudden squalls because they weren't prepared, because they'd taken chances, because they'd been stupid. Even people who could swim. Even those who'd won medals for it. And still, I couldn't make my fingers let go of the boat's sides long enough to grab up the faded orange life vest.

Alex muttered a curse when the wind came up and tried to steal the sail. He yelled for me to grab a rope, pull a knot, something I didn't understand. I didn't know how to sail. I'd never learned.

The boat rocked and jumped on sudden waves. One took us higher than expected, and when we dropped into the valley it left behind my stomach heaved into my throat. Up. Down. A roller coaster without exhilaration. Without the safety of brakes and seatbelts.

The rain coming across the water looked like lace curtains or the scrolling of the numbers and symbols on the black screen in the opening frames of *The Matrix*. It looked like the tornado from *The Wizard of Oz*, its curving dinosaur neck bringing doom.

The Skeeter was small, and it rocked when Alex shifted

his weight to bend next to me. I drew in a breath, not screaming but heart pounding so fast and hard it hurt. My fingers gripped tighter, my knuckles white.

"Don't worry!" He had to shout over the sound of the wind. "We're almost home!"

The storm reared up in full force when we were just a few feet from the shore. Alex jumped out to tie the Skeeter up onto the small wooden dock James's grandparents had built. The sail snapped and fluttered. I caught a face full of wet fabric and gasped at how cold it was.

Once we were safely on shore, my fingers unkinked. I helped him tie everything down and secure the Skeeter. The waves were storm-sized but still did no more than tickle the beach; this wasn't the ocean, after all.

The rain came down in fat, stinging splatters. Drops struck the top of my head, my arms, got in my eyes and ears. We ran into the house and skidded on the tile floor. Alex slammed the door and the sound of the storm outside muted at once. I heard heavy breathing and realized it was me.

"You're shivering." He grabbed up a dishtowel from the counter and handed it to me.

I held it for a moment, the fabric inadequate to do more than wipe my face. I did that.

"My father," I said, and stopped. My teeth chattered like dice in a cup.

Alex dripped, waiting for me to speak. Lightning from outside reflected in the puddle at his feet. I tried again.

"My father," I said, "took me out on a boat. We were supposed to be fishing. It started to get dark."

He ran a hand through his wet hair, smoothing it back from his forehead. Water ran down his face, off his nose and chin. His eyes caught the green light from the microwave.

"The storm came up fast. We weren't too far out. But I didn't know how to sail. And…he was…"

He was drinking, as he almost always was when he wasn't at work. He'd filled his cup again and again from the jug of "iced tea" in the red-and-white cooler between his feet. The sun made him thirsty, he said. I was ten and had tasted what was in his cup. I didn't see how it could quench his thirst.

Alex's shoes squeaked on the tile as he came closer. His hand on my shoulder felt heavier than it should have, an undeserved weight. He meant it to be caring, but his understanding was too intimate to be borne. I didn't want to be beholden to him for his compassion.

I shook off the memory. "We didn't drown, obviously."

"But you were scared. You're still scared, remembering it."

"I was ten. I didn't know any better. My dad wouldn't have done anything to hurt me."

Gentle but firm, Alex squeezed the tension in my shoulder. He found the trigger point. My body wanted to melt into that simple touch, to give up the coils of anxiety woven into my muscles. I didn't move, and we stayed like that, linked by the touch of his fingertips.

The flash of lightning and almost instantaneous crash of thunder made me jump. I slipped a little, but Alex was there with a hand under my elbow and a firm forearm for me to grab. I didn't fall.

The power went out with a bleat from the microwave

and came back on a moment later with a similar, electronic cry. Another rumble followed another flash, and the power stayed out. Night hadn't fallen but the afternoon had gone dark enough to cast the kitchen into shadow.

Darkness reveals as much as it hides, sometimes. We were touching, hand to shoulder, hand to arm, hand to elbow. We dripped. We breathed. My teeth had stopped chattering, because of the heat.

"He was drunk," I said.

Alex's fingers squeezed again. I never said that aloud. We all knew, my sisters and my mother and I, but we never said it aloud. I never even said it to James, the man to whom I'd bound my life.

"He couldn't get us back in. The water came over the sides and up to my knees, and I thought we were going to die. I was ten," I said again, like it was important.

Alex said nothing, but we moved closer to each other anyway. The hem of his jeans caressed the skin of my foot revealed by my flip-flop. His shirt dripped onto my bare arm, and the water was cold.

"Families suck," Alex said.

The power came back on. We moved apart. By the time James came home, I'd made dinner and we ate while they laughed together and I put a smile on and pretended it was real.

My mother was dithering. I didn't know whether to scream or take pity on her and simply remove the choices that had sent her into such a frenzy. The air in the attic was so hot it was like breathing steam.

"Mom, just pick out a couple and let's get downstairs. Or better yet, bring the boxes downstairs and we'll look at them there."

"Oh, no, no," my mother said, her hands fluttering like birds over the carefully labeled boxes of photographs. "I'll just be a minute. There are so many nice ones...."

I bit my tongue against a sharp retort and craned my neck to see the pictures she'd lifted. There were a lot of nice ones. Nobody could ever say my parents weren't photogenic, not even in the butt-ugly 1970s prairie-style wedding gown and brown tuxedo with the yellow ruffled shirt.

"How about this one?" She held up a portrait-size photo of the two of them. She had Farrah Fawcett wings in her hair and he had mutton-chop sideburns. They looked happy.

"Perfect."

"I don't know." She dithered some more, going back and forth from one to the next, the only difference between the two was the width of their smiles. "This one is nice, too...."

The heat sapped my patience; so had the lack of sleep the night before. I'd dreamed again of the weight of stones in my pockets and water closing over my head. "Mom. Just pick one!"

She looked up. "You pick, Anne. You're so good at that sort of thing."

I reached for the one closer to me. "This one." I put it in the pile of others she'd chosen for the collage Patricia wanted to put together.

"Oh, but that one—"

I gathered them up and tucked them into the manila envelope for safekeeping. "I have to get out of here before I pass out. I'll take these."

Without waiting for her answer, I ducked through the low-hanging eaves and down the set of pull-down stairs. Compared to the stifling heat of the attic, the second floor felt like the arctic. My vision blurred for a moment and I swallowed hard against a swirl of nausea. I could blame it on the attic, but I almost always felt a twinge of stomach upset whenever I stood in the place I was now.

The stairs from the first floor came out in the middle of the second level. We had no upper hallway, just a square cordoned off by banister railing surrounding the stairs. The three bedrooms and the bathroom all opened off this square. As they'd always been, the doors were cracked open to keep the breeze flowing.

Mary, at home for the summer while she waited to return to law school in Pennsylvania, had taken over the room that had been mine and Patricia's. Claire had the room she'd shared with Mary all to herself. They still shared the single bathroom, but with only two instead of four, the fighting for the shower probably never reached the epic proportions it had when we all lived at home.

The door to my parents' bedroom was closed, the only one to ever remain that way. Closed to keep in the cooler air from the shadowed side of the house, and the air from their window air conditioner. Closed to keep us out, as children, when our dad had "a headache" and needed to "rest." A closed door that shut us out but didn't keep us from hearing the shouting.

"Anne?" My mother's flushed face appeared in front of me. She wore her curls shorter than mine, in a cut that emphasized the bright blue of her eyes. She'd stopped coloring her hair and now two side streaks of white painted the dark auburn. I didn't need a time machine to know what I'd look like as I aged. I only had to look at my mom.

The world swam and I swallowed again. Dizziness swept over me and I gulped in air that no longer felt so cool.

"Sit down." She might have been held hostage by indecision at having to choose which pictures to use, but my mother didn't hesitate now. In a house full of pale-skinned redheads, fainting had been a common occurrence. "Put your head between your knees."

I did as she said, knowing well enough the warning signs of buzzing in my ears and flashing spots in my vision. I breathed in through my nose and out through my mouth with slow, measured breaths. She brought a cold, damp washcloth and laid it over the back of my neck. It only took a few minutes before the discomfort of the balustrade digging into my back was worse than the dizziness. My mom brought me a plastic cup of ginger ale, cold but without ice, and I sipped it.

"Should I ask if there's something you want to tell me?" she asked, and when I looked up, her eyes were twinkling.

I shook my head, only slightly, not wanting to send myself back into feeling faint. "It was the heat, Mom. That's all. I didn't eat breakfast, either."

"Okay, if you say so."

My mother wasn't in my face about having kids the way

Mrs. Kinney was. My mom adored her grandchildren, Patricia's son, Tristan, and daughter, Callie, but she wasn't the sort of grandma who heat-sealed photos of her grand-kids onto tote bags or wore sweatshirts that said "Grammy's Gang" and had small embroidered stick figures represent-ing each grandchild. My mom loved her grandkids and was happy to take them places and just as happy to send them home when she was done.

I sipped more ginger ale, feeling better. "Mom, I'm not pregnant."

"Stranger things have happened, Anne."

They had happened, and to me, but she hadn't noticed back then. Or if she did, had stayed silent in the face of early morning sickness and fainting spells, of sudden bursts of hysteria and long, telling silences.

"I'm not. I'm just overheated." My stomach rumbled. "And hungry."

"Come downstairs. We'll have a late lunch. It's almost four o'clock. What time do you have to be home?"

I didn't *have* to be home at any time. Alex had left the house early that morning with mention of seeing some people about projects that hadn't been my business, and James had gone to work. I expected him home around six, but I didn't have to be there when he walked in the door.

"I should leave soon. I have time for a sandwich. I think we might be going out to eat, later, when James and Alex both get home."

My mother, however, had the long-time habit of being home when my father got home. This was a useless at-tempt at restricting his drinking; if she could keep him occupied with household tasks for a while before he settled into the easy chair, he might drink less. Or, he might not. The futility of the effort didn't seem to keep her from trying.

I didn't want to be here, however, when my dad got home. There would be much joviality on his part and much tension on mine as I counted the number of times he refilled his glass of "iced tea," each time adding more whiskey and less tea. Once, as children, Patricia and I had hidden the tea bags. We thought if there was no tea, there'd be no special ingredient, either. It hadn't worked.

"Oh, James's friend's still there? How long is he planning on staying?"

"I'm not sure."

I followed her down the stairs and into the kitchen, where the ceiling fan stirred the air into a semblance of cool. It hadn't changed much, that kitchen. The same daisies nodded on the wallpaper and the same yellow curtains hung at the windows. My mother had talked a lot about redecorating, but I suspected the enormity of choosing a new paint color, new fabric for window treatments, new potholders, had proven too much for her. We tried, sometimes, the four of us, to encourage her. But what did I care if my mother never changed the pattern on her walls? I hadn't lived in that house since I was eighteen; if God was good I'd never have to live there again.

"Is he nice? Do you like him?" She pulled out plates, bread, lunchmeat, mustard. A jar of pickles.

I grabbed a bag of chips from the pantry. "He's nice. Sure. But he's not my friend, he's James's."

"That doesn't mean he can't be yours."

My mother had befriended my father's buddies, opening the house to poker games and football-watching parties. Backyard picnics. She claimed as friends the wives of these men my dad brought home, but they only seemed to get together with their husbands in tow. No luncheons or shopping trips, no ladies' night at the movies. Those things she did with her sister, my aunt Kate, if she did them at all. The rest of it was an attempt at keeping him home. If he was home, he wasn't out driving over someone's dog. Or their child.

"He's only staying for a little while," I told her. "Until he gets his new business started."

"What does he do?" My mom looked up from the mustard she was slathering on her bread.

"I...he had some sort of transportation business in Singapore." That was all I knew.

My mom finished making the sandwiches and reached for her leatherette cigarette case. Most smokers had brand loyalty, but my mom usually bought whatever was cheapest. Today they came in a plain white pack that looked sort of like a deck of playing cards. I didn't bother asking her not to light up, though I did reach to pull my plate far out of the way.

"Singapore, oh, that's very far away." She nodded and lit her cigarette, drew in smoke, let it out. "How long did you say James knew him?"

"Since eighth grade." Suddenly ravenous, I fell to the sandwich with gusto, adding a handful of crispy chips to my plate. They were kettle-cooked, the sort I never bought at home because I tended to finish the entire bag in front of an especially good movie marathon.

There's no place like home. Ain't that the truth? Home for me would always be the smells of cigarettes and cheap hairspray, and the taste of greasy, kettle-cooked chips. I suddenly felt weepy, all at once, my emotions as much of an up-and-down roller coaster as the ride I'd taken with Alex the day before.

My mother, bless her, didn't seem to notice. We had a lot of practice avoiding the discussion of sadness. I think maybe it had become habit for her to talk over the sound of surreptitious sniffles. She chattered on about some movie she'd watched and a cross-stitch pattern she was intending to try. I got myself under control by concentrating on finishing my sandwich, but it was time for me to go.

I wasn't fast enough. The back door slammed, the way it had done a hundred thousand times when I was a kid. I heard the clump of heavy boots.

"I'm hooooooome," boomed the voice of my father.

"Dad's here," my mother said, unnecessarily.

I stood. He came into the kitchen. His eyes were already red, his smile broad, his forehead sweating. He held out his arms to me and I went obediently, no choice but to suffer the embrace. He smelled like sweat and liquor, like maybe he sweated booze now. I wouldn't have been surprised.

"How's my girl?" My dad, Bill Byrne, stopped himself from knuckling my head…but only barely.

"Fine, Dad."

"Staying out of trouble?"

"Yes, Dad" was my dutiful answer.

"Good, good. What's for dinner?" He looked at my mother, who looked almost guiltily at our plates.

"Oh...are you hungry?" She began cleaning the mess like she was destroying evidence. She'd cook him a full dinner even if she wasn't hungry herself.

"What do you think?" He grabbed for her, and she giggled, flapping her hands at him. "Annie, you staying for dinner?"

"No, Dad. I've got to get home."

"Bill, she's got to get home, of course." My mother shook her head. "She's got James waiting for her. And a guest. Alex...what did you say his name was?"

"Kennedy."

My dad looked up. "Not John Kennedy's boy."

I laughed. "No, Dad. I don't think so."

"Not John Kennedy the president," my father said. "John Kennedy who's married to Linda."

"I don't really know." Leave it to my dad to think he knew Alex's parents.

"Ah, well. Doesn't matter. What's he doing in your house?"

"He's James's friend," my mother put in quickly as she pulled the makings of dinner from the freezer. "He's come for a visit. He's been in Singapore."

"Yeah, that's John's boy, then." My dad looked satisfied with himself, like he'd sleuthed the answer to some great mystery. "Alex."

It was useless to point out I'd already told him his name. "Yes. You know his dad, huh?"

My father shrugged. "I see him around sometimes."

Around. I knew what that meant. At the bars.

"He's James's friend," I repeated for what felt like the hundredth time. "He's just staying for a little while."

"But you got to get back to him, I get it. Go on. Go." My dad waved a hand. "Get out of here."

My dad opened the cupboard and pulled out a glass. Another cupboard gave up the bottle. I loved my parents, both of them, but I couldn't stay to watch. I made my goodbyes and stole away the photos of them in their youth, leaving them to what they'd made of their lives.

Chapter 05

Alex wasn't home when I returned, but James's truck was in the driveway. He couldn't have been home for long, as he hadn't even showered. I found him headfirst in the fridge, and I took the chance to squeeze his denim-clad ass.

"Hey, you—" He whirled, his grin faltering for a moment before he grabbed me around the waist. "What are you doing?"

"I should ask that of you. What are you doing home so early?" I slipped my arms around his neck and tipped my face for a kiss.

"I was waiting on a couple of the subcontractors to bring some stuff and they cancelled, so I came home." He brushed his lips to mine. "Hello."

I laughed. "Hello."

His hands crept from my waist to my ass. "I'm hungry."

"I thought we were going to go out for dinner tonight...."
The nip of his teeth on my jaw stopped me, and I wriggled.
"Have a snack!"

"I know what I want for a snack." His hand slid between my thighs and pressed upward. "Some of this, and a little of that…"

Any other time I would have opened my legs and my mouth for him. Today I pushed him away. I laughed as I did it, but it was still a refusal.

"If you want a snack get one from the fridge," I said. "If you want something else—"

"I do." He reached out, pulled me close again. Inside the worn denim of his jeans, his cock was stiff.

I didn't yield. "James, cut it out."

He got the picture. He didn't let me go, but he did stop trying to feel me up. "What's wrong?"

"Nothing's wrong. But we can't get busy in the kitchen, okay? In case you forgot, we have a houseguest who could come home at any moment."

I pushed past him to open the fridge myself. The chips had made me thirsty. I pulled out a can of diet cola. As I was popping the tab, James grabbed me again around the waist, snugging me in close to him. He tucked his chin against my shoulder, his cock hard on my ass and his hands flat on my stomach.

"That will make it more exciting," he whispered. "We'll hear his car in the driveway, anyway. C'mon, baby. I've been thinking about you all day."

"No!" I tried to sound stern, but his hands had begun roaming again. He cupped one of my breasts while the other hand rubbed my side. "James, no. Forget it. We wouldn't hear him, he'd walk right in on us. It would be awful."

"Why would it be awful?" His voice had taken on a familiar, seductive cadence, the one he used to get me to do pretty much anything.

"It would be…rude, at the very least." I wasn't winning this argument. His hands were too skilled. I wanted to please him too much.

"Alex wouldn't care. Trust me."

I turned to face him, my can of cola held out to the side to prevent spilling. "He might not. But I would!"

He stopped. Looked at me. I've always been able to read James's face, and he's never had any reason to hide anything from me. Today, though, his expression was familiar and still indecipherable.

"Think about it," he murmured. He turned me as he spoke. Put my hands on the center island. His hands went to my hips, anchoring me as he pushed my feet apart with one of his. "Think about me fucking you, right here like this."

The marble was cool under my fingertips. I pushed the soda can aside to spread my hands flat. James pressed against me from behind.

"All I have to do is take down your pants and your panties," he continued. His hand moved between my legs again, stroking me through my jeans. "I'll rub you. Think how good it will feel."

It did feel good. Pleasure coursed through me. I looked to the back door, to the small square of driveway I could see. I pushed back against him.

"It will feel good in the bedroom, too," I said. "And we don't have to worry about Alex coming home."

"C'mon, doesn't it get you hot, just a little? Thinking

about him finding us?" He rubbed a little harder. Under his fingers my body responded. I got wet for him. "Think about me fucking you, just like this, Anne. And he comes in…"

"And what?" I turned to face him, effectively saving myself from further seduction by fingertip. "What happens then in your little fantasy, James? Is he wearing a pizza delivery costume and I suck him off while you finish fucking me?"

I spoke louder than I'd meant to, and James stepped back. I felt on edge, tingly, aroused and disgruntled, too. Random fantasies were one thing, and we'd never been shy about sharing even the most ridiculous. But they'd never been about anyone real.

James said nothing. I stared. I heard the faint fizz of my soda's carbonation evaporating.

"James?"

He smiled. Smirked, actually. "Well?"

He glanced over my shoulder, and I actually whirled, expecting to see Alex in a pizza delivery costume. The doorway remained empty. I refused to be disappointed. Instead, I smacked James on the upper arm and pushed past him to stalk down the hall.

"Anne, c'mon…."

I wasn't sure what I meant to do in our bedroom, just that I wanted to get away from him. I'm sure he thought I was angry. I was acting that way. It wasn't, however, anger that urged me into pacing. It was a jumble of confusing emotions, coupled with the day on the lake and my visit with my parents. It was everything in my life. It was PMS. It was many things, but not anger.

"Anne, don't be like that." He leaned in the doorway for a moment, watching me. "I didn't think you'd react that way."

I focused on the basket of laundry waiting to be folded. "How did you think I'd react?"

He came into the room and stripped off his shirt, tossing it toward but not quite into the dirty laundry. He undid his belt and slid it from the loops, then eased open the button. My fingers smoothed T-shirts into neat squares, but my eyes followed his movements.

"I thought you might, you know, get excited."

"By exhibitionism?" I tried sounding shocked, but didn't do a very good job of it.

James stepped out of his jeans and stood in front of me in boxer briefs. "Haven't you ever thought about it?"

I straightened. "About having sex in front of someone else? No!"

"We did it with your roommate in the room," he reminded me.

"That was different. We didn't have anyplace else to go. And it was only once."

Once, making love under covers. Making sure not to moan too loudly, or rustle too fiercely. Listening to be certain the bed wasn't squeaking in a telltale way. James's mouth between my legs, licking me as I arched and tensed and came in agonized silence.

"We're too old for that now," I said.

He put his hands on his hips. God, I loved him, every piece of him. Loved the way his skin dipped so slightly between his ribs. The tufts of dark hair under his arms and around his prick. Loved the smoothness of his skin, the dark thickness of his eyebrows, the startling blue of his eyes. He could be an infuriating pain in the ass, but I loved him anyway.

"You can't tell me it doesn't get you hot, thinking about it." He was always so sure of himself. So confident he was right. "Like that time at the movies. When we sat in the back and you wore that skirt."

I turned back to the laundry. I snapped a pair of wrinkled shorts to smooth them before folding. Heat crept up my throat to my cheeks.

"You liked that," James said.

His slow stroke on the outside of my panties had made me writhe. He'd kept up the pace for an hour and a half, the entire length of the movie. He'd never even slipped his fingers inside my panties, just circled my fabric-covered clit with small, tight strokes until I'd been ready to climb the walls. He made me come as the ending credits began, just before the houselights came up. I'd come so hard I couldn't breathe. I still couldn't remember what the movie was about.

"Just because I liked that doesn't mean I want to have your friend walk in on us," I said begrudgingly. "Think how embarrassed he'd be."

James put his arms around me. He should've smelled like sweat and dirt, but he didn't. "He's a guy, Anne. He wouldn't be embarrassed. He'd be horny."

I tried not to smile at the truth of that. "He's your friend!"

James was quiet for a few seconds. "Yeah."

I looked at him. "You like that idea, don't you? Of him watching."

Not just anyone. Not a stranger. Not a delivery boy. Of Alex, watching us.

James traced a finger along each of my eyebrows. "Forget it. You're right, it's stupid."

"I didn't say it was stupid." I put my hands on his chest. "I just want to know if it's true."

He shrugged, a nonanswer that said more than words. My guts did a slow, rolling tumble.

"What is it about him?" I whispered the question so he could pretend not to hear it.

He heard me. He didn't answer, but he heard. We looked at each other. I didn't like the sudden distance between us, in a moment when we should have felt closer than ever.

We both heard the door open at the same time. We both turned our heads toward the sound. We both heard Alex coming home, but it was James who went to greet him.

Patricia's house is always clean. I've seen her vacuum her carpet to leave marks in a herringbone pattern. I've known her to scrub her kitchen floor on hands and knees with a toothbrush, just to get the grime from the grout. We might make fun of each other for various things, but none of us ever mocked Patricia about the cleanliness of her house.

Despite her compulsion to clean, she's always made it comfortable. Her kids have the run of the place. They're good kids, too, messy like kids can be but not destructive. The house is clean, but you can tell people live in it. It's not a showroom. It's a home.

So when I walked inside my sister's house and saw the

pillows scattered off the sofa and puzzle pieces littering the floor, I wasn't at first surprised. When we went to the kitchen and dirty dishes were piled in the sink and crumbs scattered the counter, I stopped to take a second look.

"I hope you brought the pictures," Patricia said from behind me. She grabbed a full mug of coffee from next to the pot and sat at the kitchen table. More crumbs there, and she barely paid them a glance. From upstairs I heard the sound of pounding feet and some shouts as the kids played.

"I did." I held up the envelope and took the seat across from her. "I brought some really good ones."

Patricia took the envelope and shook out the photos. She sifted through them, sorting them by size. I watched her efficiency and wondered if her natural sense of organization had made her a good mother, or if having children had fostered her managerial skills. I tried to remember if she'd always been so naturally precise, but I couldn't.

"Pats," I said. "Do you ever try to think about stuff from when we were kids and can't?"

"Like what?" She picked up a picture of the two of us as toddlers, dressed in identical yellow sunsuits. "I remember those outfits."

"Do you remember them because of seeing this picture, or do you really remember?"

She looked at me. "Both? I don't know. Why?"

I reached for some of the pictures. One of my parents at a party, both with cigarettes, my dad with a tall glass of amber liquid. One of Claire as a baby, the three of us clustered around her bassinet staring at her like she was a prize. I was eight in the picture. I remembered things from when I was eight, but I didn't remember this moment that had been captured forever by a camera.

"I don't know. Just thinking."

"Well," my sister said tersely, "I don't know why you'd want to."

She snapped a couple of photos down in a row, like she was laying out cards.

"Pats," I said gently, waiting until she looked at me before I continued. "Are you all right?"

"I'm fine. Why?"

I looked around the kitchen. "You seem a little tense, that's all."

Her gaze followed mine. "Yeah. Well. Sorry about the mess. I fired the maid."

I waited for her to laugh, but she didn't. "It's not a mess."

Not compared to my house, anyway, which didn't even have the excuse of children. Certainly not compared to the house in which we'd grown up, where chaos had reigned on a daily basis. Faced with too many choices, my mother often chose none. The result had been a lot of half-finished chores. I was in college before I figured out that if you fold your laundry right out of the dryer instead of leaving it in the basket for a week, you don't have to wear wrinkled shirts.

"Let's take these upstairs to the spare room. I've got all the stickers and stuff up there."

Upstairs, I heard the mutter of cartoons and peeked my head into the bonus room above the garage. Tristan and

Callie sprawled in beanbag chairs, their eyes glued to the television. I heard a familiar theme song.

"Hey, Scooby Doo," I said from the doorway.

Two small faces turned to me. "Aunt Anne!"

Tristan, six, leaped to his feet and ran to hug me. His sister, older by two years, was slower about her affection. She was growing up, getting too cool for hugs.

"What are you doing here?" Tristan clung to me like a barnacle and lifted his legs so I was forced to pick him up or fall over.

"I came to work on some things with your mom. Why aren't you guys outside?" I said, before releasing Tristan.

"It's too hot and Mommy said we could watch TV." Callie had shot up another inch since the last time I'd seen her. Now her head reached my shoulder.

I might have trouble remembering some things from my childhood, but I had no trouble remembering the first time I'd held my niece in my arms. I'd been the one to drive Patricia to the hospital when her water broke in the middle of mopping her floor. We'd met Sean at the hospital and Callie was born twenty minutes later. I'd had the chance to hold her before she was even two hours old.

"C'mere and give me a hug," I told her and squeezed her like I never wanted to let her go. "You're getting too big."

Tristan, dancing, gave me a few more pokes before attacking his beanbag with a flying leap that threatened to bust it open. I looked at the TV, which had...shrunk?

"What happened to the big screen?"

The kids were watching their cartoons on an old twenty-five-inch set with a bunch of scratches on the side. The picture was a little fuzzy around the edges, and duct tape covered one bottom corner.

"Mommy and daddy sent it back," Callie said.

"They did? Why?"

"Anne," Patricia called from down the hall. "Come on!"

The children either didn't know or care about the disappearance of the big television. I left them to their cartoon overdose and went to the spare room where Patricia kept all her craft supplies.

Usually even that room is as neatly cataloged as a museum collection, but apparently a tornado had whirled through it. Patricia pushed aside a pile of fabric squares from the desk along the wall and put the pictures there. She closed up her sewing machine and put it away.

"Been working on something?" I asked, looking around.

"A quilt." She pulled out an accordion file, then another, from the closet and set that on the table, too. "I've got lots of stickers and papers."

Patricia had inherited my mom's creative talents for sewing, knitting and baking, though she was better about finishing projects. She'd started scrapbooking. I was lucky if I got my photos in an album, much less took the time to write journal entries about them, but Patricia had several bookshelves full of albums dedicated to different topics.

"I thought you were making a collage on a piece of poster board."

She pulled out a small black album from a shelf in the closet. "I thought I'd make an album with the pictures and leave pages for the guests to write comments. There will be blank pages at the back to put pictures from the party."

She gestured at the plethora of materials spread out all around the room. It was a nice idea, the album, if a daunting one.

"What? You don't like it?"

"I think it sounds great, Pats. Just ambitious, that's all."

"I like doing it," she said.

"Are you sure you'll have time? I mean—"

"I'll have time," she said.

Tension crackled between us, and I backed off. "Okay, but if you need help…"

She smiled, looking more like herself. "Oh, right. None of you like scrapbooking. Claire would rather poke out her eyes than do something like this. No, it's fine. I like doing it. Thanks for getting the pictures."

"Sure." I paused. "Have you seen them lately?"

She looked up from the piles she was making on the table. "Who? Mom and Dad?"

I nodded. She shrugged. She had a bunch of clear plastic shoe boxes filled with markers and various scissors, the kind that make fancy cuts. She was organizing them as she answered.

"Mom came over to watch the kids last week, and I talked to her on the phone. Why?"

"Have you seen him lately?"

She looked up, her hands full of colored pens. "No."

I hadn't thought so. Patricia took her children to visit my parents, but she never left them there. When my mom babysat, she did it at Patricia's house. But, like my father's consumption of "iced tea," nobody ever talked about why.

Without answering her question, I looked through the

stack of pictures I'd brought from my parents' attic. I held up a faded Polaroid showing me and Patricia, both of us sitting on our father's lap. We were all grinning. I had my mother's hair and eyes, but I had my dad's smile, and so did my sister.

"I look at these pictures, and I just…I don't remember that." I tapped the picture. "Do you?"

She took it from me. "We were so young. You look like you were about four, which meant I was two. Who remembers anything from when they were two?"

That wasn't what I meant, but I wasn't sure I could find the words to explain myself. At least, not without crossing into forbidden territory. I looked at the picture again.

"We looked happy," I said.

My sister said nothing. She took the picture from my hands and put it back on the pile. She opened her accordion file and pulled out a package of stickers shaped like balloons. She was ignoring me.

"I just…I look at these pictures and I know they happened because I'm in them, but…" My struggle to voice my thoughts hurt my throat. "But I just don't remember any of it."

I didn't remember sitting on my dad's knee while he read to me from Dr. Seuss, or putting together the train tracks that circled our Christmas tree every year. I didn't remember the family portrait session with all of us dressed in sweaters my mother had knitted with our names on them. I didn't remember our family being happy.

"I had to be about Callie's age in this one," I said, showing her. "And I just don't remember it. I remember the sweater, you know? It itched and the sleeves were too long. I remember looking at this picture. But I just can't really remember being in it."

My sister looked at me, the eyes we'd inherited from our mother bleak. "Stop thinking about it, Anne. Just stop it, okay? We have the pictures. We were there. You were there. Memory's a fragile thing—there's a reason why people can't remember everything. We don't have enough room in our brains for all of that garbage."

"I'm just saying, that's all. Some of these things wouldn't be so bad to have in my brain. I can remember Chris Howard upchucking all over me on the bus in second grade. That's a memory I could do without."

We laughed, but it sounded strained. I helped Patricia organize her supplies until it became quite obvious to me I was hindering more than assisting. She didn't need me there.

I squeezed my niece and nephew extra hard before I left. Would they remember the times I took them for ice cream, or played Candyland? Or would those memories fade in time, too, replaced as they aged with more recent events?

It wasn't that my mind was a gaping black hole. I remembered school and visits to my grandparents' house in Pittsburgh. I remembered the sight of the three rivers joining in one place, the view from the Duquesne Incline, and not only from seeing the pictures of that trip. I remembered favorite toys and books and television shows. I remembered bits and pieces of my life before ten…but so much of it was slippery. Maybe Patricia was right, and there just wasn't enough room in my brain.

Everything had changed the summer I was ten, Patricia eight, Mary four and Claire two. There had been phone calls waking us in the middle of the night. The shouting that used to happen behind closed doors erupted in the middle of dinner. My mother burst into tears without warning, frightening me. Everything was changing, and at ten I was old enough to know it had something to do with the phone calls and my mother's tears, but I didn't know what it was. All I knew was that we weren't supposed to talk about it, that mysterious "it" that was pulling us all apart. It had been a bad summer, and I remembered all of it with crystal clarity.

My dad had always been jolly, but he became a parody of "good-time" Dad, who got on the floor and wrestled with his daughters whether they wanted to or not. The one who brought home gallons of ice cream, half-melted because he'd stopped for a drink on the way. He woke us up at dawn on Saturdays to take us fishing, or kept us up late to catch fireflies in the yard. He'd always been a drinker—we had plenty of photographic evidence of that. But that summer he was never without his glass of tea, heavily laced with whiskey from the bottle in the cupboard. Mary and Claire were too young to notice, but Patricia and I could count. The more trips Daddy made to the kitchen, the louder he got and the quieter Mom became.

I didn't want to go out on the boat with my dad, but there wasn't any way to tell him so. I didn't like fishing, putting the worms on the hooks or the boat rocking side to side. I didn't like sitting and frying in the sun that always managed to find the spots I left uncovered. I wanted to stay home, reading my Nancy Drew mysteries, but when my father shook me awake I got out of bed and dressed and went with him.

I never told anyone, until Alex, about the day on the boat when the storm came up and my father almost capsized our boat. Like the bottles we hid under the garbage and the doors closed to mute the shouting, it was one more thing not to talk about.

Two days after the one on the lake, my mother disappeared. Taking Claire, who at two was too young to be left behind, my mom went to take care of my aunt Kate, who'd fallen ill with a mysterious ailment the adults wouldn't reveal. With school out for the summer and my dad home to ostensibly handle the details, I'd been left to take care of my sisters during the day while he worked. Looking back, I can't believe my mother ever left us alone for that long, but I guess she had no choice. And she wasn't leaving us alone, exactly. She'd left us with our dad. If I had told her about that day on the boat, she might not have gone. But I'd said nothing, not then or ever, and she had left us with my father, who'd never harm us but who hadn't done a very good job of keeping us from harm.

He'd always been moody, but without my mother to temper and soothe him, he was free to wallow. Up, down, up, down. One day he'd be talking a mile a minute, serving popcorn and potato chips for dinner, playing hour upon hour of Monopoly or Clue with us. The next, he'd come home from work and disappear into the darkness of his room with a full bottle and come out with an empty one. It was like having two fathers, both frightening in their extremes.

Patricia had asked me why I wanted to bother thinking about the past. I wanted to remember good things. It was like my life had begun for real that summer, and everything I'd ever done since, every choice I'd made both for better and for worse, had been as a result. Now my life was changing around me while I stood in the middle, wanting something without knowing what it was. I wanted to remember something good so I didn't have to think about the bad, so it didn't have the power to keep affecting me. So I didn't keep making choices based on feeling like whoever I trusted would eventually let me down, so I could stop feeling like I didn't deserve good things. So I could stop dreaming about drowning.

I didn't see much of Alex over the next few days. Whatever his new business was, it took him out of the house before I was up and sometimes kept him out until after I went to bed. I knew he was in touch with James, but I didn't question my husband too carefully about it. The subject felt tender to me, like there were answers to questions I didn't want to ask, even if I thought James wanted to answer.

I'd almost got used to thinking I had the house to myself again when Alex came home one afternoon as I sat out on the deck, reading. I could've been cleaning, or doing work for the anniversary party coming up in August, but instead I'd made myself some lemonade and gone out to read in the sun before it got too hot.

"Hey." He lounged in the doorway for a second before

coming all the way out to the deck. He'd pulled his tie loose but the suit still looked sharp.

"Hi." I shaded my eyes to look at him. "Long time, no see."

He laughed. "I've had a lot of meetings. Investors."

"In Sandusky?" I made an impressed face.

He laughed again and shrugged out of his suit jacket. His salmon-colored shirt beneath looked barely rumpled, and I envied men who didn't have to fuss with hair and makeup to look good. Or pantyhose. "No. Cleveland. I've been driving to Cleveland every day."

That would explain why he'd been so scarce. "I made lemonade. I can make some lunch, too, if you want."

"Such service." He squinted into the sun. "You shouldn't have to work so hard."

"Yes, well, I haven't had any luck with hiring a houseboy."

Alex unbuttoned his shirt and pulled it from his waistband as he kicked off his shoes. I was learning something about him. He liked to be half-naked.

"Now there's an idea." He pulled off his socks and wiggled his toes against the sun-warmed wood. "You could put an ad in the *Register*. 'Help wanted. Personal Mr. Clean needed for lakeside cottage. Duties include washing windows, scrubbing floors and shiatsu massage.'"

I giggled. "Not from Mr. Clean."

He stretched his back with a groan, twisting at the waist until his spine crackled like puffed rice cereal in milk. "You've obviously never had a good massage. Christ, I'm tight. I got spoiled in Singapore. I had weekly massages there."

"From big, bald men in white T-shirts?" I watched him stretch and move, fascinated by the lines of his body. I wondered if he was going to take off his shirt. I wondered why I cared.

"No. Small, gorgeous women with the most amazing hands…" He wiggled his eyebrows and spoke in a feminine voice. "Ah, Mr. Kennedy, you like a Happy Ending today?"

I covered my mouth, feigning shock. "You didn't."

His enigmatic grin told me nothing, but that maybe he was lying.

"Wouldn't you?" He put a hand on the railing and stretched his back again.

"I don't think so." The ice had melted in my lemonade, cutting the tartness but keeping it cold. I drank, not because I was suddenly thirsty but because I found myself needing something to do with my hands.

"But you'd hire a houseboy to come and do your laundry for you and scrub your toilets. Interesting." He shook himself the way a dog does coming out of water. "Fuck, my back hurts. Would you rub it for me?"

He was already taking a seat on the foot of my lounger and pulling off his shirt.

"Does anyone ever say no to you?" I was already putting down my glass.

He looked over his shoulder at me. "No."

I opened and closed my fists quickly, stretching my fingers. I hovered my hands over his shoulder blades, my fingers spread. I didn't have to touch him to feel him.

He was still looking at me. There was no reason for me to do what he wanted, but he acted like I couldn't refuse him. Maybe I couldn't.

His skin was already warm from the sun. My fingers were

cold from the glass of lemonade. He hissed when I finally touched him, though I don't think it was from the chill.

"You've got knots the size of softballs." I kneaded them, one at a time.

"So I've been told," Alex murmured, and we both laughed.

"You have a dirty mind," I told him and dug my fingers into the tight bundles of muscle.

He moaned, low and long. "Been told that, too. Fuck, that's good."

"James's back hurts him a lot."

He moaned again and put his head down so I could work at his neck. "Right there. Yeah…fuck."

I moved closer, my knees on either side of his hips. I could smell him. Sunshine. Flowers. Something exotic. I leaned in as I worked, my eyes closing as I breathed him in.

"Hello-oh!"

The singsong greeting immediately clenched my jaw and curled my fingers. Alex yelped as I dug into him too hard. We both looked up as my mother-in-law appeared in the kitchen doorway.

Her eyes took us in, her gaze weighing and judging us and finding us guilty in the time it took for me to uncurl my fingers. Alex took his time getting up, rolling his neck on his shoulders and stretching his back again.

"Thanks, Anne," he said. "Hello, Mrs. Kinney."

"Alex." She let her accusing eyes fall on me. "Anne. I should have called first."

Why start now? rose to my lips and I bit it back. "Don't be silly, Evelyn. Would you like some lemonade?"

"No, I don't think so." She looked at Alex, who seemed intent on poking her with his every motion as he settled himself on another lounger and lifted his glass of lemonade, pinched from me, toward her with a smirk. "I just came by to drop off these magazines."

I'd read somewhere once that you should never refuse anything someone wants to give you for free, even if you don't want it, because the next time they might not offer and you'll miss something you do desire. I never wanted Mrs. Kinney's stacks of used magazines, nor her unwanted picture frames or, God forbid, the sweaters she'd replaced with new. Still, I smiled and stood.

"Oh, thanks so much. I guess you can never get enough home and garden tips."

Alex snorted under his breath and she shot him a sour look. The one she gave me was only a little sweeter. "I put them on the kitchen table."

"Thanks." I made no move to go inside and gush over them, though I knew that's what she was waiting for me to do. I found the more I could tell she wanted something, the more perverse the pleasure I took in pretending I didn't notice what it was. She wasn't subtle. I'm not dense. It was a power struggle with a veneer of shiny.

"James won't be home until later," I said. "Did you want to wait, or…?"

I trailed off with an expectant uptilt at the end of my statement, leaving it up to her to fill in the rest. I'm sure she wanted me to ask her to stay, to sit with her over coffee and chitchat, and in the past I'd have done it. I wasn't going to offer it with a smile today. It would have been lying.

I think she would have stayed if not for Alex, now stretched out full-length in the sun, his eyes closed. Instead, she pursed her mouth and shook her head. "No. I'll call later."

"Okay." I also didn't move to show her out, though I suspected she expected that, too.

Mrs. Kinney made a big deal about how family weren't guests as a reason to make herself comfortable in my house. I didn't mind, mostly, but for the way she wanted it both ways. She didn't want to be a guest but she wanted to be walked to the door. This would give her some private moments to snark about Alex. I knew this because in the early days of our marriage, Evelyn had snagged me with this divide and conquer tactic. She'd stand up to leave, and I'd walk her to the door. Separated from the pack, or even just from James, I'd be open to her wheedling or gossip. I'd learned my lesson. And I won't pretend it didn't give me a small thrill of satisfaction to thwart her, either. If she wanted to complain about my houseguest, she'd have to find someone else to do it to.

Alex waited until the thrum of her car faded before he sat up and looked at me. He clapped once. Twice. Three times. "Bravo."

"Hmm?" I turned to look at him.

"You handled her brilliantly. Bravo."

"I didn't handle her," I demurred.

Alex shook his head. "Ah, ah, ah. Don't be modest. Evelyn's a tough woman to deal with. You were perfect."

I'm always wary when anyone gives me a merit badge for perfection in any arena. "Was I?"

"You weren't rude, but you were firm. You didn't let her manipulate you into giving her what she wanted."

"Which was?" I finished off my lemonade. It wasn't cold or tart anymore, and it left me thirsty.

"I'll be fucked if I know. But I could tell she didn't get it."

It was wrong to laugh at that, but I did anyway. "You know her pretty well."

"I did. She hasn't changed, I guess."

"That's funny," I said. "That's what Molly said about you."

"She did?" I expected him to give me a sardonic look, but disappointment flashed so quickly in his eyes I thought I must have imagined it.

"Tell me what it was like. What James was like, when he was young."

"Jamie? Pretty much like he is now. A good guy." He adjusted the chair so he could sit up to look at me. His bare toes curled against the plastic woven straps of the seat.

"That's what he said about you."

"Well, one of us is wrong."

It would have been nice of me to dispute that. "I heard you wore eyeliner."

"Sometimes I still do."

"Evelyn doesn't like you."

"The feeling's mutual, I assure you." Again, the small flicker of disappointment.

I waited for him to tell me why. From where I sat, his eyes looked wide and dark. Limpid, I thought, since languid had worn out its welcome in my descriptions of him. Luminous, too. Alex's gaze had a glow that seemed unrelated to the light around him.

"Anne."

"Yes, Alex."

"Are you hungry?"

This gave me pause. "A little. Why?"

Then, the smile. The look. Heat.

"Because you're looking at me like you want to eat me up with a spoon."

I dissolved into laughter, turning my face to keep truth from showing in my eyes the way it had flashed in his. He didn't laugh, just settled back into the lounger, stretching his arms over his head. I imagined straddling him. Bending to lick the smooth curve of his arm and shoulder.

"I'm going to get some more lemonade," I said, instead, and went inside.

Chapter 06

My doctor's office was decorated with fecundity. Pictures of smiling babies and pregnant women hung on the walls, and the racks overflowed with magazines with *parent* and *family* in the titles. I waited, my purse tucked over my stomach against the curious glances of the other patients waiting, most of whom were proudly displaying bulges. Several of them came with children, small humans who ran around and wept without provocation and seemed to me both delightful and obnoxious.

"Mrs. Kinney?"

I looked up. Six years later, and I was always still a bit startled when someone called me by that name, no matter what my driver's license said. The nurse smiled and gestured.

"Dr. Heinz is ready for you now."

I gathered my things and followed her down the hall toward the brightly painted room. More photos of babies decorated the walls. The magazine selection in there was far more out of date. I undressed at her command and settled myself onto the paper-covered table, a crinkling gown covering me. My feet were cold.

I had too much time to think while I waited. Too much time to look a the jars of tongue depressors and cotton balls, to ponder the small table set with sharp and shiny instruments that looked like torture devices. Directly opposite me was a large poster displaying the signs of common sexually transmitted diseases. Suppurating pudenda stared at me. I was saved from an overload of ooze and blisters by the sharp knock on the door announcing my doctor's arrival.

I liked Dr. Heinz because she was in her early thirties. Close to my age. Her attitudes about sex, childbearing and birth control were straightforward and refreshing, never judgmental. If I'd had her for a physician when I was much younger, I might have been able to make different choices than I had. Then again, that was a long time ago, and there wasn't any point in wondering what if.

"So how are you today, Anne?" Dr. Heinz wore the traditional white lab coat, but underneath her clothes were a mix of patterns and colors that would have guaranteed her arrest by the fashion police.

"I'm fine." I sat up straighter, too, aware that beneath the paper dress I was naked.

"Good, good." She bustled around the room, preparing latex gloves, lube and the instruments while she chatted with me about my history. When at last she settled between my legs on the rolling stool, her face level with my groin, I lay back on the examining table and stared at the ceiling.

"So," she finished, "anything new?"

"No."

I drew in a breath as I waited for the invasion. Dr. Heinz also had a slow hand, an easy touch, but that didn't make it any easier when it came time for her to use it. I concentrated on relaxing my muscles. She was good. She waited until I'd let out the breath before putting her fingers inside me.

"How's the pain?" She probed.

I winced. "It's...better."

Her fingers slid out of me. "Much better or a little better?"

"Much, actually." I tensed again, waiting for the speculum's metal quack.

"Any pain during intercourse?"

"No." The chill metal slid inside me.

Once, after an E.R. visit to stitch up an embarrassingly placed puncture wound on his rear, James had complained to me about the indignity of having a stranger access his most private parts. "He didn't even buy me breakfast," was the joke, and I'd laughed even as I mentally rolled my eyes at what he thought was indignity. Prostate exams might give a man an idea of what it's like to be a woman with the yearly intrusion into our pink parts and the experiences of childbirth and nursing. Maybe.

"Just a little scrape."

It was more the anticipation of the scrape than the actual pain that made me hiss. I felt embarrassed immediately after, like I'd screamed aloud. Dr. Heinz patted my foot kindly as she swabbed the glass slide and tucked it into a plastic Baggie to be sent to the lab.

"How are your periods? One hand over your head, please."

I always wanted to giggle when she manipulated my breasts, checking for lumps and bumps. Not because it tickled, but because it felt so ridiculous. Cool, latex-covered fingers massaging my skin while paper crinkled beneath me. Laughter would have relieved some of the tension, perhaps, but I managed to never laugh.

"They're still irregular. But not so painful. I can get away with a hot bath and some ibuprofen, now."

She grinned. "Good. That's what I like to hear. You can go ahead and sit up."

The rest of the exam was swift. Heart, lungs, whatever it was she did while probing and tapping my back. Then she left the room to give me privacy as I dressed, returning in a few minutes with her clipboard and a friendly smile.

"Okay," she began. "So. No more pain during intercourse, which is fantastic. Periods are feeling better, but still irregular. That could be a side effect of the birth control shot, but then again…" She flipped through my chart. "It says you've often had irregular or skipped periods. That's also typical with endometriosis. But other than being inconvenient, are they concerning you for any reason?"

I shook my head. "No. I wish it were easier to predict them, but other than that, no."

She noted my answer on the paper, then looked up at me. "Do you have any questions, Anne? Anything about the endometriosis treatment, pain management, the shots? The meaning of life? How to make a meat loaf?"

We laughed. "No, thanks. I think I can make a decent meat loaf."

She made a gesture of wiping her forehead. "Phew. I was afraid you were going to ask me the meaning of life, and I'd have to come up with something on the spot."

"No." I hesitated, the questions I knew I should ask hovering on my lips but in the end, unasked. "Thanks, Dr. Heinz."

"Sure thing." She smiled. "Let's get you your shot, okay? And you can be on your way."

The shot didn't really hurt. Not compared to childbirth, I thought, as she swabbed my skin with the alcohol pad and stabbed me with the chemical cocktail that would prevent James's sperm from conquering my eggs for the next three months. The puncture didn't even bleed. I bid my doctor farewell and headed through the gauntlet of burgeoning bellies and out of the office.

June really is a beautiful month. The sun shines, but not with the intensity of July or outright nastiness of August. Flowers bloom. People get married. School finishes for the summer. Everything seems on the cusp of something new, a new life, a new start.

I'd had the chance in Dr. Heinz's office to make a new start. I hadn't. I had another three months to convince myself I wanted to try to get pregnant. Also, another three months to lie to my husband.

James had been patient and understanding through my bouts with the disease that caused painful menstruation and intercourse. He'd brought me medication and held my hand when the cramps had made me sweat. He'd been the one to tell me my pain level wasn't just monthly aches and pains. I'd been having the discomfort for so long, I'd convinced myself it was normal. Coming from a family with four other women in it, moaning and groaning about periods seemed matter of fact. James had insisted I tell my doctor about the problems getting worse.

I'd been relieved to find out there was something she could do for me. That my suffering was not, as I'd half convinced myself, a punishment for long-ago sins. Many women had the same condition, some far worse than I. I was lucky. Minor outpatient surgery and some medication had helped immensely. I felt better than I had in years.

It was a good time to have a baby. James had a great job. My career had sputtered to a stop, a situation I could rectify if I wanted…but why go back to work if I was only going to leave to have a baby in a few months? It was perfect timing. I could be the stay-home mother I'd never dreamed of being.

Everything seemed like it had fallen into place. Perfect. I'd have told anyone who asked I didn't want to lie to James about anything, and certainly not something as important as our decision to have children. That in itself would have been another lie. The fact was, if I really hadn't wanted to lie to him, I wouldn't. I'd have told him the truth. I was still taking birth control. I wasn't sure I wanted to get pregnant.

I wasn't sure I could.

Endometriosis, though it can contribute to it, is not a guarantee of infertility. Nor is having a previous miscarriage. I'd had both, though James knew only of the former.

I wasn't sure I couldn't conceive, but I was terrified of finding out. Choosing not to have a child was my right as a woman. Choosing to have one was up to the whim of higher powers, and I wasn't so convinced I hadn't pissed off God enough to have Him give me the big thumbs-down when it came time to procreate.

Leaving Dr. Heinz's office, I meant to go straight home, where several loads of laundry yearned for folding, and the mop and vacuum patiently awaited my arrival. I had weeds to pull and some bills to pay.

I also had a houseguest.

James and Alex had stayed up until far past midnight. I'd left them to their reunion, the occasional rumble of their laughter pulling me from sleep. James had slipped into bed sometime between when the birds began chirping and the sun came up, that predawn time when it's still possible to convince your body you haven't stayed up all night. He'd smelled of beer and cigarette smoke, a combination that would have been much improved by the thorough application of soap and water. His snoring had woken me and kept me awake.

Despite his late night, he'd been up and about in time to head out to work. The house had been quiet when I'd left for my appointment. The door to Alex's room had been closed, no sound of anyone stirring within.

Alex wasn't my friend, but James wouldn't have bothered to leave a fresh pot of coffee or a stack of clean towels and linens. I hadn't gone so far as to offer to do Alex's laundry, but I had left instructions on how to operate my diva of a washing machine and where to find the detergent. I'd done what a good hostess should do. I even planned on stopping at the grocery store on the way home to pick up some steaks and corn for grilling tonight. I filled my day with errands designed to keep me out of the house all day, avoiding going home without even trying to pretend to myself I wasn't.

We'd had plenty of houseguests. Though our house was smaller than many that lined Cedar Point Road, we had three bedrooms and a finished basement that could accommodate more. Most importantly, we had lake frontage, a small section of dirty sand beach and a small sailboat. We were also a few easy minutes' drive to Cedar Point. James and I liked to joke that our popularity increased exponentially in the summertime, when friends came to stay and take advantage of myriad touristy things to do in the Erie County area.

The difference between those days and the current situation was twofold. They'd always been *our* friends, not only James's. And I'd been working full-time. Houseguests are much easier to stand when contact with them is limited to a few hours in the evening. I hoped Alex would have gone off to another day-long meeting, but I couldn't know for sure.

The simple fact was, I wasn't sure what to think about Alex. It wasn't so much anything he'd said or done as what he hadn't said. Hadn't done. He'd skated to the edge and backed off. Flirting, I could handle. But this was something different. It was something more. I just didn't know what it was.

I forced myself into leisurely shopping for deck furniture we didn't need and I didn't want. I tested bamboo chairs for comfort and matching tables for sturdiness. I looked at sets of grill tools, shiny and new, complete with carrying cases. I told myself I didn't mind or care that James had opened our home to Alex Kennedy, but that was another lie, one I only realized this morning when I'd had to think twice before going to the kitchen in my nightgown.

"Hi! I'm Chip! I see you're looking at our Exotica set!"

This set of exclamations came from the fresh-faced young salesman who swooped down on me as I perused the expensive teak deck sets that were too large to ever fit on our deck. I saw dollar signs gleaming in his eyes when he held out his hand. Before I had time to protest, he started rattling off all the benefits of the furniture, including resistance to termites.

"I don't think we have much of a problem with termites," I told him.

"This set is also weather resistant! And I know you've got weather!" He almost, not quite, nudged me with his elbow. I was reminded strongly of Monty Python's Eric Idle and his "wink wink, nudge nudge, know what I mean?" routine. I laughed. Chip laughed, too. "Right? Am I right?"

"Yes, we've got weather, but—"

"Well, this set will stand up to anything Mother Nature can throw at you. Do you have a big yard?"

"Not really. We have a very small piece of property."

"Oh." The dollar signs dimmed.

I felt bad. I hadn't meant to make him think I was actually going to buy the outrageously pricey table and chairs. Compulsion forced me to keep talking. "It's a lake-front property, so we have mostly sand and stones."

"Oh!"

Bing bing bing! That was all Chip had to hear. Lakefront property apparently equaled big sale in his mind. I'd been looking for a reason to linger. I felt so bad, I allowed him to regale me with descriptions of nearly every piece of furniture in the store. By the time he was finished, I'd agreed on a glider swing and a brand-new set of grilling tools, neither of which we needed.

I escaped with Chip's cheery farewell echoing in my ears, and gave myself a mental kicking. James wouldn't care that I'd spent the money. He'd probably love the swing and the tools. New things made him happy. My self-flagellation came from the fact I'd allowed myself to be nudged into buying something I didn't want and didn't need simply because I felt guilty about disappointing someone.

A stranger! A salesperson! A man I'd never have to see again! I wanted to smack myself. I wanted to march back inside the store and cancel the order, but through the window I could see Chip doing some sort of congratulatory victory dance for his co-workers. With a heavy sigh, I got into my car.

Worst of all, the shopping trip had left me without the energy to keep avoiding my house. Resigned, I hit Kroger and spent more money, this time on items I wanted. And needed. I hesitated in the alcohol aisle, the one I generally didn't go down. Today, in honor of having company, I picked up a bottle of merlot James liked. After some more consideration, I also set a six-pack of dark beer in my cart. From the way James had smelled upon coming to bed last night, they'd finished the beer from the fridge downstairs. It wouldn't hurt to bring home a few more. A six-pack wasn't a big deal.

My eyes traced over the rows of bottles with pretty-colored labels. Pictures of pirates and sexy wenches, azure seas. Escape, those bottles said. Sex, they murmured. Fun, they proclaimed. A party's not a party without Bacardi.

Well. I wasn't planning a party, only a dinner for three. Beer and wine would be enough. I turned my back on the bottles and their siren's song and headed home.

Alex had gone out and returned while I was gone. His car, which earlier had been parked slantwise next to the detached garage, now sat somewhat straighter. I parked in the driveway so I'd be closer to the door, grabbed two bags of groceries, and let myself in through the side door and into the kitchen.

I stopped in the doorway, feeling like an intruder in my own house. Soft music wafted in from the living room. A jar candle James's mother had given me, and which had rested unused in a cupboard for months, now burned on the table tucked along the bank of windows overlooking Lake Erie. Pots bubbled on the stovetop and platters of crackers, cheese, vegetables and dip had been laid out on the center island.

Alex turned, spoon in hand, when I came in. He wore low-slung, faded jeans and a button-down Oxford shirt. Unbuttoned. No shoes. His bare feet peeked out from under the frayed hems of his jeans. His hair looked slightly damp, like he'd just come from the shower and swiped a hand through it. It was the color of some luxury hardwood I couldn't name, the shade of a burnished desk in an executive's office. Brownish-red with darker and lighter strands.

"Anne," he said after a moment in which I said nothing, just gaped. "Need a hand?"

I looked at the bags in my hands. "Oh. Sure, I've got more in the car."

He set the spoon into the metal spoon rest designed to prevent utensils from staining the counter. I never managed to remember to use it, setting spoons all over the place no matter if it made a mess. He reached for the dishtowel slung over his shoulder and wiped his hands.

"I'll get the rest from the car. C'mon in. Have some wine."

He pushed past me before I could respond with more than a nod. I set my purchases on the kitchen table. He'd found the wineglasses someone had bought us as a wedding gift. Ruby liquid sparkled in two of them.

I looked at the stove. Mushrooms and onions simmered in what smelled like a garlic/butter/wine concoction. I peeked beneath the lid of another pot. Rice. Corn on the cob steamed in a third. A glance through the windows overlooking the deck showed the grill, smoking. I breathed in, deep. Everything smelled delicious.

"You've been busy," I said when he came in, laden with twice as many bags as I'd be able to carry.

"Nah." He put them on the table and looked up. His hair, drying, feathered along the back of his neck and over his ears and fell in strands over his eyebrows. He picked up the two glasses of wine, then came over to me, one held out. "I figured it was the least I could do. Make dinner."

I took the glass automatically, the way people tend to do when someone hands them something. "You didn't have to."

His smile warmed me all the way to my toes, and he leaned forward, just a little. "I know."

"It smells great." I should've taken a step back, but didn't want to be obvious about it. "You found everything you needed?"

"Yeah." He sipped his wine and looked around the kitchen. "Man, this town has changed. I headed out to hit the grocery store and damn if I didn't get lost."

Before I could answer, his gaze swung around again. Pinning me. "I never would've thought good ole Sandusky would support a gourmet food market."

"I guess it depends on what your standards of gourmet are."

God, that smile. That slow, lazy smile that promised hours of pleasure. How many knees had that smile spread?

"You have high standards, Anne?" He sipped again and looked at my glass. "You don't like red? I've got some blush, too."

Somehow, I thought the only blush Alex Kennedy ever had was the kind that came in a bottle. "No, no. That's okay. I don't drink wine."

"I don't drink…vine," he said in a thick Dracula accent. "You're a vampire?"

I laughed, shaking my head. "No, no. I don't drink wine, that's all."

"Want a beer, instead? I picked up a case of Black and Tan. Let me tell you something, Anne, Singapore had a lot of things to love about it, but nothing, and I mean nothing, beats Ohio's drive-through beer distributors."

"No, thanks." I shook my head again.

He reached over to pull open one of the bags from Kroger. "You bought wine and beer, too, I see." He looked at me with an eyebrow slightly tilted. Quizzical. "You don't want any?"

A third shake of my head. "No. I don't drink."

Alex took a long, slow sip of his wine, finishing it. He put the glass on the counter. "Interesting."

Self-conscious, I placed my glass down by the sink. I couldn't bring myself to pour it away. "It's not that interesting."

The lid of the saucepan containing the mushrooms and onions began a *rat-a-tat-tat* trembling as steam fought to escape from beneath it. Alex moved. I moved. My kitchen, like the rest of my house, isn't large. The old adage about too many cooks made a lot of sense in my kitchen, and not because they'd spoil the broth. Simply because there wasn't enough room for more than one person at the stove. We danced momentarily, him reaching for the lid and me trying to back out of the way. His open shirt trailed against my arm as he stretched. He tilted the lid off the pot and turned off the flame beneath it. His other hand landed on the small of my back, not pushing or caressing. More like steadying.

The touch was fleeting, withdrawn before I had time to do more than barely feel it. He turned to face me. "I hope you're hungry."

My rumbling stomach proved the truth of that. "Starving."

"Good."

We stared at each other. The corner of his mouth

quirked. I wasn't sure I liked the way he looked at me. I wasn't sure I didn't.

"You're pretty good in the kitchen." I looked at the stove, then back at him.

Alex put a hand over his heart and gave a small, half bow that brought him close enough to me so I could smell his cologne. It was the same as it had been the day before, something spicy and exotic. Masculine and yet…flowery. He looked up at me through the fringe of his hair, smiling. Devastating. Charming. And he knew it.

"The bachelor life isn't all pizza and beer. Well, not all pizza, anyway. When you don't have anyone to do it for you, you learn how to do it for yourself."

I emptied bags of perishables and put them in the fridge or freezer. Alex stayed out of the way. I felt him watching me. "Maybe you can give James a few pointers."

"Jamie's never had to do it, that's all. He's always had someone to do it for him. Mama and two older sisters have taken good care of him. And now he has a wife."

I turned to look at him. "Yes."

"And now you take care of him." He grinned.

I couldn't decide if he was offering a compliment or an insult. "We take care of each other."

Alex went to the stove and stirred the pot of bubbling mushrooms and onions. "Poor Alex has nobody to take care of him. So I learned to cook just to save myself from having to eat takeout every night."

I took a long sniff of the delicious smells coming from the stove. "Well, I'm impressed."

"Then my evil plan has worked," he said. "Bwahaha."

The funny thing was, I couldn't be certain he was kidding. He didn't give me the chance to ponder it, though. Alex straightened, put a hand on my shoulder and guided me out to the deck, where he sat me in the comfortable lounge chair and urged me to put my feet up. I was laughing, self-conscious at the attention again, but he just smiled.

"I'm a full-service agent," he told me. "You sit. I'll bring you something to drink that you will drink."

He flipped the steaks on the grill and disappeared into the kitchen. He returned in a moment with a glass of iced tea and the platter of cheese and crackers, which he put on the small table next to my chair.

"I could get used to this." I took the glass from him. It was too early for dusk, but the breeze off the lake was chill. It would be a good night to light a fire in the clay chiminea shaped like a carp.

After checking the steaks again and turning off the grill, Alex eased into the chair opposite mine. One long leg crossed over the other as he leaned back. His shirt fell open, revealing his chest and belly. I didn't know how he could stand to wear those jeans so low, but I wasn't unhappy that he could.

"Mind if I smoke?"

I didn't care for the smell of cigarette smoke, but I shrugged. "Go ahead."

Both my parents had always smoked. They still did. The stench of cigarettes clung to their clothes, breath, hair, skin. I hadn't smelled anything on Alex but his cologne and the scent of garlic, butter and wine.

He lit up, drawing the smoke deep into his lungs and

holding it for a moment before letting it seep out slowly, in twin streams from his nose. I watched, admiring the talent. Just because I'd never acquired the habit didn't mean I couldn't appreciate a sexy man with smoke curling around his head....

"Sorry?" He'd asked me a question.

"I said, what time is our darling Jamie due home? The steaks are done and so's everything else."

I glanced at my watch. "He usually gets home around six. Sometimes later, if he's tied up on the job."

Alex made a little *O* with his lips. "Ooh. Tied up, huh?"

The way he said it made me laugh. I seemed to do that a lot around him. He didn't laugh, but that smile tilted his mouth again.

I had my glass of tea raised halfway to my mouth when it hit me like a two-by-four. Alex's smile, its quirking, smirky tilt. It was the smile James wore when he was trying to be sexy. It was as different from James's normal easy grin as night from day and sat on his face like an imposter. Now I knew why.

He'd stolen it from Alex.

This realization made alternating hot and cold flashes ripple down my spine. I finished the gulp of iced tea that had been arrested halfway down my throat. It burned, and I blinked rapidly against the blurry edge of tears.

Alex smoked, and I watched him. He looked out over the lake, toward the glittering lights of the roller coasters. "Did you ever work there?"

"No." My family lived on Mercy Street, way across town. "I didn't have a car."

"Me neither. I rode my bike."

"So you grew up in town." James and his sisters had grown up in a house in one of the nicer neighborhoods. His parents still lived there. His sisters and their husbands had stayed in the area.

"Yeah. My mom and the old man still live here."

I'd been layering a cracker with thin-sliced Gouda, but at this revelation I looked up. "They do?"

He smiled around his cigarette, eyes still looking toward the park. After a moment he looked at me, heavy-lidded. A little sly. "Yeah."

But he was here, with us. With James. With me.

There could be a thousand reasons why he wasn't staying in his childhood home. I didn't need to even guess one of them. "Families suck" had pretty much said it all. Even so, my face must have shown something of my surprise, because Alex let out a slow, grating laugh.

"We don't get along, the old man and me."

"That's too bad."

He shrugged and finished the cigarette, stamping it out in the empty cola can on the arm of his chair. "I haven't seen him since before I left for Asia. My mom calls once in a while."

"Do you get along with your mother?"

"Do you get along with yours?"

I blinked at his tone, just this side of mocking. "I get along with both my parents."

"And Jamie's, what about them?"

"I get along with them, too."

"Ah, ah, ah," Alex scolded, raising and moving one finger from side to side. "Anne, it's not nice to lie."

My feelings toward my husband's mother were complicated and made me uneasy. I shrugged again. "You've known them longer than I have."

"Yeah." He flicked the top on his square silver lighter and lit the flame, but didn't take out another cigarette. The flame flickered and died, and he lit it again. "But I didn't marry Evelyn's wittle boy."

"She means well." The cracker and cheese were dry as dust in my mouth, and I had to swallow more tea to wash it down.

"Sure, she does." Alex got up and went to the railing. Leaning over, one foot propped on the bottom rail, he stared out over the water. "Don't they all?"

I heard the rumble of tires on gravel. James. Relieved, for the conversation with Alex had definitely taken an awkward turn, I got up to greet my husband. He came through the kitchen like a dervish, grabbing up a handful of baby carrots and leaping through the screen door hard enough to slam it back against the house.

"Honey, I'm home!"

He wasn't looking at me when he said it.

Alex turned, rolling his eyes. "It's about time, fucker. We're starving."

"Hey, sorry, man, we can't all be independently wealthy bastards."

James slung an arm around my neck in a way I've always hated because it snags my hair and weighs me down. He kissed my cheek. I smelled carrots.

"Bitch, please," said Alex. "I worked my ass off for

that company. Taking a month or two off doesn't make me a bastard."

"Hell, no," James said. "You were a bastard long before that."

Alex snorted, moving closer. The three of us made a triangle with Alex at the apex. Two handsome men and me. What woman wouldn't enjoy being part of that party?

"Damn, that smells good." James sniffed the air and kissed my temple, half-distracted. "What is that, steak?"

"Alex cooked," I offered.

James let go of my neck to lift the grill lid and hoot in approval of the three huge, juicy steaks inside. "Dude. Nice job."

Alex slipped his lighter into the pocket of his jeans. "Let's eat, asshole."

Asshole. Fucker. Bitch, even. Women might tease each other with bitch, but you had to be very, very good friends with a very, very good understanding of how that word was being used. Men tossed off insults like they were pet names.

We ate on the deck, the three of us knee to knee to knee around our small and somewhat rickety table. The food wouldn't have tasted any better if we'd been sitting on teak. The men talked. And talked. And talked some more. I stayed mostly silent, listening, searching for the key to this friendship.

What made it tick? What had kept it going all these years? What had nearly ended it? And what had brought it around again?

"Ho-lee-shit." This was said by James in a tone of utter

awe as Alex brought out a layered dessert made of cake, custard and fruit. "Look at Julia Child."

Alex put the dessert, which had been assembled in the footed glass trifle bowl we'd received, like the wineglasses, as a gift. Seeing the layers of goodness inside, I couldn't believe I'd never used it.

"Fuck you, man." Alex flipped James the bird, right in his face.

James swatted the hand away. "And the horse you rode in on."

Alex sat and stuck a spoon into the bowl. "Serve yourself."

I caught his eye. He didn't look displeased with James's teasing praise. Both had drunk wine with dinner, but now Alex had opened a bottle of beer. He sipped, set it down and leaned forward to grab the spoon again.

"But Anne first."

"I'm stuffed," was my first protest, but neither James nor Alex would hear it, and I ended up with a serving anyway.

"Dinner was delicious, Alex. Thank you."

He waved an indolent hand, his attention on James. "Don't mention it."

"I still think you should give James some lessons," I said casually. "He can barely make oatmeal."

"That's because his mommy packed his lunch for him until he went away to college," Alex said, though fondly. "And mine was usually too much of a mess to cook anything at all."

Another moment of awkwardness fell over us, and it took me a second to understand I was the only one feeling it. Whatever Alex's home life had been, it was obviously something he and James had been quite used to.

"You're a long fucking way from grilled cheese and bologna sandwiches, man." James licked the tines of his fork. "Man, when we were kids, Alex used to make the best fucking GC&B."

They both laughed. I made a face. "Grilled cheese and tomato soup I've had. But grilled cheese and bologna? Ew."

Alex drained his glass. "At Jamie's house we got stuff like PB&J with the crusts cut off and Cracker Jacks."

"At his house we got grilled cheese and bologna and Jack Daniel's."

They laughed again. James finished off his dessert. Alex had pushed most of his aside. I looked up from my plate. When Alex had said he didn't have anyone to take care of him, I'd assumed he meant now.

"You're kidding, right?"

Alex had been looking at James, but now he favored me with his gaze. "No. I have the dubious honor of being the first person to ever get our little Jamesy-Wamesy fucked up."

"How old were you?"

"Fifteen." James shook his head, still eating. "We drank half a bottle of Jack we snuck from Alex's dad and read porn mags and smoked a pack of shitty little cigarillos we bought off some kid at school."

"Black Market Pete."

"Who?" I looked from one to the other. The conversation was losing me.

"This kid who could get anything for anyone." James laughed. "Black Market Pete."

I was content enough to listen to them talk and trade

stories. It was sort of like listening to secrets. I was fascinated by these glimpses into my husband's past.

"How did you two meet, anyway?" I asked.

James looked to Alex, who answered. "Homeroom. Eighth grade. Mrs. Snocker."

"Good old Hocker Snocker." James snickered.

"Heather Kendall had moved away the summer before school started." Alex gestured, expansive. He filled his glass again and put the bottle, empty, aside. "The rest, as they say, is history."

"Kennedy, Kinney," James explained. "He sat in front of me. First day of school, Alex shows up in this fucking leather jacket with fucking zippers all over it like Michael Jackson—"

"It was black, fucker," Alex said without animosity. "His was red."

"Anyway. Ripped jeans, white T-shirt, black motorcycle boots and black fag jacket."

Alex's eyes flashed. "That you borrowed from me every chance you could get because your mommy wouldn't let you dress like all the other boys."

"Cold, man. Cold." James drained his beer.

I felt like I was at a tennis match, listening to the volley of their words. Fag jacket? I'd never heard James call anything or anyone *fag*. The word had a harshness to it that didn't sound right coming from his mouth. He didn't even tell ethnic jokes.

Alex didn't seem offended. "Jamie's mom used to make him wear the queerest madras shorts and polo shirts. And deck shoes. Jesus. And sweaters over the shoulders. Good

Christ, it was like he walked out of the frigging Buttfuck Sailor catalog."

By this time James was laughing so hard all he could do was wave his middle finger in the air. Alex, who appeared to be trying to keep a straight face throughout the description of James's teenage wardrobe, finally burst into a flurry of guffaws. Their conversation deteriorated into gasping insults while I looked back and forth, amused.

"...frigging reject from *Grease...!*"

"Mr. *GQ*, pretty frosted hair all slicked back! Mr. Pink Izod shirt!"

"Fuck you, man, that shirt was cool!"

"Sure, sure. So you say. Let me guess, Anne's taken over dressing you, cuz you sure as hell look a lot better than you used to."

"Excuse me, America's Next Male Model."

The insults faded into chuckles and obscene hand gestures. In unison they turned to me. I was caught, not sure what they expected me to say.

"You dress him, don't you, Anne?"

"I don't, actually." I looked at James, who was now flipping a triumphant bird. I hadn't realized how many emotions could be conveyed with one single hand motion.

"She doesn't." James sat back with a sigh, hand on his stomach. "Fuck. I'm stuffed."

I looked at his work clothes, a pair of grimy jeans and an equally stained T-shirt that bore the logo of his company. Kinney Designs. A baseball cap or hardhat often completed his outfit along with a pair of steel-toed work boots. But when he wasn't working, James knew how to dress really well. It had been one of the first things I'd noticed as I got to know him, how much time he'd spend coordinating his clothes. I looked from him to Alex, and back again. I wondered if James had learned his sense of style from the same place he'd lifted that smile.

"Thanks for dinner, Alex. It was delicious." I stood to gather plates and napkins.

"Hey, Anne, don't do that."

I looked up. "What?"

"Don't clean up. Sit with us for a while." Alex reached for another cigarette and lit it, sucking in smoke and blowing it away from the table before looking back at us. "Talk."

I sat, though I had nothing much to say. They had years of history of which I had no part. It was a little hard to keep up my end of the conversation. I didn't mind, really. When I got together with my sisters or old school friends it was the same way. I understood it.

"Look at that water." James patted his stomach again.

We all turned to look. Night had dipped along the lake, though the sky was clear and the moon and stars gave enough light to reflect in the water. It was lovely and reminded me anew why I loved living by the water as much as I didn't like being on it.

Alex stood. "You know what we've got to do, man."

James started laughing. "No. No way."

"Yes. Way." Alex leered. "C'mon. You know you want to! Anne, tell him he wants to."

"What does he want to do?" I asked, wary but laughing, too.

"No way, man! We've got neighbors!" James held up a hand against Alex's grabbing fingers.

"Come on, ya pussy!" Alex hooked the edge of James's shirt and tugged. "You want to do it."

Obviously James did, because he got up, batting away his friend's hand. "All right, all right!"

"What are you going to do?" Their antics were both amusing and alarming.

Alex stripped off his shirt. His hands went to the button on his jeans. He looked at me. He smiled. I swallowed, hard.

"You up for it, Anne?"

I looked out at the water, rippling so gently under the moon. "Swimming? Now?"

"Skinny-dipping." James snorted lightly and tugged his shirt over his head. "She doesn't swim, Alex."

"She can swim."

Our eyes met. Alex's fingers slid open the button and undid the first couple notches on his zipper. It felt like a challenge, one I lost because I let my gaze go to his crotch before swinging back to his face.

James pushed his jeans over his hips and stood in his briefs. Hands on his hips, he jerked his chin toward the lake. "C'mon, pussy. Thought you were going in."

"I'm waiting to see if Anne's coming, too."

"No." I shook my head, our little moment lost. "You boys have fun."

"Sure I can't convince you?" He put on more charm.

"I don't swim in the lake," I said, keeping the smile on my face and meeting his gaze head-on without flinching.

James had spent enough nights being woken by my

dreams to understand why I wasn't going to join them, even if he didn't know the reasons for the dreams themselves. He reached to stroke a hand down my hair. I looked at him, and he bent to kiss me.

"C'mon, man," he said. "Let's go."

Alex had made himself a portrait, a moment frozen in time. He cocked his head and watched us, his fingers still lingering at his crotch. His pupils looked like they'd swallowed the rest of his eyes. Darkness. I waited for him to ask me why, though he must have known.

The moment passed. Grinning, he shoved his pants over his hips and thighs. I squeaked and covered my eyes at the sudden nudity, which made them both laugh. I heard the pounding of feet on the deck, then whoops and splashes as they ran down the beach into the water.

I got up to lean on the railing to watch them. They roughhoused a little bit, splashing and wrestling. Then Alex ducked all the way under the water and came up a moment later, shaking his hair. James did the same. They swam and floated. I heard the rise and fall of their conversation, though not the words.

I cleaned up the table while they swam. I brought out towels, lit the chiminea and made coffee, too. At last they ran dripping out of the lake and back to the deck, where naked James grabbed me and dipped me for a long, thorough kiss.

"You're wet!" I protested, squirming.

"Are you?" He whispered, naughty, his eyes gleaming.

"Anne, you're a goddess," said Alex upon discovering the towels and the pot of coffee on the table. "Jamie, move out of the way and let me have my chance."

I must have looked alarmed, because James laughed and set me upright on my feet again. He wrapped the towel around his waist and stood between me and Alex. "Put some clothes on first, man."

"Both of you put some clothes on," I said. "You're going to get sick."

Alex saluted. James bowed. They moved in unison without even noticing how alike their mannerisms had become. I turned my back and poured coffee to give them both time to dress, my heart pounding a little at the thought of Alex having his chance.

For what?

Chapter 07

I didn't get to find out, because by the time they had both pulled their clothes on again Alex seemed to have forgotten his intentions to show his appreciation in any physical manner. Dinner and swimming hadn't tired either of the men, though I was yawning behind my hand. James tugged me next to him on the lounger and wrapped us both in a large throw blanket against the chill coming off the lake. I'd bought some scented long-burning cords for the chiminea, and they gave off a steady, woodsy fragrance the package had called Forest Fresh.

"Smells kind of like ass, to me," said James. "Sweaty ass."

Alex smirked. "And you know this how?"

I'd tucked my feet up on the edge of the chair, the better to snuggle close for warmth. James's shoulder made a bony pillow but I rested my cheek there, anyway. It brought me close to him and let me see Alex at the same time.

"Yes, James. I want to hear the answer to that." Beneath

the blanket, his hand moved between my thighs. His fingers were a little cool but quickly warmed.

"I'm just saying. It's not 'fresh' anything. Hey, man, give me one of those." James gestured at Alex's pack of cigarettes.

Alex tossed him the pack. James pulled out one of the slim tubes and held it up to me. "Anne?"

The look I gave him was one he'd fondly termed the what-the-fuck look. As in, what the fuck are you doing, asking me if I want a cigarette?

"Let me guess," Alex said as he sucked in smoke and held it. "You don't smoke?"

"I don't. James doesn't, either. Do you?" I sat up, putting some distance between us.

"Only when I'm drinking, babe." He lit the cigarette and drew in some smoke, but let it out in a small fit of coughing.

"Ha! Ya fucking pansy." Alex grinned and blew a smoke ring.

They traded more insults, and to my relief, James stubbed out his cigarette without taking any more drags. He pulled me back down next to him. His hand slid beneath my arm to cup my breast. His thumb eased back and forth across my nipple, bringing it to a tight point. His lips found my temple and lingered.

Across from us, Alex had fallen into shadow lit by the occasional flare of his cigarette and the square of light from the kitchen window. He and James had been matching each other bottle for bottle, and now he lifted another to his lips.

"Don't swim. Don't drink. Don't smoke," he said in a husky voice. "What *do* you do, Anne?"

"That's me. Goody Two-shoes." It wasn't true. Didn't feel true, anyway.

"Just like Jamie." Alex propped his feet up on the edge of our lounger, one between James's toes and the other along the edge of mine. His feet dented the blanket tangling around our heels.

"Why do you call him Jamie?"

Under the blanket, James's hand kept up the slow stroking. He'd moved it beneath my shirt, his fingers skating the edge of my lace bra. I was pretending not to notice, though it was impossible to ignore.

"Why don't you?"

It didn't seem fair that they were both drunk and I wasn't, yet I was the one left without a witty answer. "Because...his name is James."

"Alex is the only one who calls me Jamie." James's mouth moved against my temple.

A chill skittered down my neck at the combination of hot breath and tweaking fingers. I shifted, which pushed my foot against Alex's but allowed James the chance to slip a hand between my thighs again. He put it much higher, this time the edge of his thumb pressing against my clit.

"Why? Why not Jimmy? Or Jim?"

Alex couldn't see what James was doing to me and might not have cared. James had drunk enough beer to make certain he didn't. I was the one who ought to have had more restraint. I didn't have the luxury of blaming booze for my lack of composure.

"Because his name's Jamie," said Alex, like that explained it all.

Maybe to both of them it did, but I was still on the outside. I hadn't heard half of their inside jokes and didn't understand the ones I had.

James left off pressing between my legs to shift my hand over the bulge in his jeans, then returned his hand to its previous spot. His cock pushed against the denim. His thumb pushed against me. His other thumb dipped inside my bra to fondle my nipple.

I wasn't drunk, but I was feeling a bit lightheaded. I wasn't averse to a little subtle poke or pinch now and again, but James was full-on trying to get me off.

It was working, too. My clit had gone as tight and hard as my nipples, even though there were two layers of cloth between his hand and my body. It was the steady push-push against me that was doing it. It hit me just right. It was…perfect.

James and Alex kept talking, sharing memories, though I noticed they avoided any further mention of Alex's parents or the years after high school. They mocked each other mercilessly, saying things I'd have bet would have earned other men a punch in the face.

They talked. James stroked and kneaded me and every now and again pushed his crotch with growing insistence into my hand. My arousal grew slowly, like the first drip-drip of melting ice that threatened to become a torrent.

It was my husband touching me, but his friend whose face I watched as my pussy got slick and my clit throbbed. The two of them, James so light and Alex his dark counterpart, seemed to work together. James's hands, Alex's voice as he told us stories about living in Asia. About the sex shops there, where you could buy anything you wanted.

"I thought Singapore didn't have sex shops. I thought they were illegal." How did my husband know about Singaporean sex laws?

"In Singapore, yeah...but not in other places. There are always places to find it, if you want it."

"And you wanted." James's voice had grown hoarse.

The night had grown downright cold, though beneath our blanket James and I were hot enough to start a fire. Alex didn't seem to mind the chill. He'd buttoned his shirt up to the throat but seemed otherwise unaffected.

"Who wouldn't, man?" came Alex's shadow-voiced answer. "Find a girl, find a boy. One of each. You'd find your houseboy there, Anne."

My inner thighs were trembling, my breath coming short and shallow as the sneaky seduction orchestrated by my husband's hands did its work. It wasn't exactly what he was doing, as the stimulation would likely have left me wanting under other circumstances. It was the sheer length of time he'd been at it.

"Anne wants a houseboy? That's news to me." James didn't sound like he was about to dissolve into orgasm at any moment. Then again, my occasional pressure on his cock was probably only enough to tease.

"Yeah, she wants a houseboy in a thong to cook and clean for her." Alex's chuckle was low and naughty. "But, hell. Who wouldn't?"

"I never said...he had to wear a thong." I shifted and

put a hand over the one between my legs. James didn't get the hint, didn't stop what he was doing. A slow, inexorable press-press, release against my clit that had me biting my lip and wanting to moan.

"She doesn't need a houseboy. She's got me." James nuzzled the side of my neck. He nipped. I felt tongue. I closed my eyes.

"You, my friend, don't cook."

"You're right." James's laughter buzzed in my ear. Press-press. Release. "But you do. And now she has you."

I was only paying half attention to their half-drunk conversation, focused too much on the building pleasure between my legs. My fingers gripped down on the arm of the lounger. I was timing each breath to coincide with the infinitesimal motion of James's hand. In. Out. Press-press, release.

I was going to come, hard. Inevitably. I couldn't stop it, not without forcing away James's hand and leaping to my feet to get away from him, and even then I'd reached the point where something as simple as the pull of my panties against my clit would finish me off.

"She's not listening."

I heard Alex's chair scrape the deck and felt our chair shake a little as he pulled his feet off it. My eyes opened, wide. Startled. He leaned forward, hands on his knees, and the motion brought his face completely into the golden light shining from the kitchen.

"She's listening," James said.

And I came. Not fast, like lightning, but in slow, easy waves. Climax rolled over me in a tightening and trembling of muscles, in a stifled, hitching breath, in the flutter of my eyes as I fought not to give any outward sign of my orgasm. My eyes went wide, though, as my fingers dug into the arm of the chair and I bit the inside of my cheek to keep from crying out.

We were looking into each other's eyes, when I did it, Alex and I, and no sooner had the last spasm coursed through me than he leaned back in his chair, one bare foot resting on his denim-clad knee.

"I know she was," he said. "But I look like shit in a thong."

Warmth flooded and abandoned me, leaving behind a chill that had nothing to do with the night air. My illicit orgasm should've left me relaxed but had instead created greater tension. Silence hung between the three of us for what seemed too long for comfort.

Then Alex stood. "Well, ladies, I'm off to bed. I need my beauty sleep."

I began to disentangle myself from the blanket and James's arms, meaning to get up and bid our guest goodnight in the polite way. I hadn't managed to get very far when Alex leaned over us both, one hand on each arm of the chair. I smelled him again, something like the bite of cedar with a hint of exotic flowers. Smoke and alcohol, too. His scent was a layering as complicated as the man himself seemed to be.

Light from the window cut across his face, highlighting his eyes, which were large and round. I'd thought they were brown, but now I saw they were dark gray. He smiled, lopsided, weaving a little.

"Good night," Alex said. He brushed his lips against

my cheek, then did the same to James without a pause, adding a pat to both our heads as he withdrew. "See you in the morning."

"Night," I replied, my voice somewhat faint.

I watched him as, holding the doorjamb for momentary balance, he went into the house. A minute later the lights in the kitchen went out, leaving us in darkness. James pulled me closer at once, his mouth seeking mine.

"Baby, I've been waiting all night to do this." He nibbled my lips and urged my mouth to open, sweeping his tongue inside.

"James…" My protest was feeble, no more than a hand on his chest and a turn of my head to fend him off.

His hand slid between my legs again. "I couldn't stop touching you."

I looked at him. "You're drunk."

That smile, that copy of his friend's. James had worked hard on it, I could tell, but it was still something that didn't belong to him. It was too hard for him. Rapacious.

Yet I couldn't deny what that smile did to me, how it made me feel. How seeing it, I'd know exactly what he was thinking about doing, and how much I always enjoyed what he did.

James moved his hand a little. "You liked it, didn't you?"

I had. "That was impolite, at the very least."

He laughed, pulling me closer and kissing me again. I tasted beer. I turned my face again, slightly, when he attempted to capture my mouth once more. He satisfied himself with mouthing my jaw and neck.

"But you liked it, Anne."

"I don't know what to think about that," I whispered

with a glance at the house. The light in Alex's room, which I would've been able to see from the deck, hadn't gone on. "He's your friend! It was…"

"It was fucking hot," he murmured against me. "Touching you like that, getting you off. Sort of like the time in the movie theater. Sort of like when I came over that weekend at school and your roommate wouldn't leave."

"Yes, but that was…those were…" I couldn't exactly think what I meant to say.

"This was better," James whispered with a little growl. He bit at my neck, gently, but still with a press of teeth that made me hiss. "My cock's so hard I could lift bricks."

That was certainly true. He groaned a little when I touched him. When I slipped a hand inside his jeans, he muttered "fuck," and leaned back against the lounger with an arch of hip that pushed his cock harder into my hand.

"Suck it," he whispered. "I've been thinking about you sucking my cock all night, Anne. Put it in your mouth."

I undid the button, then the zipper, slowly. I folded open the denim and freed his erection. It pulsed hot in my hand. James lifted his hips so I could pull down the jeans a little. When I pumped my curled fingers up and down his shaft, he moaned.

"You want me to suck you?" I asked, quiet, mindful of the neighbors and our presumably sleeping houseguest. "You want me to put you in my mouth?"

He liked to hear me say it. I liked to say it. During sex was the one time I never had to pretend, never had to be polite. Never had to bite my tongue against saying what I really thought and felt.

"Yeah," he moaned, carding his fingers through my hair. "Suck my cock the way you do. So good."

Normally the way he was slurring his words would have turned me off. I'd have put distance between us, real physical distance as well as mental, the way I always did around someone who'd overindulged in alcohol. Tonight, all the rules seemed to have changed. James wasn't melancholy or belligerent. He wasn't going to be driving and therefore taking his life and the lives of the world around him into his hands. Alex and James were drinking. They were drunk. And though it normally would have settled my stomach firmly into my throat, tonight, somehow, it was different.

Maybe because Alex was so charming with his stories. Or the way he got drunk but not sloppy, not spilling or stumbling. He drank like it was a skill, like bowling. Or golf. And James, who didn't drink much and tended to get sloppy and silly when he did, seemed to take Alex's lead. He wasn't sloppy or silly, but apparently, he was horny.

I made myself comfortable, the blanket around my shoulders and my body stretched out along the lounger. His prick might not have been able to lift bricks, but it was admirably erect. I traced the rim of the head with the tip of my tongue. I took him into my mouth inch by inch instead of all at once, accustoming myself to his girth.

I've never found monstrous penises attractive. Bigger is not always better. Huge, vein-encircled members the size of a baby's forearm, like the ones they show in porn films, always left me feeling half-horrified and wanting to clamp my legs closed. I've never found the idea of fucking a tree trunk appealing.

James has a thick penis, shorter than some I've seen but beautifully proportioned. I can take him all the way to the back of my mouth without choking. Sucking James is a treat, a pleasure for both of us. I love the sounds he makes when I cover him with my mouth that first time.

He made that noise then, a low half gasp mingled with a groan. The hand in my hair tangled tighter, not quite pushing me down but almost ready to.

I'd spent hours with my mouth between his legs, sucking and licking. This was not the time for that. No teasing, no lingering. He'd been hard for hours as he rubbed me surreptitiously, getting me off in the presence of his friend. He was already pushing upward as I sucked him. Already close.

I pulled the blanket over my head, shielding myself against the night. I made love to him with lips and tongue, with a hand stroking his shaft while I sucked the head of his cock. Even in the darkness I knew him. The shape and taste of him. The way he moved as his orgasm approached. Even in the dark I couldn't really pretend I was sucking someone else's cock.

Could I?

There's no shame in fantasy. If imagining you're in bed with your favorite movie star or rock singer helps make you come, who's getting hurt? It only becomes a problem when the fantasy becomes the only way to find pleasure, not just one way to enhance it.

I'd had my share of celebrity-inspired daydreams, but this time the face that filled my mind had large gray eyes and deep brown hair feathering over his ears. He had a lazy smile and smelled like sin. I wasn't thinking about some unreachable fantasy. I was thinking about Alex.

"So good," James said.

I thought of his smile, the one he'd stolen. My hand crept between my thighs, inside my panties, found hot slick flesh already satisfied once but far from sated. My fingertip settled without faltering on my clit. The hard nodule rolled easily, already wet.

I thought of his smile. His scent. I thought of low-slung jeans. Bare feet. Bare chest.

My body hummed with pleasure. My hand moved in time with my mouth. James moaned and thrust. My belly tightened, thighs trembled. Clit pulsed. My cunt was alive with humming, buzzing pleasure.

I sucked and licked and stroked. I was close. He was close. The world faded away, nothing but blackness under the blanket, nothing but the smell of sex, the sound of sex, the taste of it.

His smile. His laugh, low and somehow sly. The burning wink of a cigarette in the dark.

James let out a hoarse cry and thrust inside my mouth. I swallowed him, his taste flooding me. I came for the second time that night, sharp and hard, something inside me snapping. The chair squeaked as we shuddered together.

Eyes closed, I rested my cheek against James's thigh. He pulled away the blanket and fresh air bathed my face. His hand stroked softly down my hair.

"Holy shit," he murmured, slurring a little. "I wanted that so much. You don't know how much."

I waited a moment or two more before we got up and folded the blanket and took ourselves inside to bed. I paused outside the closed door to the guest bedroom, James already having stumbled down the hall and into ours.

I'd been thinking of Alex when I came, a thought I might have felt guilty about, but for one thing—I thought James might have been thinking about him, too.

Morning came way too early, and I hadn't even been drinking. Despite that, James was up and out of bed at his usual time. I woke to the sound of the shower running and a voice singing.

James was…singing? I propped myself on one elbow to listen. He was rocking out to something by…Duran Duran? And not early-90s-comeback-tour double Duran, but classics from the 80s. He was singing something about blue silver when I pulled the covers back over my head in protest and tried to go back to sleep.

It was useless. In the light of morning, albeit the barely glimmering light of dawn, the night before seemed more like something I'd dreamed than a real event. I waited to feel embarrassed. Or guilty. What was keeping me on edge wasn't my flirtation with Alex, because after all, who could've blamed me for reacting to his practiced seduction? No, what had my eyes popped open wide despite my intense desire to return to slumber was, in the end, James.

James singing Duran Duran. James drinking. James insisting on a frantic blow job.

"Morning." Still damp from his shower, he slid into bed next to me for a kiss. "How'd you sleep?"

"Fine." I wriggled to turn on the pillow and look at him. "You?"

"Like a rock." He grinned and kissed me again, then hopped out of bed to dress.

I watched him. "You feel all right today?"

He glanced over his shoulder as he slid into jeans and a T-shirt. "Yeah. Why?"

"Because you had a lot to drink last night. You both did."

Grabbing up his socks, James sat on the edge of the bed to put them on. "Alex can hold his booze, babe. And I can, too. Don't worry about it."

"I'm not worried about it." I got on my knees behind him to put my arms around his neck and kiss his cheek.

He patted my arm and turned his face to kiss me properly. "I haven't seen him in a long time, Anne. We're just having fun. It's fun having him here."

I didn't agree or disagree. James got up and swiped back his wet hair with one hand as he put on a baseball cap with the other. He grabbed up his leather belt and slid it through the belt loops, buckling it with swift fingers. He put his cell phone into the belt clip and his wallet in his back pocket. His boots, probably caked with dirt from the construction site, would be by the side door.

"Gotta run," he said. "Love you. Have a good time today."

I must've looked perplexed because he grinned. "With Alex. On second thought, Anne, don't have too good of a time. Don't get into trouble."

I rolled my eyes. "As if."

He laughed. "If I come home and he's wearing a thong—"

I threw a pillow at him. "Shut up!"

James caught the pillow and tossed it back. "See ya."

"Have a good day." I remembered something. "Oh... James, tomorrow I'm having dinner with my sisters, remember? To go over plans for the party."

He shrugged as he slid his arms into a windbreaker. "Okay. We'll go out, maybe. Hit the sports bar for wings or something. Don't worry, honey, we're big boys. We'll keep ourselves occupied."

Why did that thought give me another twinge of uncertainty? "I know you will. Just..."

He paused and turned in the doorway. "Hmm?"

"Be careful," I said, the admonition failing to convey what I really meant.

"Always." With a wink, he was gone.

I waited until the rumbling sound of his truck faded away before I got out of bed to face the day. I wasn't quite sure what I was going to do with Alex this morning, but I was one hundred percent certain it did not involve a thong.

As it turned out, I didn't have to do anything with him. I spent the morning on the computer, researching local caterers and pit roast beef suppliers. I love the Internet. Once I'd seen a bumper sticker that said *The Internet: it's not just for porn, anymore.* I totally agreed.

I also loved being in a house so quiet I forgot I wasn't alone. I made coffee, browsed the Net, read my e-mail, chatted for a few minutes with a school friend who lived so far away I never saw her but with whom I talked almost daily. I updated my résumé and thought about adding it to a job search site, but I'd only managed to begin setting up my login account with one of them when the doorbell rang.

The morning had become afternoon to my astonishment as I looked at the clock. I wasn't expecting anyone and was doubly surprised to find my sister Claire on the doorstep. Today she wore black capri-length pants with a matching black top dotted with a pattern of tiny skulls, and funky black-and-red striped shoes. She'd tucked her hair under a brimless red cap. She looked paler than usual, but I figured she'd overdone it on the pale foundation.

"Hiya," she said, pushing past me and heading for the kitchen without waiting for me to say a word. "I'm starving."

I followed her. "You know how to open the fridge. Help yourself."

She did, grabbing a container of cubed melon and then a fork. She ate a few bites, quickly, and I swore I saw a faint blush of color return to her face.

"Sit." I pointed at the table. "Coffee?"

"I'll have water."

I'd already been pouring her a cup and now looked up. "No coffee?"

Claire made a face. "You need a hearing aid or what?"

"Fine, water." I shrugged. "Help yourself."

She did that, too, then sat across from me with a sigh. She'd also found a box of crackers that had to be stale, but she ate them anyway.

"I thought we were all meeting tomorrow at six," I said.

"We are." She licked crumbs from her lip and drank some water with a sigh.

"So…?" I raised a brow.

"So nothing." Claire shrugged. "I needed to get out of the house. Dad's got some sort of use-it-or-lose-it vacation time, so he's been hanging around."

"Yeah, so instead of taking Mom somewhere fun, he's doing what?" My words were critical but I was careful to keep from sounding bitter.

"He's spending a lot of time in his workshop." Claire wasn't as careful. She didn't bother to hide her expression, either, the curled lip and wrinkled nose.

That was never good. Our father had two hobbies. Bowling and making birdhouses. His team was one of the top in the league, and he made beautifully detailed replicas of famous buildings as birdhouses. Sadly, neither hobby seemed to bring him as much joy as the drinking that accompanied both.

"I can't believe he's never cut off a fucking finger or something," Claire said.

"Claire, God. Don't wish for that."

"Right. Because then Mom would just have to wait on him even more," my sister said.

She stabbed melon and ate it. I reached for a piece myself. It was sweet and good, and juice ran down my chin. We giggled as I wiped it.

The soft pad of bare feet on the wood floor made us both turn. Alex wandered into the kitchen. His hair stuck up, rumpled all over. He wore a pair of Hello Kitty pajama bottoms that hung even lower than his jeans had, and again bare feet. When had the sight of a man's toes become so erotic?

He disappeared behind the open door of the fridge as he rootled inside for something, coming out with a plastic container of leftover steak and rice. He popped off the lid and put the bowl in the microwave, set the timer and poured himself a mug of coffee, all without so much as a smirk in our direction.

He'd obviously been saving it for when he could give us his full attention. When the timer beeped he pulled out the food and, mug in hand, swaggered to the table and took the empty seat next to Claire. He looked from her to me and back again, then sipped his coffee. He made a long, low noise of enjoyment.

"Mmmmmmm," he said. "Coffee."

I've been known to be at a loss for words, but I couldn't remember the last time I'd seen Claire so gobsmacked. We both stared, our mouths agape, at the entire proceedings. Having the advantage of already having met him, I recovered first.

"Claire, this is Alex Kennedy. James's friend. Alex, this is my sister Claire."

"Hello, darlin'." Alex gave her a slow, lazy grin and checked her out from head to toe without trying to hide the examination. He even leaned to the side to look at her feet.

"Sweet shoes," he said as he returned to his full and upright position.

"Nice pants," Claire said.

Alex grinned. So did Claire. I just shook my head.

Alex swiveled his gaze to me. "And good morning to you."

"It's almost three o'clock," I told him.

He sipped coffee. "Jet lag."

Claire leaned in and gave him a sniff. "Sure it's not hangover?"

"Could be a bit of that, too. Jamie make it off to work all right this morning?"

"He did." I sipped my own coffee, which had become cool.

"James was boozing last night, too?" Claire made a face. "Interesting."

"Alex cooked us all dinner," I explained. "There was…wine. And beer."

I've never banned drinking from my house. We're all grownups, and just because I don't indulge doesn't mean I have a problem with anyone having a glass of wine or beer with dinner.

"Interesting" was all my sister said to that. She shoved the melon toward Alex. "Here."

"Why is that so interesting?" I demanded. It was the same thing Alex had said, almost.

Claire shrugged. Alex let out a small, conspiratorial chuckle. I wasn't happy the two of them seemed to be ganging up on me, especially since while Claire might feel mistakenly entitled to judge me, Alex didn't know me well enough to have that right.

"Have you talked to Patricia lately?"

Leave it to Claire to change a subject she didn't want to discuss.

"No. Should I?"

Claire gave an artless shrug. "I dunno. Maybe. I think we need to kidnap her."

I gave Alex a glance, not sure I wanted this conversation to continue. It sounded like it was going to touch on private issues. He dug into his plate of leftovers.

"Kidnap?" he said around a mouthful of steak and rice. "Sounds like fun."

"Our sister Patricia's married to a big asshole."

"Claire!"

"What? He is. Sean's been an ass lately, Anne, you know it, too." To Alex, she said, "She needs to get out away from her kids for a night. Besides—" back to me "—we've got to get together again to talk about the party."

"You're having a party?" Alex looked interested and stabbed another bite of steak.

"For my parents. My sisters and I are planning it for August. It's their wedding anniversary."

"The Four Musketeers," Claire put in.

"More like the Four Stooges," I said.

Alex swallowed his food and wiped his mouth with the back of his hand. "I have three sisters, too."

I'd known he had sisters. Just not how many. "Really?"

"Poor you," said Claire. "Your house must have been one big fucking PMS bitchfest growing up. But I guess that explains your taste in pajamas."

They laughed together, leaving me out.

"Where'd you get those, anyway?" Claire tilted her head much like he'd done earlier to peruse her outfit.

"A friend bought them for me."

"A girlfriend?" She reached over and snagged a bit of steak off his plate while I watched, appalled and half-envious at her easy manner.

"No."

"Boyfriend?" She grinned.

Alex grinned, too. "No."

"Tell me it was your mumsy, and I'll have to barf."

"Claire, God, what's with the third degree?" I glared at her. She rolled her eyes at me.

"Oh, Anne, lighten up. Dude's got on girl pajama bottoms and looks like sex on a stick. I'd like to know who bought them for him."

Alex smirked and pushed away from the table. He took his plate to the dishwasher and refilled his coffee mug. I exchanged glares and "I don't know what the big deal is" looks with Claire.

"It was a lover." He lifted his mug toward Claire. "It happened to be my birthday. Hello Kitty amuses me."

Claire gave him a thumbs-up, but his answer didn't sit right with me.

"A lover isn't a girlfriend?"

He looked at me, but it was Claire who answered. "Oh, Anne. C'mon."

I gave her a look she couldn't misinterpret. "C'mon, what?"

She shook her head. "A lover isn't a boyfriend or a girl-friend. It's someone you're fucking."

I looked at Alex for confirmation. He didn't say anything, but his lack of answer was confirmation enough. He watched me over the rim of his coffee cup.

"Oh," I said, feeling stupid. "I guess I'm just out of the loop."

"Don't worry, big sissy," said Claire, getting up to pat me fondly on the shoulder. "You don't need to worry about it, anyway."

She gave me a squeeze. "I'm going to the mall. I heard that new boutique's looking for help."

"You're actually going to get a job?" I wasn't being sarcastic. I was genuinely surprised.

Claire scowled. "Yeah, well, having no money sucks. So does living at home. I've got one more semester of school and until I can get a real job or qualify for an internship, I guess working at the mall is the best I can do. Unless I meet up with some handsome sugar daddy who'll support me in the manner to which I'd like to grow accustomed."

She turned and batted her eyelashes at Alex whose sultry return stare made me want to turn on the ceiling fan. "You got someone in mind, darlin'?"

Claire laughed. "You offering?"

He was a flirt. She was a flirt. I knew that about both of them, and yet watching him make goo-goo eyes at my sister sent a barbed arrow of jealousy straight through me.

"I'm not sure I'm in the market for a love slave," said Alex, his tone intimating he was, in fact, looking for exactly that. "What are your qualifications?"

"I'd tell you, but my sister's in the room. We might burn her ears."

That sultry stare shifted my way. "I bet she can handle it."

Claire held up her hands, laughing. "Ew, ew. Ew. Dude. So not going there. Okay? Anne, I'll see you at dinner tomorrow. Alex, nice meeting you. I'm outties."

She sauntered past him, reaching out to flick the end of the tie at his waist. "Your lover had good taste."

Then she let herself out the back door, leaving Alex and me alone in the kitchen. He lounged in my kitchen like he'd always been there. On the one hand I was glad he felt enough at home to act that way. On the other…well, on the other he looked a little too much like he belonged in my house, and I wasn't at all sure I wanted him there.

"So," he said when the door slammed, "that was your sister."

"That was my sister." I got up. "We're not very much alike."

"You don't think so?" He stepped aside to let me put my mug in the sink. "I see a resemblance."

"I didn't mean the way we look."

There we were, dancing again, and I straightened, determined not to let this rattle me. I held out my hand for his mug, which he handed me, and I put that in the sink, too. He leaned back against the counter again.

Sleep rumpled hair. Nipples like two copper coins against skin the color of expensive linen writing paper. Small tufts of hair beneath his arms and a thin line of the same starting just below his belly button and disappearing into the waist of his cartoon-printed drawers.

Damn it.

"It's Friday," he said, and I tore myself away from my mental cataloging of his body.

"Yes?"

He smiled, and though I tried not to let myself be sucked up into it, I failed. Miserably.

"A friend of mine's DJing at a club in Cleveland. Let's go tonight."

I hadn't been dancing in ages. James and I went to

dinner and the movies, and he sometimes went out for wings at the local sports bar, but dancing…

"I'd love to. It'll be fun."

"More than fun," Alex said. "It'll be fan-fucking-tastic."

Chapter 08

From the outside the club looked no different from the rest of the industrial buildings lining the block. Some of them had been turned into luxury apartment complexes and condos. The rest had been transformed into nighttime hot spots.

The line of people waiting to get in reminded me of an amusement park queue, though here the people themselves were the entertainment. Most wore black. Leather. Vinyl. Spandex. Many of them wore sunglasses, even though it was night.

"Should I be wearing a garlic necklace?" I muttered to James, who laughed.

We didn't have to wait in line. Alex flashed a card and mentioned the name of his DJ friend, and we were waved immediately inside to an almost pitch-black anteroom. At one end was an arched alcove flanked by two burly, bald men dressed in black and wearing the obligatory sunglasses. Inside the alcove, floor-to-ceiling hooks and racks held what I hoped were fake weapons.

"Guns. We need lots of guns," said Alex with a laugh.

"Welcome to Wonderland," said a voice from just inside the door. "Care to take the red pill?"

The voice belonged to a very tall man in full drag regalia, including two-inch-long eyelashes and glittering red lipstick. He looked like a cross between Dr. Frank-N-Furter from *The Rocky Horror Picture Show* and a character from *The Matrix*. Which, I suddenly realized, the club was supposed to represent.

"I thought it was Wonderland like Alice," I said. "Boy, do I feel stupid."

Our "hostess" chortled. "Don't eat any mushrooms inside, honey. Ooh, look at the three of you! Thing One, Thing Two and Miss Thing!"

Alex, who was already handing her a couple of bills from his wallet, grinned. "You like?"

"Mmmhmm," she said. "Bookends. Can you handle them, Miss Thing? Because if you can't, I'd be happy to step in and offer a…hand."

Her leer suggested just what sort of hand she'd like to offer. I laughed, not sure what to say. I hadn't paid attention until just now that Alex and James had dressed a lot alike. White T-shirts and black pants, though Alex's were leather and came with a studded black belt. Both had slicked back their hair, and in this weird lighting the difference in color wasn't as easy to see. Similar though not identical in height and build, they did look like bookends.

"She can handle us," said Alex when I didn't answer. "But we'll keep that in mind."

The hostess handed Alex three red tickets. "Take these

to the bar, sweetie. And I'll hold you to that. You come find me if you need anything, you hear? N. E. Thing."

That was, I realized, her name. She blew us a kiss as we walked toward the alcove and the guards.

"No weapons in the club," one said, and if the weapons on display were just for show, they were utterly serious in patting us down.

"That's more action than I've had in months." Alex nudged James with his elbow.

"Have a good time," said the other guard.

They stepped aside, and we pulled open the large, ornately carved double doors and went inside the club itself.

It really was Wonderland. Outside in the antechamber it had been dark and fairly quiet, the benefit of superb soundproofing. Once we opened the doors, however, the heavy thumping bass was enough to pound the pulse in my wrists and throat, to reverberate in the pit of my stomach. Flashing lasers bisected the multiple dance floors. There were cages in which scantily clad figures writhed, and raised platforms where more of the same gyrated. It took me a second to figure out these weren't paid performers, but regular club-goers taking their turns on display.

"Let's go get some drinks!" James shouted in my ear. "The bar!"

Alex was already heading that way. He held out his hand without looking to see which one of us grabbed it. James did, then grabbed mine, and we made a chain through the crowd toward one of the three bars set up around the club's outer walls.

"Don't waste a ticket on my drink," I told James. "Just get me a soda."

Alex had already ordered, two rounded glasses of something red, and a squat glass of brown fizzy cola. "Cheers," he leaned over to say into my ear with a tickling whisper. "Drink up, Miss Thing."

"What do you guys have?"

"They're called Red Pills," said Alex. "Want one?"

James sipped his and let out a little oof. "What the hell's in this?"

"Vodka, grenadine and cranberry juice." Alex grinned. "Anne, you want one?"

"No." I held up a hand. "I can smell it from here."

Their identical smiles disturbed me less than before, maybe because here with the music pounding away at us nothing seemed too important. Maybe because they both looked so handsome. More likely was that they both were directed at me.

Alex tossed back his drink and put the glass on the bar. James followed suit. Not wanting to be left behind I finished my drink, too, though the carbonation sank directly to my stomach and wanted to lift itself right away. I stifled a burp with the back of my hand, not that anyone could have heard it over the music.

"Let's dance!" Alex pointed toward a small section of the floor less crowded than the others. Again, he held out his hand, this time grabbing mine. I grabbed James.

We hit the dance floor just as a remix of Soft Cell's "Tainted Love" began its distinctive beat. The crowd surged around us, bouncing, wiggling. Grinding. Clusters of dancers joined and broke apart, making starfish patterns. Couples and triples moved in unison. The entire atmosphere had gone feral. I'd joked earlier about wearing garlic, but looking at some of these people, I really expected to see fangs.

I didn't worry about it, though. Snugged up between James to the front of me and Alex to the rear, not even a bloodsucker could've reached me. It really was fan-fucking-tastic.

I'd danced with James at weddings and holiday parties and sometimes in our living room. A few times we'd gone out to clubs but had never been to a place like Wonderland. So, though I'd danced with him before, we'd never really…danced. Not like this. Not this undulating, rocking, fucking with our clothes on.

James put a knee between my thighs, his hands on my hips. Behind me, Alex at first kept a bare distance, but as the music kept coming and the crowd kept growing, he moved closer until he was as tight against me in the back as James was in the front. Alex put his hands on my hips, too, just above James's.

Me, I had to do nothing but let them both move me. They found a rhythm, somehow. Something that worked for three. One pushed as the other pulled, keeping perfect time.

If I've had more fun in one night, I can't tell you when it was. With two gorgeous men pulling me onto the dance floor, bumping and grinding, one in the front and one in the back, I'd have had to be dead not to enjoy myself. Laughing, I looked at my husband. Grinning, he bent to kiss me.

No sweet, gentle peck, either—a full-blown, mouth open, tongue-searching kiss. He'd always been affectionate, hugging or holding hands in public. But I couldn't remember him ever French-kissing me in front of other people. I'd have been embarrassed if a dozen other people around us hadn't been doing the very same thing.

I should've felt more awkward about being ground like coffee by my husband's friend, and if James had shown any sign that it bothered him, I'd have stopped. Not only did James not seem to mind, he pulled me closer, which moved Alex closer. Their hands slid together on my sides and then…they linked. Their fingers tangled, thumbs pressing my back and belly. Against my back I felt the chill kiss of Alex's belt buckle as the hem of my shirt rode up. Against my front, James's thumbs stroked along my bared belly.

Everything was heat and sweat, bump 'n' grind. Stroke and sigh. The music changed to something with a more Latin beat, sensual, urging hips to shake. James let go of one of my hips to cup the back of my neck. He tugged the clip holding up my hair. Kinky curls tumbled down around my shoulders, and he stroked his fingers through them for one moment, making them frame my face.

Neither of them faltered. Other couples and triples around us merged and broke apart as the music flowed from one song to the next, but the three of us stayed perfectly in rhythm. Together they moved to bend my body back, supported by Alex, while James licked my throat. Together they pushed me up again, effortlessly. I was never once afraid I'd fall. Together they turned me in the circle of their embrace so I faced Alex, and James pressed his face to the slope of my neck from behind. He pressed his teeth against my skin, and the music swallowed the sound of my cry.

Sweat gleamed on Alex's face and molded his white T-shirt to his chest. His belt buckle, so cold against my back, now pressed my belly. James snugged up tight against my ass. Nobody but James had touched me this way in a long time. I hadn't wanted anyone to.

Maybe it was because they'd dressed so much alike, or because they had such similar mannerisms. Maybe it was because James had given me unspoken permission to enjoy Alex's hands upon me. Or maybe it was Alex himself, his charm and innate sensuality that kept me there. Maybe in the end, it had nothing to do with James.

Alex didn't kiss me. I think that would have been too much of an assumption, even for him. He did, however, put his face to the side of my neck not being tantalized by James. Two men, both nuzzling and groping and writhing against me. I was, indeed, well and fully bookended.

I loved it.

What woman would not? Two sexy, gorgeous men paying her the utmost attention? Four hands, teasing? Two mouths, tickling? The music filled us all and swept us away.

We couldn't go on like that forever, and the next time the song changed, Alex disengaged himself from our cozy little pretzel.

"Drinks," he shouted toward James, who gave him a thumbs-up.

With Alex gone, it felt somehow odd to dance with only one person. James put his hands back on my hips and kissed me again. He dipped me low and back up, the way Johnny does to Baby in *Dirty Dancing,* a move that made the people around us hoot and holler. Laughing, I gripped his shirt when he tried to do it again, forcing him to keep me upright. We moved off the dance floor, toward a dark corner.

"Are you having a good time?" James wiped his forehead with the hem of his T-shirt, exposing a stripe of muscled belly I wanted to lick.

I nodded. James leaned against the wall and pulled me against him. We aligned just right, my cheek to his chest, his thigh between mine. His hands were strong on my back, holding me close, and as always in his arms I felt safe.

It took me a second to realize that I'd been feeling unsafe.

James buried his face in my hair and breathed deep. "Mmm…I hope Alex gets here with the drinks."

I looked up at him. "James—"

I meant to ask him if it was really okay, what we'd been doing. If it didn't bother him that another man had been putting his hands all over me. I meant to ask him why he didn't mind…and why he didn't seem to care that I didn't mind. Before I had the chance, Alex appeared with two more Red Pills and another cola for me.

"Thanks, man." James dug in his pocket for his wallet, but Alex waved him off.

"My treat."

"Oooh," said James with a laugh, lifting his glass. "Big spender."

"Hey, you guys are letting me stay in your house. A couple of drinks is no big deal."

They both drank. I drank my cola, which was too sweet and didn't quench my thirst, though I downed it in almost one gulp.

"I'm going to get some water," I said, and held up a hand when both men started offering to serve me. "I have to go to the ladies' room, anyway."

"Hurry back," said James.

"I'll keep him out of trouble," promised Alex with a smug smile that was a kind of trouble all its own.

"Be good," I told them both, and wove my way through the crowd toward the restrooms.

Two doors faced me, one marked with the symbol for female, the other for male. And, wonder of wonders, there was no line of the sort in which women are accustomed to wait. As I pushed through the women's door, I saw why at once.

The doors might have been marked to separate the sexes, but the occupants themselves didn't appear to give a damn. Men and women mingled at the sinks and used the stalls. When I bent to peer under the doors to see which were open, more than one showed two pairs of feet...and some more than two.

"Well, hello, Miss Thing," drawled a familiar voice from the leopard-print sofa along the wall. "We meet again."

I flashed her a smile. "They let you take some time away from the door?"

"Listen," said N. E. Thing, "a girl's got to use the facilities once in a while, if you know what I mean."

I wasn't going to argue with the fact she wasn't exactly a girl. "Yeah."

"Hurry up in there, you sluts!" she hollered, reaching over and banging on the nearest stall with a strong-knuckled hand. "Someone out here actually needs to take a piss!"

Laughter from inside the stall echoed—the door opened and two slender young men stumbled out. N.E. snorted and rolled her eyes. They both gave her the finger.

"It's all yours, sweetie," she told me. "I can hold it."

She burst into a gale of infectiously throaty laughter at that. "And when I say I can hold it, I mean it, honey."

Laughing, I went into the stall and was relieved to discover the lock functioned, and no matter what had been going on in there before I entered, it was reasonably sanitary. I did the squat-and-spray quickly, glad I'd worn a skirt that I could hold up out of the way instead of having to risk dropping my pants on the floor of dubious cleanliness. It only took me a minute or two, but by the time I came out, the bathroom had become jam-packed.

I waited my turn for the sink behind two women loudly discussing something they called packing, and which I was pretty sure didn't apply to suitcases. The three guys behind me were gossiping about someone named Candy, who apparently didn't understand the difference between vegan and vegetarian, which didn't matter anyway because "we all know that bitch eats meat!" A straight couple had taken N.E.'s place on the sofa, and if they weren't actually going to fuck right there, they were going to do their best to make it seem like they were.

When I finally made it to the sink I felt a bit like Alice

tumbling down the rabbit hole. I washed my hands and dried them and followed a surge of people abandoning the pleasures of the lavatory for more drinking and dancing… and, I suspected, groping in dark corners.

At the bar I paid for my water and gulped down half the bottle before making my way back to where I'd left Alex and James. It took me a couple minutes to find them, as the crowd had changed again and I didn't have a clear view. My gaze glanced over them twice before I realized I was looking at them. I'd been searching for two men in white shirts. From where I stood, I could see only one.

Alex stood in front of James, who leaned against the wall. Alex had one hand planted up high, fingers splayed, next to James's head. His other hand held his drink, which I was close enough to see glimmering red. As I watched, he leaned in to say something into James's ear that tipped his head back in laughter.

Two men, hands in each other's back pockets, pushed past me. James laughed again, his eyes gleaming. I'd seen him look like that before, mouth slightly parted and eyes half-closed. He'd looked that way at me the first time we went to bed. Alex turned his head, his profile clear to me, and drank. His throat worked as he swallowed. When he put his hand down and turned back to James, I could no longer see either of their faces.

I froze, water bottle forgotten in one hand until someone else pushed by me and tipped it enough to splash on my hand. The drops felt electric, sizzling, like my skin had been a griddle.

I waited for them to touch, but they didn't. I waited for

them to move apart, but they didn't do that, either. They stayed there, two men standing too close to be just friends and not quite close enough to be lovers.

I must have moved, because I was in front of them, though I didn't remember putting myself in motion. Alex turned to look at the dancers. Blue-and-green flashes from the laser lights glittered in his eyes that looked alternately light and dark. Sweat had wet his hair, spiking the part at the front and making the longish bits over his ears feather forward the tiniest bit on his cheeks. Around the back of his neck, sweat-damp hair clung to his skin.

He turned, catching me looking. He smiled, a man used to being watched. I could have turned away and pretended I wasn't staring. I think he would have laughed but said nothing. I didn't look away.

Shadows suited him. On James they skittered and fled, even in the dark, leaving him bright and shining. On Alex they clung and caressed, dressing him in mystery.

I looked at him, and he looked at me, and when he put down his empty glass and reached for my hand, I reached for his without hesitating. Only for a second, though, before I looked at James, who was smiling and looking also at Alex. Too late, Alex took my hand, his palm warm and slightly sweaty against mine. He pulled. I moved. Looking over my shoulder at James, who did nothing more than give a little wave, I let Alex pull me out onto the dance floor.

He wasn't a better dancer than James, just different. Smoother. He was a little taller and at first I didn't know where to put my hands. We shuffled with an awkwardness that hadn't been there when we'd been three, but one-two step and we'd picked up the rhythm once more.

The song was bouncier, our dance not quite such a sensual onslaught. I was glad. Though we were still touching, he was grinning, not spearing me with an intense glare. I relaxed a bit, until he pulled me close and turned me, my back against his front. He jerked his chin toward James, watching from the sidelines.

"He looks lonely. Should we take pity on him and invite him back?"

My hands had fallen into perfect place on top of his, crossed over my belly. "No."

"No?" He turned me to face him. His hands settled just above my ass, in territory that could not be misconstrued as innocent but wasn't outright lechery, either. He was good at that. Walking the line.

I'm not blind to the effect I can have on men. Just because it had been a long time since I'd bothered flirting didn't mean I didn't remember how to do it. Flirting was a game, like any other. There were rules.

I slid my hands around the back of his neck and linked my fingers together. He smiled at this and hitched me closer. I didn't hear the music anymore, though I still felt the pound-pound-pulse of it in my stomach. It was the same as my heartbeat. He put one hand between my shoulder blades, in exactly the place James would have, had he been the one holding me, instead.

"No," I repeated, looking into his eyes.

"Should I be flattered?" His mouth tilted on one side, a half smile.

I glanced over my shoulder. James still stood against the wall, one leg straight and one bent, sipping his drink. If he noticed me looking, he gave no sign of it. I thought I might see him looking at people as they passed, but he didn't let that distract him. He stared at us, but I couldn't really be sure who'd so captured his attention. I looked back at Alex.

"Are you gay?"

His gaze flickered, but his smile didn't change. "No."

"Then why are you trying to seduce my husband?" I demanded, blunt and forthright and making it very clear I expected an answer.

"Is that what I'm doing?" He looked neither offended nor surprised, and his gaze never left my face.

"Isn't it?"

"I don't know," Alex leaned in to say into my ear, his breath sending a quiver through me. "I thought I was trying to seduce you."

Three heads swiveled to stare at me when I dropped the little bomb of what Alex had said. Patricia was the only one to look horrified. Mary looked distracted. Claire, typically, was laughing.

"You told him that was never going to happen," said Patricia as though there could be no other answer.

After a moment, when I said nothing, Claire snorted. "Of course she didn't. Did you fuck him, Anne? I bet he's got a nice prick."

"She didn't have sex with him," Mary said with a small shake of her head.

"But she wants to." Claire sipped from her iced tea, a regular one for once, not a Long Island. "Who wouldn't? I'm not surprised James wants a piece of it, either."

"I didn't say he did." I sipped my own drink. These three women, as much as we might sometimes clash, were my most trusted mirror. We reflected each other, flaws and all.

"Of course he doesn't." Patricia tore open a package of sweetener and added it to her tea. "James isn't one of them."

This time, the three of us turned to stare at her. Patricia didn't look perplexed. She shrugged. "Well, is he?"

"Gosh, Pats," said Mary, disgusted. "One of 'them'? What the heck does that mean?"

"She means a fag." Claire lolled back in her chair and exchanged grimaces with Patricia.

"James isn't gay." The remains of my meal had lodged in my gut, heavy like a stone. "Alex says he's not, either."

"So he's bi." Claire shrugged. "Plays for both sides, doubles his chances of getting laid."

Mary frowned. "That makes it sound like something you'd choose."

"Isn't it? You can't tell me they don't want to do it." Patricia's tone grew haughtier, and I turned to look at her again. She'd always been the prim and proper one, but lately…

"What bug has crawled up your ass?" Mary snapped. "Who on earth would choose to be different than everyone else? Who would choose not to be what everyone else considers normal? God, Patricia, you can be such a stuck-up bitch sometimes!"

Silence in the aftermath. Patricia folded her arms across her chest, face set in a glare from which Mary didn't back down. Claire and I exchanged glances about the showdown.

"I don't know what you're getting so upset about," said Patricia at last. "We're not talking about you, for God's sakes, Mary."

"So," Claire said brightly. "Shrimp cocktail or caviar?"

She'd pasted on a bright and shiny smile quite unlike her usual grin. It was a doll's smile. Plastic. She added a head-tilt and blank gaze.

"For Mom and Dad's party," she added when we all lacked an answer. "Shrimp cocktail or caviar?"

"As if Dad would eat caviar." I laughed at the thought and admired Claire's clever manipulation of the sisterly dynamics to avoid a fight. "We can get bulk shrimp from the seafood market."

"And see if the beef people will steam them. They have to have a pot big enough to handle quantities that large." Patricia the practical.

I clicked my pen and made a note. "I'll call about it."

The conversation continued, discussing the merits of kaiser rolls versus plain burger buns and different sizes of napkins. This party was growing into an epic pain in my ass, a gut-clenching, nail-biting, tension-headache maker. The guest list alone had taken a couple hours of wrangling. Our father had a lot of friends, most of whom I didn't really want as guests in my house.

That thought brought me back to thinking of my current houseguest, the place my thoughts hadn't strayed far from since last night. I hadn't told Alex to fuck off, but I hadn't taken him up on the offer, either. Mary and Patricia had both been right.

Claire, however, had been right, too. I wanted to let Alex seduce me. I wanted him to put his hands on me again, to feel his mouth on me. I wanted his face between my legs. I wanted him to fuck me. What disturbed me wasn't that I wanted him to fuck me. What had my mind racing like a hamster on a wheel was that I didn't feel guilty about it. Or that it no longer seemed a question of if, but when.

"Anne?"

I'd been drifting on daydreams of cunnilingus, but now snapped back to reality. Again, three faces stared at me, waiting. I looked down, pretending to study my notes.

"Music," prompted Mary. "Do we want to hire a DJ or just have music on the stereo?"

Claire laughed. "Hey, maybe you can get Alex's friend to come do the party. I bet that would liven things up. Get old Arch Howard grooving with Stan Peters. Oh, man, I think I just threw up a little in my mouth."

"Alex's friend is a club DJ. I doubt he's available for parties, anyway." Still, I took down the suggestion.

Patricia leaned over to look at my list. Childishly, I wanted to shield what I was writing from her, but my better nature won over. "Well, if we did go with a DJ, I'd want to hear him, first."

"Field trip! Let's all go to Wonderland!" Claire nudged Mary. "You up for it? Hot girls, hot guys...hell, maybe I'll get lucky and find myself a nice little Neo look-alike for some bullet-time action."

Mary let Claire's nudging rock her a bit in the chair, but she smiled. "I think my vinyl's at the cleaners."

"Aw, c'mon," Claire said, looking around. "It's been ages since we all went out together. It would be fun."

"I've been to Wonderland." Mary said it like she was revealing a secret. "Last summer. Betts came up for a visit and we went."

"And you didn't take me?" Claire popped Mary on the shoulder. "Bitch."

Mary shrugged. "You go plenty of places without me."

"Well, I don't think it sounds like my sort of place, even if I could go, which I can't." Patricia stirred her tea like she'd rather be stabbing it.

"You'd have fun," I told her. "Maybe Sean would watch the kids?"

Patricia kept her gaze on the swirling tea. "I don't want to go to Wonderland. If you all want to go, fine, but I don't really want to go to a place like that. Gross."

"What's gross about it?" Mary challenged.

"The way Anne described it was gross!"

"Never mind," Mary muttered.

The talk steered back to the party details, though by this time I was as sick of the party plans as I was of the drama between Patricia and Mary. Claire kept the conversation moving with a fewer than usual number of wisecracks, which was as disturbing in its own way as the animosity between my other sisters.

We were at a table full of secrets. I knew mine. I could guess at Patricia's—trouble with Sean. Of Mary and Claire

I had no idea, but it was easy enough to guess their minds were as far from planning the party as mine was.

"How are we going to divvy up?" said Mary at last when the bills for dinner came. "I think we should all put our shares into a fund and draw from that. Patricia penny-pincher can take care of the details."

"I'm not a penny-pincher!" Patricia's voice was louder than I expected, and I flinched. So did Claire. Mary only looked smug.

"Why don't we divide up the different things we need to buy and just turn in the receipts at the end," I suggested. "Divvy it up then."

"Because Claire will never remember to keep receipts," Claire said. "Don't bother saying it, Pats. We know."

Patricia tossed her napkin onto her plate. Her voice quivered. "Why don't you all just back off? Why are you all riding me?"

"We're not riding you." I'm sure Claire meant to sound soothing, but it was so out of character I wasn't surprised Patricia didn't hear it that way.

"You are! And I'm sick of it!" Patricia stood, body straining like she meant to flee until her gaze caught the flutter of the bill on her plate.

I watched her physically restrain herself from shoving away from the table. She read the bill and pulled out her wallet, counted out the money carefully. Even exact change. She added the minimum, exact tip and settled the small piles of bills and coins on the table. We all watched her in silence as she went through this ritual. Patricia had always been precise, but she'd never been cheap.

"What?" she cried, chin lifting. "That's right, isn't it?"

"Sure," I told her. "If it's not, I'll cover it, don't worry."

"I don't need you to cover it, Anne." Patricia hiked her purse over her shoulder. "I'll pay my own!"

"Okay, sure. Don't worry about it." I exchanged looks with Claire again. Mary, face clouded, stared at her own bill like she meant to burn a hole in it with her eyes.

"I have to get back. I had to get a sitter, and she's expensive." Patricia edged past my chair.

"Where's Sean?" asked Mary without looking up. "Working again?"

"Yes." Patricia looked like she meant to say more, but didn't. "Anne, I'll call you."

Her keys jangled as she pulled them from her purse and strode away. Like good sisters, we waited until she was out of earshot before we fell to talking about her.

"Since when does Sean work on Saturdays?" I asked.

"Since he's at Thistledown watching the horses." Mary sounded less smug now.

Claire looked surprised. "No! Sean? You think so?"

"Yeah. I do." Mary looked at each of us. "I think he's lost a lot of money lately. She told me they're not going on vacation this summer. She said it was because of Mom and Dad's party, but you know she's lying. Sean never gives up his trip to Myrtle Beach."

"Unless they can't afford it," I said. It made sense. "God. That sucks."

"But…he's such a nice guy!" Claire sounded more than surprised. She sounded forlorn.

It took me a second to remember that she'd only been

fourteen when Patricia had started dating Sean. To Claire he was the big brother the rest of us had never had, no matter how many times she might have called him asshole.

"Just because he's nice doesn't mean he doesn't have a problem, Claire."

We were all silent for a moment after that. I don't know what they were thinking, but I was thinking of our father. Everyone who ever met him thought he was a nice guy. Life of the party. And he was. They didn't know the man who sat in the dark with a bottle of Jack Daniel's and a pack of cigarettes, the one who sat and wept and talked about the taste of a pistol.

"If we just have music on the stereo, that will save money," Claire said quietly. "We can hook up my iPod or something."

"Yeah." Mary nodded. "That would be better."

We said our goodbyes, and I took my notes and headed home. The radio might have distracted me, but I drove in silence. Thinking.

The past doesn't change no matter how much time you spend thinking about it. Good and bad all add up to the whole. Take away one piece, no matter how small, and the whole changes. Whether it's optimism, pessimism or fatalism, I don't spend my time wishing for the past to be different so the present would be different, too. I control my future with what I choose now. I'm the only one who does.

My sisters and I had grown up in the same house, had the same parents, gone to the same schools, yet we were all different. Our tastes in clothes, music, political leanings, faith, all scattered in scale. We were as alike as four strangers, yet we all had one thing in common.

Our desire for perfection.

Patricia was the perfect mother, the kind who bakes cookies and hand-sews Halloween costumes. She was the mom who drove the carpool and waited at the door for the school bus with snacks that weren't too full of sugar or caffeine. Her children were clean and well-pressed and if, upon occasion, they were also little terrors, it wasn't because she didn't discipline them with a firm but gentle hand.

Mary, until recently, had been the perfect virgin. Saving herself for marriage or Jesus, one or the other and now neither. She volunteered in soup kitchens and gave blood. She went to church every Sunday and almost never swore.

Claire had rejected perfection and become the perfect rebel. She'd have been a parody of clothes and hair and attitude if she hadn't also believed it of herself, the wild child. The one who didn't care about what other people thought.

I played at being perfect, too. The perfect daughter, the one who took care of everything. Who had everything. The house, the car. The husband. Everything bright and shiny.

And yet, like my sisters, I, too, failed at being perfect. I didn't have children to resent, or an image of myself to uphold, and I didn't secretly care desperately about being liked. No. I had a perfect life. Car, house, husband, shiny.

But how could it all be perfect when I wanted it to change?

Chapter 09

*I*t took me a long time to drive home. I had a lot to think about. When I finally got there, the tang of cigar smoke made me sneeze. I heard laughter rumbling from the den and sought the source. I watched them from the doorway for a while without their noticing.

They were playing cards. James, in sleep pants and a T-shirt, gripped a cigar between his teeth while he dealt a fresh hand onto the coffee table between them. Alex, in those damnably sexy jeans and an open Oxford shirt, lolled on the couch with a glass in one hand and picked up his cards with the other. His cigar squatted in a make-shift ceramic key-holder ashtray. The open windows and ceiling fan had kept the smoke from gathering too thickly, but it was still pungent enough to tickle my throat. A green bottle of what looked like wine was on the table, too, along with a silver spoon and a box of sugar cubes.

"One-eyed Jacks wild." Speaking around the cigar, James tapped the deck to even out the cards and set it down. He fanned out the cards in his hand.

"Aren't they always?" Alex gulped the remnants of the liquid in his glass. It didn't look like wine. "Ever since the first time I taught you how to play poker, man, you make one-eyed Jacks wild."

The tickle in my throat forced its way out as a cough. They both looked at me. Slow smiles spread across their faces. Side by side, there were differences in them. Not identical, as I'd thought.

"Welcome home." James took his cigar out. "C'mere."

I did, picking my way around sofa cushions that had been tossed to the floor and a newspaper that had been strewn about. I bent to kiss him. I tasted smoke and licorice.

"What are you drinking?" This close, I could smell it on him, too. Anise. His eyes were bright and a little red.

James laughed and cut his gaze from mine. "Umm… absinthe."

I looked at the bottle, which had a picture of a fairy in a green dress on the front. "Like in *Moulin Rouge?* You're drinking absinthe?"

I picked up the bottle while James and Alex laughed like boys caught with their hands in the cookie jar who know they're charming enough not to get in trouble. I looked at the spoon and the sugar and the lighter next to them.

I looked at Alex. "Isn't this illegal?"

"Illegal to sell," he said. "Not to drink."

"But…doesn't it have wormwood in it? I mean…isn't absinthe poison?" I handed Alex the bottle when he reached for it.

He poured a small amount of bright green liquid into

the glass, then balanced a pair of sugar cubes on the spoon. Dipping a finger in the absinthe, he dripped the liquid on the sugar and lit a flame beneath it. It flamed blue. The sugar started to melt. He grabbed up a pitcher I hadn't seen from the floor and poured water over the sugar, dissolving it. The green liquid in the glass turned a milky white. He swirled it and held it up to me.

"Try it."

"She doesn't drink," James said, though I already had the glass in my hand.

"I know she doesn't." Alex leaned back against the couch.

They both watched me. James looked curious, like he was waiting, but Alex's expression was inscrutable. I swirled the liquid in the glass.

"What does it do? Make you high?"

"The Bohemians drank absinthe." Alex re-lit the end of his cigar.

"The last time I checked, we were not Bohemians." But I didn't put down the glass. It smelled good.

"Vive la décadence!" Alex said, and he and James laughed.

I looked at my husband, who was definitely not acting like himself. His gaze flittered over Alex's face like a butterfly sipping at a flower, never lingering. He looked at me, next, and reached out a hand to pull me onto the couch next to him.

Absinthe sloshed on my hand and I licked it. I'd expected the bite of alcohol but tasted only fine black licorice. James slipped an arm around my waist and nuzzled at my shoulder.

"You don't have to drink it if you don't want to, baby."

"I know." I didn't put it down.

Alex fixed himself another with a glass from the wet bar in the corner. He added more absinthe this time. The sugar flamed higher. Like children watching fireworks, we oohed and ahhed.

"Are you in, or are you out?" Alex said when he returned to the sofa across from us. "One-eyed Jacks are wild."

"I'm in," I said.

I thought the absinthe would burn but drinking it was smooth and warm. Sort of like eating candy. Sweet. I wanted to drink all of it, which was why I put it aside after two sips.

Alex noticed but made no comment. We played cards, betting pennies we shook out of the wine jug that had been James's since college. We all cheated.

"I'm out," said Alex after a while and tossed down his hand. "I got nothing."

We'd all moved onto the floor, the low table between us. James had an arm around me, fingers doing a familiar dance along my bare arm. He put his cigar in the ashtray.

"And you're broke, man."

"I am broke," said Alex. "Flat-out broke. Busted. Damaged beyond repair."

"I'm out, too," James said. "What you got, baby?"

I showed them my hand. Winning was easy against men fuzzed by alcohol. "I've got a pair of kings."

Alex buffed his nails on his bare chest. "You certainly do."

I looked at the cards in my hand, the queen of hearts nestled between the king of clubs and the king of spades. No wonder she was smiling.

"Pay up, boys," I said to both of them.

"We're both broke." James nuzzled against my ear again. "I'll have to pay you in sexual favors."

I turned to look at him. He smiled, his cheeks flushed and his eyes so bright a blue beneath the darkness of his brows. "That's fine for you, but what about Alex?"

We both looked at Alex, whose attention had been captured by picking up the scattered cards. He looked up at the sound of his name, and it was the first time I hadn't seen him look completely in control of his expression.

For most of the night we'd been two and one, but now, as we had in Wonderland, we became three again. Three points of a triangle. A trinity.

"I guess that's up to you," James said finally, voice a husky whisper.

I had the chance for things to stay the same. To choose perfection over change. I could've said no, and we all would have laughed and gone to sleep in separate beds. I could've saved us all a lot of grief.

But I wanted him, and unlike the absinthe, I didn't put him aside.

Alex had been our pivot point, but all at once I found myself the focus of two very sharp gazes, one bright blue. The other deep and smoky gray.

"Anne..." James said.

I thought he meant to call it off. End the game. I thought he meant to save me from myself, but in the end all he said was, "Do you want him to kiss you?"

I wanted it so bad I shook with it, but I needed to be sure it was all right. I turned and put my mouth very close to James's, so close our lips brushed with each word. "Do you want him to?"

James's tongue flicked out to wet his lips and caught mine, too. Our mouths parted. We breathed, in and out, but we didn't kiss.

"Yeah," came his answer, finally. "I want to watch him kiss you."

I put aside any notions I had about what both of them really wanted. I wanted both of them. I could have what I wanted. Did it really matter how we got there, or why, when we'd all have what we wanted in the end?

"You're drunk," I whispered against James's mouth.

"You're not," he whispered back.

I fell, spiraling, into his eyes and his smile brought me back. "You want this?"

His hand stroked my hair and tugged it free of its clip. "If you want it, baby."

He looked over my shoulder at his friend. "If there's anyone else I trust you with, it's Alex."

I turned to look at Alex. This time, I needed no red pill to tumble me to Wonderland. I only had to lean across the table. One hand supporting myself, the other linked with James's, that's what I did.

James had asked me if I wanted Alex to kiss me, but that first time, I kissed him. I owned that moment. It was mine.

I tried keeping my eyes open but at the last moment courage failed me and I couldn't look. His mouth was warm, lips fuller than James's. He didn't move toward me, but his mouth obliged me by opening right away.

I couldn't hold that position for very long before it

cramped my wrist. That was okay. It was long enough for a first kiss, that tentative exploration I'd expected nervousness to make less exciting. I pulled away and opened my eyes.

Alex had closed his eyes, too, and this made me feel unexpectedly tender toward him. He looked softer like that, a prince awaiting true love's kiss to waken him from slumber. But only for a second, because then his eyes opened. His gaze flared.

He took the second kiss with a hand to the back of my head, holding me in place. Alex kissed me breathless, almost bruising my mouth but pulling back at the last moment.

The table was still between us, digging into my stomach. My hand still linked with James's. The kiss went on and on and ended before I'd had enough.

This time when I opened my eyes, he was already looking at me. "Now," he said. "Let me watch you kiss him."

I looked at James. I leaned in close. "Is this okay with you?"

He put his arms around me. "Do you want to do this?"

"Do you want me to do this?"

The hands that threaded through my hair and slid over my shoulders and down my arms to capture my hands were shaking. He pressed our palms together, our fingers linked. James took a slow, shuddering breath. His gaze went over my shoulder. I don't know what he saw when he looked there, but it was enough for him to smile when he returned his eyes to me.

"Yes. I do."

I'd never been unfaithful to my husband. I had no reason to suspect he'd been unfaithful to me. Yet now we were inviting another person into our bed. I'd have been insane not to feel some trepidation.

Lust won out over good sense, as it had done in the past, when my body ignored the wise counsel of my mind and heart. I'd grown older, but not, apparently, smarter.

I stood between and above them, a queen with two kings. They looked poised on the edge of leaping, their bodies arrested in waiting for my command. They didn't look alike and yet at that moment were indistinguishable.

"Come on." My voice dipped low and husky, but they both heard me. I crooked a finger and turned, not looking to see if they followed.

I went up the two steps from the sunken den to the kitchen, down the hall toward our bedroom and through the door. My buttons slid from their holes. My zipper unlatched beneath my fingers as I walked. By the time I got to the bed I'd tossed my shirt aside and stepped out of my jeans. In bra and panties I stopped at the foot of our bed and turned.

Waiting.

I heard them in the hall, the soft whisper of bare feet along wooden floors. The rasp of zippers and shush of cloth sliding on skin. I waited to see who would come through the door first. Would James be a good host and allow his guest to enter before him?

They showed up in the doorway together, shoulder to shoulder, both bare-chested. Alex's jeans had slid even lower over his hips, the zip undone and allowing a hint of dark hair to show through. The front of James's sleep pants was already tented, and I smiled.

Like teammates who've played together so long they can anticipate each other's moves, James and Alex both shifted, each making a half turn toward the other so they could both slip through the doorway at the same time. Their bodies aligned and parted as soon as they were through. Though it had taken less than the time it took my eyelashes to flutter, the sight of them face-to-face like that burned in my brain.

Anyone who says women are not turned on by visuals the way men are is full of shit. The sight of them dried my throat and started my heart pounding. My clit pulsed. My body grew hungry for touch, ached for it.

I held out my hands, one to each of them, and they took them. I pulled and they came toward me. I put my arms around their waists. Theirs went around my shoulders. No longer a triangle with sharp and unforgiving points, we made a circle woven of limbs and held together by desire.

I kissed them, one and then the other. When James was on my mouth, Alex found the sweet spots of my throat and shoulders. When Alex's tongue danced with mine, James ran his hands over the slopes of my breasts and freed them from my bra so he could suck my already tightened nipples.

We were dancing again, this time to a beat much slower than the music Alex's DJ friend had played. James knew me and Alex knew James, and together they discovered the best places on my body to stroke and touch and lick. Four hands covered me, and if I closed my eyes I couldn't tell which belonged to whom.

They removed my panties and spread my legs as I stood. I let my head tip back, the ends of my hair tickling my shoulder blades as two mouths traced the curves of my hips and rounded belly.

They talked to each other, in low murmurs, words I couldn't always decipher. They had a secret language of sighs and laughter. I opened my eyes, anchoring myself with sight.

I put a hand on each of their shoulders and pushed them to stand next to one another. Stretching to kiss James, I hooked my fingers in his waistband and pushed the sleep pants over his hips and down his thighs. Without breaking the kiss, I used my foot to push them all the way to the floor. His cock sprung up between us, heat on my belly, and he muttered against my lips. When I turned to Alex, those sleepy eyes were gleaming.

Alex's skin was warm when I put my hands on his chest. His heart thumped steadily beneath my palm. He wasn't burnished by the sun, like James. His abs and pecs weren't hard with muscle from physical labor, but from reps on a machine in some expensive gym. He had a body suited for designer suits and worshiping hands. He tilted his head and slid a hand into the hair at the base of my neck.

We paused like that for a heartbeat. No going back, not now. James's hand on my hip, his fingers loosely curled, urged me to move. I slid my hands down Alex's chest to his hips. My mouth followed the path my hands had made. I knelt in front of him and hooked my fingers into his jeans, pulling them down slowly to savor the anticipation.

At first I couldn't look at his penis, and I closed my eyes to nuzzle his thighs as I pushed his jeans to the floor where he stepped out of them. His erection brushed my hair, then my cheek, and I ran my hands along the backs of his calves and knees.

I straightened, still on my knees, and opened my eyes. I looked up at both of them, my two kings, waiting for me.

And I fell in love.

With James it was all over again at the look of pride and adoration on his face. With Alex it was with the glimpse of vulnerability and the tenderness with which he pushed my hair off my face.

My doubts, of which I'd had many even though I'd been ignoring them, fled. Whatever this was, it really was okay. For them. For me. For us.

I took Alex first, easing his unaccustomed length into my mouth with my hand gripping the base to control the pace. His fingers twisted in my hair. His moan was the sexiest noise I'd ever heard. He pushed his hips forward and I took in the rest of him. His cock was longer but not as thick as James's. It was beautiful. I worked my lips and tongue over the head and down again, caressing with my hand on the upward stroke.

James waited patiently, but I was impatient to taste him, too. I opened for him, my mouth adjusting without effort to his proportions. I moved faster on him, sucked harder. He jerked a little, and laughed. I love the sound of James's laughter when his cock is down my throat.

It was sloppy, this making love to two at once. It was wet and uncoordinated, and more than once I got an eyeful of erection meant for the more welcoming orifice of my mouth, or my hands slipped when they meant to slide. Their laughter broke with sighs and moans. Their cocks stayed stiff in my grasp. Their tastes mingled on my tongue and sent bolts of electric excitement through me.

I didn't know who stopped me first, whose hands urged me to stand, because when I did, both were holding me. They pushed me gently onto the bed, where it was my turn to be worshipped.

They were better coordinated than I'd been. Without having to say anything, they moved along my body with their mouths and hands. I didn't have to do anything but give up to them.

Time melted for a while as we wriggled and writhed, twisting and tangling. I laughed under my breath, listening to them.

"Touch her here."

"See if she likes…yes. Like that."

"Move over, man. Let me…"

"Do that again."

And they did it again. And again. They did everything, separately and together. The pleasure built until it became almost pain, until I thought I might break from it. Until I wanted to break from it, if only to find release.

Until I drowned in it.

As if on cue, with no more than a look at each other, they withdrew. The sound of our breathing was very loud. Sweat gleamed on all three of us, and the air was heavy with the scent of sex.

"Jamie, sit up. Anne, move here." Alex's voice was rough, but not hesitant.

How many times had he done this? Enough to feel confident in choreographing us. We did as he said, James pulling me against the front of him. His cock throbbed against my back as I settled between his legs. When he lay back, I went with him. My back arched. His mouth found my cheek as my hands gripped our headboard.

I was so wet, so ready that it took only half a minute of careful maneuvering to slide onto him. We had made love this way before, though never prone. I'd always been sitting on his lap, facing away from him. Reverse Cowgirl was what the positions book my friends had given me as a bachelorette present called it. It worked this way, too.

James gripped my hips, thrusting slowly. The angle was different. His cock stroked my cunt in places I wasn't used to. I arched, taking him deeper.

I wanted to come so much my muscles leaped and jerked, but doing it this way didn't give me the stimulation my clitoris craved. I shifted. James bit into the back of my shoulder. The sweet pain made me yelp.

I cried out louder at the flick of wetness on my clit. My eyes flew open, and I looked down. Alex knelt next to me, his prick in his fist. He pumped it slowly as he bent again to flick his tongue against my cunt.

I gasped. The sight of it, that dark head bent over my pussy while hands held me from behind and a cock filled me, sent a surge of pure pleasure rocketing through me.

James pushed my hips, supporting my weight and shifting the angle so he could thrust even deeper. I let go of the headboard with one hand. I licked my palm and took Alex in my fist. He groaned, hot breath puffing over my equally heated flesh. I jerked him slowly, then faster, making a cunt of my fist for him to fuck.

Everything rippled like a silk banner in a gentle breeze. We moved. We fucked. We came, the three of us together, one man inside me, the other in my hand.

In the silence, after, sweat cooled on our bodies in the night air from the windows. Sleep beckoned, though there was no temptation of dreams we'd already lived. The bed was big enough for three, but sometime in the night when I awoke, only one body lay beside me.

I should've been able to tell who it was, should have known even with a blindfold of darkness it was James. I should have known it without question, but caught between oblivion and consciousness, even running a hand along his body didn't assure me.

I wasn't sure who'd stayed and who'd gone, only that one of them had…and it didn't matter to me at that moment which one it was.

Chapter 10

I woke early and crept to the shower where I crouched on the floor with my arms around my knees and let the hot water pelt me as I gave in to panic. What had I done? What had *we* done? What would happen, now?

I understood sex and pleasure. I understood desire. Love. I loved my husband. He gave me pleasure, and I tried to do the same for him. But last night had not been about love. It had been about lust and passion. It had been about yearning.

I knew about that, too.

At seventeen I'd fallen in love for the first time. Michael Bailey, never Mike. He played baseball and football. He was homecoming king. He was beautiful and good-natured, and I wasn't the only girl who had a crush on him.

Algebra brought us together. We had first period study hall our senior year, and we sat next to each other. Math wasn't my strong suit, nor his, but by working together we found we could usually struggle through the homework. Our first date was at his kitchen table, where we studied for a big test and ate cookies his mother served warm from the oven.

He wasn't supposed to like me, quiet, studious Anne Byrne who wore glasses and never got in trouble. Jocks dated the popular girls, just like in the movies. Except life isn't a movie, and somehow it seemed the most natural thing in the world for him to hold my hand as he walked me home. To bend and kiss me goodnight as he dropped me on my front porch and turned to stride away, a boy who'd shot up into manhood almost overnight.

I never invited Michael inside my house. Compared to Michael's, mine was a lunatic asylum, where my sisters yelled and stole my clothes and we fought like cowboys and Indians. Nothing ever stayed clean, it all smelled of smoke, and meals could be embarrassingly boisterous or excruciatingly silent as we all tiptoed around my dad's moods.

I fell in love with Michael's family almost as much as I did with him. Mrs. Bailey was the perfect mom, always home, always freshly coiffed and made-up, even when she was mopping the floor. His dad was pleasant and bespectacled, and tended toward puns that made Michael groan but I adored. He had an older brother off in college who I never saw but whose photo looked like a slightly older version of Michael. Nobody swore. Nobody smoked. Nobody drank.

The Baileys took me in easily, seamlessly, as if I was no different than any of the other dozen of girlfriends Michael'd had. I guess, to them, I wasn't. But I wanted to be. I wanted them to like me more. I wanted him to like me more than he had any of those other girls. Love me more.

I was Catherine. He was my Heathcliff. If all else

perished and he remained, I'd have continued to be. Michael was the sun, the moon, the stars, my alpha and omega. He was the ocean and I tossed myself into him, not caring if I drowned.

There was no question I wouldn't go to college. I'd been looking forward to it since ninth grade when we took our first set of aptitude tests. I'd applied to several schools but had settled on Ohio State because it offered the best financial aid options for me. The spring of my senior year I turned eighteen, got accepted to Ohio State and started counting the days until I could leave home. The only thing holding me back from complete anticipation was knowing I'd have to leave Michael, but since he'd applied to Ohio State, too, I harbored the hope we'd still be able to be together.

Sex was something everyone wanted to do and some people did, what all the boys bragged about and no girl would admit to. I did everything he wanted me to do. He came in my hands, my mouth, between my breasts. Between my thighs. I gave up my virginity to him without a second thought, without even a pretense of putting him off. I'd have given it to him sooner, had he asked, but I guess he assumed I'd say no.

The perception is that the first time is always awful, but it wasn't for me. We'd spent an hour making out and touching each other. There's no foreplay quite like youthful exploration, when each undone button is cause for exaltation. I'd spent more time going down on him than he'd done for me, but that night he'd put his mouth on me for quite a while. I tasted myself on his lips when he kissed me.

We were naked by then, his penis hot and hard on my belly.

We didn't talk about doing it. It just happened. We kissed. We moved. Somehow, a shift of hips and thighs, and his erection slid against me. I arched. He pushed. I was wet and slick and open. It all happened so slowly and naturally, I don't think either of us really noticed until he thrust inside me all the way. It didn't hurt, and when he started moving, I was already so close to coming I couldn't hold back from gripping his ass and forcing him harder against me. He moaned my name into my ear as he bucked and shuddered, and hearing it sent me over the edge. We came within moments of one another that first time, the only time it happened. We had plenty of sex after that, but it was never like the first time.

In the aftermath of the rise of AIDS, the use of condoms had been pounded into our heads, and we always used them. Except that first time. But, as they say, it only takes once, and we were caught.

I think I knew I was pregnant the first time I woke up and had to run to the toilet to dry heave. Because my periods had always been irregular and painful, I convinced myself that my tender breasts and the nausea and light-headedness were just signs of PMS. I couldn't be pregnant. God wouldn't do that to me.

Except, of course, it hadn't been God but my own stupidity.

We were three days away from graduation when I told Michael. As seniors, finished with our finals, we'd been released from attending regular classes. We'd taken advantage of his house, empty while his parents were at work, to make love with wild abandon in his single bed with the wagon-wheel headboard. The sex was good the way it is when you're desperately in love and everything your partner does is like Christmas and the Fourth of July. I came more from luck than any skill either of us had, but orgasms can't really be quantified.

He lay on top of me, his hand on my belly that hadn't yet begun to grow. He smelled like sunscreen. We'd been out by the pool. I loved him so much my heart wanted to burst with it.

I'd struggled to find the perfect moment and the perfect words, but what came out was, "I'm pregnant." Flat. Simple. I could have been telling him I was hungry or tired.

I couldn't see his face, but his body, so relaxed on top of me, strung suddenly as tight as a guitar string. He didn't ask me if I was sure. He didn't say anything. He pushed himself off me and went into the bathroom next door, where he closed the door with a sharp, final click.

Minutes passed as I waited for him to come back. Through the wall I heard the deep, strangled sound of him vomiting. I got up and dressed and left the house without waiting anymore.

He didn't call me. My heart broke like a glass someone drops onto brick, too many pieces to find, and I cut myself trying to pick them up. I saw him at graduation. In photos we are standing on the same riser, but we are both staring straight ahead.

I was two months gone, with three months before I left

for college. I had a summer job, waitressing to help pay for school. I had my life stretching out in front of me, escape in sight without even Michael to hold me back now, and it was all slipping away from me.

Suicide was too melodramatic to consider. I didn't have the money for an abortion, not to mention what it would have cost my immortal soul, had I believed I had one. I got as far as looking up *Adoption* in the phone book before my palms started to sweat and I had to put the phone away before I passed out.

It was a nightmare worse than the ones I had about drowning. Anxiety stabbed me, over and over, every time I ran my hands over my stomach, or the phone rang and it wasn't Michael. It never let up, either, the way terror eventually always does.

I knew it was wrong, but I drank the first shot, anyway. It burned my throat. I stood in the kitchen with my dad's bottle in my hand, and I waited to feel what he did. What he must, in order to keep doing it. I waited for oblivion or something, anything, to take off the edge of hysteria that built day by day.

I felt nothing.

So I took another shot, straight up, coughing and choking but keeping it down. It settled into my gut like an old friend. I drank another. By the third, life didn't seem so bad, and I began to understand the allure. Later, on my knees in front of the toilet, vomiting so hard I burst a blood vessel, I would think *I'll never drink again*.

Two weeks later, while I lifted a particularly heavy tray of steaks, a twisting stab of pain erupted inside me.

Another followed. They passed long enough for me to serve the food, but an hour later they started again. I went to the employee restroom and found a dark clot of blood the size of my thumb in my underwear. I stifled my burst of tears with both hands, scrambled for a thick sanitary napkin, and went back to work.

I made it through my shift. At home, I stood in the shower watching the blood run down my legs and swirl into the drain. My laughter sounded like sobs. I didn't know what to do, only that God had answered prayers I hadn't even sent.

In August Michael came into the place where I worked. He ordered a soda, which I brought him in a glass with a slice of lemon in it. I gave him a straw without his having to ask, the paper still covering the end out of which he'd drink, like my fingers touching it could ever have in any way contaminated him.

"How are you doing?" he asked with shifty eyes, though it was in an off hour and the only other patrons were seated in another section.

"Fine." I tried to remember what it was like to love him.

"How's…?" His eyes finished the question with a look at my abdomen.

"It's gone," I said, like our baby had been a pesky rash cleared up by ample applications of medicated ointment.

I didn't begrudge him the relief on his face. I'd felt the same thing. But it hadn't been him watching the blood, or dealing with the cramps, just like it hadn't been him who'd dealt with the situation at all. Perhaps it wasn't fair of me to judge him like that. We were young, and I'd have run if I could, if the problem hadn't been inside me.

"Oh. Well. That's…" He trailed off. His soda sat untouched. He cleared his throat and made as if to reach for my hand but didn't. "Was it expensive?"

I wanted to be angry with him, but since my love for him had burned to ash, I couldn't find anything to mold into fury. When I didn't answer, he seemed to think I meant yes. He nodded, shifty eyed again.

"I'll give you the money for it. And, Anne…I'm sorry."

I was sorry, too, but not too sorry to tell him the truth. Not too sorry to give him back the money. I needed it for school. Five hundred dollars paid for my books that first year.

Steam parted like a curtain as I stepped from the shower and reached for a towel. All of that had been a long time ago. It had left a scar, but so had a lot of other things. Except sometimes I wondered what might have happened if I hadn't wished so hard to lose that child. I'd been diagnosed with endometriosis, which can cause infertility. One had nothing to do with the other, yet in my mind they'd linked. Useless to ponder.

I dried myself and stood at the bathroom door wrapped in a towel. I listened to two male voices, rising and falling in conversation that included a lot of laughter.

I knew why I'd thought of Michael today. It was the yearning. I loved James, but I'd never burned for him. Not like I had for Michael.

Not like I was for Alex.

They both looked up when I opened the door. Two

gorgeous men with smiles trying hard to be identical. I smelled coffee. Alex reached out a hand.

"Anne," he said, "come back to bed."

And I did.

I was locking my car in the diner parking lot when I saw Claire leaping out of a black car two spots away. She slammed the door with all her might and added a flip of the bird as the car pealed away. She turned, spotting me.

"Men suck!" she cried. "Fucking suck donkey cocks!"

I wasn't inclined to disagree with her just then. "Who was that?"

"Nobody," she told me. "And I mean nobody as in loser, white-trash, moron fucktard."

"I thought you said you didn't have a boyfriend." I was trying to make her laugh, but Claire only glowered.

"I don't." She looked in the direction the car had gone. "And if I did, it wouldn't be him."

An unfamiliar car pulled into the spot next to mine, and Patricia got out. She locked the door and slung the keys into her purse. Seeing us looking, she gave her shoulders a little straighten.

"The van got terrible gas mileage. We traded it in for this."

My sister hadn't driven a used car in her entire life. I looked at Claire, who wasn't paying attention. Like in a comedy of errors, Mary pulled up at that moment in my mother's car.

"Where's the Beetle?" Claire said.

"It needed new tires." Mary's ever-present phone beeped at her through her purse. She reached inside to press a button or something. The bleating stopped. "Are we ready? I'm starving."

With the party only a few weeks away, the RSVPs had begun rolling in. I handed over a pile of postcards with *Yes* or *No* checked on the back.

"God. Everyone's coming." Claire looked through a few more cards and put them back in the pile. "Holy shit, you guys. This is, like, two hundred people."

"We're going to have to call the caterer." This from practical Patricia.

"Where are they going to all fit?" I asked, not expecting an answer.

"Oh, it'll all work out." Mary's cheerful answer made us all turn. She looked surprised. "What? Won't it?"

"Okay, Mary Sunshine," said Claire with a roll of her eyes. "If you say so."

"Sure, why wouldn't it?" said Mary blithely.

I looked at her closely. Flushed cheeks. Bright eyes. Small smile tugging the corners of her lips. Something was up with her, too. With all of us. It was a summer for secrets. At least Mary's looked like a good one.

We divided up the final chores. Paper goods, decorations, party favors. We debated the pros and cons of hiring someone to help clean up after, and decided not to waste the money. The catering team would take care of their own mess and there wouldn't be dishes to wash if we went with paper goods.

"We can rent a big trash bin," said Patricia. "They come pick it up the day after the party."

"You should rent a Portaloo, too," put in Claire. She

snagged a few more fries from my plate, since she'd finished hers. "Two toilets for two hundred asses ain't gonna cut it."

That wasn't a bad idea, either. Our meeting went well, with no squabbles. Patricia was uncharacteristically quiet, Mary uncommonly bubbly. Claire excused herself suddenly halfway through the meal, looking pale. My other sisters turned to look at me, like I had an explanation.

I held up my hands. "Don't look at me. Mary, you see her more than I do."

"Not lately." Mary dipped a fry in ketchup but didn't eat it. She just smiled at it. "She's been working a lot and I've been out of town."

"Out of town? Where did you go?" Patricia was counting out exact change for the bill again.

"I went to stay with Betts for a few days. I wanted to scout out apartments for the fall when I start school, and I had some paperwork to do."

Patricia looked up from her pennies and dimes. "Ah-ha. Let me guess. You saw that guy again."

Mary looked confused. "What guy?"

"She means the one you slept with," I said.

Mary made a face. "Joe? No."

"Something put the pink in your cheeks." Patricia stacked her coins in neat piles on top of the dollars.

None of us said anything. Patricia froze for a minute. Mary's chin lifted, almost a challenge.

Wow. I got it, just then. So did Patricia. I didn't dare look at her.

"Fucking hell," said Claire as she slid into her seat again.

"Men fucking suck donkey cocks all the way down to the fucking hairy root. And the balls, too!"

She looked around the table at the rest of us, but we'd all found something to occupy our attentions. "What the hell happened here?"

And still, we said nothing, like we'd all been trained so well to do.

It wasn't until much later that James remembered to ask me about the doctor's visit.

"It was fine." I leaned closer to the mirror to layer my lashes with mascara. "She said it was good that I wasn't having the pain anymore. The surgery worked."

James had shaved and now smelled of the rosemary-lavender lotion he'd rubbed into his cheeks. "And what about getting pregnant?"

I didn't even blink. "She said we could do that, any time."

He grinned. "Great."

I capped the silver tube and put it in my makeup bag, then turned to face him. "I'm not so sure this is actually the best time to try and get pregnant, James. Think about it."

His toothbrush paused on the way up to his mouth. "If you don't ever fuck him, I don't see the problem."

I crossed my arms over my stomach. "I can't believe you just said that. We've gone to bed together twice. What makes you think eventually we won't do more than just suck and jerk?"

"Just…don't, that's all." James shrugged, like it was no big deal. Like watching his wife take another man's prick down her throat was fine but watching her take it inside her pussy wasn't.

Somewhere in our house, Alex waited for us to be ready to go out to dinner. Somewhere between us he stood, even when he wasn't in the room. I frowned, but James seemed unmoved.

"That seems a little unbalanced," I told him.

He touched my cheek lightly, then started brushing his teeth. "He understands," he said through the foam.

I took a second or two to process this. "Explain that."

James spit and rinsed, then stuck the toothbrush in the holder before he turned to hold my upper arms. "He's cool with it. He knows we might want to be having kids. He's fine with not fucking you."

"You talked about this?" The words caught in my throat but I forced them out. "Without me?"

Guile didn't sit well on James's face. "It's not a big deal, Anne."

I jerked away from him. "It *is* a big deal. How dare you discuss something like that without me? What were you doing? Negotiating?"

Something that wasn't quite guilt drifted across his expression. "Baby, don't be like that."

"What did you guys do? Make rules?"

He shifted his gaze from mine. "Something like that. Yeah."

I felt the color drain from my face. "What are they?"

"Aww, c'mon, baby…."

I shook off the hand he tried to put on me. "What. Are. They."

James sighed and leaned against the bathroom counter. "Just…he can't fuck you. That's all. Anything else you want to do is fine, just not that."

I had to pace while I considered this. They had discussed this without my knowledge. They'd talked about me.

"He can go down on me?"

James rubbed his face, but answered. "Yeah. If you want."

"And I can suck his cock?"

"Only if you want, Anne," James said patiently. "All of this is only if you want to."

"How long?" I kept my voice steady.

"How long what?"

I'd seen him do that before. Play dumb to keep from answering questions. It was a trick he'd learned to deal with his family, and it irritated the ever-loving shit out of me that he'd try it with me.

"How long have you been talking about this?"

He reached for me and I put a hand up between us to hold him off. He sighed and ran a hand through his hair, spiking it. He backed off, not meeting my eyes.

"Does it matter?"

For a moment I had to struggle to find a voice with which to answer him. "Yes, it matters! Of course it matters!"

"A while." He turned back to the sink to scrape his razor along his cheeks, though he wasn't scruffy. "Once, when we were talking it just came up."

"Please explain to me how the subject of letting your friend fuck your wife came up in conversation, James," I said. "Oh, excuse me. Of letting your friend *not* fuck your wife."

He turned back to me. "I found that survey you took in one of those magazines in the bathroom, okay? I thought I was doing something you wanted."

If I'd thought he was just trying to defuse my anger I probably would've snapped, but his sincerity took me aback. "What survey?"

"The one about fantasies. You answered that your top fantasy was to be with two guys at the same time."

I was thrown so off-balance I felt like the floor had tilted. I grabbed the counter for support. "I have no fucking clue what you're talking about."

Surrounding a lie with truth can make it believable. James wasn't good at lying, but I believed he was telling me at least part of the truth.

"That's what it said," he told me. "And I thought you wanted it. So…"

"So you set this up? All of this was a setup?"

He shrugged, palms up. I had to turn away to keep from slapping him. "I can't believe you'd pimp me out!"

"It wasn't like that," he said quietly. "I didn't know he was going to come and stay until he called that day. But it just seemed like a good time to try it…. I knew he'd be up for it. And I wanted to give you something I thought you really wanted."

"Oh, sure, like the golf vacation?" I asked in reference to the trip he'd planned for our third wedding anniversary, despite the fact I don't play golf.

"Huh?"

"Never mind." I pushed past him and went into the bedroom to finish dressing.

"I thought you'd like it," James said from the doorway. "And you did."

I whirled, my throat tight with emotion that couldn't decide if it wanted to be fury or humor. "You never even told me you were in touch with him, James! For years you talked about him almost like…like he was dead! You never told me you were talking to him! You let me invite him to our wedding and let me think you hadn't talked to him in years!"

"Because I hadn't!" he yelled, too loudly for the small space. "He called me to congratulate me on getting married. We started e-mailing once in a while. Sometimes he'd call me. It was no big deal!"

"What did you fight about?" I asked him. "When you were twenty-one and in college, and he came to visit you at school. What did you fight about that you didn't talk for so long? He was your best friend. What did you fight about?"

James went to the dresser and yanked out a pair of socks. He sat to pull them on. He didn't look at me.

I'd been on my knees for him plenty of times, but this time there was no crackle of arousal between us to cushion me. I put my hands on his thighs and tilted my head to look at his face. When he straightened to meet my gaze, his brows knitted together, and his mouth had been sewn shut by clumsy fingers.

"I have the right to know this," I said to him.

He sighed, then, and stopped looking angry. "I hadn't seen him for a while. I was off at school and he was working at the Point. We weren't in touch, really, but every once in a while he'd call or I'd see him when I came home on break. He'd changed. He was going to clubs. Meeting people. I was trying to graduate on time. Things weren't the same with us, you know. People grow up."

I nodded. "I know."

"So I get this call from him, out of the blue, in the middle of studying for finals. He wanted to come out for the weekend. So he came out and...well, I knew something was up with him but I didn't ask, you know? Because he was, like...vibrating, almost. I thought maybe he was high, at first, but he said he wasn't on anything. So we went out. Got drunk. Got back to my apartment and he told me some guy he met was offering him a job in Singapore, and he was going to take it."

James took a long, slow breath.

"I thought I didn't care. But...we were drunk. Fuck." He ran a hand through his hair. "Then he told me this guy wasn't just some guy, but a guy he'd been fucking, and...I just...I just lost it."

This wasn't the story I'd been expecting. "Oh, you didn't..."

"We had a big fight. We broke the coffee table, and the bottles on it." He rubbed his scar, absently. "We were both shit-faced drunk, Anne. I've never been so wasted. I got cut. It bled like a motherfucker, all over the place." He gave a weak laugh. "I thought I was dying. Alex hauled my ass to the E.R. The next day he left."

I looked at him. "And you offered him a place in our bed without even bothering to ask me what I thought. You went behind my back and invited him to seduce your wife, and you watched him eat my pussy, but you don't want him to fuck me."

He flinched. "I thought—"

"You didn't think," I snapped.

We stared at each other. It was the first time we'd ever fought about something more important than who forgot to take out the trash. I got off my knees, but he stayed sitting.

"If you don't want this," James began, but I stopped him again.

"I do want this." My voice sounded very far away. "I want it."

I blamed James more than Alex in their little collaboration. After all it was James who'd married me, James who'd made it okay for Alex to come to stay with us. James who'd ever-so-cleverly introduced the idea of voyeurism and exhibitionism and ménage à trois. James knew me. Alex didn't.

I should have held tight to my fury, but knowing James had come up with the idea didn't change the fact I'd wanted Alex Kennedy almost from the first moment I'd met him. Or that having two men was just as fabulous in real life as it was in the fantasy I hadn't filled out in any survey. What it came down to was whether or not I chose to believe my husband's motives for this little adventure, or if I wanted to dig down deep and possibly drag up things that should stay buried.

I chose to believe him.

I found the magazine he'd meant tucked under a pile of reading material in the basket next to the toilet. Someone had, indeed, circled the "two men, one woman" scenario as their top choice, but it wasn't me. I took the magazine into the bedroom and threw it at James. The fluttering glossy pages hit him square in the chest. He grabbed it up.

"There's your survey," I said, managing to sound angry, though I wasn't, really. "I didn't fill that out."

"Who did, then?" He held it up.

"Gee, I don't know," I said, finger to my chin in mock innocence. "Who gave me the magazines? Could it have been...your mother?"

He looked stricken and disgusted, and flung the magazine from him like it had grown eight legs and crawled out from under a rock. "Anne, God!"

I couldn't help it. I laughed. James looked like he wanted to scrub his eyeballs.

"Think about that," I said.

"No. I don't want to." He shuddered.

I went over to the bed and straddled him, grabbed up his wrists and pinned them above his head. That he could have easily pulled away was not the purpose. Making my point was.

"If I ever find out that you did something like this again," I said sternly, "I will never forgive you. Do you understand?"

He looked up at me. "Yes."

I moved my hips a little. The shift of his cock as it began to get stiff rewarded me. "If you're going to talk about things like this, you have to include me."

"Done."

I moved again. His pupils dilated a bit. His hips lifted, and I pushed down, squeezing his sides with my thighs.

"And when he leaves, it's over," I told him. "It's a few

weeks, only. Just for the summer. It's not something you're going to offer to anyone else, you got it? No inviting Dan Martin back here for some wine, cheese and a hand job from Anne."

"Jesus, no," James said. Dan Martin was one of his crew members. A nice enough guy, although I preferred men with teeth.

He lifted his hips again, but I wasn't ready to give him what he so plainly sought. "I don't want this to come between us, Jamie, I'm serious."

He smiled, and I realized I'd called him by the name Alex gave him. I let go of his wrists, and he put his hand on my cheek. We sat that way for a moment.

"It won't come between us. But if you want it to stop, all you have to do is say so. And it's done."

I considered this. "I just need to know why. Really why."

"I told you why." He shifted under me, his cock still hard and probably getting uncomfortable. "Because I thought you wanted it."

I shook my head. "Not the answer you think I want to hear. The real reason."

His hands on my hips tightened. "Why did you do it?"

"Because I wanted to."

He moved me against him, rocking. "You wanted him to touch you?"

"Yes."

"Like this?" His hand cupped my breast.

My breath caught. "Yes."

"And here?" A hand went to my ass, squeezing.

"Yes. There, too."

"And here?" He touched between my legs.

My back arched a little as I pushed forward at his touch. "Yes, James. There, too."

He pulled me down and rolled me beneath him. His mouth found mine, already open. His tongue plundered me, tasted and retreated. He pulled away to look into my face.

"You wanted him to kiss you. And touch you. It got you hot."

He was doing all of those things as he spoke, and I was getting hot. "I already told you, yes."

His expression was closed to me. He stopped his exploration of my body with his hands and looked into my eyes. He brought his mouth close to mine, but though I strained to reach him, he didn't kiss me. His breath gusted over my face.

"Watching him go down on you, I knew just how you tasted. How you felt inside when he put his fingers inside you. How you get so hot, so wet. And tight. And I knew how good your mouth felt when you put it on his dick. Seeing you suck him while I fucked you..."

His voice hoarsened, got deeper. "You have no idea how beautiful you look when you're coming."

I wanted to dig deeper. Ask him more. I wanted to get under the surface, the shiny. "If we're going to do this, we have to be honest with each other."

"Of course." His whisper in my ear made me shiver. "Absolutely. I promise I won't talk about you with him again...unless it's to plot new ways to get you naked."

I smiled automatically. "I mean it, James."

"Call me Jamie," he murmured, licking my throat.

Somehow, he'd unbuttoned my jeans and slipped a hand inside. "I like it."

"Jamie," I whispered. "I mean it."

He reached for my hand, and I let him take it. "I'm not gay."

I started to tell him it didn't matter to me if he was, that it wasn't his preference in genitalia that made me love him, but a noise from the doorway made us both turn. Alex stood there, watching. How long he'd been there, I didn't know. He looked at our hands, linked, but he showed no expression.

"I came to see if you guys were ready to leave," he said, tone as beige as the walls.

James got up, his arm around my shoulders. "Yeah, man, give us a minute."

Our eyes caught and held. Alex nodded once. Then he turned and left us alone again.

Chapter 11

$\mathcal{T}$he next morning I found Alex sitting with his laptop at the kitchen table. His hair was sleep rumpled, chest and feet bare. He wore his Hello Kitty pajama bottoms. I'd never seen him wearing glasses. They changed his face. Made him a stranger again. Somehow, that made it easier to approach him.

"We need to talk."

He looked up, then closed his laptop. "Okay."

"James told me everything." I wasn't going to gild this conversation, or keep it pretty for the sake of peace. There were things I needed to say.

"Did he?" Alex crossed his arms over his chest and leaned back in his chair.

"Yes. He did."

Aggression doesn't come naturally to me, but I must have seemed threatening despite my pajamas and equally disheveled hair. Maybe it was the mug of coffee I brandished like a weapon, or the way I towered over him while he was seated.

"What did he tell you?" He could say so much with just the slightest quirk of brow and lip.

"About the rules you two laid out."

He waited a beat before answering. "Did he tell you that, or did you ask him about it?"

"A little of both."

He made a small noise. I sipped my coffee. He looked somewhat blank, but I thought that was on purpose, not because he didn't get what I was trying to say. Not that I was, at that moment, saying anything.

It was hard to force a discussion like this, but like ripping off a bandage all at once, I figured I'd better give it a shot.

"He told me about how you talked about what you could and couldn't do."

Damn him. He wasn't giving me an inch, not doing one damn thing to make it easier for me. He didn't even nod.

"I don't like it," I finished firmly, albeit lamely.

This got a reaction from him. Scornful charm trickled into his eyes and tilted his mouth on one side. He leaned back more in the chair with a small shake of his head to clear the hair off his forehead.

"You don't like what?"

I gripped my coffee mug in two hands and tried to keep my voice neutral. "The rules the two of you made."

I stood my ground even when he was on his feet with one smooth motion, like a cat. He took the mug out of my hands and put it on the table. I didn't back up, not even when he stood so close I could count the individual hairs surrounding his nipples.

"Which ones don't you like?"

He moved forward and I back, slowly, like ripples in water. We stopped when my back hit the small section of wall between the window seat and the door to the deck.

My heart began a familiar thump-thumping that echoed in my wrists and odd places like the backs of my knees and behind my ears. The places I'd put perfume, if I wore it. The places I'd want someone to kiss.

Alex put a hand on the wall next to my head. "Tell me something, Anne. Do you not like the rules or the fact you didn't make them?"

I took a breath to steady my voice. "You negotiated me like it didn't matter what I wanted."

He was looking down at me. The weight of his gaze surrounded me, but I didn't look up. Warmth rose from his skin, but gooseflesh humped my arms.

"You're right," he murmured. He didn't sound smarmy or condescending, but it wasn't quite sincere, either. "We should have asked you what you thought. So tell me. What do you think?"

He was waiting for me to look into his face, but I cut my eyes away. Sunlight and shadow dappled the deck outside the windows. A breeze swung the chimes Patricia had made for me out of old silverware. I saw them move but couldn't hear them.

When I didn't answer, he moved his hand closer to me, the heel of it brushing my shoulder. The other one went to the wall next to my hip. He caged me with his arms.

"Is it all right if I kiss you?"

I swallowed, my mouth dry. It didn't seem to matter that I didn't answer. His breath stirred a loose tendril of my hair.

"Is it all right if I touch you?"

But he wasn't touching me, the bastard, though my entire body vibrated with the tension of waiting for it. I could have moved a hairsbreadth in any direction and met his skin with mine, but I was frozen. Between my legs, my pulse throbbed. I was bare beneath my thin pajama pants, and every small shift, every breath, shook the fabric against me.

"Is it all right if I put my mouth on you?"

My clit leaped. I remembered the feeling of his tongue against me, his lips pressing my flesh as he slid a finger deep inside to stroke me. My lips parted. A sigh escaped. I could have inclined my head an inch and kissed his chest, could have licked him without even straining. I felt like I was shaking all over, but my body remained still.

"Anne," he whispered, bending his head to speak directly in my ear. "Is it all right if I fuck you?"

I jerked my head up at that, looking at him at last. "You know it's not. That's the one thing he said no to."

Then he touched me, oh, God, and it was good, the way he cupped his hand against my cunt and pressed just hard enough. "Then it's a good thing there are so many other things to do than fuck."

I think I said his name, but it might have only been a moan. Whatever it was, his kiss swallowed it up. My arms went around his neck. He crushed me to the wall, every part of him pushing against every part of me. His mouth slid from mine to my neck, my shoulder. His hands roamed my body, kneading and squeezing, hooking under my leg to pull it up around his waist, reaching around to cup my ass.

Is it adultery when it's not a secret? When there are rules? Can you be unfaithful to someone who's given his permission?

Alex moved down my body with his mouth, his hands tugging the pajamas down my hips and thighs. He bared me to him, and parted my legs. He knelt in front of me and put his face between my thighs.

I covered my mouth to mute the cry when he kissed me there. When he licked my clitoris and forced my legs open wider to accommodate him. The wall was smooth and cool on my back and rear, and he pinned me to it with his tongue.

Orgasms are like snowflakes, no two alike. The first one jittered up and down my legs, making them shake and curling my toes. My fingers twisted in his hair, soft and thick. I watched him as he memorized my pussy with his mouth, as his eyes opened and he looked up at me. He smiled, and I came again in slow, rolling bursts of pleasure.

I tasted myself when he kissed me. Me, mingled with him. His tongue stroked mine like it had stroked my clit. He pulled back, breathing hard. So was I.

His cock demanded my attention and consideration, and with my body still boneless from climax I was eager to return the favor. I rubbed him through his pajamas. I liked the way my touch made him shudder, how he put both hands on the wall like he needed the support.

"Fuck, you have a gorgeous mouth."

I can't adequately describe how freeing it was to get on my knees in front of him. We had no baggage. I wasn't thinking about the mortgage, or laundry, or an argument we'd had. All I had to think about with Alex was how he felt in my hand when I stroked him, and how he tasted when I opened my mouth to take him inside. There was nothing but the yearning, and I gave in to it as I sucked him.

I did my best for him. He came with a shout before my jaw had time to ache, and the speed surprised and pleased me. I swallowed him as his balls pulsed in my cupped hand. Then I got to my feet.

James would have kissed and hugged me and we'd have shared a moment of intimacy, but Alex and I didn't reach for each other. We hadn't broken any rules, but it still felt illicit, which was probably part of the appeal. We weren't strangers but we didn't really know each other, either. I wondered if he wanted to know me just then, or if it really only is women who let their minds work overtime.

"I'm sorry," he said, surprising me. "I didn't know he hadn't told you. I thought you knew."

This piece of information didn't sit any better with me than learning about the whole plot in the first place. "I'm not sure I'm glad I found out. It's not nice to find out someone you love hasn't been truthful."

"Jamie's never been a good liar," Alex said with a grin. "He's not a rascal like me."

I smiled a little. "Maybe not, but he's not as good as he thinks he is, either."

The words came out sounding more bitterly than I'd meant them to. Alex looked confused.

"I also didn't know you'd been in touch after our wedding. As far as I knew, you hadn't spoken since your big fight in college."

"He told you about that? The fight?"

"Yes," I said. "He told me that, too."

"And you're—"

I didn't get the chance to find out what I was, because the backdoor handle jiggled. I think we both jumped ten feet in the air. We scrambled to rearrange our clothes and sprang apart like polarized magnets.

It probably wasn't far enough, but the door flew open and Claire stumbled in with her arms full of bags. The door banged against the wall and started to close on her, and Alex moved forward to catch it.

"Thanks, handsome," my sister said automatically, without even really looking at him. Flirting by rote. "Can you give me a hand with these?"

He did, handling with one hand the bags she'd needed two to hold. The plastic looped over his fingers and he lifted them. "Where should I put them?"

"Ooh, nice pecs," Claire said a little more perkily. "On the island, I guess. Hey, Anne, do you have any ginger ale?"

Alex deposited the bags while I gestured toward the small closet. "In the pantry."

"Thanks." She opened the door to help herself.

Alex and I shared a look, half relief and half amusement. His hair still looked rumpled, but now I knew it was from my touch and not from sleep. His mouth was still wet from mine.

"Jesus, it smells like burritos in here." Claire wrinkled her nose and popped the tab on her soda. She looked at both of us, back and forth.

We stopped looking at each other. Alex went back to his

computer. I busied myself with emptying the bags. Claire had brought bags of balloons and spools of curling ribbon, along with several boxes of plastic utensils that looked like metal.

She sipped from her can. "I found them at the party supply place. They look like real silverware."

Alex picked up the laptop. "I'll get out of your way."

"You don't have to leave on my account," Claire told him. Again, she looked back and forth between us. "Don't mind me."

"I don't mind you at all, sweet thing," Alex said with a wink and a saucy grin. "But I've got to take a shower and get on the road. I've got an appointment."

"Oooh," she flirted back. "Hot stuff."

They laughed, mine trailing half a second after, like a badly timed soundtrack. Alex walked behind me, barely brushing me as he passed, and headed down the hall toward his bedroom. Claire waited until we heard the door shut before she turned to me.

"Does James know you're fucking his supposed best friend?"

I squished the plastic bags into the holder in the cupboard under the sink. I wasn't ignoring her. Just answering with silence.

"Anne!" Claire sounded shocked, no small feat.

"I'm not fucking him." Technically speaking.

"You are doing something with him. I know that look. That just-fucked look. And you've got DSL."

"What?" I turned, then.

"Dick-sucking lips," my sister said. "Holy shit, Anne. You were giving him a BJ, weren't you?"

"Claire…" I sighed and forced my hands not to stray to my face and hair or to straighten my clothes as evidence of a guilt I didn't even feel. "It's really none of your business."

"Well, excuuuuuuse me!"

From elsewhere in the house we heard the creak of doors opening and closing, and the far-off hiss of running water. I looked back at her. Faint shadows circled her eyes, a very goth look but one I didn't think she was affecting on purpose.

I thought of how she'd been acting lately. "Are you okay?"

She drank soda and avoided my eyes. "I'm fine."

"You're not acting fine."

"Is that your spidey-sense acting up again?" She scoffed, but it sounded forced.

"It's a big sister's prerogative."

She smiled but rolled her eyes. "Yeah, okay. Whatever."

"Claire. Are you sure you're okay?"

Her face crumpled. A sob snuck out, though I could see she tried to hold it in. Alarmed, because Claire never cried, not even at sappy movies or at Hallmark card commercials, I moved around the island toward her.

"What's wrong?" I asked, but as she broke down against her will, even pressing her hands to her eyes to keep the tears from coming, I thought I knew.

"I'll be fine." She sounded like she was trying to convince herself more than me. "I'll be fine. I'll be fine."

"Come here. Sit down." I took her by the elbow and forced her over to the table's bench seat. I sat beside her, my hand on her shoulder. "Are you in trouble?"

Trouble covered a lot of ground. But when she didn't

answer at first, it was obvious the kind she was in. My heart sank, and I rubbed her shoulder gently.

"Claire?"

She got her tears under control and grabbed up a napkin from the holder to wipe the streaks of mascara from her cheeks. She took a few deep breaths and blew them out. She looked at the ceiling for a minute, her mouth trembling.

I waited. She took a few more deep breaths and wiped her eyes again. Then she looked at me.

"I'm pregnant."

"Oh, Claire." I didn't have much more to say.

"I knew it!" she cried. The tears came back, swimming in her blue eyes and melting the black eyeliner. "I knew you'd be disappointed in me!"

I wasn't disappointed in her. How could I be? I shook my head. "I'm not—"

"I didn't want to tell you because I knew you'd think I was stupid." She put her face in her hands. "I wasn't stupid, Anne. It was just an accident—I was on antibiotics for a UTI and the condom broke…."

"Claire. Shh. Stop. I don't think you're stupid."

She buried her face in her arms and let go. Sobs wracked her shoulders and shook the table. I put an arm around her shoulders and said nothing, letting her cry.

Even as a baby Claire hadn't been much of a weeper. Patricia had been sensitive, bursting into tears when teased. Mary had been a whiner. I'd been stoic, not crying even when I'd felt like it, but Claire had always just been…Claire. Upbeat. Sassy. Seeing her this way, I didn't quite know what to do. Sisterhood didn't come with a handbook.

"I *am* stupid!" she wailed. "I should never have believed him when he said he loved me! That son of a bitch!"

More sobs dissolved her. I got up to pour her soda into a glass with ice and stuck a straw in it, then set it in front of her along with a box of tissues and a cold, damp cloth. She looked up. Her tears had washed away the last of her eye makeup, and without it she looked so much younger it made me want to cry, too.

"Thanks." She wiped her face and kept the cloth pressed over her eyes for a minute.

"You're welcome." I gave her a minute. "What are you going to do?"

She laughed like it hurt. "I don't know. He says it can't be his. Can you believe it? Fucking bastard prick. Of course it's his. Fucking married bastard fucking cocksucker!"

Another flurry of sobs sputtered out of her. I didn't say anything. After a moment, she swiped at her face.

"I didn't know he was married, Anne. Swear to God. Fucker told me he was divorced. He lied. God, why do men have to suck so much?"

"I'm sorry."

"It's not your fault," she said. "Not every man can be perfect like James."

"Is that what you really think?" I shook my head. "Claire, don't give him that much credit."

She gave me a small, waterlogged smile. "Is that why you're giving his friend blow jobs in your kitchen while he's at work?"

Claire was the only one of my sisters who wouldn't have judged me for it. "It's complicated."

"Well, shit."

I rubbed her shoulder again. "Yes, he knows."

"And he's okay with it?"

"He's the one who set it up." Bitterness twisted my mouth with the words, though I wasn't sure why. I had wanted this, and if he hadn't given it to me I wouldn't have taken it.

"I knew you were kinky." She wiped her face again with the cloth and blew her nose in a tissue. She took a long sip of ginger ale.

One laugh slipped out. "I'm still not sure I qualify as kinky."

"Anne, two dudes? Kinky. And hot."

We heard doors open and close again as Alex left the bathroom and went back to his room. Claire sighed, her thin shoulders rising and falling. She slumped, forehead resting in her hand.

"I don't know what I'm going to do, Anne. I have one semester left of school. I have a shitty job. I can't tell Mom and Dad about this, they'll freak."

"Do you need money?"

She looked up. "You mean for an abortion?"

I nodded, silent. Her brow furrowed, and she looked at her hands. She rubbed a spot where her black polish had chipped off her nails.

"I don't think I can do that."

I took her hand and squeezed it. "Then you don't have to."

She started to cry again, and this time I knew what to do. I pulled her close so she could sob on my shoulder. I rubbed her back over and over. Her tears wet my shirt.

"Whatever you decide, Claire, I'll support you."

"I'm so scared," she whispered, like she was ashamed. "You don't even know."

I had to close my eyes then, my throat closing tight against my own tears. "Yes, I do."

She looked up at me, then down the hall. "Not—"

"No. Michael Bailey."

"But you were only in high school," she said.

"And I *was* stupid," I told her.

Claire sniffled. "Did you tell Mom and Dad?"

"No."

"Did you have an abortion?"

I shook my head.

"Did you...you didn't have the baby!"

"No. I had a miscarriage. Maybe because of the endometriosis. Maybe not. I don't know."

"Wow." Claire looked stunned. "I never knew."

"Nobody did. I didn't tell anyone. As it turned out, I didn't have to."

"What did he do?"

I sighed. "He didn't do anything. We broke up."

"I remember when you did," she said. "I could hear you crying at night."

"Ahh, good times, good times," I said with fake fondness.

We laughed. She hugged me, and I hugged her back. She drank the rest of her soda.

"Does James know?"

I shook my head again. "I never told him."

She nodded, like that made sense. "You'd better be on the

pill *and* use a diaphragm," she said seriously with another look down the hall. "Imagine how fucked up *that* would be."

"I told you, I'm not fucking him. It's an…arrangement."

Claire made one of her distinctive faces. "Uh-huh."

"If you need a good doctor, I can recommend one." My change of subject didn't even play at being subtle.

"Jesus. A cooch doctor. God." Claire put her face in her hands again. "I need one that will work on a sliding scale. I'm fucking broke."

"She does. And she's great. And if you need money…"

She looked around at my shabby kitchen in a house valued for sale at half a million dollars. "You're not exactly a fountain of cash, sissy."

"You're my sister. If you need help—"

She shook her head and gave me a watery smile. "I'll keep that in mind. Right now, I just need to figure out what I'm going to do."

Whistling alerted us to Alex's return. Wearing a dark suit with a deep red shirt and black tie and smelling of the same rosemary and lavender lotion James wore, he came into the kitchen. He looked professional, but his smirk was anything but.

"Ladies," he said. "Try not to drool."

Claire rolled her eyes and gave him the finger. He put a hand over his heart and staggered back. "Ouch! That hurt."

"Act like a cocky bastard, you run the risk of being treated like one," she said smoothly.

I was interested to see that her flirting, no matter how little she might have meant it previously, had stopped. Claire even flirted with James, though without intent. Yet she'd backed off from Alex. She wasn't being rude to him. Just...not flirting.

He got it. I liked that about him, that he was sharp. Fast. It could be intimidating, but it was also very sexy.

"Anne, I'll be out late tonight. So don't hold dinner for me or anything, okay?"

"Sure. See you later."

He nodded and saluted Claire, grabbed his car keys from the hook by the door and left.

When he was gone, she said, "My, my, my. What a picture of domesticity."

"He was being polite, that's all. He's still a guest in our house."

"Uh-huh," she said. "Funny, but he doesn't impress me as the sort who'd bend over backward just to be polite."

For some reason, this annoyed me. "You don't even know him."

She shrugged. "He's a Kennedy. And not one of the ones who fucked Marilyn Monroe, if you know what I mean."

"I don't, actually." I frowned so hard it gave me a headache.

"He's got how many sisters? Three?"

"Yes."

"Big-time sluts," Claire said. "Into drugs. His mom works at Kroger."

"How do you know this?" I'd gone to the same high school as James and Alex, but five years behind. We'd never been there at the same time. If Alex's sisters had been there, they'd have been before or after me, because I didn't remember any of them.

"We were in school together, me and Kathy, the youngest one. We were on the drill squad together. She used to talk about him. Alex. He used to send her weird candy bars and stuff like canned pig's feet from wherever he was in China."

"Singapore," I corrected. "And that still doesn't mean he can't be polite."

She shrugged again. "I'm just saying, his sisters were slutty and his dad's one of those guys that hangs out down at the VFW on disability."

I gave her a long, steady look, and to her credit she did look faintly ashamed. "I don't think I'd be judging anyone else so harshly if I were you, Claire."

"Yeah," she said in a low voice after a moment. "But at least nobody pretends it isn't true."

Claire had been two the summer everything changed. I don't think she could have remembered our family any differently than it was. In a way I envied her not having the comparison.

"This fucking party," she sighed. "I can't wait until it's over."

"Yeah. Me, too."

"Okay. I'm totally raiding your fridge." She got up to sidle past me, but stopped. "Anne. Just...be careful. Okay? With that whole thing."

"I will," I assured her, though I wasn't at all certain I could. Even if I wanted to.

I discovered the power of an orgasm at sixteen. I'd fallen headlong into the teenage girl's habit of spending hours staring at my face in the mirror wishing I looked more like the women in the fashion magazines and less like myself. I took long showers, standing beneath the water until it ran cold and I faced the wrath of my sisters who'd had to wait their turn. I washed my hair, shaved my legs and the places on my body where hair still seemed such an odd thing to have. I hadn't thought much about the handheld shower other than it made it easier to rinse the shaving cream from my skin.

It felt good, that first unintentional burst of water against me. So I did it again, and held it there. A few minutes later, fireworks exploded inside me. I had to sit on the floor of the shower because my legs shook so much I thought I might fall.

I learned quickly how my body worked after that. At night, beneath the blankets and in the shower, I traversed my lines and curves and discovered all the places that felt good to touch and stroke. I learned how to prolong the pleasure until I couldn't stand it anymore, and a mere squeeze of my thighs could keep me on the edge of coming for an hour or longer. How finally letting go could take me high and sink me low almost at the same time and leave me breathless and spent.

Michael wasn't the first boy who kissed me, but he was the first to kiss me after I'd learned what sexual pleasure felt like. It was easy for me to put two and two together, to think about how my own hands could make me writhe and tremble and automatically assume his could do the same. In that way I was both lucky and unfortunate; my best girlfriend, Lori Kay, had also begun seriously dating a boy who wanted to push her into sex. She didn't want to do it, not because she thought she ought to wait until she was married or anything like that, or that she was afraid of getting pregnant, because she'd been on the pill to control her periods since eighth grade. No, Lori didn't want to fuck her boyfriend because he gave her no reason to think she'd enjoy it.

We had shared stories sitting under the big tree in her front yard, or in her basement during sleepovers. Her boyfriend was happy for her to go down on him but when he fingered her all she felt was irritated.

"Kissing's great," she confided. "But when he puts his hand between my legs it's like he made a mistake on his homework and he's trying to erase it. Rub, rub, rub!"

We laughed at that, and she marveled at my description of how Michael used his hand to make me come over and over. I didn't tell her I already knew how it felt to climax. She'd said she never had one. We didn't talk about masturbation.

So I was lucky in that learning my body had opened me up to having someone else know it, too, but looking back on it and the way things turned out, it might have been better if I'd been like my friend, who successfully put off losing her virginity until college.

After Michael I was sure I'd never fall in love again. I never wanted to lose myself inside someone like that again. I lost the desire to touch myself. Sex, even of the solo sort, had been ruined for me. The thought of kissing, touching, making love, turned my stomach so fiercely I couldn't even watch romantic movies without feeling my mouth twist into a frown.

I went to college, relieved to escape my house and smiles we all put on to hide the truth. I worked hard in my classes and at the work-study programs I found to help support myself. I made friends with my roommate, a beautiful girl who had a boyfriend "back home" but who nevertheless found a lot of time to "hang out" with the entire Delta Phi Delta Fraternity on weekends. I made other friends, too, girls and guys. My dorm was co-ed and for the first time, since I had no brothers, I learned what it was like to live in proximity with boys.

I wouldn't say promiscuity was rampant, but in college it was certainly easier to admit you'd fucked somebody without the stigma of high school when girls who had sex were whispered to be sluts. Hook-ups were frequent and most often initiated by alcohol consumption. Getting drunk was as much a part of the dorm life as eating fries at every meal or ordering pizza at 2:00 a.m.

I went to parties in the basements of frat houses, where the floor had churned to mud that left permanent stains on the hems of my jeans, and the music was so loud it was impossible to hear conversation. I didn't need to talk to the boys who offered me beer. I didn't want to. But I could dance with abandon, splashing in puddles of beer mud to songs that had been popular years ago but somehow managed to be played at every party.

Hey! Hey, what! Get laid, get fucked!

And everyone was getting laid, getting fucked, getting hand jobs and blow jobs.

It happened for me, again, finally, after a party. I'd gone at the invitation of my sophomore-year roommate, who was dating a theater major. We'd gone to some ramshackle Victorian mansion on the edge of campus. I wasn't sure how many people actually lived there, but there must have been at least twelve. The rest of the guests were familiar enough with the house and its residents to act as though they lived there, too, helping themselves to food from the fridge and booze from the cabinet. Compared to the wild frat parties I was used to attending, this gathering was like a cocktail party where people actually sat around and had discussions, and the music playing in the background was heavy with The Cure and Depeche Mode, groups with lush instrumentals and heavy-duty lyrics about love, lust and life.

They served wine, which I tried to refuse without looking like a geek but ended up taking. It made me feel backward and awkward to hold the fragile-seeming glass, and to compensate I sipped regularly. My glass was refilled before it was ever empty. I was quickly deep into the alcohol haze. I went quiet with it instead of raucous, so I didn't stand out among the serious conversations about acting methods and playwrights.

I knew nothing about theater, so when the tall boy with the long dark hair asked me if I was going to try out for *Waiting for Godot,* I blinked slowly before answering.

"I don't know," was my answer. It sounded more clever than it should have.

He smiled. His name was Matt. He was a theater major, a junior, and he intended to work with special effects. He offered to show me some of the models he was building for an independent film feature he was making with some of his friends. He called them his little monsters, and until

I saw the small clay and wire figures, I thought he was referring to his friends.

We talked for a long time, sitting in the darkness of his room lit only by a black light. He'd put up velvet posters of Elvis and unicorns that glowed with vibrant, surreal luminescence in a rainbow of colors. When he leaned over to kiss me, I was surprised that he wanted to. I'd stopped thinking of myself as the sort of girl boys wanted to kiss, even though I'd fended off my share of groping hands and come-ons. I'd chalked their interest up to the beer and the darkness, because after all, why else would anyone be interested in someone with whom they hadn't even spoken?

Matt had condoms in the drawer next to his bed and I didn't dissuade him from using them, though I'd gone on the pill my freshman year and was adamant about taking them. He pulled me close and kissed me, his hands roving. I floated on the cushion of wine and soft music, on the sonnets he murmured. On his confidence that didn't come off as cockiness. When he slid a hand between my legs, my thighs opened almost of their own accord, like my body had been waiting for so long for a touch that my mind could no longer overrule it.

We had sex and there were no bad consequences of it. I didn't get pregnant again, or a disease. He didn't break my heart.

I'd had sex again and my life hadn't changed.

It was the last time I'd ever had more than a few sips of alcohol. Nothing bad had happened, but nothing would have happened at all had I been sober. It wasn't hard to figure that out.

Two years and several lovers later, I met James. I was in my last year of college and doing an internship at a women's shelter, and he was spending a summer shadowing his uncle part-time in the real estate business that had an office next to ours and spending the rest of his time overseeing his first construction crew. We were the ones sent to fetch lunch and coffee. We often met outside with our hands full of bags from the diner around the corner.

I didn't fall in love with James. Falling sounds like an accident. Falling hurts. I'd fallen in love with Michael, fallen hard like slipping off a cliff and hitting the rocks below. Falling in love was something I'd vowed never to do again.

I chose to love James.

My life was better for it. We fit, two small puzzle pieces inside a much larger picture. I could laugh with him. I could cry with him. When he held my hand, I knew it was being held, and when he hugged me I felt embraced. He listened to me when I talked about my dreams and goals, and he told me about his. His easy confidence, his utterly unshakeable belief that the world would never fuck him over, attracted me. I wanted what he had, and I wanted him. I didn't fall in love with him, but that didn't make my feelings for him any less. They were made greater for being chosen, for being given on purpose. Individually there were things we lacked, but together we were perfect.

I never imagined falling in love ever again. I never imagined yearning. I had everything a woman could want with James. In our marriage, our house. Our perfect life.

Until he gave me Alex, I hadn't realized something was missing, but until he gave me Alex I didn't know I wasn't the only one who missed it.

Chapter 12

$\mathcal{I}$ didn't tell Claire's secret, and she kept mine. I wanted to ask her what she was doing about hers, but because she pretended not to remember she'd figured out I was not fucking Alex, I pretended not to know she'd been knocked up by some married loser who'd led her on.

It wasn't as easy to pretend we didn't know something was wrong with Patricia. Of the four of us she'd always been the best at keeping in touch. Now we had to leave several messages before she'd call us back, even about the plans for the party that was edging ever closer. It wasn't like her not to be on top of stuff like that. So we did what sisters do. We ganged up on her.

Mary brought coffee cake. I stopped at the diner and picked up one of their boxes of coffee to go, an ingenious invention that provided hours of hot coffee in a container the size of a box of wine. Claire, typically, didn't remember to bring the doughnuts she'd said she would, but she had re-membered to bring the DVD version of several kids' classics and a bag of dollar-store markers and coloring books.

"From your favorite aunt," she said to Callie when she opened the door to find the three of us standing on the stoop.

Mary snorted. "Nice."

Callie grinned. "Auntie Claire's our favorite aunt for bringing movies. You're our favorite aunt for taking us to the park, Auntie Mare."

"So diplomatic," I complimented, holding out my arms for a hug. "What about me?"

"Oh..." Callie was stumped. "You're our favorite aunt for hugs."

"That's good enough for me. Where's your mom?"

"She's upstairs in her office, working." Our niece let us all in. "Me and Tristan are watching cartoons."

"I'll put on *Totoro* for you." Claire held it up. "We have to do some stuff with your mom for a while. Can you rug monkeys be quiet? It's worth a trip to McDonald's for you, later."

That was bribe enough. Claire set off to take care of the kids while Mary and I dropped off our offerings in the kitchen. We found Patricia in her office. She had the photos I'd picked up from our mom spread out on the desk. Paper, scissors and colored pens scattered the surface. An album waited for her creative touch, but she wasn't writing in it. When we gathered in the doorway, she was hunched over her desk, her face in her hands. She was crying.

"Pats?" Mary was the first to touch her shoulder. "What's wrong?"

When you love someone, seeing them in pain can be harder than being in pain yourself. At the sight of my sister's tears, my own throat closed. We all went to her, gathering around her in the small space.

"You guys didn't tell me you were coming over!"

"What's the matter?" Claire propped herself on the desk. As always, she was the first of us to get right to the point. Maybe the only one of us capable of doing it. "What did he do to you?"

Patricia looked toward the still open door, and I closed it. Mary rubbed Patricia's shoulder. Claire crossed her arms and looked stern.

Patricia looked for a moment like she meant to put on a brave face, or try to detour us with anger. It only lasted a moment before her face crumpled further and she buried her face in her hands.

"He's lost all our savings," she said, each word weighted with shame. "He's lost almost everything. He says he can win it all back if I just give him time. He says he's got a good tip on a horse and he only needs a few thousand to cover him, and he'll win it all back."

She looked up, face bleak. "But we don't have a few thousand. We don't have anything. He's going to lose the house, and I don't know what to do! He's missed so much work his boss is going to fire him, I know it, and then what will happen? What will I do? How will I go back to work? Who will take care of the kids?"

She quashed her sobs behind her hands, like weeping was somehow more shameful than what had caused the tears. I knew how she felt. Giving in to tears meant you had to admit something was wrong. That not everything was bright and shiny.

Mary handed her a box of tissues, which Patricia took. Claire looked fierce. For a few minutes nobody said anything, Claire and Mary giving me small, expectant glances.

I didn't know what to say. I wanted to denounce Sean and call him names, but Claire could do that better than I. I wanted to offer my shoulder to cry on, but Mary was more skilled at that. I was somehow expected to be able to make things better, to solve the problems or offer a course of action, but the problem was, I just didn't know what advice to give.

"How much in debt are you?" I asked, finally, though talking about finances seemed as personal and invasive as if I'd asked her how often they had sex.

Patricia wiped her face and sighed. If my question offended her, she didn't show it. "Between the savings and the bonds he cashed in...twenty thousand dollars."

"Hole-ee shit." Claire's jaw dropped.

Mary made a small noise. My stomach lurched. "That's a lot of money."

Patricia pressed the heels of her hands to her eyes. "I know."

"How'd this happen? I mean...how long has he been...?" Mary trailed off.

"I just found out about four months ago. I started bouncing checks and couldn't figure out why. I checked our statement online. He'd made a few large withdrawals. I asked him about them and he said he was making investments."

Patricia's laugh was so bitter I could taste it, sour like milk gone rotten. "Investments. I thought he meant for the kids' education. For retirement. Something. I didn't know he was down at the track when he was supposed to be working late."

Her next laugh lurched into a sob. "I thought he was having an affair. Late nights, lame excuses. He came home smelling of smoke and beer when he said he was having meetings with the sales team. I found receipts in his pockets. He started bringing me presents. Flowers and jewelry, mostly. I thought he was trying to keep me from suspecting something, and he was, but it wasn't another woman he was fucking. It was our bank account."

Claire scowled. "Fuck. What an asshole."

Patricia, for once, didn't defend him. "What do I do? I'd divorce him but it costs money, all of which he's lost. The kids need new clothes and they want to go to the Point, and I had to tell them we couldn't get season's passes this year.... What am I going to do about my kids?"

She looked up at us. "If we lose the house, what will we do?"

That was the worst of it for her. The effect this would have on her children. I grabbed her hand and held it, tight.

"You've got us." I said this without a doubt. "You know you have us, Pats."

I think we all started crying then, four grown women sobbing like toddlers. But it cleared the air, because we cried and laughed at ourselves for crying and shared the box of tissues all around so we could wipe our eyes and blow our noses. Patricia gestured at the scrapbooking supplies spread out on the table.

"I could sell this stuff," she said. "God knows it's

worth a ton of money. Or I could get a job as a consul-
tant, if I had to."

"Selling this crap?" Claire lifted a package of paper cut
into the shape of balloons. She looked at the small price
tag on the back. "Holy shit, Pats. People pay that price for
this stuff?"

Patricia snagged the package back from Claire. "Yes.
And consultants can make good money. It's just the time
I'd have to spend doing parties. Someone has to watch the
kids. And even if I managed to book two or three parties
a week, it's not enough to cover the money Sean's lost."

She let out a small, helpless groan but didn't start crying
again. "Twenty thousand dollars. Oh, God. It's more than
our first car cost. How could he lose twenty thousand
dollars without me knowing? I feel so stupid!"

"Don't feel stupid. You're not the one out there doing
it. Put the blame where it belongs," Mary said firmly. "And
if you want a divorce, you can get one."

"Ms. Law School would know." Claire waggled her
eyebrows. "Too bad you're not done with school, Mare,
you could take her case Sonny Bono."

"That's pro bono, you moron." Mary rolled her eyes.

"Duh," said Claire. "I know. I'm just trying to make Pats
laugh."

Patricia smiled, a small one but a smile nonetheless.
"Thanks, you guys."

"You should have told us, Pats. We'd have helped you out."

She looked at me with a more familiar Patricia-look on
her face. "What could you have done? By the time I
figured it out, he'd already done the damage. I thought he

really could make it up. I wanted to believe it, you know? That he'd somehow win the lottery, or pick the winning horse like he said he was going to. I wanted to imagine this fairy-tale ending where we ended up millionaires or something. I couldn't face the truth, that we're broke. Worse than broke. We owe so much money...."

"Stop," said Mary. "We'll get you through this. First you should see a debt counselor. And a marriage counselor, too. Anne, you must know someone."

"I have some friends who specialized in addiction counseling," I said. "I'll find out from them what they suggest, okay?"

Patricia groaned again, hiding her face. "People are going to know. Oh, God, the neighbors will know. Everyone's going to know!"

This wasn't quite as bad as how it would damage her children, but I knew it had to be a close second. Worse than the actual gambling, worse than the debt and the lies. Worse than the problem itself was having people know.

I squeezed her hand. "Nobody has to know. Besides, you can't tell me none of them are up to their eyeballs in debt, too."

It wouldn't be much consolation, but I was trying. Patricia squeezed my fingers and nodded. "You're right. It's just...not the same."

I knew it wasn't. We all did. It was the difference between our friends' fathers' chug-a-lugging a few brews while grilling up burgers in the backyard and the sort of drinking our dad did. It was the same, maybe, on the surface, but not underneath, where it counted.

"Sex toys," Claire said. We all looked at her. "You should sell sex toys and lingerie. Now *that* would make you a shitload of money."

"How much is a shitload, exactly?" asked Mary wryly.

Patricia sighed. "I'm sure it's not twenty thousand dollars."

"No. But it's something. I could be your demonstrator." Again, Claire wiggled her brows. "Now, ladies, this little baby's called the Humdinger. Runs on a car battery or plugs right into the wall for a never-fail buzz that's guaranteed to keep you humming all day long!"

The first giggle slipped from Patricia's lips like a teenager sneaking home past midnight. The second followed a moment after it. When Mary laughed, Claire laughed, too, and soon we'd all burst into relieved guffaws.

"It will all work out, Pats." I wanted to make her believe it.

"One way or another." She nodded. "I know. I just can't believe he'd do this. I can't...I can't believe I married a man who can't control himself."

Silence fell between us at her words. Not awkward, not exactly. It felt more like we were all standing outside a door, listening as we waited for it to open.

Patricia looked around at each one of us. "I swore to myself I wouldn't marry anyone who couldn't control himself. I couldn't understand how any woman could stand to be with a guy who didn't know when to stop. How any mother could let someone do that to her kids, you know? Let them down again and again? But here I am. And part of me just wants to serve him with papers and walk out of his life. But then I see him with the kids. He's a good dad. A great dad. He's there for them. He listens to them, he loves them. He doesn't ever push them away. But now I'll always be waiting for him to start. For him to miss a birthday because he's got to go to the track. Or forget about taking Tristan to Boy Scouts."

"Has he done any of those things?" I asked.

"No. Not yet. But I'm waiting for him to do it. I'm waiting for him to let us down."

I knew what she meant. So did my other sisters. We all knew what it was like to be let down, over and over, until it became the expectation instead of the exception.

"Divorce the fucker." Claire's no-nonsense answer made Patricia shake her head.

Mary gave Claire a mean look before turning back to Patricia. "She loves him, Claire."

"I don't know. I kinda sorta think that a dude who put me twenty grand into debt and is lying to me about it might make me stop loving him pretty damn fast."

Her sarcastic tone wasn't abnormal, but it irritated me just then. "And we all know how much experience you have with love. Oh, excuse me. That would be that you have more experience than all of us with sex. There's a big difference, Claire."

I'd meant to sting her a little, out of sympathy for Patricia, who didn't need Claire's forthright assessment of her marriage. Claire didn't flinch. She turned a mocking gaze on me.

"Nope, big sissy, I'd say you've got me trumped on that, now."

"We're talking about Patricia, here. Rein it in, Claire, for God's sake. They're married, she loves him, getting a divorce isn't as easy as closing a bank account."

"I don't know. I had a fuckall hard time closing my bank account."

"Mary's right," I said. "Pats, you know I'll help you find a good counselor, if that's what you want."

Claire hopped down from the desk and put her hands on her hips. "Sure, so she can work on their problems together, which are really his problems? So he can cry and beg her to forgive him and give him another chance, until the next time the track calls his name and he goes and blows his load? How many times does he have to bend her over a chair and fuck her up the ass with this before it's okay for her to cut her losses and just get out?"

The venom in her tone sucked the air from the room and left us breathless. It wasn't that what she said didn't make sense. Nor was it unexpected, not coming from Claire. But it brought back too many memories to be pleasant.

"What would you know about it?" said Patricia in a slightly strangled voice. "We've been married ten years. We have two children together. It's not that easy to just walk away, Claire. You'd think it would be, but it's not. And unless you're in the situation yourself, you just don't understand."

"Understand what?" Claire shot back. "That you're going to let him keep screwing up your life because he has a little 'pwobwem'?" Her voice sunk into mockery.

"Patricia needs our support right now. If you can't give

it, maybe you should leave." I could have given the same lecture. I felt the same way. But it wasn't what Patricia needed to hear, not then.

"You said it yourself, Pats. You never wanted to be with a man who couldn't control himself. You didn't want to do that to your kids. Well, you're doing it," Claire said. "And unless you want to end up like Mom, I think you should kick his ass out and hire yourself a good lawyer."

Patricia didn't say anything, just stared. Mary and I looked at each other. I couldn't take sides because I saw both of them. And I liked Sean, but liking a person and not liking the way they behave are two separate issues.

"Hate the sin and love the sinner," said Mary after a moment. "I think she should help him get help, first. You don't just stop loving someone because they've fucked up."

"Good one, Mare." Claire made a checkmark in her palm with a fingertip. "So how long should he fuck up before she should give up on him?"

Mary hesitated.

"That's for Patricia to decide. Not us." I squeezed Patricia's hand once more, but she pulled it away.

"Claire's right," Patricia said. "She is right. But I just can't up and leave him. I can't."

"I know," I told her. "We all know it. Claire knows it, too."

She'd have had to be endowed with superpowers to stand up to the combined force of three sisterly glares. Claire sighed and hung her head for a minute, then tossed up her hands in defeat.

"Fine. But when I'm the goddamned voice of reason, there is some serious shit going wrong. Some serious shit."

Patricia sighed, looking around. "I won't be able to do my share for the party. Just the scrapbook. All this stuff's already paid for."

"Don't worry about it," I said.

Mary nodded. "Yeah. It'll be fine."

Claire also sighed and chimed in to the feel-good moment. She leaned over, looking at the album. "You're doing a good job, Pats. This is really nice."

It wasn't all fixed, but Patricia gave her a small smile. "Thanks."

The squabble of raised voices in the hall dispersed us. Claire went to referee the argument over who got the red marker. Mary's phone beeped and she left for privacy to take the call. Patricia and I looked at each other.

"Tell me I'm not like Mom, Anne."

"You're not. It's not the same."

But we both knew it really was.

James was once again not home when I got there, though the soft sound of music and smells of good cooking greeted me. Spaghetti sauce bubbled on the stove, and garlic bread tempted me to break off a piece, though I wasn't really hungry. I grabbed a glass of iced tea and sipped it as I shucked off my shoes and found a hair band in the junk drawer to pull my hair off my neck.

"Hey." Alex appeared in the doorway. "Jamie's going to be late. I guess they got caught on some job with some cement or something…something like that."

I smiled. "Sounds familiar. You made dinner again?"

He grinned. "I have to make sure you don't mind having me around."

I studied him over the rim of my glass. "Uh-huh."

He moved closer. "It's not working?"

I pretended to think about it. "How are you with cleaning toilets?"

He leaned closer. Sweet tension flared, but he didn't move to kiss me. "Give me a thong and I'll do what I can."

I needed to laugh after the afternoon with my sisters. Patricia's situation had done more than make me sad for her, it had called up a whole mess of garbage we usually kept locked away. I looked into his dark gray eyes.

Alex offered escape, if I wanted to lose myself for a little while. Yet we stood, somehow shy, like we hadn't already tasted each other coming. He nodded toward the stove.

"It's almost ready, if you're hungry."

A few minutes earlier food had been the last thing on my mind, but now my stomach rumbled. "Yes. There's salad in the fridge, too. I'll get that."

"It'll take a few minutes for the pasta to boil. Why don't you go take a shower?"

My lips curved upward. "Do I offend?"

"No." Alex reached out to twine a stray curl around his finger. It bounced back like a spring when he let it go. "But you look like you could use a few minutes alone."

I gaped, astounded. The next moment I was in his arms, my face pressed to the front of his T-shirt as tears burst out of me. James's T-shirt I realized, but it smelled of Alex now. Alex stroked my hair and put his chin to the top of my head.

He said nothing, questioned nothing, made no effort to draw out my troubles. He was simply there in a way James, who'd have tried to get me to talk, wouldn't have been.

I didn't cry long. The emotion was too intense to maintain and quickly replaced by a different, more selfish feeling I'm a bit ashamed to admit. I tipped my face, which I was sure was red and swollen, to look at him.

"Sorry."

"You don't have to be." He pushed my hair off my forehead with one fingertip.

"Don't you want to know what's wrong?"

Alex leaned back, his hands on my upper arms as he looked at my face. "No."

This made me pause. "No?"

"If you want to tell me, you will." He shrugged, then smiled. "If you don't want to talk, that's fine, too."

It was a simple answer. I didn't know if I wanted to talk or not, what I wanted to say. How much I wanted to share. Giving him my body was one thing. Giving him myself was something altogether different.

"It's my sister," I said, and the story seeped out of me in fits and starts. I didn't share every detail, particularly the parts about how her story paralleled our mother's. I paced while I talked, and he leaned against the counter, listening with his arms crossed.

"I'm worried about what will happen to her," I said finally. "I want to help her, but I don't know what I can do, really."

"Sounds like you're doing the best thing for her, which is to be there."

"It doesn't feel like it's enough."

"Anne," said Alex after a moment. "You can't fix every-thing."

I'd been watching my fingers trace the swooping pat-terning of flecks in the countertop, but at that I looked up. "I know that."

He had so many different smiles. This one was a small lift of lip and brow. Something like a smirk but not as smug. "No, you don't."

"What's that supposed to mean?"

"It means that you think you should be able to fix your sister's life. Fix her problems. You want to fix everything, and you hate that you can't."

My mouth worked as denial tried to come out. "That's not true."

His brow lifted a bit higher. "Sure, it is."

I shook my head. "Absolutely not. It's just that she's my sister and I want to—"

"Fix it." The smile had grown vastly more smug.

"Why are you so convinced you know me?" Irritated, I grabbed up a dishcloth to wipe down the already clean counter. It gave me something to do with my hands and a place to focus my gaze so I didn't have to look at him.

He didn't say anything for a minute, but I refused to look up. "Maybe it's not you," he said at last. "Maybe it's just me."

He'd snared me. I threw the cloth down and gave him my gaze. "What?"

I'd thought maybe he was just playing games, but his face looked serious. "Wanting to fix things all the time. Make things better."

"Well...is it?"

Tension unfurled again, tinged with something I couldn't quite identify. He rolled his head on his neck, cracking his spine. This time, he was the one avoiding my eyes.

"Forget it. You're right. I don't know you. I'm just talking a lot of bullshit. I'm good at that. I shouldn't have said anything."

Sometimes the picture someone else paints of us is a more accurate portrayal than a reflection. What we see in the mirror is always reversed. A portrait not only allows us to see our own faces, but how it looks to others.

"I can't fix everything." I said it aloud, knowing it was true.

He looked at me. "But you'd like to."

"Wouldn't anyone?"

Alex ran a hand through that silky hair so it fell in rumpled smoothness over his forehead. "But not everyone blames themselves when they can't do it. Most people understand the entire universe doesn't rest on their shoulders. Most people, Anne, understand that just because you want to make something better doesn't mean it's your fault when it doesn't happen."

"You have sisters," I said.

"Three, all younger."

"And you never felt like you had to help them out? Give them a hand? Protect them, or make it better?"

He made a small noise. "Fix them? All the time."

"And could you?"

"No." Again, he ran his hand through his hair, then crossed his hands over his chest, tucking them under his arms like he wanted a way to keep them still. "And I feel like shit about it, too."

We both smiled in mutual understanding. The song on the stereo moved into something slow and sweet. We stared, saying nothing. Alex untucked a hand and held it out to me.

I took it. He pulled me closer, step by careful step, until our bodies pressed against one another. His shirt was still damp from where I'd wept, and I closed my eyes to breathe in the scents of fabric softener and soap mingled with his own unique smell. He held me for a while until we started moving slowly to the music.

We danced. One song blended into the next. It didn't matter about the lyrics or the artist, not even the beat. We found our own rhythm there in my kitchen. We moved in perfect time, one step leading to another and the next without hesitation or bumbling. The music played on as we swayed.

We danced in silence. Not because there was nothing to say, but because we didn't have to speak aloud to understand each other. We didn't have to talk to explain ourselves. Right then, there was nothing wrong.

We had nothing to fix.

It's amazing how quickly things became familiar. How easy it was to adjust. The tidy little life James and I had formed melted and re-formed to include Alex.

There were benefits to it. Sex. A third set of hands to help around the house. Another bank account to draw from; for Alex was generous in his contributions to our budget. A less tangible but more appreciated benefit was the way having Alex with us kept James's mother from dropping by as she'd been wont to do for the first six years of our marriage. She even stopped calling the house, preferring instead to reach James on his cell phone.

There were drawbacks, too. Two other bodies in my bed, both snoring. More laundry to wash and fold and put away—though Alex never asked me to wash his clothes, they had a tendency to end up strewn around in odd places, and I never knew what jeans belonged to which man until they were already in my basket. When we weren't all tangled up together, I sometimes felt like a third wheel, not privy to their in-jokes or moronic forays back to adolescence. It was sometimes like living with Beavis and Butthead.

"Why do you do that?" This came from Alex. James wasn't paying attention, his eyes focused on the television where their lame and loud video game was blaring. Alex had brought home the latest game system and they'd been playing nonstop for hours.

"Do what?" I stopped on my way out of the room.

"If you want us to stop playing the game, why don't you just say so instead of getting all frowny?" He actually looked interested in my answer, unlike his cohort who was hooting with glee at the cartoon carnage.

"I did say so, about twenty minutes ago."

"No, you asked us if we wanted to go to dinner and a movie tonight." Alex let go of the controller completely, which did get James's attention, since that meant Alex's character was no longer shooting. A monster came and ate his head. James grumbled.

"And obviously you don't." I folded my arms. The video

game system had way underwhelmed me. I didn't care how many bytes of memory it had or what sort of graphics card, or how hard it was to get.

"See? Why do you do that?" Alex unfolded himself from the floor in a long, lean motion. "Now you're pissed off."

James looked up. "Huh? What's she pissed about?"

"Because we're ignoring her," Alex told him.

"Huh?" James seemed honestly stumped. "No, we're not."

"Yes, fucker, you are." Alex tried to take me in his arms, a ploy I resisted without success. "We're ignoring our Anne, and it's pissing her off. What I want to know is, why do you walk away like that instead of telling us to get the fuck off our lazy, immature asses and take you out to dinner and a movie?"

PMS had made me cross and weepy. I tried pulling away from him, preferring to sulk, but his hands gripped my upper arms firmly. I went stiff and unyielding, instead.

"Jamie, turn off that damn game and get up here. Anne wants to be taken out to dinner and a movie. You're not treating her like the queen she is."

James scrambled to his feet at once. "Why didn't you say so, baby? We'd have turned it off."

I managed to roll my eyes. "Just forget it. I don't need to be treated like a queen."

"Yes. You do."

"Alex," I said, less pissed off and more exasperated. "I'm not a queen."

"You are." He pulled me closer. "A queen. Am I right, Jamie?"

James grinned and moved behind to hold me from behind. "Yep."

"A goddess."

They moved closer, sandwiching me.

"The light of our lives," said Alex. "Breath in our lungs. Mustard on our hotdogs."

"If you say the wind beneath your wings, I will punch you both in the face."

"See?" said Alex. "That's what I mean. Why don't you say stuff like that more often?"

It was hard to concentrate with James licking the back of my neck and Alex's thigh nudging between mine. "What? That I want to punch you in the face?"

"If that's how you feel. Hell, yes. Jesus, sometimes I want to punch the ever-loving shit out of Jamie over there, especially when he fucking farts under the covers and acts like he didn't."

"Hey," James protested. "Fuck you, fucker. Sleep in your own bed."

Alex wiggled closer, dipping to nuzzle my jaw. "My bed doesn't have Anne in it."

Between them I lost the anger over the video games, but I wasn't quite ready to give up. "You're both pains in the ass, you know that?"

He pulled away to look at me. "See? Doesn't that feel good? Say it again."

James snorted lightly behind me. Alex reached around to poke him. "Shut up." He looked back to me. "Go on. Say it again."

"You're both pains in the ass." I waited a second.

Neither of them looked concerned. I tried again. "And if I walk into the bathroom one more time to pee in the middle of the night and find the seat up, I'm going to scream."

A sly smile slid across Alex's mouth. "See? Doesn't that feel better?"

It did feel better. James wrapped his arms around me and rested his chin on my shoulder. I leaned back against him, letting him take my weight.

"Are we really pains in the ass?" James asked.

"We are, man. I'm sure we are." Alex didn't sound upset. Just resigned. "Men are pigs."

I laughed, finally. "You're not that bad."

James tugged me until I turned to face him. "You want dinner and a movie? We'll give you dinner and a movie. Jeeves! To the limo!"

"Wait, wait, I'm not ready—" I protested around laughter as James tickled my sides.

"What do you mean, you're not ready? You look ready to me." James looked me up and down.

"You're an ass," said Alex. "Don't you know anything about women?"

"Since when are you an expert?"

I put my hands up, one on each of their chests, pushing them apart and away from me. "Gentlemen. Enough with the banter. Give me ten minutes in the bathroom. Alone," I said to Alex, who didn't have the same sense of bathroom privacy as I did. "And I expect to be taken to a nice restaurant, not some burger joint."

"What madam wishes, madam shall have." Alex took

my hand and lipped the back of it, a silly gesture that still managed to make my stomach do happy flip-flops.

Later, we came home to an empty house after an exquisite dinner and an enjoyable movie. We stumbled down the hall, hands roaming, mouths meeting, clothes strewn once more in odd places. I had two men doing their best to please me, over and over, and their best was pretty damn good. Lying between them as the chorus of snores began, I looked up at the ceiling and wondered how it was that Alex, who didn't know me, knew me so well, and James, who should have known me better than anyone in the world, didn't.

Chapter 13

I shouldn't have answered the phone, but when it jangled my hand reached automatically and cradled it to my ear before I'd even opened my eyes. "'lo?"

"Anne. It's your mother-in-law."

As if I couldn't guess by her voice, or wouldn't know who she was if she called herself by her name. "Hi, Evelyn."

"Are you still sleeping?" Her voice insinuated that anyone still in bed at this hour was a lazy good-for-nothing.

I cracked open an eye to look at the clock radio. "It's only eight in the morning."

"Oh. I thought you'd be up by now. Doesn't James have to be up early to go to work?"

"He leaves around six-thirty, yes." I covered a yawn with my palm and rubbed my eyes, which someone had apparently filled with sand. "Was there a reason you called?"

God, I hoped there was. I wasn't in the mood for idle chitchat, not that I ever was. But today, particularly, I felt grouchy and out of sorts, my belly bloated and threatening to cramp.

"Yes. The girls and I are going shopping today and we thought you'd like to come along. We'll pick you up at nine-thirty."

Fuckity fuck in a duck-colored bucket.

I sat straight up in bed. "Where are you going shopping?"

She rattled off a list of stores, outlets, the mall and some nail salon I never frequented. "Nine-thirty. You'll be ready, won't you?"

"Actually, Evelyn…" I rolled over to look at Alex, his face buried in James's pillow. Heat rose off him, comfortable in the early morning coolness. I stroked a hand down the satin skin of his bare back. "I'm busy today."

Dead silence for the time it took for me to count to five. "Really."

"Yes. I'm sorry, but I've got other plans today—"

"Oh." Her voice shifted, staying pleasant as it always did but with an undercurrent of tension. "What are you doing?"

"I've got some errands to run, that's all."

"Well, you're going shopping, then." She sounded pleased. "Just come along with us."

I didn't really have any errands, had no plans but for starting the day off with Alex's dick in my mouth and his face buried in my pussy. That was hardly the sort of thing I could tell my mother-in-law. I tried to think of something to tell her, anything. Alex stirred, lifting a squint-eyed face and looking deliciously rumpled.

"I don't really want to go shopping with you today. I'm sorry." I wasn't.

Another silence. It was easy for me to picture her expression. The slightly curling lip, the flared nostrils like she'd scented something foul. I always wondered if, in her mind, she was smiling and somehow the signals got crossed between her intent and what actually ended up on her face.

"Well. If you don't want to spend time with us…" She trailed off, clearly waiting for me to protest.

And, of course, I did, because it was expected. It turned my stomach to acid and forced my mouth into a tight frown, but I did it. "Of course I want to spend time with you. It's just that I've made other plans today."

"Of course you did. Well. Another time, then."

Meeting the Queen might have been more important than going shopping with Evelyn and her daughters. Being awarded the Nobel Peace Prize, perhaps took precedence. Abduction by aliens might have been excused. Anything else just didn't cut it.

I sighed. Alex rolled onto his back, an arm behind his head and the other rubbing his sternum lightly. Up and down. Hypnotizing me. His fingers drifted lower, my gaze following them. When I looked back at his face, he was smiling.

"Can you give me until ten?"

"I don't want to take you away from your plans."

"I'm sure I can rearrange them, but I won't be ready by nine-thirty. If you want to go on without me…"

"Oh, I'm sure we can all wait."

Great. I was going to be beholden to them the entire day because they'd waited for me. "I don't want to hold back your plans, Evelyn."

"Don't worry about it." *Because I'll hold you accountable for all eternity.*

I sighed again. Alex was smirking and moving his hand like a puppet's mouth, mocking my conversation. I turned away so I didn't laugh, and he pounced on me. He mouthed my neck and cupped my breasts from behind, tweaking my nipples to hardness. I let out an oof!

"Anne?"

"I'll be ready by—" his hand was between my legs beneath the hem of my nightgown, finding bare skin "–ten…."

"Tell her to make it ten-thirty." He gave a low, evil chuckle as his fingers stroked my curls.

"Is someone with you?" Mrs. Kinney asked. "I thought you said James went to work."

"He did." I tried wriggling away from him, but he was strong enough to hold me in place. "Alex just popped his head in to tell me something."

"Oh. He's still there?"

She knew he was, of course, because I was sure she called James at least every other day. "Yes."

He pulled me back against his erection. His fingers stroked me, slowly, circling. I was wet for him. My body ached at his touch.

"We'll see you at ten, then." She hung up and I hung up, then collapsed back against Alex with a groan.

"You're wicked."

"I told you, I'm a rascal." He kissed my earlobe. Hot breath made me shiver. The hand on my breast caressed my nipple, while the one between my legs kept up the steady motion. "Good morning."

I turned to straddle him, my nightgown the only barrier

between us. My arms linked around his neck. His hands drifted to my ass, holding me closer.

"Good morning."

"You'd better go get ready. She'll be here soon."

"I know."

Neither of us moved. Our breathing shifted, his going in while mine went out. My clit throbbed, and I rocked slightly against the heat and hardness of his cock. Alex bent his head to trace my collarbone with small, light flickers of his tongue.

I ran my fingers through his hair, the strands tickling the back of my hand. "Did you get up earlier?"

He nodded, mumbling against me. "Had breakfast with Jamie. Came back to bed."

I hadn't even woken when James got out of bed this morning. "You're the better wife."

He looked up at that, his lips glistening. Those gray-dark eyes flickered. He licked his mouth. His hands grabbed my ass harder, pulled me tighter. "I didn't know it was a competition."

I hadn't meant it that way, but once the words were out there was no denying them. "Is it?"

His lips pursed, looking sly. "You tell me."

He let go of my ass to grab a handful of fabric at my belly and pull it upward until nothing was between our bodies. Bare skin to skin, his cock trapped between his stomach and my cunt. I couldn't move for a moment. It felt so good. Heat from him, slickness from me. It would only take a small shift, the tiniest arch of back and thrust of hip, and he'd be inside me, if he wanted. If I wanted.

We didn't move.

His hands kept pulling until the nightgown came off over my head. My nipples brushed his chest. Alex put his arms around me again, while I adjusted my legs to close around his waist.

The air might still have been morning cool, but all I felt was heat. I put my hands on his face, tipping it up. I held him still while I looked down into his eyes. My thumbs reached the softness of his mouth and traced his lower lip. He turned his head just a bit and kissed my palm.

When he looked at me again, I lost myself in his eyes. Deep and dark, not like James's bright blue summer sky gaze. "Do you love him?"

"Everyone loves Jamie."

"Then why are we doing this?" I whispered against his parted mouth. I breathed in his air, took him inside me in the only way allowed.

I moaned when he put his hand to the back of my head and forced my mouth to his. When he kissed me so hard our teeth clashed. When he twisted to push me down on top of the tangled mound of sheets, and when he covered me with his body. His erection stroked along my inner thigh, tantalizing my flesh with his.

"Because we can't stop ourselves."

The perfect answer, if not one that made me happy. I didn't have time to reply because he was kissing me again. He rubbed himself on me. The friction built. My hand found his cock, fingers curling into a tunnel he could fuck into. Our mouths bruised each other. He bit the soft skin of my shoulder, and I cried out. Sweat coated us, making us slick, helping us slide.

There were, he'd said, lots of other things to do besides fuck, and he was right. We did them all. Hands, mouths, skin on skin, my body making places for him to fill. I held my breasts together so he could slide his prick between them as I used my mouth at the same time. We lay head to foot, licking and stroking. He got behind me, thrusting against the groove of my spine while his hand stroked me closer to climax from the front.

We tangled, we writhed. We contorted. But we ended up face-to-face, mouths open, concentrating too hard on what was happening between our legs to even kiss. He pushed into the space between my hand and hip, while he used two fingers inside me and a thumb on my clit.

The position was awkward. He was pulling my hair. His arm had to be falling asleep. We didn't care. Too close to coming to stop, to move, to breathe, we moved together until the headboard banged the wall.

"Fuck," Alex breathed. "Just like that..."

My fingers curled tighter. He groaned and buried his face into the curve of my neck. I shuddered, lifting my hips to meet his thrusting fingers.

He spoke, low muttered words muffled into my skin. How much he loved to fuck my mouth, how good my pussy felt around his fingers, how much he wanted to make me come. Mostly he whispered my name, over and over. Cementing me to him, making it impossible for me to think he didn't know me, or that I could have been anyone.

Anne, he whispered. My name. My body beneath him. My taste on his tongue, my breath in his lungs. He said it again and again until I answered with his. We were joined.

Pleasure filled me like water in a well, bubbling up from some place deep inside. It filled all my crevices, every inch. I shook with it. I was lost in it, swallowed up in it. James had been right about him. Alex was like the lake, and I was drowning in him.

We came within seconds of one another. Slippery, sticky fluid coated my fingers. The smell of it made me gasp. Spent, breathless, we eased to stillness and relaxed inch by inch.

Alex, face still tucked against me, moved off me just enough so I could breathe. His arm lay across my stomach and his leg stayed over mine. His breath tickled more now that passion had passed. We stayed like that for a while. Quiet.

"This is more than it was supposed to be," I said, staring at the ceiling.

Alex, so vocal a few minutes before, stayed quiet. His body replied in a way his voice did not, with a small, swift tension all over. He rolled onto his back, then away from me, and he got out of bed and padded down the hall without saying a word. I heard the hiss of the shower a moment later.

I looked at the clock and hopped out of bed with a curse. I had ten minutes to shower and dress before they arrived to take me shopping. I had no time to ponder what Alex's lack of response had meant, and I was glad. That meant I didn't have to think about it, either.

The shopping trip with Evelyn wasn't as disastrous as it might have been, despite her repeated attempts to engage me in discussions about when I might consider having a child. I managed to smile and grit my teeth and fend her off with vague answers. By the time I got home, my eyes throbbed with a tension headache as well as PMS.

"Oh, look. James is home." She sounded like she'd won the lottery. Instead of just stopping to let me out, she turned off the ignition.

"I guess you're coming in." I couldn't manage to sound welcoming.

"Of course!" She was already out of the car and opening my kitchen door.

I'm not sure what she saw, since by the time I came in behind her all that was left were the guilty looks, but whatever Alex and James had been doing it was awkward enough to make Evelyn stammer. Since this was a woman who prided herself on having a response for all occasions, watching her stumble and fumble for words was quite a sight.

"Mom," said James. "What are you doing here?"

"I took Anne shopping and I'm dropping her off. I saw your truck and I thought I'd come in and say hello." She straightened her back and patted her hair, though it wasn't messed up.

I looked hard for evidence of what she'd seen. Nothing seemed out of place. A cigarette burned in an ashtray, but though I didn't allow smoking in the house that didn't seem scandalous enough. Alex was giving James small sideways glances and looking away quickly like he was afraid he might laugh. James was ignoring him.

"Yeah, I just got home. About twenty minutes ago." There was something off about James's grin. It was too broad. Too silly. Too something.

"How was work?" Evelyn didn't move far from the doorway, so I pushed past her.

"Great. Really good. Really, really good."

Whatever they'd been doing, it wasn't something they'd intended for anyone to see. They looked like they'd been caught with their hands in the cookie jar...or down one another's pants. I looked around my kitchen, but other than the cigarette sending up its small plume of smoke, nothing was out of place. Alex looked like he was getting himself under control and stood up to give Mrs. Kinney a too-innocent smile.

"Hi, Mrs. Kinney, how are you?"

She gave him a glance. "Fine, Alex. You?"

"Great. Really, really great." His smile got broader.

I'd have been suspicious even if I hadn't seen her reaction. I shot James a narrow look he missed completely. Now they were both pressing their lips together like they were trying to keep from bursting into laughter.

"Well. I'll just be going, then." Evelyn paused, but James just waved at her.

"Bye, Mom. See ya."

"Buh-bye, Mrs. Kinney." Alex wiggled his fingers.

James and Alex stood shoulder to shoulder, smiling and waving, and Evelyn took her leave without another word. I watched her go to her car, watched her slide into the driver's seat and put the keys in the ignition. I waited to see if she'd let down her guard when she thought she wasn't being watched, maybe break down, but she didn't. She drove off, and I turned to them.

"What was that all about?" James burst into guffaws.

Alex's laughter was smug. I stared at them. "Oh my God. You're high."

I sniffed the air. The smoke from the regular cigarette was masking the tang of pot, but it was there. James opened the fridge and pulled out another ashtray, this time with a joint in it. It had gone out.

"You're smoking pot? James?"

They were laughing about the snuffed joint, paying no attention to me. I raised my voice.

"James!" They turned to look. "Why did you have pot in the refrigerator?"

"He put it in there when his mom came in." Alex snickered.

"Did she see you smoking it?"

"I don't think so." James cleared his throat and gave Alex a cautious glance. "We were sort of…fighting over it when she came in, and I…"

"He grabbed it out of my hand and stuck it in the fridge right away."

"I'm sure she saw you." I put my hands on my hips, not wanting to see either of them acting like boys.

They gave each other another glance, guiltier this time.

"She didn't see the pot," James said firmly.

"Then what did she see?" I demanded. "You two acting like teenagers? That's not shocking. She looked like she'd seen a murder!"

Alex snorted lightly. "C'mon, Annie, it wasn't that bad. And Evelyn always looks like that."

"We were just fooling around." James came from behind

the island to put his arm around my shoulder. "Just acting crazy. That's all."

Something a little cold settled in the pit of my stomach. Fooling around could mean many things. Had they been roughhousing, fighting over the joint? Or had they been standing closer than she'd expected them to stand, maybe touching a little too long? Had they been kissing?

Alex lifted the joint to his lips and lit it, sucking in smoke while his eyes squinted shut. He breathed in. Held it. Let it out. Offered it to me. "Want some?"

"No."

"Jamie?"

I looked at James. He looked at me. Then at Alex. "Sure."

I said nothing, just left them in the kitchen to giggle and wrestle or whatever the hell they were doing. I went to my bedroom and shut the door against the sound of their laughter. I pulled out a book I tried to read but on which I couldn't concentrate.

Had they been kissing? Should I care if they had? How could I be jealous of something they might have done that Alex and I had definitely done?

Was it a competition after all?

It could've been easy to lose sight of my marriage, having a husband and a lover, but I didn't. Part of it was James's unquestionable lack of jealousy about Alex and his unstinting belief that no matter how many times Alex licked me to orgasm, I loved James best. It was his complete self-confidence in the matter that allowed the three of us to enjoy what we were doing so well…and so often.

James wasn't jealous of his best friend, so how could I be jealous of Alex? Their small secret jokes that left me out, their memories? Both were here with me now, both were attentive and passionate. Sometimes too attentive and passionate.

"Enough," I said that night when cramps and bloating and a day with Evelyn had made sex seem like a chore rather than some exotic adventure. "Not even with Brad Pitt's dick."

"Damn, that's cold." Alex leaned back against the headboard, his shirt undone but his pants still zipped. He looked over at James, who'd just come out of the shower. "Did you hear that, man? She's comparing us to Brad Pitt's prick. Unfavorably."

I didn't want to laugh, I wanted to soak in the tub with a scented candle burning and a good book to read. "I wasn't. I was just saying I can't do it tonight. You've both rubbed me raw in half a dozen places. And I have cramps."

"Orgasms are good for cramps." James came up behind me and put his arms around me to nibble my ear.

"Didn't you just hear what I said?"

"Something about somebody's dick," he murmured with a low laugh, sliding his hands up to cup my breasts. "I like it when you talk dirty. Say it again."

From his lounging spot sprawled out on our bed, Alex made a shooing gesture. "She doesn't want to, Jamie. Forget it. She doesn't love us anymore."

"No?" James tweaked an upright nipple. "Are you sure?"

I gave a disgruntled sigh and slipped out of his arms. "I'm tired, James. And sore."

"Is that a compliment or an insult?" Alex asked from the bed. "Blaming us?"

I turned to give him a glare I had to work at maintaining. "You're both insatiable satyrs, and I want to take a hot bath and read a book. I do not want to have sex. Not with you. Not with him. Not with both of you."

"Not with Brad Pitt, either, apparently." James tossed his towel onto the chair and strode, comfortable in his nakedness, to the dresser to yank open a drawer. "Hey, babe, do I have any clean boxers?"

"I'm sure you would," I snapped, "if I had time to do some laundry instead of spending all my time in bed with the two of you!"

Alex stretched. "To be fair, Anne, last time it wasn't in bed. It was on the living room floor."

I'd been trying to make lists for the party. James had seduced me with a foot massage. Alex had joined in with a back rub. It hadn't been difficult from there.

James turned, still naked, a pair of shorts in his hand that he tossed to the bed. "These are yours, dude."

"Hey, I've been looking for those." Alex snatched them up. "I probably have some clean ones that belong to you."

Neither of them were blaming me, but hormones had sent me down the slippery slope to irrationality. "Well, pardon me! It's not the underwear fairy who delivers your clean laundry, you know! It's me! And you both wear the same size! So pardon me! Maybe next time you can both do your own damned laundry!"

The outburst made me feel better at once. Identical looks of surprise greeted me, and I revved up again.

"While you're at it, you can take over the toilet cleaning, because I'm sure not the one who can't aim!"

Blink. Blink. James, still naked, took a step back. Alex sat up higher, looking like he meant to speak, but I cut him off before he could.

"And if you're horny," I shouted, "you can just take care of yourselves! Or each other! Because I'm not interested!"

With that, I stomped through the door into the bathroom and slammed the door behind me so hard it knocked a picture off the wall. It was an ugly picture, some wretched picture of kittens in a bathtub that Evelyn had given me when she'd redecorated her powder room. It fell to the tile floor. The frame split in half, along with the pane of glass, which fortunately didn't shatter but stayed in two pieces.

I took a couple deep breaths and waited for guilt to assail me. It didn't. I still felt good. The outburst had been silly, even I knew that. I wasn't even mad about the laundry. I wasn't even really mad…which somehow made my shouting all right.

Yeah. That was fucked up, and I knew it, but I smiled as I picked up the kittens and tossed them in the trash. That felt even better.

"Fuck you, kittens in the bathtub," I whispered.

I calmed as the water filled the tub. Had I really told them to take care of each other? Would they do it?

So far no matter how tangled our bedtime arrangements, Alex and James hadn't had sex. I'd done everything a woman can do with each of them, separately and simultaneously. They'd been side by side and facing each other. Even back to back. But they hadn't kissed. Hadn't touched.

Maybe that was another one of the rules they hadn't bothered to share with me.

I drained the tub and threw on a robe. When I flung open the bathroom door, I again got two identically startled looks. Alex and James had sprawled out in my bed, both wearing only boxers. The television was set to the sports channel. They both had beers lined up along the nightstands. They could have been any long-married couple, comfortable with each other to the point of not noticing when one of them belched or picked his nose.

"Why don't you guys ever touch?" I demanded.

Blink, blink. Blink.

James was the first to answer, I think because Alex was wisely keeping his mouth shut. "What?"

I went to the bed and grabbed up the remote, turning off the television. "Both of you. Why don't you ever touch each other when we're fucking?"

I'd never seen James blush. He might be a butterfly, flitting back and forth or spinning in place, but he was never put out of sorts. Now I watched his chest turn blotchy and a column of red spread up his throat to turn his cheeks pink.

Alex, interestingly, looked unconcerned. He stretched a hand up behind his head, emphasizing his lean torso, and gave me a steady look. Also, an enigmatic smile, like the Mona Lisa's but dirtier.

James cut Alex a glance. The way he moved away was subtle, but spoke volumes. Alex must have noticed, as I did, but he kept his eyes on me.

"Well?" I lifted my chin toward them.

"I'm not queer," James said, adding hastily with a look at his friend, "not that there's anything wrong with that."

Alex didn't look offended. "He's not queer, Anne."

The response deflated me a little. I wasn't sure what I'd expected—or wanted—to hear. What I wanted to know. James was self-confident enough not to wonder, but maybe I needed to hear something like this to prove he loved me best.

"And I'm not polyamorous," I said. "But I'm fucking two men."

"Poly-whosee-whatsis?" James was still blushing.

"Polyamorous. It means have more than one lover, not just sexually but, like, in a relationship." Alex spoke coolly, like we were discussing the weather.

James's brow furrowed. He looked from me to Alex, then back to me. "That's not what this is."

I crossed my arms, the bulky fabric of my robe making it difficult. "Isn't it?"

James shook his head. "This is just..."

Alex and I both looked at him. We waited. James gave a small, assured grin. "It's just fun. A fling. Something fun for the summer." His brow furrowed again. "Right?"

Alex and I didn't look at each other. "Right, man," he said.

I didn't answer.

"Anne?"

I bit the inside of my cheek until I tasted blood. "Sure. Of course."

James got up and came around the bed to take me in his arms. "What's wrong, baby? I thought you liked this."

I shook my head. "Nothing. It's nothing."

James kissed me, a caress I allowed but didn't return. "C'mon. Tell me. Why are you so grouchy? Do you want us to stop watching TV in here so you can go to bed?"

A month ago he wouldn't have been so perceptive. We

had Alex to thank for that. And that, somehow, annoyed me twice as much as if he'd been oblivious.

"No," I snapped.

"Then what?" He was still trying to soothe, but I wasn't having any of it.

"Then nothing!" I cried, stiff and unwilling to yield in his arms. "Just...nothing!"

Alex got up from the bed and made to move out the door. I turned on him. "Where do you think you're going?"

He shrugged. "Giving you some privacy."

I laughed, mocking. "Privacy? You can stick around when it's time for me to put your prick in my mouth, but when I'm in a bad mood you're out the door, is that it?"

"Jesus, Anne," said James, shocked maybe by my vehemence. "What's the matter with you?"

"I'm going to go out for a while. Give you two some time alone." Alex made for the door.

I knew it was stupid, that I was getting myself worked up over nothing. Blaming hormones doesn't excuse my behavior. I knew it, and I did it anyway.

"What are you going to do? Go out clubbing? Pick up some guy and give him a blow job in the back alley?"

"God, Anne. What the hell?" James looked sick.

Alex's face had gone cold and distant. Far away. He was dismissing me, and I hated it. "Is that any of your business?"

"I think it is, yes, when you're coming back here to my house, and my bed, and my...and my husband!" I hurt my throat from shouting. James recoiled.

Alex didn't look affected, not even a flicker in a gaze

that had gone more brown than gray. "Anne, if you want me to leave, all you have to do is say so. You don't have to turn into a raging bitch."

I gasped, I know I did. I waited for James to defend me. I looked at him. He was staring at the floor. I looked back at Alex, whose smirk held a hint of triumph I wanted to smack.

Without another word I turned on my heel and threw myself back into the bathroom where I ripped off the robe and threw it on the floor. Looking down, I let out a string of curses at the sight of blood trickling down my leg.

"Pissdamnshitfucktits!"

If the kittens hadn't already met their doom, I'd have smashed them. Instead, I contented myself with slamming the cupboard open and shut as I got out a tampon. I cleaned myself up, fighting tears. Feeling stupid.

And jealous.

And insane.

I was washing my hands when someone tapped on the door. James came in a moment later. I sniffled, wiping my face and expecting a well-deserved lecture.

James looked sad. "If you want him to go, Anne—"

"No. It's not that." I heaved a sigh and splashed cold water on my face. "It's a lot of stuff. My parents' party. The stuff going on with Patricia."

"What stuff going on with her?"

I hadn't told him, a glaringly obvious omission I hid with a quick explanation. "So she doesn't know what she's going to do."

"What can we do?" James looked concerned, and my

love for him rushed up inside me so fast and fierce it was like a tidal wave. "She knows we'll help out, right?"

I held out my arms to him and he let me mold myself against him, though I didn't deserve it. "And I have cramps and a headache, and I got my period."

His face said "ah, that explains it all," but his mouth wisely stayed shut. He rubbed my back and I put my face back against him so I wouldn't have to look at his. He massaged the kinks and knots I hadn't even known were there until he started kneading them.

"And it's your mother."

His fingers prodded and pushed tight muscles. "What did she do?"

"The same thing she always does. Steamrolls me into going shopping and then proceeds to make me feel like a third wheel. And she won't let up about the kids. She just doesn't let up!"

"She doesn't mean it. You can't let her bother you so much, Anne."

"She does mean it," I said with sudden viciousness. "And the next time she asks me when we're going to start having babies I'm going to slap the question right out of her mouth."

The words were nasty and tasted bitter. James stopped rubbing for a second, then started again. I pressed my face to his chest, my eyes closed, hating feeling this way but somehow not able to stop.

"I wish you wouldn't let her upset you like that," he said finally.

I sighed. We were quiet for another minute, until he

pushed me gently away. He looked down into my face, then kissed me so tenderly I wanted to cry again.

"Are you disappointed?"

I had no idea what he meant. "About what?"

"About getting your period. That you're not pregnant."

We weren't always on the same page, and it would have been unrealistic to expect us to be. Still, I'd never felt so far away from him than I did just then. I could only shake my head, speechless.

"It might take a while," he continued. "A few months. Some people try for a long time."

We were standing on opposites sides of a very deep abyss. One I'd caused. I hadn't told him I'd gone off the shots, but I hadn't mentioned staying on them. How even if I'd wanted to start trying for a baby right now my body was so pumped full of hormones the chances of conceiving were nearly negative. There was more. I hadn't told him I wasn't ready to start trying, and he clearly thought I was.

"James." I stopped, uncertain of the right words. Honesty could wound as much as lies. I didn't want to hurt him. "I told you, it's not the best time for us to be trying for a baby. When the summer's over and Alex goes…"

He looked relieved and brushed my hair off my face. "That's better. I was afraid you were upset about it."

"James, no…" I shook my head, fighting to make myself heard, but his kiss stopped me. I could have fought it, or pushed him away to give myself the chance to say what I should have told him already. I let him kiss me, instead.

It was a long, slow and thorough kiss, just like ones in

the movies. It was a kiss perfect in length and pressure and emotion, but unlike in the movies it didn't make everything all better.

Chapter 14

ames and I rarely fought, and our anger never lasted long. He was too convinced he could do no wrong and I was too interested in keeping things smooth for us to clash. The few times we had argued, a kiss and an apology had made it all better.

I didn't know how to make up to Alex. The boundaries of our relationship had never been set. Fluid, they'd changed every day without our discussing them. Lust and sex had come naturally enough. We'd never negotiated emotion.

There was too much of it. I wasn't trying to be clever when I told him this had become more than it was supposed to. I'd yearned for his body and burned for his touch, but somewhere along the way I'd come to crave his smile and his laugh just as much. I'd grown accustomed to him beside me in bed, in the way he looked wearing James's clothes, how he smelled.

I didn't want to love him, but I didn't want him not to love me.

In the week after the argument Alex kept to himself. He

was still having meetings that kept him out of the house for much of the day, only now it was every day instead of just a few. For all I knew, he was out fucking his way through Cleveland. He came home at night still wearing his suit and tie, looking tired, but he hardly said anything and disappeared into his bedroom before I could ask him about his day.

It hurt.

I made myself scarce so we could all pretend we didn't know he was avoiding me. I heard them at night, James and Alex, talking. Sometimes their voices got loud. Other times I couldn't hear them at all, not for hours, and when James came and slid into bed next to me, I strained to catch a whiff of Alex on his skin. I never could.

It was only a week, but the longest I'd ever spent. My period ended, always a relief. James's company started a new project and his hours changed, bringing him home earlier in the day so we could spend more time doing household things like working in the yard and setting up the new glider swing.

It was like the summer would have been had Alex arrived but we'd never started the affair. He was a perfect houseguest. Polite. Distant. He'd become a stranger, and it was killing me.

I tried not to let on how it was eating me up inside. How his dismissal of me stung like thorns, like a splinter I couldn't worry free. I couldn't look at him for fear it would show on my face. The yearning. I couldn't risk letting James see just how much I wanted things to go back to the way they were.

It was Claire, surprisingly enough, who turned out to be my shoulder. In the past I'd have told Patricia how I felt, but since I hadn't revealed to her the fact I was sleeping with Alex, I couldn't admit how torn up I was over what couldn't even really be called a breakup. I'd never talked very much with Mary about sex, and she'd gone back to Pennsylvania for a week to make arrangements for school. And possibly other reasons, as well, which we didn't discuss.

So it was Claire I ended up talking with over lunch one day at my house. She'd come by to drop off some more things she'd picked up for the party. The house was quiet. I'd been working on my résumé and getting little accomplished. My fingers tapped the keys but my mind had been far away, and I'd made a lot of mistakes.

I was glad to see her at my door, because it meant I could put aside what had become a useless task. She handed me a bag of tomatoes from our mother's garden and a couple invitations that had been dropped off at our parents' house instead of sent in the mail to me.

"Because, you know, the price of that stamp is really gonna put somebody out of dinner or something," she said as she helped herself to food and drink from the fridge. She piled everything on the counter and began making sandwiches.

"Everyone really is coming. God. I hope we have enough space for all of them."

"Don't worry about it. Dad's friends will all be so plastered they won't notice, and the Kinneys have sticks so far up their asses they'll probably leave right away."

Thinking of the Kinneys mingling with my parents and their friends made my stomach tighten unpleasantly. "Don't remind me."

"How is the gruesome twosome, by the way? Evy and

Frank." Claire laughed as she made a face that looked quite a bit like James's dad. "Can't wait to see them. I think I'll wear my belly shirt, just to get them all riled up. See how long it takes her to ask me if I've put on weight."

"God, Claire, you wouldn't. At Mom and Dad's party?" She carried her plate to the table, and I followed. "I might."

I watched her take a big bite. "Have you decided to keep it?"

It took her a minute to finish the food in her mouth. She nodded. "Yeah."

"And what about school? Money?"

"I'm only three credits away from finishing. I can earn those with a final internship. I've already started looking at unpaid positions here in town. I'll get a job, too. It will all work out."

She sounded far more confident than I would have been. "And you'll be able to do all that? Afford it?"

She chewed a few more bites before answering. "I'm getting some money from the fucktard wanking bastard piece of shit who didn't tell me he was married and knocked me up, anyway."

The curses tumbled out of her mouth as sweetly as sugar kisses. She smiled. It was sunny and bright. It was shiny.

"He's giving you money?"

"Fifteen grand."

I coughed. "What? Claire, God, how the hell did you get him to agree to give you fifteen thousand dollars?"

"I told him I could prove the kid was his with DNA testing. Which I can," she told me. "And I said that not only would I tell his wife, his wife's parents and the school board about it, but about how he liked me to dress up in a schoolgirl outfit and bend me over his knee to get spanked."

I wasn't sure what to say to that. "And that's worth fifteen grand to him, to keep his secret?"

Her smile got harder. "I have pictures. I also have proof he's a pothead who's not afraid to take a cut of the deals made at his school."

"His school?"

"He's a principal," she told me. "He fucked the wrong psycho bitch, Anne."

"Wow." I wasn't sure if I should be impressed or scared of her. "Sounds like quite a scandal."

"He shouldn't have lied to me." She sounded cold. "It could have just been fun, no big deal. But he told me he loved me, and the motherfucker lied. So as far as I'm concerned, he can pay for this kid."

"And you want to keep it?" I watched her finish her sandwich.

She looked up at me. "Yeah. I want to keep it. Because its father might be a fucktard, but…it's mine."

"Have you told Mom and Dad?"

"Mom knows. She guessed. Dad's clueless, of course. I'll wait until after the party. No sense in ruining all of that." She shrugged.

"Sounds like you've got it all planned out."

My sister chuckled. "We'll see, won't we? You want another sandwich?"

I hadn't even started my first one. "No, thanks."

"So what happened?" she asked as she piled on the

thick slices of bacon, tomatoes from our mother's garden and lettuce onto white bread. Mayonnaise squished out the sides in a gloppy mess. She licked her fingers, one by one.

"With what?" My own sandwich had the same ingredients, just fewer of them.

"Not with what. With who. With him." She made the word sound ominous. "Alex."

"Nothing happened with him." I took a bite and chewed, waiting to enjoy it. I didn't.

She made a derisive noise. "Oh, please. You're such a bad liar, Anne."

"On the contrary, Claire, I'm a very good liar." I grabbed some cheese curls. I didn't enjoy them, either.

"Says you. So spill it, sissy. What happened? James get mad?"

"No."

She waited, expectant, her mouth full of food. I sipped some cola. I played with my napkin. She chewed, swallowed, took another bite. Waiting me out.

"It just fell apart, that's all. Don't things like that usually do?"

"I wouldn't know. I've never done it." She guzzled half a glass of milk and wiped her mouth daintily. "Well. I mean, sure I've fucked more than one guy at a time, but, like, they never knew each other."

"That's not helpful, Claire."

She grinned. "Sorry. So if James didn't get mad, what happened? Don't make me torture you with the belch of doom, Anne. I'll do it."

She might be exasperating, but she did know how to get

me to smile. "I told you. It fell apart. I don't know. When it's just Alex and me, he's fine. But when he's with James they act like a pair of schoolboys."

"Huh. Not sexy."

"Not really. And they have all this history that I'm not a part of," I said. "But it's not just that. I mean…it's just a lot of stuff."

We ate in silence for a few minutes while I tried to think of what to say, how to say it that wouldn't paint me in a bad light. How I could admit to jealousy and lies and still look shiny to my sister.

I shouldn't have bothered to try. Claire cut right to the heart of it, surprising me with her perception. "You want them both to yourself, but they have each other, too."

"Yes." I pushed the sandwich away. "Does that make me a possessive bitch?"

"Probably." She flashed me another grin. "But a normal one, I guess."

"We had a fight. I had a fight. He didn't fight. He just walked away from it. From me," I said and had to stop to swallow against the lump in my throat. "Now he's acting like we barely know each other."

"What about James?"

"He hasn't said anything to me about it. If they've talked about it, he hasn't said anything."

She laughed. "Anne, dudes don't 'talk.' They shoot the shit, but they don't 'talk.'" Her fingers made quotes in the air around the word.

I smiled. "I know. But they do talk. I hear them, sometimes. But I don't know if they talked about me."

"What do you think he could say?" Claire sighed and leaned back to pat her stomach, which only looked rounded if you were looking to see the bump. She belched, long and slow. "Ah, that was a ten."

"It's like I didn't mean anything to him." It felt both better and worse to say it aloud. "Like it was just the sex."

Claire looked a little sad. "Annie. Maybe it was."

I had no right to cry about it, but I did, anyway. I shielded my face inside my hands, embarrassed by my tears. "But why? Why doesn't he love me the way he loves James?"

She patted my shoulder. I hastily dried my tears with a napkin. She reached for another handful of cheese curls, and I was grateful for the time she gave me to recover.

"Sorry."

Claire shrugged. "I wish I could tell you what to do, sissy. Do you love him?"

"Alex?"

"No. The King of England."

"There is no King of England."

"Duh," said Claire. "I know that."

I sighed and toyed with the food on my plate. "I don't know."

"Hey, listen, it sucks big hairy donkey balls when someone doesn't love you, even if you don't love them."

I looked at her. "So elegantly put."

"When's he leaving?"

"I don't know. Soon. He's been here for two months."

"You could kick his ass out," she suggested. "Get rid of him. Then you won't have to think about it."

If only it were that easy. "Thanks."

"Anne," Claire said with a sigh. "What bothers you more? The fact he might be in love with James, or the fact he's not in love with you?"

"I just feel like the biggest fool," I replied in a low voice. "They planned this, the two of them. I'd have been angrier about that, except I wanted it, too."

"Told you. Kink-ay!"

I smiled. "But then it got to be more than I expected...for me. But not for him."

"Are you sure about that?"

I gave her a good imitation of one of her looks. "He's barely talked to me in a week. After I told him I thought this was becoming more than it was supposed to. After I asked him why we kept doing it, and he said because we couldn't stop."

She perked up, leaning forward with her elbows on the table. "That's an interesting thing to say. That you couldn't stop."

"He was right. I couldn't stop. Even though I knew I should, that it wasn't just sex anymore. That I...felt...something." I refused to let myself cry again. "I know why he's Jamie's best friend, Claire. I know why the Kinneys never liked him. Because James around Alex is like a different person, almost. Like the only thing around him is Alex. No wonder Mrs. Kinney hates him. He took her baby boy away, and unlike me, Alex doesn't let her walk all over him."

"Do they fuck? Did they ever?"

Because she asked so matter-of-factly, I could answer. "I don't think so."

"Maybe they should. Get it over with. So they can stop thinking about it all the time."

I pressed my fingertips to my lids to hold back the tears that just wanted to keep on coming. "I think the only reason they both slept with me was because they couldn't sleep together. Alex only wanted me because...because he couldn't have James. He never really wanted m-m-me at all."

There it was. The worst, for me. I'd given up and given in to longing for someone who didn't even want me. I'd been a substitute for something they both wanted and neither could have.

James snored beside me, but I wasn't asleep. We'd gone to bed hours ago. Alone. Alex had gone out and hadn't come home. Now I waited in the dark for the sound of tires crunching on gravel, the door opening. A familiar footstep in the hall.

I sensed him in the doorway as much as I heard him. He'd come in with the sort of purposeful quiet a drunk person has, which is to say not very quiet at all. He'd hit the doorjamb, possibly with his shoulder. Now he stood over my side of the bed. His gaze pressed down on me, though I couldn't see his eyes.

His buckle clicked. Leather slid through belt loops. Metal teeth purred as he slid his zipper down.

The scent of whiskey slung around his neck like a scarf, fit his fingers like gloves. I wanted to drink him. I wanted to drown myself in him.

Fabric slithered to the ground. He grunted lightly as

buttons on his shirt gave him trouble, and a moment later I heard them *plink-plink* on the floor. I opened my eyes wide, but shadows frustrated me. I could see the shape of him, but not his features. I wanted to see if he was looking at me.

I reached for him first. My hands found his thighs. My mouth, his cock. I took him as far as I could, making no sound even when his fingers tightened and pulled in my hair. He was so hard, so thick, I'd have choked if I didn't grab the base of his penis. I anchored him there, guiding his thrusts.

I wanted more, but he pulled my hair hard enough to stop me. Both of us were breathing hard. His erection brushed my cheek as he leaned close. He tipped my head back. Now I could see him in the light from the window. A hint of the soft mouth, the sharp nose. The glint of his eyes.

"Wake him up." His voice was still in shadows, deep and harsh from too many cigarettes.

"James," I whispered, then louder, when Alex's fingers tugged my hair again. "James. Wake up."

James snorted and snuffled, rolling toward me but not waking.

"Jamie," Alex said. "Wake up."

From behind me I heard James's annoyed grumble. Alex let go of my hair. His hand went to my shoulder, pushing me back onto the pillows as he followed. I lifted my mouth for a kiss, but he didn't kiss me.

James got up on one elbow. "Hey, man. Where the fuck have you been?"

"Out." Alex knelt with his ass on his heels between us, a fist slowly pumping his erection.

"No shit." James sounded annoyed, and I didn't blame him. He hadn't been waiting, like I had.

"Anne. I want to see you sucking Jamie's dick. Jamie. Get up here."

James laughed, but he knelt, too. "You're drunk."

I didn't laugh. I reached for James, his penis already stirring. I stroked him to full hardness in a second or two. Then I took him in my mouth the way I'd done for Alex just a couple minutes before.

He groaned when I sucked him. I envied them their easy arousal, how simple it was for them to come. Already James was thrusting in response to the motion of my tongue and lips against him. I slipped a hand down to cup his balls and press the spot along his perineum that made him jerk upward.

I left James's cock to find Alex's next to it. I sucked him, too, my mouth mapping the differences in their bodies. Back and forth I moved until my jaw began to ache and I knelt, too, and used my hands to jerk them both at the same time.

Once more we'd made a triangle. Three. I slid slick fingers over erect penises as I leaned to lick and suck and bite James's nipples and chest. Alex put his hand on the back of my head. I lifted my face and kissed my husband, then my lover. Back and forth. They kissed me. I stroked them. Hands found my breasts and hips, my thighs. My clit. Two hands held my waist, two hands slid between my legs.

We pressed so close my hands were trapped between us. Filled. They moved, pushing into my fists. I kissed

James, his mouth wet and open. I kissed Alex. One and
the other, while we moved together, the sound of slapping
flesh making music with the creaking springs. Someone
left the heat of my pussy and trailed wet fingers along my
hip to grab my ass and grind me closer. My clit pulsed with
every motion, rubbing against a palm, a knuckle, a thumb.
It didn't matter. I was going to come.

Everything got tight, pulling in, coiled. I pulled away,
back arching as my hips thrust forward. Our triangle got
bigger, the back and forth of my kisses paused as my
orgasm rushed over me. James cried out, low, and his hips
pumped forward as his hand gripped my shoulder hard
enough to bruise. Alex made a noise, too. His cock pulsed
in my hand. It was his hand between my legs, rubbing, and
it became too much all at once. Too much sensation. I
made a noise of protest but then I was coming a second
time, pleasure like hard, bright sparks arcing through me.

Alex put a hand on the back of James's neck. I knew
how it felt, there, how it felt the times he'd done the same
to me. They were already so close they could have felt the
brush of each other's lashes. A groan stuttered out of me
on a long breath I'd been holding for too long. I had to
lean back to catch a new one, and I gulped at the air as I
shook with release.

I was leaning back. They were leaning in. My eyes were
open. Both of theirs were closed. I had been kissing back
and forth, one and the other, meeting their mouths with
mine. But now I wasn't there.

They both moved at the same time. Heat and wetness
filled my hands and covered my stomach as they came.

They both moved toward each other, mouths open and ready.

But it was Alex who pulled back.

He opened his eyes. He let go of James, whose eyes fluttered open. In the moonlight, James looked dazed. His mouth closed, parted a second later by the swipe of tongue.

"Alex," he said, voice hoarse, but Alex let go of both of us like we'd burned him.

Alex broke the triangle. He pushed away from us so fast James had to pull me close to keep us from tipping, unbalanced. Alex got off the bed. He stood, staring, while we said nothing. Then he gathered up his clothes and left.

James let go of me and sank back against the headboard. His fingers rubbed the scar over his chest, over and over. I stayed frozen, my knees stiff and my body shaking, but no longer from pleasure.

"What. The. Fuck." James's voice was flat.

I looked at him, but shadows cloaked him and I couldn't read his expression. I heard the bathroom door open and close from down the hall. The shower came on some time after that, all while we didn't know what to do with ourselves.

James reached for my hand. Our fingers linked. I waited for him to speak, and when he didn't, I kissed his hand. I got out of bed. I grabbed up a nightgown from the chair and pulled it over my head as I went down the hall.

Alex was in the shower, the curtain moving faintly with the spray. I pulled it aside to look in. He was on the floor, crouched on hands and knees, his forehead pressed to the molded plastic tub.

I got in. There wasn't much room for two, but we managed. I reached for him, and he put his arms around me. The curved plastic fit to my back as Alex buried his face against my neck. The water pounded down on top of us. It felt good. Like rain.

"I didn't know parents could really love their kids until I met the Kinneys," Alex said. "My old man's a mean bastard when he's sober and a nasty fucker when he's drunk, which is most of the time. He broke a wooden spoon on my ass, once. Then he switched to the belt. I started fucking guys because I knew it was the one thing that would send my old man into a stroke."

"What did he say when he found out?"

"Nothing. I never told him." He looked up at me, those gray eyes like storm-churned lake.

"Why not?"

Alex's smile looked like it hurt. "Because I knew he'd hate me."

I pulled him back to me and stroked his wet hair and said nothing.

"But at Jamie's house, everyone was nice. All the time. Mrs. Kinney made cookies. Mr. Kinney played ball with us boys. They took me in and made me feel like they loved me, too, because I was Jamie's friend. They threw birthday parties for me when nobody else remembered. They picked me up from work when it was raining so I didn't have to ride my bike. I practically fucking lived in their house for four years, until Jamie went away to school. Four years, Anne. And the day after Jamie left, I went over there to see if Mrs. Kinney wanted me to run any errands for her. I got my first car, see, and I wanted to be able to go to the store for her. If she needed."

"She didn't."

He took a long, deep breath. "She opened the door and didn't let me inside. She told me that James wasn't at home, and I should come back when he was. And she shut the door in my face."

"What a..." I wanted to say bitch, but the word stuck behind my teeth.

"I never told Jamie. When he came home, I went over there like nothing was wrong. But when he went back to school, I forgot they even existed. If I saw them around town, and I did, I looked the other way. Jamie never knew. I never told him."

"I'm sorry, Alex."

"Jamie's the only person in my whole fucking miserable life who ever made me feel like I was worth a goddamned thing. When you asked me if I love him...how could I not love him? Jamie's the only person who ever made me understand what it was like to love someone. From the first time I saw him in that fucking pink alligator shirt with the collar up, I think I loved him."

Alex got up and turned off the water. He grabbed two towels and we got out of the shower, our clothes dripping. He sat on the toilet while I wrapped one around me. I used the other to rub his hair and dry the water from his skin. He waited until I was done, then took my hand. I sat on the edge of the tub, an uncomfortable perch that pressed our knees together.

"When I went to see him in college to tell him I was

leaving the country, I wanted him to ask me to stay, you know? To have one person want me not to go. But he was excited for me. Told me he was proud, thought this would be a great chance for me to make something of myself. We both knew I'd never be anything in Sandusky. Never get a good job. But I still wanted him to ask me to stay here. So I told him the truth, all of it. That the guy giving me the job wasn't just somebody I met, but somebody I was fucking."

"And he got mad. You fought. I know."

A small smile that had little to do with humor curved his lips. "I don't think so. When you told me he'd told you the story, I thought you got it. You understood. But I don't think you did."

"So tell me."

"We got shit-faced, and I got what I wanted. He asked me not to go. He got mad, yeah. He wanted to know how I could take it up the ass for somebody else, how could I fuck just…some guy. That's what he said. How could I fuck some guy. How could I kiss some guy. And he tried to kiss me."

I studied his face. I believed him. "He didn't tell me that."

Alex laughed. "Jamie couldn't hold his liquor. He tried. I didn't let him."

"Why not?"

"Because," Alex said. "Jamie's not…that's not him."

"Obviously it is."

He shook his head. "No. I don't think so. He's not going to suddenly come out of the closet. He's not queer, Anne. And I loved him, yeah, but not…not in a way that would end up being very good. For either one of us. I'm a fuckup.

I can't make things work. And I didn't want us to screw trashed out of our heads and lose everything we had."

"And the fight?"

"Oh, we had it. He punched me in the face and called me a fucking fairy faggot queer. We both hit the coffee table, and he got tore up. I took him to the E.R. The rest is the same."

"And you left for Singapore."

"I went back to the Kinneys' once before I left," he said. "I wanted to find out how he was. Mrs. Kinney told me I wasn't worth the dirt under Jamie's shoes and that I should consider myself never welcome in their house again. I'd known she didn't like me, but I'd never realized until then that she hated me. I don't know what he told her, but it was enough to make her crazy."

I smoothed his hair off his face. "Alex. I'm so sorry."

"I wanted to come to your wedding. I could have. I could've taken the time, no problem. But when it came right down to it, I didn't think I could see him again for the first time in so long walking down the aisle. So I waited, sent a gift."

"It was very nice. We still have it." I smiled.

He smiled, too. "I sent him a card. We kept in touch. I ended up here. And once again, I've fucked it all up."

"No, you haven't."

He reached to put his hand on the back of my neck, to pull me just a bit closer. Our foreheads touched. I closed my eyes, waiting for a kiss that didn't come.

"I didn't count on you."

A small, hitching sob leaked out of me. "I thought you—"

"Shh." He put his arms around me.

It was awkward, and uncomfortable, but I wouldn't have moved for a million dollars.

"What are we going to do?" I whispered.

"Nothing."

"We have to do something." I pulled away to look at him, to cup his cheek. "This is something."

He pulled away. "What you and Jamie have is something. This is just…nothing, remember? A little summer fling. I'll leave. You'll forget it ever happened."

"No. I won't. He won't, either."

His smile was crooked. "You'd be surprised what Jamie can forget when he wants to."

"I won't forget," I said fiercely, tears stinging my eyes. "I won't ever forget."

He kissed my forehead. "Yes, you will."

"Will you?"

When everything changes we learn who we really are. What's really important. What we want most. We discover the truth in moments of disarray.

My heart waited to break.

He kissed my forehead again, softer this time. "Anne, I already have."

Then he got up and left me alone.

Chapter 15

*G*ood things, by their nature, are fleeting. It's those that bring us grief that linger. Alex was gone in the morning, the only sign he'd been there a pile of used towels in the laundry basket and the faint scent of him on the pillowcases in the guest room. The house was quiet, James had already gone to work. There was nobody to hear me if I sobbed aloud, but still I pressed the pillow to my face to muffle my weeping. I breathed him in for a long time before I stripped the bed and washed the sheets, removing the last trace of his presence.

I ordered Chinese delivery for dinner and left it on the counter for James to find when he got home. I went to bed early, exhausted by a day I'd spent scrubbing the floors on my hands and knees, bleaching the mold from the deck, cleaning out the fridge. I'd sought to occupy myself with tasks I'd been putting off for weeks. It hadn't worked.

I couldn't sleep. James came to bed sometime later, slipping in beside me onto fresh sheets that smelled of nothing but fabric softener. He was damp from the shower.

He put his arm around me, tentatively, and I rolled toward him to press my face to the comfort of his bare chest.

"What happened last night?" he whispered, like he was afraid something might break if he spoke too loudly.

"I told him he had to go." The lie was as easy as any I'd ever told. "And he left."

I wondered if he'd question me. Or argue. He sighed, instead, and drew me tighter against him. We said nothing more. After a few minutes his touch became less tentative, more possessive. The familiar strokes and caresses seemed foreign to me now. With only one set of hands, one mouth, one body next to mine, something seemed missing.

We made love more awkwardly than we ever had. Nothing fancy or complicated, no exotic positions, and still we fumbled. His mouth sought mine and I turned my face. James thrust inside me so long it began to rub me to rawness. My involuntary sounds could have been mistaken for pleasure, but they came through gritted teeth, and when I raked my nails down his back it was not from passion. He came inside me with a grunt and collapsed and I waited half a moment to push him off me.

I waited until I heard the pattern of his breathing tell me he was asleep before I rolled away from him to stare into the night and wish I *had* been the one to tell Alex to go.

Claire looked around the waiting room as I took a seat. She twirled the rack containing various pamphlets about local social services, adoption, tests during pregnancy and other related subjects. Her fingers played with the creased white brochure from Lamb's Wool Adoptions, and she plucked it out.

She sat next to me and opened it. "How come most adoption organizations are religious?"

"I don't know. Maybe because they're the ones who don't believe in abortion, and they want to offer women an alternative." I'd picked up a months-out-of-date gossip rag, but the articles inside held little appeal.

Claire snorted, flipping the page. "This one says they'll place your 'little blessing in disguise' with a local 'Christ-oriented family.' What about the non-Christ-oriented families? Don't they deserve the right to adopt kids?"

I put down the magazine and shifted in my chair to look at her. "I thought you were going to keep the baby. What do you care about adoption services?"

"I don't." She put the pamphlet back. "I'm just making conversation."

She was nervous, I realized, and trying not to show it. Her eyes flicked around the room, but nobody else was paying any attention to her. She put her hands on her belly, a gesture that seemed unconscious but was very telling.

"You'll come in with me, won't you?"

"If you want me to."

She'd had care already, from the free clinic, but I'd convinced her to come to Dr. Heinz. This was her first visit. There were, I supposed, going to be tests of some sort, and possibly an ultrasound. I'd have wanted someone with me, too.

When they called her name, Claire looked up. For a

second, I thought she wasn't going to move. I tugged her sleeve as I got up. "C'mon, Claire. You'll like Dr. Heinz."

Even bravado couldn't hide the fact Claire's answering chuckle was nervous. "You go on. I'll ketchup."

"That joke is so bad it makes my stomach hurt," I told her. "C'mon."

Together we followed the medical assistant back to the same room I'd been in just over two months before. The posters on the wall had been updated with new ones, from a different drug company. The magazines were the same. Claire undressed and took her place on the paper-covered table while I waited behind the drawn curtain until she was done.

"What do you think?" she asked, pointing to the front of the flowered gown. "Is it me?"

"It's a new look." I smiled to reassure her. "Relax."

She took a deep breath, in and out. "Do you know how many things can go wrong in a pregnancy?"

I didn't, not from experience at least. "You'll be fine, Claire."

"Before I found out I was pregnant, I kept drinking. And smoking. That can really mess up a baby."

Telling her it would be all right felt like a lie, but I said it anyway. She took another deep breath, looking younger than she was. I was reminded of her as a toddler in a sagging diaper, following me around our backyard. She'd stopped dying her hair and an inch of strawberry-blond roots had crept out.

She saw me looking and put a self-conscious hand to her part. "I look like a skunk."

"It's not bad. It's kind of punk, actually."

She smiled and looked across the room into the mirrored cabinet on the wall. "You think so? It's better than dark roots and blond hair, I guess. At least this looks almost like I did it on purpose."

A discreet *tap-tap* on the door interrupted our discussion. Dr. Heinz waited for Claire to tell her to come in, then stuck in her head before entering the room all the way. She smiled and held out her hand for Claire to shake.

"Miss Byrne?"

I don't suppose it occurred to Dr. Heinz that Claire was my sister. She has a lot of patients, after all, and my name's not Byrne anymore. So when she did a double take at seeing me sitting to the side, we all laughed.

"Anne's my sister. She recommended you." Claire's voice didn't betray whatever nervousness she'd felt before. She sounded mature. Focused. She shook Dr. Heinz's hand firmly.

"It's good to see you, Anne." Dr. Heinz smiled warmly and turned her attention back to my sister. "Now. Let's see what we can do with you."

I didn't have much of a role to play aside from providing moral support. I listened quietly from my spot in the corner as Dr. Heinz went over the things Claire could expect from pregnancy and childbirth, about the tests and changes her body was going through. Claire asked intelligent questions that showed she'd done her research. I was proud of her. She might not have intended to get pregnant, but her answers to Dr. Heinz clearly showed she was taking full responsibility for it now.

I'd seen ultrasound pictures from when Patricia was pregnant with Callie and Tristan, but everything changes including technology. The picture that showed on the screen of the little creature swimming inside Claire's tummy made a small noise bubble up from my throat.

"That's amazing," I said.

Dr. Heinz moved the wand over Claire's bared bump. "You can see the head, here. Arms. Legs."

Claire oohed. "It's got fingers!"

Tiny webbed digits, but fingers nevertheless. And eyes. Ears. A nose, mouth...it was a baby. A real baby, even this small.

I'd been less than three months along when I'd wished away my child. I'd been happy at the time. Overjoyed, in fact. Immensely relieved. I'd been glad to see the blood and know the life inside me had ended without my having to take it. I hadn't mourned the loss of my baby then.

Confronted with the truth of what I'd lost, I mourned it now.

I excused myself to use the bathroom, where I splashed cold water on my face over and over until my cheeks stung. I gripped the cold porcelain sink and contemplated being sick, but nothing in my stomach wanted to come up. I wet a paper towel for the back of my neck and closed my eyes until the dizziness went away.

How might my life have changed had I not lost the baby? If I'd have found the money and the courage to terminate the pregnancy, or if I'd decided to have the baby. If, one way or another, I'd found the strength to actually make a decision instead of fate stepping in to make it for me.

If I'd had a child ten years ago, would I have met and married James? Unlikely. The path my life took would surely have been different had my child been born. Even if I'd given it to someone else to raise, my life would have changed. I'd never have married James.

I'd never have met Alex.

And it came back to that. My sense of loss doubled in an instant, the feeling that somehow, the choice had been taken from me. Fate had determined the course of my relationship with Alex the way it had determined what happened with my one and only pregnancy. It had given me what I wanted but then taken it away.

Alone in the washroom I didn't have to fake the shiny. Didn't have to put on a happy face to keep anyone from knowing the truth of how I felt. I was torn up, shattered and battered, my bruises on the inside but no less painful than if I'd worn them on my skin.

The woman in the mirror tried to smile. "I love him," she mouthed.

"I know you do," I whispered in return.

"I shouldn't."

"I know that, too."

"I hate him," I said and closed my eyes so I didn't have to look at my own face.

"No," she whispered, "you don't."

I got it together, of course. I always did. I pushed away what shamed me and made me unhappy, and I smoothed out the rest to make a pretty, perfect surface. It was getting harder and harder to do.

Claire looked much more relaxed when I came back into

the room. She'd dressed and had a handful of papers as well as a cute diaper bag covered with bunnies and ducks.

"Look, Anne!" She held up the bag, which bulged with goodies. "I got swag!"

"Nice." I peeked in the bag. "Binkies, diapers…you're all set."

She laughed, looking into the bag. "Oh, sure. If only."

"Are you all done? You ready to go?"

She nodded, then patted her stomach. "I'm starting to show. I asked Dr. Heinz if she thought it was baby or if it was the hot fudge sundaes I've been eating."

I stepped back to look at her. Claire had been the thinnest of all of us, the sister with the body closest to the male idea of bodacious. "Your boobs are even bigger, too."

She hefted one. "Hell, yeah."

I managed a laugh that sounded natural. "Your belly's not that big."

She stood, keeping her back straight and turning to the side so I'd be sure to see the bump. "Look at it."

"Hot fudge sundaes," I told her, just to tease.

She gave me the finger. "You're just jealous."

I broke the moment of awkward silence that followed her statement by saying, "Tell me that when you're in labor and I'm not."

Claire gave me a real smile, not a smirk, and patted my shoulder. "C'mon, big sissy. I'm taking you out to lunch."

"We can go to lunch. But you don't have to treat me." I followed her from the room.

She glanced over her shoulder at me. "No worries.

I've got some cash from—" She probably meant to call him by the names she'd given him before, but there were a lot of people in the hall. "Him. I can cover a burger and fries."

"Fine." As I sidled past a medical assistant carrying a pile of folders, Dr. Heinz called my name. I turned. "Yes?"

"Can I talk to you for a minute?" She gestured, and we ducked into a small exam room. "Since you were here with your sister, I took a quick look at your file. I can give you your shot today so you don't have to come back in, if you like."

It was considerate of her to offer, and I meant to say yes. But after a pause that felt like an eternity, I shook my head. "No, thanks. I'm going to stop taking it."

She smiled. "Do we need to set up an appointment to get you started on something else?"

I returned her smile. "No. My husband and I are going to start trying for a baby."

"Ah." She nodded. "I'll write you a script for prenatals, pick them up at any drugstore, okay?"

I was. We shook hands. She wished me luck. Claire and I went to lunch, where she paid the tab and talked on and on about many things, none of which I could later recall.

For the next two weeks, James and I talked but said nothing. Not about Alex, who might as well never have existed as far as our household seemed concerned. Not about much else. Our conversations were brief, pleasant, neutral. I couldn't remember much of what we talked about, probably because I wasn't paying attention. Looking at James reminded me too much of betrayal, though

I couldn't quite figure out who'd done the betraying and which of us had been betrayed.

Every night I made love to James with a fierceness that had nothing to do with longing. We fucked fast and hard. I came every time. I knew why I was doing it. I didn't ask James why he responded the way he did, why he branded me with his mouth and cock and the imprints of his hands. Our fucking left me bruised and aching. I meant for it to fill me, but it left me empty, too.

I don't know how Evelyn found out Alex had gone, but she started her thrice-weekly habit of phone calls again. I let James answer. If he wasn't home, I let the answering machine take her call, and I erased the message without listening to what she'd said. When he asked me if I minded if his parents came to dinner, I said I didn't, but when they came I pleaded a headache and stayed in my room until they'd gone.

"Maybe Anne ought to see a doctor," I heard her saying the second time they came for dinner and I used the same excuse. Her voice carried from the kitchen down the hall, like a drill in my ear. "She's been sick a lot, lately."

I didn't wait to hear James's answer. I locked myself in the bathroom and stood under the shower for as long as the hot water lasted. By the time I came out, they'd gone.

He caught me the next day as I stood at the sink, wrist-deep in soapy water and washing the dishes he'd left undone from the night before.

"Anne."

I turned only halfway, gave him half my attention. Half of myself.

"Are you ever going to be happy again?"

It took a long, quiet moment for me to answer, and when I did it was with a shrug. I turned back to the dishes. "I don't know what you mean."

He sighed. "Are you ever going to smile again?"

I shook my hands free of suds and dried them. I took my time doing it, getting each individual finger. I faced him. I smiled, hard and sharp.

"You mean like this?"

"That's not what I meant." He looked smaller to me than he had a few minutes ago.

I did it again, the way I'd done so many times. Tilting lips, crinkles at the corners of the eyes. Slow and easy. A smile.

"Like this?"

Feeling flickered in his eyes, a stream of emotions passing over him so fast I couldn't have determined them all even if I'd been trying.

"That looks more like you. Yes."

I turned back to the sink. From behind me I heard him move closer. I tensed, waiting for his touch.

"Are you ever going to smile at me like that again?"

"I just did, James."

"Are you ever going to mean it again?"

My fingers slid through soap and grease and found the sponge. I circled it in the pan, over and over, hypnotizing myself with repetition. "I don't know."

When he put his hands on my shoulders, I went stiff. "I wish you did."

I wanted to let myself melt back against him, to let him ease me with his touch the way he was trying. I didn't. "I do, too."

He kissed the part of my shoulder exposed by the neckline of my T-shirt. My hands stung from the hot water, and I lifted them out to put one on each side of the sink. The scents of lemons and last night's dinner bathed my face. I closed my eyes against it. I waited for James to put his arms around me and pull me close, to force me to forgive him so I could forgive myself.

"I'm going to run out to get a new pair of work boots. Do you want me to pick up anything for you?"

"No."

He squeezed me with gentle fingers and withdrew. I scrubbed the dishes until my fingers ached. James came home much, much later, smelling of beer and cigarettes.

I didn't ask him where he'd been.

With only two weeks to go until the anniversary party, I expected life to feel a little hectic. Certainly it seemed to affect my sisters that way. There were plenty of calls back and forth about the caterer, the decorations, who was going to pick up what. A few months before I might have been as hyped up and stressed out as the three of them, no matter if I didn't show it, but now I was genuinely calm about the entire affair.

"It's fine," I assured Patricia, who was almost in tears about the scrapbook, because she couldn't decide whether or not to include a place for guests to write congratulations. "Put the pages in."

"But then I'll have to put the book out where people can get to it, and you know someone will splash barbecue sauce on it!" she cried. "It will look awful!"

I cradled the phone against my shoulder while I stirred a pot of chicken soup. I didn't have much appetite. James had called to tell me he was going to be late. I hadn't asked him why.

She sounded tired, but she'd told me things with Sean were getting better. He'd come up with the cash for the mortgage, though she hadn't said from where. He was coming home earlier, not missing work, not going to the track. He'd agreed to counseling, though they hadn't yet gone.

"Just put out one page at a time near the drinks table," I told her. "Check them during the party and when they get filled, put out another. That way you'll only add the ones that have all the messages on them, you won't have any blank pages and you can keep the scrapbook someplace out of the way so nobody spills something on it."

"I guess that will work." She sighed. "I will be so glad when this party's over."

"I think we all will. It's been a stressful summer."

"Tell me about it." Patricia made a rueful chuckle. "I think the only one who hasn't had disaster strike's been you."

"Lucky me."

"I don't know what Claire's going to do," she continued, moving away from the scrapbook and party plans into the far juicier realm of sisterly gossip. "She's not ready to have a kid. But she says she's going to keep it, and she does seem on the ball. I would never have expected it of her, Anne, but she's doing all the right things."

"She is."

"But Mary...I'm not sure what's up with her, that whole moving in with Betts thing. What if that doesn't work out?

I mean, I know she's trying to save money and everything, but…what if it doesn't work out?"

"Patricia, I'm sure she and Betts have talked about all of it."

Patricia's sigh sounded loud, even through the phone. "It's just craziness, that's what it is."

"Oh, Pats. C'mon."

"Well, at least we know *she* won't get pregnant."

Her dry comment hit me right between the eyes. It took me a second to laugh, but once I started the guffaws ripped out of me, one after another. On the other side of the phone, she started, too. We laughed together, and it felt so good I didn't notice I'd started to cry until the distinctive sound of the call waiting tone beeped.

"Hold on," I said, my voice hoarse. "Got another call."

"Anne. You need to come over here right away."

I didn't recognize Mary's voice at first. She sounded like she was whispering into the phone while standing in a closet. Maybe she was.

"Mare?"

"You have to come over here," she repeated. "I don't know what else to do, and you're the one who deals with him when he's like this."

My guts churned. "Wait a minute, what's going on?"

"It's Dad," she said, and I didn't ask any more questions, just hung up with her and switched back to my other sister.

"I'll be there in twenty minutes," Patricia said at once. "The kids are spending the night with Sean's parents. He's at a meeting. I'll be there in twenty."

We hung up without even saying goodbye.

We pulled into my parents' driveway at the same time, even though she lived farther away. Mary's car was parked by the garage, along with my dad's. The one my mom usually drove was gone. Patricia and I got out, both of us pausing to listen for voices inside the house. I didn't hear anything, but that didn't mean anything wasn't going on.

Claire opened the door as soon as we got on the front porch. She'd pulled her hair back from her face in a high ponytail and wore no makeup. Her eyes were red, but if she'd been weeping she wasn't now.

"It's Dad," she said. "He's gone fucking nutso. You have to talk to him, Anne, you're the only one he'll listen to. He just went ballistic."

Patricia and I shot glances at each other, then followed Claire into the house. Most of the lights were off, making each room dim. Back through the dark hall we saw a golden square of light falling from the kitchen doorway. That's where Claire took us.

In the kitchen my father sat at the kitchen table. A bottle, mostly empty, of his favorite whiskey sat in front of him. So did a glass, also mostly empty. His eyes were red-rimmed, his hair askew. He looked up at us as we came in.

"There she is," he said with a nod at Claire. "Did she tell you? What she's done?"

"Yes, Dad," Patricia said. "We know."

My father gave a harsh, nasty laugh. "Goddamned whore's what she is! Shows up here, flaunting her belly like she's got something to be proud of…."

He filled his glass. He drank. We all watched him. Mary

leaned against the counter, arms folded tight over her stomach. Claire filled a glass of water from the sink and drank it almost defiantly. Patricia and I moved to opposite sides of the doorway. Our father put his glass down with a sharp crack of glass on wood.

"I oughta throw your ass right out on the street!"

"You won't have to," Claire said. "I told you, I'm getting my own place." She looked at me. "I told him I was getting my own place, and he asked me why."

"Because she thinks I was too stupid to notice before," he said with a scowl. "Everyone else in the world knows, but not me. Not your dad."

"Because I knew you'd act like this," Claire cried and tossed up her hands. She was the only one who'd ever talked back to him this way.

"And now she tells me she's planning to keep the bastard!"

"Dad, for God's sakes," Claire snapped. "Nobody calls them bastards anymore!"

He turned on her. "Shut your mouth, you little tramp!"

The insult had to sting, but she put on a show of rolling her eyes and making a whirling motion with her finger on the side of her head. Our father got up from his chair so fast it fell back with a crash against the linoleum. He picked up his glass and threw it at Claire's head. It missed but hit and broke against the wall next to Patricia, who yelped and jumped aside.

Our father pointed a trembling finger at Claire. "You goddamned little slut! Just like your mother!"

"Don't you talk about Mom that way!" Claire screamed. "Don't you dare, you asshole!"

My father, when drunk, had often been melancholy or temperamental. He'd been careless, suicidal, morose or sometimes vicious with his mouth, but he'd never hit any of us. When he advanced on Claire I really thought he meant to strike her.

"Little bastard bitch." The alcohol had made him slow, and he stumbled. Mary put herself between him and Claire. Patricia and I flanked him. "Little goddamned whore."

We stayed like that, a tableau of family dysfunction, until he turned. His arms swung, catching me and Patricia with unintentional blows. He went back to the table and drank directly from the bottle, finishing it.

"Where is your mother, anyway? Run off again?" His muttered words were directed at the bottle, not at any of us, but he turned in a shambling half circle to confront us all. "Well? Where is she?"

"She went to the grocery store," said Mary.

His laughter made the hair rise along the back of my neck. "Did she? Annie, c'mere."

I didn't want to, but my feet moved by themselves.

"Give your dad a hand upstairs. I need to lie down."

"You need to sober up," snapped Claire.

He whirled on her, reaching out for my shoulder to keep from falling. I staggered under the sudden weight. We both might have fallen but he caught himself at the last minute.

"What did you say?" he demanded with all the righteous indignation of a falsely accused man.

Claire turned away. "Nothing."

He looked around at all of us. "Any of the rest of you have anything smart to say?"

Nobody said anything. He snorted, derisive. "I thought so."

What is it about our parents that can send us back to childhood with a few words or a look? We'd stood this way before, in this same room, with my father leaning on my shoulder to help him upstairs. With Mary and Patricia cowering in opposite corners of the kitchen. For an instant my vision blurred and wavered, showing me them as they'd been that summer. Little girls with wide eyes, ready to but afraid to cry.

Claire hadn't been there, and it was seeing her that reminded me more than anything that we weren't children anymore. We didn't have to be afraid to show our feelings. I didn't.

"C'mon, Dad, let's get you upstairs."

I'd made this journey many times before, though it was easier now that I was taller. In the bedroom I led him to the bed, where he flopped with a boozy sigh and swung his legs up on the bed. I untied his shoes and slipped them off, and put them away neatly in the closet.

He wasn't snoring, but his breath came in wheezing sighs. I drew the shade to keep out the light. I turned on the air conditioning unit to cool the room. I was ten again, and eight, and five. I was waiting for my mother to come home and make it all better. I was waiting for him to fall asleep so we could be sure he was finished for the night.

"You always were a good girl, Annie." His whiskey-thick voice floated in the darkness.

"Thanks, Dad."

"I'm sorry I yelled at Claire. You'll tell her, won't you?"

"You should tell her yourself."

More silence.

"Where's your mother?"

"She went to the store."

"When's she coming back?"

"I don't know."

Cold air pushed the warm eddies across my face. It swirled over me like water in the lake. Like currents that could sweep me away.

"She left me once, you know. You remember that? That summer?"

"I do. Do you want a blanket?"

He wasn't listening. He was lost somewhere. "I loved that woman so much I wanted to die from it, you know that? Did you know that, Annie? Loved her like it was burning me up from the inside."

I hadn't known, but how could I? Why would I? "No. I didn't know that."

He sighed and was silent. I thought he'd passed out. I pulled a blanket from the closet anyway, in case he did need one.

"She ran off and left me, and I wanted to die."

The wool of the blanket scratched my palms as I put it on the bed by his feet. He reached out faster than I'd have thought he could, finding my wrist with unerring ease despite the dark. He pulled me closer, until I sat on the edge of the bed.

"You remember that summer, don't you?"

"I do, Dad. I told you that."

"You were always a good girl. Took care of your sisters. Little Mary, sweet Mary. And Patricia. You were such a good girl. She went away and left us all, remember that?"

I sighed and patted his hand. "Yes, Dad."

"But she took Claire. Baby Claire." He laughed, and the bed rocked. "Who's going to have a baby of her own, sweet Jesus."

"Do you need anything else? Because I'm going to leave now."

"You'll tell Claire I'm sorry, won't you? I didn't mean what I said."

The circular conversation wasn't new. Instead of feeling annoyed, I felt only sad. This man, for better or worse, was my father.

"Sure. I'll tell her."

"I don't think she's a whore."

"I know you don't."

"You're a good girl, Anne."

"I know, Dad. I've always been a good girl." The words sounded bitter, but he was beyond noticing. "I'm going, now."

"That summer, I took you out on the boat."

My stomach did a slow, sick somersault. "Yes."

"That was a good day, wasn't it? Just you and me, out there on that boat. Riding the boat. Out on the water. Out on the waves. That was a good day."

I hadn't thought so. Not then. Not now.

"Maybe the last good day."

My mother had left with toddler Claire two days after the boat ride. It had been a bad summer, but for me it hadn't started when she left. It had started the day we almost drowned.

"There have been other good days," I said.

"I should just do it," he said. "Just finish myself off."

I said nothing. He wasn't talking to me, not really. Or maybe he was, but it was ten-year-old Annie Byrne he meant to tell, not Anne Kinney.

"Just put the pistol in my mouth and pull the trigger. Just be done...with...all of it." His words got more slurred. "Be better off for everyone. If I just did it."

I'd heard this before, more than once. Sometimes like this in the dark. Sometimes through the closed door while my mother begged him not to.

"I should just do it," he said again, and I answered the way I always had.

"No, Daddy. No, you shouldn't."

"Why not?" he asked, voice deep and slow and far away.

Tears pricked my eyes and stung my throat. "Because we love you."

I was sure he'd passed out, then. The wheeze of his breath had settled into a steady in and out, and his hand fell limp from mine. I let it go and got up to leave. His voice stopped me at the door.

"Annie, did you ever learn to sail?"

"No, Daddy. I didn't."

"You should," he muttered. "Then you wouldn't be so afraid next time."

Then all I heard was snoring, and I left him there to sleep it off.

Chapter 16

$\mathscr{T}$he day of my parents' party threatened rain, and Patricia called me to moan before the sun had fully risen. James answered the phone and passed it off to me after a mumbled hello. I took it, and he got out of bed to shuffle to the bathroom, where I heard him peeing for a very long time.

"It will be fine, Pats. That's why we got the tent."

"The tent will only cover the food," my sister said. "What about all the guests? They can't fit in your house!"

"Maybe we'll get lucky and most of them won't show up."

"Very funny, Anne."

I wasn't laughing. I wasn't really even joking. I yawned and looked at the clock, which showed an hour far too early for my taste. "Pats. Calm down. It will be fine, I promise you."

She sighed. "You're so good at this, you know that?"

"Good at what?"

"Being in charge of things. Making it all better. Fixing it."

Through the half-open bathroom door, I could see my

husband scratching himself in places I didn't need to see scratched. I turned on my side. "No, Pats. I'm really not."

She sighed again, and was silent for half a second. "It's only a chance of thunderstorms, right?"

"Only a chance."

"And…we just have to get through this one day, and we're fine. We'll be done."

"All done."

She laughed. "I'm sorry I'm such a pain in the butt. I know it. I just…I'm just…"

"I know." I did. There was a lot going on, not just this party. There'd been a lot going on for a long time. "It will be great. Mom and Dad will have a good time. Their friends will be here. We'll be held up as bright and shining examples of what good daughters do, and we'll be done for the next thirty years."

I wasn't sure exactly what she was doing, but the noise didn't sound quite like laughter. Maybe a snort. "Sure. Right."

James came back to bed, his eyes still half-closed. He slid between the covers and reached to pull me back against him. I allowed the embrace because it would have been too difficult to disentangle myself from him while I was on the phone. When he nuzzled into my hair and his hand came up to cup my breast, I let out a low, annoyed noise. He didn't get it.

"Everything will be fine," I said for what felt like the millionth time. "The sun will come out. The rain will hold off. The people will come and eat and leave, and tomorrow this will all be a pleasant memory. Go back to sleep for a while, Patricia. God knows I'm going to."

"How can you sleep?" she protested. "What time do you want me to come over? Is there anything I can bring? What about—"

"Noon, like we agreed. And no. Goodbye," I said, and hung up even though she protested.

"Patricia?" James asked.

"Yes." I didn't move out of his arms, but I didn't exactly nestle, either.

"She's freaking out?"

"Yeah." There'd be no going back to sleep for me. I had over a hundred people arriving at my house a few hours from now, and though I'd told Patricia it would all be all right I wasn't as assured.

The barometer hanging on the wall in my kitchen didn't make me feel any better. The blue water in the tube had risen nearly all the way to the top, portending storms. I looked outside. Blue skies didn't necessarily mean anything. A storm could fly up at any time.

Despite the concerns about the weather, the tent arrived on time and was set up without problem. The caterer came with his portable pit beef spit and all the other gear. James had already set up the outdoor speakers to play a mix of songs from our iPod. "Build Me up, Buttercup" wafted over air steamy and humid and smelling of cooked cow. It was two hours to party time, and though Patricia and Mary had shown up, Claire was nowhere to be found.

"She said she had to meet the asswad," Mary told me as she helped me set out paper plates and plastic utensils on the long trestle tables set up in my teeny tiny yard. "Something about getting some money, or something?"

"I think you mean the fucktard." I surveyed the yard. Everything looked okay.

"Yeah, him." Mary laughed, her eyes scanning the driveway. "And she's going to drive Mom and Dad. You know, so…"

"So he doesn't have to drive. Yes." I watched her. She fumbled with the stack of plates, picking it up and setting it down, and arranging the spoons so they tucked neatly inside one another.

James appeared on the deck, moving chairs. He was a very good husband, I thought, shading my eyes to watch him move. He'd been helping all morning without complaining. He'd even run out twice to pick up things we'd forgotten. He was cheerful about it, too. I loved him. So why did looking at him make my stomach drop like I was falling?

"Are you okay?" Mary waved a hand in front of my eyes to capture my attention. "Earth to Anne. Hello?"

I shook it off and gave her a smile. "Fine. You?"

"Fine."

We looked at each other, both aware we were lying, but only Mary confessed. "I invited Betts to come. I hope that's okay."

"Of course." I thought I should say more.

"Thanks." She fussed some more with the plates and spoons before she crossed her hands tightly over her stomach. "Anne…"

I'd been watching James again, my hand raised in a small half wave in return to the one he'd given me. "Hmm?"

"How'd you know you wanted to spend the rest of your life with James?"

I was still looking at him when I answered. "I didn't."

"What do you mean, you didn't? You married him."

She sounded so astonished, I had to look at her. "I knew I loved him, Mary, but I didn't know that it would be the rest of my life. I hoped it would be, but I wasn't convinced it would last."

"Why not?"

It was my turn to fuss with the plates, though there was nothing wrong with the way they'd been arranged. "Because good things don't last, do they?"

"Gosh," she said quietly. "I hope you're not right about that."

I shrugged.

"Anne?"

I looked up. "Mare, I want to tell you that you'll know love when it hits you, and it will all be great and you'll find that one person who makes your heart sing, the end, happily ever after. I want to do that for you, I really do. But I'm just not that person. I'm sorry."

She blinked and cleared her throat, looking chagrined. "I thought you and James had a perfect thing going on."

"Yeah. Well. Like I said, things don't last. Good things don't last."

"I'm sorry."

She looked sorry, and I felt bad for putting the damper on her enthusiasm. "It's not your fault. And it could be different for you, Mare. It really could."

"Are you guys having problems?" She shook her head. "I mean…obviously, I guess you're having trouble, but… bad trouble? Divorce trouble?"

I searched the yard for James and found him down by the water. He was doing something with a beach umbrella. I wanted to holler at him to forget the stupid, single umbrella—what could it do for a hundred people? But he was trying to help, and no matter what had happened between us, I didn't need to be unkind.

"I don't know. I don't think so. We haven't really talked about it."

"Wow. I just had no idea. I'm sorry, Anne."

I smiled at her. "I think you've been a little tied up with things of your own, haven't you?"

She laughed. "Yes. I guess so."

We looked the most alike, Mary and I. The same curly auburn hair, though she wore hers longer. Our mother's blue-gray eyes. We were about the same height, too. We looked a lot alike, but I'd never felt we were much alike.

"Listen, Mare. Don't let what I said keep you from trying to find something that will make you happy, okay?"

"Is this going to be a 'make your own kind of music' lecture?" She shot me a grin.

"What the heck's a 'make your own kind of music' lecture?"

"You know. Sing your own special song, blah blah blah, find your own shiny star, be your own person. You know what I mean. That feel-good sort of thing."

I snorted. "Okay, so I'll pass on the lecture."

I did wish I had better advice for her. According to Patricia, I was supposed to be good at fixing things. Mary didn't seem concerned, though, as she came around the table to sling an arm over my shoulder.

"It'll all work out," she said confidently. "I know it will."

"How do you know this, oh wise one?"

She looked out across the lawn, where James was now talking with the pit beef crew. "Because you love each other."

Tears are such unfortunate things. They never quite make everything all right. Sometimes they make everything worse.

I had no time for self-indulgent weepiness, not even with a shoulder all ready to cry on. There was a party to put on, families to deal with. My marriage to save. I didn't have time for sorrow. I took it anyway.

Mary, even if she didn't understand all the reasons I was crying, was a good enough sister to hand me a napkin and say nothing while I sobbed into it. I'm sure I got a few odd looks from the caterer, but I kept my face hidden so I didn't have to see them.

"Maybe you should go lie down for a while," Mary said after a few minutes. "Patricia and I can handle things from here. Maybe you need a break."

I wiped my face. "No, no. That wouldn't be fair to you guys. I'll be fine, really. I'm okay."

She shook her head. "Anne—"

"I said I was fine, Mare." My voice brooked no argument. I was fine. I would be fine. I would put on the smile, and I'd make it all shiny, because goddammit, it was what I did. I was a good daughter. I was not going to let my personal fuckups ruin this party. It had too many chances at ruination already; it didn't need my having a breakdown, too.

A car pulled into the drive. We both turned, Mary's face

first lighting then getting dark when she saw it was the Kinneys. I'm sure mine didn't look much better.

"Why does your mother-in-law always look like she just stepped in dog poo?"

Laughter, too, can be an unfortunate thing.

"Hello, girls," Evelyn said. "What's so funny?"

"I'm going to go see Pats about the…stuff…with that… thing…."

Mary abandoned me. Evelyn smiled. I smiled back. She waited, but I had nothing to say to her. She was early, like she often was. Frank had already disappeared into the house. I wondered if she was waiting for me to greet her with a hug. She'd be waiting a damn long time, I thought. Still smiling.

"I came early to see if you needed any help," she said.

"Nope." Cheer came out of me like blood from an artery, great spurts of it. "Everything's all taken care of."

She looked around, eyes scanning the tent, the yard, the tables. "Everything looks nice."

She was, I think, trying to be nice. I think she meant to be. At least, I wanted to give her credit for the effort, because assuming she was really just trying to make me feel inadequate on purpose would have made me a nasty person.

"Thanks. James is in the house."

"So. It's thirty years for your parents?"

I nodded, still smiling brightly. My face ached. "Yep."

She might not have been calculating my age, twenty-nine, with a birthday coming up in April. She might not. She really did look like she'd stepped in poo.

"That's a nice accomplishment," she said, like they should get a gold star. "Frank and I will have been married for forty-five years in December."

She looked around again at the yard and toward the house. "A party is such a nice way to honor your parents, Anne."

No way was I planning an anniversary party for Frank and Evelyn Kinney. No way. She had a son and two daughters, all fully capable of taking the matter into their own hands, if they thought of it. Which they probably wouldn't. Shit. Shit, shit, shit.

"James is in the house," I said again. Still smiling.

She gave me an odd look. "Yes, you told me that."

"Don't you want to go see him?"

Something in my gaze must have seemed sour, because she frowned a little. "Anne, are you feeling all right?"

"Yep, yep, dandy. Just fine. Just have a lot to do, that's all, why don't you go ahead inside and I'll just talk to the caterer over there." More smiling. Fierce. I was getting a headache.

I smiled.

Fortunately, she backed off. Maybe I scared her. Maybe I wanted to.

Guests began arriving, filling my driveway and parking along the somewhat narrow street. We'd invited the neighbors—the ones we liked and the ones we didn't—so there'd be no problems about the extra vehicles. The sun came out, hot as could be expected on a late August afternoon. A breeze came up every so often from the lake, though, and the tent and our scraggly trees provided shade. Some people waded down in the water, splashing and laughing.

There was plenty of food, despite Patricia's worries. Cascades of carved beef slathered in tangy horseradish and barbecue sauce. Mountains of crusty rolls. Buckets of potato and macaroni salads. Coleslaw. Desserts by the dozen. People ate and talked and mingled. They drank.

My father held court on the lawn, a plastic lawn chair his throne and a bottle of beer his scepter. My mother ran back and forth to serve him, bringing him platters of food and cans of cola he didn't drink. He started off with beer but soon had switched back to his favorite: tall glasses of iced tea that gradually contained less and less tea and more and more whiskey.

Mary spent most of her time with Betts, discreetly. Patricia buzzed between the house and the catering tent, supervising the food. Children played under Claire's watchful eye. She was an unexpected babysitter, but the kids loved her because she played games with them like Simon Says and Red Light, Green Light. Today she wore a clingy summer skirt and shirt that were perfectly modest yet managed to show off the newly sprouted bulge of her tummy, leaving no question as to her pregnancy.

The party was an absolute success. Friends and family had gathered to celebrate what would have been a happy occasion for any couple; for my parents it seemed equally as remarkable as it did joyful. I mingled with people I hadn't seen in years. Family friends complimented me on my house and the party. Most commented on how much I'd grown up, how they'd remembered me as that "quiet little girl with the book in her hand."

"You always had a book. What were you reading,

anyway?" said Bud Nelson. I remembered him as a hefty, red-faced man with a boisterous laugh who always had a quarter in his pocket for a girl who'd run and fetch him "another cold one." He'd gotten sickly thin, with scrawny arms and legs poking out beneath his too-large Bermuda shorts. His skin drooped on him like it had melted. His eyes and teeth were yellowed.

"Nancy Drew, probably." I smiled. Always smiled.

"Girl detective," Bud scoffed. "That Nancy got herself into some trouble, didn't she? Always had to have her dad bail her out."

That wasn't the way I recalled the stories, but I wasn't going to debate it. "They were only stories."

Bud laughed and dug in his pocket. "Hey, Annie. How about a quarter for you if you fetch me—"

"Another cold one?" I said before he could finish.

He nodded and settled back in his chair like it had been an effort just to dig for the money. The quarter gleamed in his palm. I closed his fingers over it.

"You don't need to give me a quarter, Bud."

"You're a good girl, Annie. Always were."

"So I've been told."

He was being kind, and he wasn't the only one. I heard it over and over again that day. Annie, you were always such a good girl. A quiet girl. Annie, fetch me another cold one. Annie. Annie. Annie.

I hadn't been Annie to anyone but my dad for years, and suddenly I was that girl again. Fetching cold ones. Smiling. They only figuratively patted my head now instead of literally, but it was the same feeling.

The party was in full swing, with people beginning to dance on the deck and the lawn. The food had been decimated, like a plague of locusts had marched through. The day had turned sweltering, with the unrelenting pressure of humidity added to the heat. Clouds had started drifting in from across the water. Still white for now, but hinting at darkness.

I went into the house to find some cold air and a glass of ice water and maybe just a few moments to myself. Patricia, who'd been on the verge of a breakdown for weeks over this event, had spent the day beaming from ear to ear and laughing. I, on the other hand, was slowly becoming a wreck.

It wasn't the party, really, but the entire summer that had weighed me down. It was Evelyn. It was Alex and James. It was fixing things that had caught up with me all at once. I sought the quiet of my bedroom, looking for just a few minutes' peace. Time to catch my breath and not have to talk or smile. All I wanted was a minute. Just one.

The house was as full as the yard. The noise level, higher. I wove my way through the kitchen and down the hall, hoping at least that nobody had migrated into my room. I'd closed the door before the party started but left all the others open. Most people would have understood what that meant. A closed door meant privacy. Keep out. Most people, when they enter someone else's home, understand boundaries.

This part of the house was marginally quieter. Most of the guests had gathered in the living room, den and kitchen. One of my cousins sat in the quiet and clean guest bedroom, nursing her baby. We smiled at each other but didn't say anything, and I pulled the door most of the way closed to give her some privacy. The bathroom door was closed but opened as I passed. Laughing, I danced for a minute with the person who came out until we moved in opposite directions.

At the end of the hall, my door was no longer closed. It was cracked open an inch or so. I put my hand on the knob, but paused at the sound of voices inside.

"...well, no wonder," said a familiar voice. "And that sister of hers is pregnant, it's so obvious. I didn't see a ring on her finger, either. And the father! I knew he had some...issues...but I had no idea he was a drunkard."

God. Did people really use that word, anymore? Apparently Evelyn Kinney did.

For about ten seconds I almost turned around. Let it go. Ten seconds in which I contemplated just being the good and quiet girl with a smile on her face and walking away. On the eleventh second, my hand pushed the door all the way open.

Things got worse. Much worse. Extravagantly, extraordinarily, infuriatingly worse.

Evelyn stood next to the small writing desk beneath the window. It had once belonged to James's grandmother, and though I didn't often sit at it to write, I did keep my private correspondence in its drawers. Sentimental cards from James, certain photos, my calendar. Not the one I hung on the wall in the kitchen to chronicle things like doctor's appointments and when it was time to rotate the tires. It was a small journal-style calendar with a small block for each day. In it I wrote brief notes or summaries of what had happened that day, just a few lines to remind me what I'd done or felt. It was the best I could do at keeping a diary.

Evelyn put it down when I walked into the room. Margaret, who was eating a brownie without a plate beneath to catch the crumbs now scattering my floor, had the grace to look guilty.

"Anne. Hello."

For an instant I saw nothing but white, like a flash of lightning that faded and left a burning blue afterimage. And I stopped being a good girl.

"What are you doing in my room?"

"Oh." She tittered. "Well, your sister Patricia told us there was a scrapbook of your parents for the party that we had to sign."

"It's in the living room, on the table."

"Well, she didn't tell us that." Mrs. Kinney's nostrils, at odds with her sugary smile, flared.

"So you came looking in my bedroom for it?"

"I wanted to show Margaret the desk. She might want some of these pieces. James said to go ahead."

I didn't even attempt to believe her. Margaret swallowed the brownie and wiped her fingers on the napkin. With flushed cheeks she edged toward the door, but she had to get by me to escape, and I wasn't moving. She turned sideways and fled.

Coward.

"So you came into my bedroom and helped yourself?"

She wasn't expecting confrontation, and I understood that. After all, I'd kept my mouth nice and shut for a long time. She hadn't expected to be caught, either.

"I was looking for the scrapbook." She drew herself up.

"And you thought it might be inside my desk? Does that seem a likely place to put it?" Each word came out clipped and sharp, but I didn't raise my voice.

Inside I was shaking, but I kept my back straight. My hands loose at my sides. It took every effort I had not to clench them.

"Anne, really, this isn't necessary."

She recoiled when I laughed. "Oh, I think it is. Tell me something, Evelyn. Does that look like a scrapbook to you?"

She made a break for it. I expected as much. Nobody likes their misdeeds flung in their face. I'd have respected her more if she'd flat-out admitted she was a snoop. I'd probably even have stepped aside to let her pass if she'd just said she was sorry, she'd made a mistake. But my mother-in-law didn't admit to mistakes, a nifty little trait she'd handed down to her son.

She didn't go so far as to shove me, and we stood at an impasse. I was taller than she was, though she was broader.

"Does it look like a scrapbook to you?"

She shook her head. Stubborn. "I don't have to listen to a lecture from you."

"Why not just answer the question?"

Hot color had spread up her throat and cheeks. I was glad to see her that way, squirming like a worm on a hook. I was glad to see her made to feel uncomfortable for once.

"Does it look like a scrapbook?"

"No!"

"Then why would you have picked it up?"

Her mouth worked, but heaven help her, she wasn't going to admit to wrongdoing. "Are you accusing me of snooping?"

"I don't think it's an accusation. I think it's true."

She sneered. I'm sure she felt righteous in her indignation. Most people who know they've fucked up manage to find a way to justify themselves.

"You are a disrespectful—"

I lost it. All of it. The final, shredded threads of my control. If my hair had turned to snakes, writhing and hissing and dripping venom, I wouldn't have been shocked.

"Don't you *dare* talk to me about being disrespectful. You came into my house, during my party, and you helped yourself to my room and violated my privacy. Don't you dare talk to me about respect, because you don't have a clue."

My wrath must have been horrific to behold. I know it sent Evelyn reeling. She must have thought I meant to strike her, though I still hadn't raised my voice.

"You're trying to paint me out as some evil person, and I won't stand for it!" she cried, indignant, crocodile tears glimmering.

"I don't think you're evil," I said in a voice thick with ice. "I think you are incredibly arrogant and self-absorbed, and if you really think that you are not in the wrong, then I guess you must be stupid, too."

She opened her mouth. Nothing came out. I had done what I'd have said was impossible, rendered Evelyn speechless. It only lasted a moment, but it was immeasurably sweet.

"I would say I can't believe you'd say something like

that to me," she said in the tone of a woman soaked in gasoline who's just lit the match. A martyr.

Was it wrong of me to assume she took an especial, private satisfaction in this conversation, just as I did? That it somehow relieved her to be right about me? That I had acted in the way she always knew I was capable, had treated her horribly, and, therefore, her forgiveness and acceptance of me could be construed as a laudable act of charity? Because she might still have managed to save herself in my eyes if she'd only managed to rein herself in.

But, no. She went there.

"But I suppose you can hardly be expected to know any better," she added with the simpering, sanctimonious tone that had always made me want to puke, "taking into consideration your family background."

I was done with her. There was no going back after that. No cooling down, no finding a way to smooth this over. I was done.

"At least in my family we understand how to behave in someone else's house. You are not allowed to judge my family," I told her. My calm dismissal seemed to set her more aflame than my anger had. She couldn't defend herself and be affronted against dismissal the way she could against fury. "Not in my house. Not to me. You need to leave."

"You can't throw me out!"

"Then get your panties in a twist and storm out on your high horse. I don't really care how it happens. Just get out of my house. You are not welcome here anymore today. Maybe not anymore, ever."

"You...you can't..."

I leaned toward her, not because I wanted to intimidate her, but because this was something best said up close and personal. "My life," I said, "is not any of your business."

"Anne?" We both turned to see Claire in the doorway. "Dad's going to give a toast."

She looked at us curiously. Evelyn pushed past me and my sister with a sniff. The clack of her heels was very loud in the hall.

"Holy shit," Claire whispered. "What did you do to Mrs. Kinney? Threaten to throw a bucket of water on her?"

In the aftermath my legs shook. Feeling sick but lighter, too, like an immense burden had been lifted, I sank onto the bed. "Let's just say I got some things off my chest."

Claire sat next to me. "She looked like someone had served her a big old bowl of worms and told her it was angel hair pasta."

"That's probably what it felt like." I covered my face with my hands for a minute, taking deep, shaky breaths. "God, she's such a bitch."

"That's not news, I hate to tell you."

That first laugh felt like acid in my throat. "I don't think she's ever going to forgive me, Claire. What a mess."

"Forgive you?" My sister made a nasty noise. "For what? Calling her on the carpet for behaving badly? Anne, you never do anyone favors by letting them be assholes."

"I could've just kept my mouth shut about it. We'd have pretended it didn't happen. But I couldn't, Claire. God. I saw her standing there with it, and I just couldn't hold it in anymore. All those times she got in my face about things, poking her nose where it didn't belong, acting like she was so perfect...I just lost it."

"What the fuck did she do?"

I told her.

"No!" Claire sounded fascinated as well as horrified.

"Yes. I don't know how much she'd read, but she was definitely looking through it."

"No fucking way!" Claire shook her head. "And you didn't knock her on her ass?"

"I wasn't going to hit her, Claire."

She put her hand over her mouth for a second, looking at the desk. "I'd have bitch-slapped her."

"Oh, Claire." I laughed again, and it came easier this time.

"Seriously. I don't blame you for being pissed. What a nosy bitch."

"Yeah. Well, unfortunately, she wasn't smart enough to lock the door behind her so I didn't see her doing it. Or maybe she really feels entitled to sift through my drawers, I don't know." I told her the rest of what had happened.

"And she had the nerve to insult our family?" Claire was outraged. "Oh, you wait. I'll be all up in her shit. You wait."

"Oh, God," I said, but laughing. "Don't!"

She laughed, too. "Honestly? Not worth the effort. She's a pain in the ass, Anne."

"She's James's mother."

"Then let him deal with her."

I rolled my eyes but said nothing about that. I got up. "C'mon, we're probably missing the toast."

"I'm not so sure that's such a tragedy. They're all getting up and toasting. It's a fucking slosh fest out there. Besides, Sean's getting it all on that nice new video camera he showed up with today. You can watch it all in vibrant color at your convenience, later."

I groaned and flopped down on my bed. "God. Will this day ever end?"

"Yes," my sister said simply.

I listened for voices but heard nothing. "Why have I so messed up my life, Claire? Can you tell me that?"

"Telling off Mrs. Kinney didn't mess up your life."

I looked at her and sat up. "That's not what I meant."

"Oh." She nodded, after a second. "Alex?"

"That, too."

"There's more?" She grinned. "Damn, woman. You've been keeping secrets."

I was so tired. Of everything. All of it.

"Claire, you don't remember the summer Mom left. You were too young. And she took you along. You don't know all the stuff that happened...." My voice twisted, got tight. I swallowed against the barbed wire in my throat.

"I know some of it. Mary and Pats told me things. You never did," she said. "But...I'm sure it was bad. Wasn't it? I mean...it's never really been good, has it?"

"It used to be. He didn't drink so much. He and Mom didn't fight. Before that summer, he was better."

She pulled her knees up and curled her arms around them. "Gah. Belly's getting in the way." She relaxed her posture a bit. "Dad's a drunk, Anne. It's the way it is."

"But it got worse after she left." I pulled a pillow onto my lap, kneading it. "I never told Mom about how we'd gone out on the boat, or the storm. How the boat almost capsized because he was too drunk to sail. If I'd told her, maybe she'd have stayed, and he would've managed to get it together. Keep it together. Forget it. Forget I said anything."

Claire was staring with wide, wet eyes. Her mouth, painted today in a demure shade of pink, trembled and turned down at the corners. "You can't blame yourself for anything he did. Or she did. That was a long time ago, and you were just a kid. It wasn't up to you to do anything."

"I know. I know," I said, fingers digging deep into the pillow's forgiving softness. "But like you guys always said, I'm the only one who could ever deal with him."

"Oh, Anne," Claire said. "Don't make yourself sick over this."

"I've read the journals and studied about it," I told her. "Alcoholism is a disease. It's not my fault, or yours, or anyone's. Nothing I did made him drink. I know it."

"But you have to believe it," she whispered and took my hand.

We looked at each other.

"Yeah," I said finally. "That's the hard part. Sometimes I just think, if I'd told her about that day, she'd have stayed. He wouldn't have tipped over like he did. She'd have stayed instead of going to take care of Aunt Kate."

Claire's fingers twitched. She wiped glittering wetness from one eye, then the other. "She didn't go to Aunt Kate's, Anne."

I wasn't sure I'd heard her correctly. "What?"

Claire shook her head. "She didn't go to Aunt Kate's

that summer. That's just what everyone told you, but it wasn't true."

"Well...where did she go?" The bottom had fallen out of my basket already today. I couldn't do more than blink at this news.

"She went to stay with some guy named Barry Lewis." Claire looked more uncomfortable than I'd ever seen her. "She was having an affair with him. She left Dad that summer. She meant to divorce him."

Chapter 17

*E*velyn had not left the party, despite my sweetly worded suggestion. I spotted her on the far side of the yard, talking to James. He looked supremely unhappy. Then he looked angry. I couldn't hear what they were saying.

I hadn't missed the toasts. Someone had given my mother a pull-tab necklace and crowned my father with a hat made from a paper plate with plastic forks poked through the rim. I heard a lot of laughter as, one by one, friends and family got up and said a few words and lifted a glass to mark my parents' accomplishment.

It all seemed more like a lie than ever. I'd never thought my parents had a good marriage. One that worked for them, one that limped along pretending to be satisfactory. But good? No. Not by the standards I'd set for myself.

My mother'd had an affair. She'd left my father for another man. Knowing this exonerated me, but I didn't feel better. She hadn't only left him. She'd left us, too. She'd left me behind to take care of him when he should've been taking care of us. She'd left us, and he'd fallen apart, and nothing had ever been the same after that.

Laughing and shaking her head, my mom refused to get up and speak. My dad had no such false modesty. He stood, glass held high. He surveyed the crowd. There was no anticipatory hush, but the murmuring of conversation dimmed.

"What a day, huh? What a day."

"You said it, Bill! You tell 'em!"

"Way to go, Bill!"

Some people clapped. A few whistled good-naturedly. Over by the tent, Evelyn folded her arms across her chest and looked like doom.

My dad started out by thanking everyone for coming and my mother for being with him for so long. James appeared and put his arms around me from behind, his cheek next to mine. I tensed, waiting for him to say something about his mother. He didn't. She was watching us, her displeasure obvious to anyone who wanted to look. Her expression made me angry all over again. This wasn't her day, but somehow, she was trying to make it all about her.

"And to my daughters, Anne, Patricia, Mary and Claire," said my father. "For planning this party for us."

The crowd sought us out, the four. Patricia, with her arm around Sean's waist and her kids circling her like satellites. Mary, standing just far enough away from Betts. Claire, deep in conversation with a tall guy I didn't recognize. And me, looking out from the dubious safety of James's arms.

They seemed to be waiting for something.

"They want you to talk," James whispered. "Go ahead."

"No," I said, but he linked his fingers through mine and squeezed, and I somehow found the strength.

"About six months ago," I began, "my sister Patricia came up with this crazy idea for an anniversary party. So if you're all having a good time—" lots of cheers "—you can thank her. If you're having a horrible time…thank her."

Laughter greeted that. I continued. "We're glad you could all come today to help us share thirty years of marriage for Bill and Peggy. There've been some good times. And some not so good times."

I faltered, then, with tears in my throat. James squeezed my hand again. Just a gentle touch, letting me know he was there.

"But that's what family is all about. Good and bad times. Sticking together. Sharing the happy things and being there to lend a hand during the unhappy ones."

I wanted to be more eloquent but with what felt like every eye upon me, I could only come up with cliché after cliché.

"Some of you have known my parents for the past thirty years. You've known me and my sisters for almost our whole lives. Some of you we've just met, but that's okay. You're not exempt from the craziness. If you're here, you're all part of the family. Be prepared to help clean up after the party."

More laughter.

"So…a toast to my parents, Bill and Peggy. To thirty years together." I didn't have a glass to lift, but there were enough raised in my stead. "And to twice as many more."

"Good job," James whispered and kissed me.

He folded his arms around me, holding me tight. I let him. I didn't want to let go of him, not ever.

"I love you," I whispered against his chest.

His hand came up to cup the back of my head and stroke the heat-frizzed mess of my hair. "I love you, too."

"James." Evelyn's voice interrupted our quiet moment. James didn't let go of me. "Yeah, Mom."

"We're leaving. Now."

He kept me circled within his arms. "Bye. Thanks for coming."

"I said we're leaving," she repeated, as though hadn't heard her.

"I heard you," said James. "Goodbye."

It seemed as though the second wave of eating had begun, with people drifting back into the house in search of the brownies and cookies Patricia had baked. We got a few curious looks as they passed by, probably from Evelyn's tone. I didn't give in to the temptation to speak to her. I wasn't sure what would have come from my mouth.

"Aren't you going to walk us to the car?"

James didn't even turn toward her. "I think you know the way."

I pushed away a bit. "If you want to—"

He shook his head. "No. I'm fine. Bye, Mom. I'll call you."

"Will she let you?" The comment was nasty, even for her.

James kept his temper better than I would have. He answered her with silence, which I had to admit was the best way to deal with her, after all. It gave her nothing to respond to. Evelyn turned on her heel and left. As soon as she was gone around the corner of the house I took a deep, relieved breath.

James patted my back. "We can talk about it later."

I didn't think I'd ever want to talk about it. "Okay."

"Get a room," commented Claire as she climbed the two steps to the deck and propped herself up next to us by the railing. "Ya buncha exhibitionists."

James ruffled her hair and she ducked away with a scowl. "Look who's talking."

Claire put on a hoity-toity attitude. "I'm not into public displays of affection, thanks. That's tack-ay."

Patricia popped her head up from the yard below. "Hey, should we bring out the cake?"

"Cake!" Claire clapped. "I vote yes."

"I vote yes," said James.

Mary showed up, too. "What are we voting on?"

"Cake," I explained.

"A definite yes," she answered. "I'll help. C'mon, Claire."

"Hey, that's not fair, making the pregnant woman work!"

"Sit on it" was Mary's suggestion.

"The cake?" Patricia cried. "Don't you dare!"

"God help me," I murmured, sinking back against my husband. "It's a madhouse around here."

My sisters went inside to bring out the cake, a reproduction of the one my parents had served at their wedding. It got lots of oohs and ahhs when it was unveiled. Compared to the elaborate cakes I'd seen at more recent weddings, theirs was a simple three-layer with white icing and a plastic bride and groom on the top.

My sisters corralled my parents into cutting it. Claire

had cued up "Hit Me With Your Best Shot" from the iPod, and they smashed the cake into each other's faces. Watching my dad lick icing from his fingers and my mother help clean him up with a napkin, I saw something.

They really did love each other. No matter what had happened in the past, they still did. They'd made it this far, made their choices. They didn't need anyone to step in and give them a hand. They could do it all on their own.

The party wound down as the sun started setting. We said our goodbyes and packed food in foam containers provided by the caterer. We settled bills and helped tear down the tent. By the time it was all done and everyone had gone home, night had fallen.

"The rain held off." James cracked open one of the remaining bottles of beer and took a long swallow. He looked out over the water. "Some party, Anne. Good job."

I collapsed with a groan into the swing glider. "It wasn't all me. And you did your share, too. Thanks."

He plopped down beside me. We rocked. He finished his beer and put his arm around my shoulders, inviting me to rest my head against him. The night had no stars, hidden by the clouds that had promised rain but not delivered. The night was muggy, though every so often a fresh and cooler breeze would spring up and make me shiver.

He yawned. "I'm going to sleep until noon tomorrow, I think."

I toyed with the buttons of his shirt. It wasn't pink. The material felt scratchy under the pads of my fingertips. "That sounds good."

His fingers crept up to scratch my skull, through my hair. It felt good. I knew why cats purred when petted.

"So you and my mom went at it, I hear."

"I came into our bedroom and found her standing with my calendar in her hand, James."

His fingers kept working my skull and down to the base of my neck, easing knots of tension. "She told me you said she wasn't welcome in our house and she had to get out."

"Well…yeah. After she tried to tell me she wasn't being a snoop and then insulted my family."

James gave a heavy sigh. "Anne, you know my mother."

"I do know your mother." I looked up at him. "I really hope you aren't trying to defend her."

He paused. "No. I guess not."

"Good. Because from now on, she's your problem."

A small smile quirked his lips. "Like she never was before?"

"I mean she's not mine. I'm not going to keep smiling like some kind of ventriloquist's dummy when she gets on my nerves."

"Nobody ever said you had to, honey." He moved down to my shoulder, his strong fingers massaging the aches.

"Good. Because I'm not doing it anymore."

"My mom just wants you to like her, that's all."

I sat up straighter. "Is that what she said?"

He shrugged. "Yeah."

I laughed. "Oh, right. That's why she's been so open and accepting of me all these years. Why she's embraced me fully with open arms."

"She thinks you don't, that's all."

"She knows it today because I told her off after I found her invading my privacy, James."

"Are you sure she wasn't just—"

"What? She tripped and fell and caught herself with my journal? And it just happened to flip open and she had to read it?"

"I didn't say that." He withdrew his arm and sat back.

The swing moved us back and forth, and I put a foot down hard onto the deck to stop it. "I guess you don't think it's as big a deal as I do."

His expression told me that was true. "I guess not. It was just a calendar, right?"

I got off the swing. "Not just a calendar. It was where I marked down important events, or things that happened. Snippets of thought. It was personal, and it was private. If I wanted the world to read it, I'd have set it out on the coffee table for everyone to flip through."

I could tell he still just wasn't that upset about it. I put my hands on my hips. He rocked the swing, bringing the edge dangerously close to my shins but never letting it hit me.

"I wrote down everything in that calendar, James."

It took him another second. The swing stopped. "Every-thing."

"Yes. All of it. Everything about you and me…and Alex."

"Shit."

"Yeah, shit. Funny how important it suddenly becomes when it's about you, isn't it?"

"That's not fair, Anne!"

He sounded angry, and I poked him just a bit more. "It

might not be fair. But it's true. Isn't it? You didn't see much harm in your mom reading about my fight with my sister or how many drinks my dad had, or when I got my period or how much my sandals cost. Those things she has a right to. But when it comes down to you and your love affair—"

He stood, menacing. "It wasn't just mine."

"You're right. It wasn't. But I guess the difference is I don't really care if anyone knows I gave Alex Kennedy a blow job. And you do."

I think he was more surprised than I when he grabbed me. I'd taunted him into it. James didn't like to think of himself as a man who could be pushed that way.

"And it wasn't a love affair." His fingers gripped my upper arms. "Was it?"

"You tell me," I said in a low voice.

"If you have something to say, maybe you'd better just say it."

"He told me what really happened the night you got that scar." I poked it, and he captured my hand, squeezing my fingers into a fist.

"I told you what happened."

"Apparently, you left out a few things."

James pulled me so close I had to tip my face back to look up into his. "What did he tell you?"

"He said you got upset when he told you about the guy he was fucking."

"I did!"

"Why?" The question came out quieter than I'd expected it to, and less accusatory.

We both were breathing hard, our anger mixing into a

different kind of tension. One more familiar. We hardly ever fought, but we'd fucked plenty.

"I was surprised."

"Were you, really? He was your best friend. You'd known him for years. Was it really a surprise when he told you?" I slid my hands up his chest to curve over his shoulders. "Or were you just disappointed it wasn't you?"

James let out a low, shuddering breath. "Jesus, Anne. What a hell of a question."

I waited patiently for an answer.

"He dated girls. Fuck, Alex got more pussy than I ever did. He was sleeping with senior class girls when we were sophomores."

"So you were jealous."

"Yeah, a little. He got any girl he wanted."

I smiled. "That doesn't surprise me."

James made a face.

He still hadn't really answered my whole question. "You didn't get mad about that."

"Hell, no."

"But you got mad when he told you he was sleeping with a guy?"

"He threw it at me out of the blue. What was I supposed to do?"

I shrugged. "Understand? He was your best friend."

"I didn't even know he liked guys," James said. "We were drunk. Maybe things got a little out of hand."

I put my hand over the scar beneath his shirt. "Or a lot out of hand."

There was a long, long moment while the world

revolved and we went with it. He kissed me, soft and slow and sweet. He hugged me, too, folding me close to him. I put my arms around him, my cheek to his chest. Beneath the scar his heart thumped steadily.

"I'm sorry," he said. "I never thought it would end up this way."

"I know you didn't."

We swayed together to the music of the wind and water. James nuzzled my hair and the side of my face. I opened to his kiss and tasted beer.

I put my hand to his chin, arresting the kiss. I looked into his eyes. "I don't love him the way I love you, James."

He smiled like I'd given him a gift. He'd been slowly dancing me back toward the kitchen door as we spoke. Now my heels hit the threshold, but I didn't trip. The small step brought me just high enough that I didn't have to tip my head to look directly into his eyes. His hands slid down to cup the curve of my ass and pull me against him. I put my arms around his neck and he lifted me, carrying me over my laughing protests back to the bedroom. Darkness made it hard to figure out where we were going, and I flung out a hand to hit the wall switch as we passed.

We fell onto the bed in a tangle of limbs and scattered pillows everywhere. His body on mine felt different, somehow. Heavier and more solid. He felt real to me, finally. For the first time in as long as I could remember, I didn't feel like I was waiting for all of this to go away.

He looked down at me. "Everything's going to work out all right. You'll see."

I pulled his mouth to mine for a kiss that got hungrier

as it went on. He stole my breath and gave it back. Our lips mashed, bruising as our tongues tangled. He slid a hand into my hair, pulling my head back. His other hand went beneath the small of my back, lifting my hips against his. He ground his erection on my belly.

"Do you feel that? Do you feel how hard I get for you?" he whispered against my lips as he rubbed the bulge in his shorts against my crotch. "That's for you, baby."

I put my hands under the hem of his shirt and into the waistband of his shorts, finding the twin dimples on the sides of his spine. I rubbed them, then moved down over the slope of his buttocks. "Take these off."

He reached between us to undo the button and zipper and together we worked to shove the material down over his thighs. He wore his favorite boxer briefs beneath, the soft fabric outlining his cock as it strained the front. When he lay back down on top of me, I felt his heat.

I ran my hands over the clinging material covering the mound of his ass. I hooked my fingers in the elastic at his waist and tugged it down. He kissed me harder, pressing me into the pillows as his hips lifted so I could make him naked. We wriggled and writhed, working off our clothes as fast as we could without letting go of each other's mouths for any longer than it took to pull our shirts over our heads.

Naked at last, James covered me again. The hair on his legs rubbed my smooth skin, while the patch on his lower belly teased and tickled. My nipples could have cut glass. When he slid down my body to take one into his mouth, I moaned, arching.

"I love the way you sound when I do that." He slid

lower, urging another soft moan from me when he nipped at my hip. "And that."

He paused between my legs to look up at me. I ran my fingers through his hair. His eyes gleamed in the light from the bedside lamp. They looked incredibly, particularly blue tonight against the flush of his cheeks and dark arches of his eyebrows.

"What are you thinking?" he asked, not a typically male question. Not a typical James question.

"How blue your eyes look." I rubbed the black wires of his brows with a fingertip.

He planted a kiss on my belly button. "Good."

I passed my hand down his face to his cheek. Warm skin. We were both sweating. "What did you think I was going to say?"

"I thought you might be thinking about him."

"Oh, James." I could have said something perfect, but I said something honest, instead. "Not this time."

His eyes closed. He pressed his lips to the curve of my stomach, his hands curled under my thighs. He breathed out, his sigh a gust of moist heat on my skin. Then he kissed me softly. And again. Small, light, feathering kisses that tickled and tantalized. He moved lower.

In the early days of our lovemaking I'd often been content to lie back and allow him to do as he pleased…even if what he was doing missed the mark. It had taken his asking me to tell him what I liked and wanted. Here. There. How hard, soft, the pattern and rhythms to which my body best responded. Like this. Like that.

Now I could lie back as James did what he pleased, and

I didn't have to show him how I liked him to touch me. We'd grown together over time. We'd found the places on each other that felt best, learned what pleased the other.

Yet as he bent his mouth to my clit and licked me, I could feel the differences the past few months had wrought. My body no longer leaped the way it had before. I'd changed, but so had he. We'd both learned new things.

He slid a finger inside me, pressing upward as he licked me. Pleasure jumped inside me. Electric. James shifted on the bed, rolling to his side so I could see as he fit his fingers around his cock and stroked it with the same thrusts he made with his hand.

Watching him, I wanted to touch him. I wanted to taste him. I wanted to fill him up and be filled up. I murmured his name and he looked up. I pulled him toward my mouth so we could kiss. His penis lay against the side of my leg, and that wasn't close enough. I wanted it in my hand, mouth, cunt, between my breasts.

I pushed his shoulder so he rolled onto his back. I was no longer satisfied to lie back and allow him to have his way with me. I needed more. I wanted everything, all of it. All of him. I needed all of him with a sudden desperation I understood but didn't want to think too closely upon.

Straddling his thighs, his cock jutting between us, I took him in my hands. Using both, I stroked him up and down. James lifted his hips a little, moving my weight as though it were nothing. His back arched. His hands reached for the spokes of the headboard and grabbed them.

We'd done a lot of things that couldn't be discussed

even in impolite company, but we hadn't ventured into any sort of dominance and submission games. I didn't have a scarf to whip out from a drawer to use as a blindfold, nor handcuffs lurking to bind him. I had only the power of my words and his willingness to obey.

"Don't let go of the headboard," I told him. "Not until I say you can."

James uncurled his fingers but tightened them immediately. "Is that what you want?"

"It is."

I left his cock and ran my hands up his chest to pinch his nipples lightly. I loved the way they tightened under my fingers. I also loved the way his cock bobbed against my stomach as I leaned forward.

"I won't be able to touch you," James said.

I looked at him. "When I want you to touch me, I'll let you know."

There wasn't any menace in this command. I hadn't turned into a dominatrix. But I needed this, to be in charge of our lovemaking. I'd spent the past few months with hands and mouths and pricks doing everything I could have ever wanted. I'd taken that pleasure as a right, gorged upon it. Sated myself with it. Now I needed to be the one who held back a little bit.

"Take down your hair," he whispered. "I want to feel it on me."

I unclipped the mass of curls I loathed and loved in equal amounts. My hair fell just past my shoulders, refusing to behave. I shook it a little and ran my fingers through the strands.

"You look so fierce when you do that. Like you should be carrying a spear out in the Amazon somewhere."

"Do I?" I shot a look into the mirror across the room, but the angle wasn't right and I could only make out a blur.

"Yeah. You look like a warrior."

I never in my life had felt like a warrior. I threaded my fingers again through it, pulling out some tangles. "Does that...turn you on?"

He pushed upward with his thighs. "What does it look like?"

I looked down at his prick, straining upward. I took it in my hand and gave a gentle, downward stroke. His breath hissed out.

"Should I go and get my spear?" I murmured, stroking.

It was good to hear him laugh. To be amused with each other instead of angry, or so caught up in the physical pleasure we knew how to give each other that we forgot about the importance of connecting mentally, too.

"If you want to."

"I think I left it at the cleaners." Stroke up. Stroke down. His penis got harder even as I touched it. Impossibly hard.

"Can I let go of the headboard now?"

I looked up, gaze sharp. "No."

I meant to take the time to relearn his body, to imprint him on my hands and mouth and between my legs. I wanted to replace the memories of anyone and anything else with him. I didn't intend to torture him, but I won't deny there wasn't some small measure of satisfaction in listening to him moan as I took him in my mouth, or traced his body with my lips and hands.

He was good. He didn't let go of the headboard, even when I took him close to climax and eased off. And again. Not even when his muscles strained and he muttered curses at the way I sucked and stroked him, then pulled away to straddle him and made him watch me touch myself.

Then, at last, I couldn't take anymore. I was torturing myself as much as him. I'd spent hours filling my senses with him. There were no more shadows between us.

"Put your hands on me," I said, and he did.

It was old and new, familiar and strange. For me, it was a reinvention of our marriage. One that wasn't quite so invested in being perfect.

Later, with the overhead fan stirring the air over us, I unstuck my skin from his and turned on my side to face him. "I never get tired of looking at your eyes."

James yawned, which somehow ruined the moment since he closed his eyes when he did. "How romantic."

"It's not romantic, it's true. They're amazing. I hope our children have your eyes."

He looked at me, then reached to twirl one of my curls. "I hope they have your hair."

"I don't. It's a mess and so hard to take care of. And I'm not so sure I want a bunch of warriors running around the house."

"The color, at least," he told me. "A bunch of little sunset-colored heads running around."

"Sunset?" That was very sweet and made me smile.

He yawned again. "Yeah. Gold and red. Like a really good sunset."

"It's settled then." I snuggled into the pillow and slung a leg over his. "They'll have your eyes and my hair."

"And my sense of style."

I laughed. "What sense of style?"

"Hey." He looked offended. "I clean up pretty good."

"Yeah," I said fondly, caressing his cheek. "You do."

He kissed my fingers. "A bunch of little mini-me's running around. I can't wait."

His sentiment touched me. "Jamie, I have to tell you something."

He was already drifting toward sleep, but honesty couldn't wait. If I really wanted a new start, it had to begin now. I pulled the blanket up over us, tucking us up in a little cocoon. He waited, and I was sad to see how wary he looked.

"I stopped taking the birth control shots."

"I know."

I shook my head. "No. Just a few weeks ago."

"I don't understand." His brow furrowed. "I thought you stopped—"

"I know. I didn't tell you otherwise, and I should have. I just let you assume I had because we'd talked about it, but when it came time for my appointment I just couldn't do it. And then things got so hectic around here, I just never told you."

"You let me think there was a chance you could get pregnant and you didn't tell me?"

I couldn't figure out if he was angry or hurt. Or both. "I'm sorry. I wasn't ready to try for a baby."

"So why didn't you just tell me that?"

"Because you were so gung-ho on the idea, and I

just…" I faltered. "I just wasn't ready. I wasn't sure I could get pregnant. As long as we weren't trying, I couldn't fail."

With a hand on my hip, he pulled me closer. "Baby, it wouldn't have been failing."

"I'm an idiot. I know it." I managed a watery smile.

"The doctor said the chances were good that the surgery took care of everything and you'd have no trouble."

"I know. But…there's more."

So I told him all of it. About Michael. About the long-ago baby that hadn't survived, and how I'd wished so hard for it to go away I felt responsible even though I'd done nothing to make it happen.

He listened to my story without interrupting. I thought I might cry, but it came out without tears. Somehow I'd become distant from it. It didn't hurt so much any longer.

I told him, too, about the day on the lake with my father, and how my mother had left us. I told him how it had felt to be responsible for them all, for making things work. Fixing. How I had needed to keep everything so bright and shiny, polishing the reflection, so that's all anyone saw and nobody looked underneath to the way our lives really were. I told him why I dreamed of drowning.

And I told him how hard I'd tried to be perfect, even when I wasn't sure exactly what being perfect was.

I talked for a very long time. He listened. The room grew cool as the night deepened outside, but in our cocoon and with each other, we didn't get cold.

"I'm sorry," I said when I was finished. "I felt like I was

lying to you. I didn't want to keep it hidden, anymore. I want us to be honest with each other, always."

He hugged me close and stroked my hair. He said nothing for a long time, and though his embrace was strong and unfaltering, I thought he might be struggling with what he meant to say. When he finally spoke, though, he didn't sound uncertain. He was James, sure of himself and of me.

"You don't have to be perfect, Anne. I never expected you to be. I don't want you to be. I want you to be happy, with me. With our life, the way it is."

"I'm afraid of being happy," I told him. "Because I'm afraid that it will all just…go away."

"I'm not going anywhere," he told me.

I believed him.

Neither of us intended to wake up early the next day, but the phone demanded it of us. James groaned and put the pillow over his head. I looked with bleary eyes at the caller ID box. Patricia. I made a disgusted noise and followed James's example.

I heard the machine click on in the kitchen. She didn't leave a message. I started dozing again, but within one minute the phone rang again. This time I let out a string of muttered curses that James laughed at from beneath his shield of cotton and down.

"This had better be good," I growled into the receiver.

"Anne?" Patricia's tremulous voice at first annoyed me.

"Pats, it's godawful early. What?"

"It's…" She broke down.

I sat up at once. "Pats, what's wrong? I can't understand you. Calm down and tell me what happened."

"Anne, it's Sean," she managed to say, her voice a horrible croak. "He's been arrested."

Chapter 18

*W*e gathered at Patricia's house so she wouldn't have to worry about what to do with the kids. My mom and Mary had taken over the chores of making coffee and sandwiches nobody wanted to eat so early in the day. Claire, who'd kept up a steady stream of insults and invectives about Sean and his latest antics, had been banished to the upstairs bonus room to keep Callie and Tristan entertained and out of the way. My dad paced uncomfortably around the kitchen, getting in everyone's way. James and I shared the table with Patricia, who looked shell-shocked.

"I knew it was bad, but I didn't know it was this bad." Patricia sifted through piles of bills and credit card notices, though she'd gone over them all so many times she must have had them memorized. "I didn't even know…. I feel so stupid."

She put her face in her hands. I took the scraps of paper away from her, which made her look up. I thought she was going to grab them back, but despair settled in the lines of her face. She put her hands back over her eyes.

"Oh God, what am I going to do?"

My mom slid a cup of coffee in front of her. "Drink this."

Patricia shook her head. "No. I feel sick to my stomach."

Mary gave her a ginger ale, already poured into a glass of ice. "Sip this."

Patricia sipped weakly. "He's got four credit cards I didn't know about. They're all maxed. It's only another twenty thousand…but that's not all of it…."

"Take a deep breath," I told her when her voice shook again. "This is all going to work out."

Sean had been arrested for drug trafficking, of all things. So deeply in debt from his gambling habit he couldn't get out, he'd turned to a "friend" he'd met at the racetrack to help him get some easy cash. The friend had turned out to be the sort of idiot who talks big and takes risks with other people's lives. He'd hooked Sean up with a man who needed some packages delivered. Sean, in turn, drooling at the promise of an easy couple hundred bucks he intended to turn into thousands at the track, was caught carrying forty Baggies of premium marijuana, enough to put him behind bars at once.

This was his version of the story, filtered through an almost-hysterical Patricia. What he'd failed to tell her was that not only had he wasted their savings on the ponies, he'd also been failing to make their mortgage payment for the past six months. He'd had the statements forwarded to him at work so she didn't see them. He'd also taken large withdrawals from their household credit card. She hadn't discovered the four cards he'd opened only in his name until she'd been searching through his briefcase for the password to his computer.

"He told me it was all fine," she said now. "He told me he was getting help. He was seeing a counselor. The bills were being paid. I checked them online! They were being paid!"

She deteriorated into sobs again. My dad paced and opened the fridge, rooting around inside and pulling out a can of beer. We all looked at him, but only for a moment. Patricia was taking up our attention.

"He was using the credit cards to pay off the bills, just trading balances and opening up new accounts when he maxed out the old ones. Who are these goddamned morons that kept sending him credit cards?" she cried.

I was happier to see her angry than despairing. "We will work this out, Pats. First things first, okay? First we have to find out how much bail's been set at."

"Or leave him in jail to rot," said Mary.

It was a very Claire thing to say, and my mother tutted. Patricia groaned and slumped into her hands again. James looked like he was biting his tongue, but said nothing.

"The bank wants fifteen hundred dollars to start," came Patricia's muffled answer. "They told me that right away. So I went to the checking account, but I knew we had nothing in there. We were slowly building it back up now that he'd stopped gambling. So I thought. I mean, every paycheck we'd add a bit more back in."

On the surface, anyway. In the meantime Sean had been throwing money hand over fist into other places. I looked at the pile of statements in my hand. At least the morons who'd given him new credit cards had capped his limit at five thousand.

"So I went to see if I could use one of those checks the credit cards are always sending. But when I called to find out how to get some, they told me if I used one, I'd be over our limit. They offered to raise it for me!" She laughed, incredulous. "Because we were such good customers! Can you believe it? We've been carrying a near-maximum balance for the past year and paying the minimum payment, and they wanted to raise our limit!"

"Anything to get you to spend money," my mother said. "They don't care if you don't pay it all off. They can charge you interest then."

"Well, at that point I knew we couldn't afford to be defaulting on our credit card," Patricia said. She sipped more ginger ale. Some color seeped back into her cheeks. "What an idiot!"

I wasn't sure if she meant Sean, or herself. "You can't blame yourself for this, Patricia. Sean was lying to you."

"I knew there was a problem. I just didn't want to see it was so bad. I wanted to believe him," Patricia said. "I wanted to trust him."

Mary rubbed Patricia's shoulders a little. "Of course you did. Nobody knew he was in this deep."

"I just don't know what I'm going to do!" Patricia wailed.

As we clustered around her, trying to find ways to make her feel better and offer our support, my dad still paced restlessly. Finally, he grabbed up his car keys from the table. My mom looked up, leaving Patricia's side to follow him to the front door. I went, too.

"Where are you going?" I demanded.

They both turned.

"I'm going out for a while. I'll be back."

My mother nodded, lifting her face for a kiss, but I scowled. "Dad, Patricia needs you to be here."

"She doesn't need me," my dad said.

"It would be nice if you were here to offer her support," I said evenly, "instead of going out to get hammered so we all have to worry about where you are and when you'll be home."

My parents both went straight and stiff. My mom's expression folded in on itself. My dad looked like he couldn't believe I'd just said that. I couldn't believe it, either.

"What a thing to say. How could you say a thing like that to me?"

"Because it's true, Dad," I said. "Because it's always true."

I turned on my heel and left them at the front door. I didn't have the energy to take back what I'd said. I didn't want to see his face as he decided to leave, anyway.

Mary and Patricia didn't look at me when I came back into the kitchen, but James did. He reached for my hand. I've never been so grateful to have him as I was just then.

"How much money do you owe, with everything?" James asked my sister, breaking the silence that threatened to undo us.

"Just over seventy thousand dollars. Seventy. Thousand. Dollars." She mouthed each word like saying them that way would make them less real. Or more.

"Holy cow," whispered Mary.

Patricia's mouth twisted. "He doesn't even make seventy thousand dollars a year! And he told me over and over I shouldn't get a job. No, I shouldn't work."

"You work. You take care of this house and your kids. That's plenty of work," I said. "And even if you'd had a job that paid money, you couldn't have stopped him from doing all of this."

"What am I going to do?" Patricia whispered, sounding sick.

Mom returned to the kitchen and helped herself to a cup of coffee without speaking to us. We didn't look at her, though glances flew between the four of us at the table. Patricia picked up her glass but put it down without drinking.

"I can get you the money," James said.

We all looked at him. Pride filled me, first at his willingness to help my sister. Uncertainty followed. Kinney Designs was profiting, but slowly. Most of our assets were tied up in the business, and even if we'd liquidated everything immediately, I doubted we'd come up with that sort of cash.

"We don't have that kind of money."

He shook his head. "No. But I can get it."

Patricia grabbed his hand. "We'll pay it all back, James. You know we will. No matter how long it takes."

He patted her fingers. "It'll be okay. We'll figure that out later."

I could only think of one place James could find that sort of money. One person who would be able to make a loan like that. "But how will you—"

"I know where he's staying."

"Who?" Patricia asked.

I answered for James. "His friend. Alex."

"Really? He's got that kind of money? And he'll loan it

to me?" For the first time since her phone call had woken us, Patricia sounded hopeful.

"He'll do anything for Jamie," I said, knowing it was true.

When James got up to leave, he bent to kiss me goodbye. I turned my face at the last minute, giving him my cheek instead of my mouth. I pretended it was because I was giving my attention to my sister. I didn't fool James, or myself.

My dad didn't come back. James came back briefly to give Patricia a check for enough to cover Sean's bail and assurances that as soon as the banks opened on Monday she'd have another to cover the rest of his debt. I think he was relieved to escape with her to go pick up her husband. All the tears and hugging discomfited him.

The kids were packed off to bed before Patricia returned with Sean and James. My mother put out the sandwiches nobody had wanted before. Claire had sacked out on the couch, a victim of pregnancy hormones, and Mary's phone had lured her out to the backyard for private conversation.

I wasn't hungry, but picked at the food anyway. My mother nibbled some pretzels and drank coffee, glancing at the clock every other minute. I rolled a pretzel stick in my fingers like a cigarette, then drew an imaginary puff of smoke on it.

"I'll give you a ride home, Mom."

"Your dad will be back to pick me up."

"Then Claire can drive you both home." My pseudo cigarette was stale. I bit the end anyway.

"I think Claire's going to stay here for a few days," my mother said. "To help with the kids."

"Then Mary or I or James will drive you," I said firmly. "But you're not getting in a car with Dad."

"Anne," said my mother sharply, "I think I can decide that for myself."

"Not if you're going to be stupid about it!" I snapped. "You're lucky he hasn't killed you both or someone else already!"

"You should watch your mouth."

"I'm an adult, Mother," I said. "And you know I'm right."

She didn't say anything at first, just looked down into her coffee cup. "Your dad's fine."

"Look. I don't care what he does at home or at the bar. But getting behind the wheel of a car when he's been drinking is not only stupid, it's selfish and irresponsible. If he wants to screw up his body with booze, that's his business. But when he puts other people in danger, I'm not just going to sit back and be quiet about it anymore. He's careless when he's been drinking, and he takes chances, and the worst part of it is, he never admits when he's had too much. He could get as wasted as he wants to, but he should have the goddamn balls to admit it."

My mother's face went hard and tight. "Your dad—"

I held up my hand, no longer in the mood for denial. "Mom. Save me the bullshit stories, okay? If you want to pretend that what I said isn't true, fine. I've had too many nightmares about drowning to listen."

"About drowning? What does that mean?"

I gave a heavy, heavy sigh. And, much like I'd told James everything I never had before, I told my mom about the day out on the water. She listened, her hands going tighter around the coffee cup.

"I didn't know," she said. "I never knew it was so…"

"Bad?" I shrugged. "Well. It was."

"You never said anything."

"Because you were gone. And when you came back, well, he got better again. Didn't he? Aside from the drinking and the bouts of depression and the times he just didn't show up for things like dance recitals or birthday parties. The times when we counted on him and he just wasn't there. Things got better. Didn't they?"

"Oh, Annie," my mother said.

I knew I'd sounded bitter, but I didn't bend even when guilt threatened to throttle me with its bony fingers.

"I hope it was worth it, Mom."

"Anne, you don't know—"

"Claire told me you were with another man that summer. Is that true?"

My mother lifted her chin. "Claire needs to learn to keep her mouth closed."

"Is it?"

"Yes."

I sighed, my head drooping. "I thought if I'd told you about Dad and the boat, you'd have stayed. But you wouldn't have, would you?"

"Maybe," she said. "I might have…"

She trailed off. I looked at her and saw myself in another twenty years. I hoped I wouldn't have to look so sad.

"I was in love with another man," she said. "I don't have to explain myself to you, but I will. Your father was always difficult to live with. He was a good provider, but he was moody. Up and down, all the time. He was possessive and jealous, too. He was convinced I was having an affair on our honeymoon."

I stopped myself from asking if she was.

"So I decided to prove him wrong. I just wanted him to stop berating me all the time for something I wasn't doing. I met Barry at the bowling alley. He started giving me lessons. He was your dad's friend, and interestingly enough, the only man your dad didn't accuse me of sleeping with."

"So you had an affair with him?"

"We didn't mean for it to happen, Anne. It just did." My mother sipped her coffee, which must have gone cold long before. "And I fell in love with him."

"So…you went with him. You left us behind."

"I didn't know if things were going to work with Barry. I didn't want to drag you kids back and forth. I needed a while to sort myself out. Being a mother doesn't mean you're perfect," my mother said. "I made mistakes. Barry and I didn't work like I thought. I loved your dad too much to leave him behind. Should I have dragged you kids out of your house, away from your dad and introduced you to some other man, all when I wasn't sure he was the right choice for me to make?"

"You left us!" I cried. "And he drank, all summer long! And he told us about how he was going to put rocks in his pockets and go out in the middle of the lake, or how he was going to take a gun and shoot himself in the head!"

"I'm sorry," my mother said, her fingers spread like she sought absolution. "I'm sorry, honey. I didn't know. And all I can do now is be sorry I didn't."

She was right, of course. All she could do was be sorry. She couldn't make any of it better, or take it away, or change the past.

"Why'd you choose Dad?" I asked her. "Did you really not love Barry, after all?"

"No. I did. As much as I loved your dad, but in a different way. I was a different person with Barry. But that person was a woman who didn't have four daughters and a history. He let me be someone new, but in the end…it wasn't being new that I wanted."

I had never given my mother credit for being able to express herself with such eloquence. I felt bad for dismissing her all these years. "Do you ever regret the choice you made? Do you ever think about what might have been different?"

"Of course I do. But I don't let it hold me back."

I nodded, looking down at the table. "I'm sorry, Mom."

She made a small, surprised noise. "For what?"

"For not being a better daughter."

"Oh, Anne," my mother said with a laugh. "Don't you know that to me you're perfect? Each of you is perfect?"

She hugged me then, and we cried some more. We must have been loud enough to wake Claire, who padded into the kitchen rubbing at her eyes. She put a hand on her hip.

"What the hell's going on in here?"

"Mom thinks I'm perfect."

"Screw you, bitch," said Claire. "I'm the perfect one."

My mother sighed. "Claire, for God's sake. The language. Don't talk to your sister that way."

But Claire and I were laughing and giving each other obscene hand gestures. My mother, outnumbered, could only shake her head and toss up her hands in defeat.

"You're a perfect bunch of pains in the ass," my mother said.

That was good enough for me.

Everything was working out for my sister, thanks to James's help and Alex's money. Fixing Patricia's problem, however, had created one for us. I'd promised honesty, and he'd given me lies.

Lies of omission, true, but I'd taken as much responsibility for mine as if I'd out and out told him an untruth. He'd let me believe Alex was gone. Out of our lives. Well, he'd been out of mine, all right. Just not my husband's.

The thunderstorms that had threatened all weekend hovered all day Monday, too. I stood on the deck, watching the lake grow choppy and the clouds get darker. A breeze whipped the ends of my hair, tangling it, but I didn't tie it back.

I wanted to be a warrior.

James came home from work as the first drops of water splattered on the wood at my bare feet. I didn't turn to greet him. I pulled the sleeves of my oversize sweatshirt down over my hands and tucked them close to my body. The rain made dark circles on my jeans.

"You should have told me" was all I said when I heard his footfalls in the doorway.

"You told me you'd made him go. I didn't know you'd care. I thought you wanted him gone."

"But you didn't."

"No," said James. "I guess I didn't. If I thought you could handle him being around, just not the whole sex thing, I'd have told you."

I whirled. "Fuck you!"

He recoiled. "Anne—"

I stabbed my finger at him. "No. Shut up. Fuck you, James. You say that like it was something silly. 'The sex thing.' Like it was some stupid game or something."

"That's not what I meant!"

"Then what did you mean? Oh, silly Anne, she got all tangled up with Alex because of 'the sex thing.' And then she couldn't deal with it, so she tossed him out and made him leave, but you just didn't think that was important, did you? So you kept seeing him? Behind my back? What did you boys do together, James? Get high and play video games? Did you look at porn and jerk off together? Oh, wait. I forgot. You're not queer." I sneered the last.

Rain spattered harder, still individual droplets and not a downpour. Each was cold and stung my skin. They beaded on the deck, beginning to make puddles.

"I didn't want to upset you, that's all!"

I wanted to shake him until his teeth rattled. I wanted to scream. I wanted to fill my mouth with rain so I never had to talk to him again.

"He came into our house and into our bed and he fucked with our marriage—"

"Alex didn't fuck with our marriage."

"You are absolutely right," I said. "That was you."

He lifted a finger to point, accusing, but dropped his hand. "You've already judged me. There's nothing I can say that will change your mind, so I'm not going to bother."

The wind, cold, ripped through me. I bit down to stop my teeth from chattering, and said through a clenched jaw, "You did this, James. You did it."

"And you wanted it," he snapped back. "I saw it the first time you looked at him. Like you wanted him to strip you down right there. I'm not fucking blind, you know."

"So what? You gave me to him so he wouldn't take me?"

He didn't answer.

"I wasn't yours to give!" I shouted, advancing on him. "I wasn't some princess in one of your goddamned video games, James!"

"But you wanted it!" he shouted. "Dammit, Anne, you wanted it! You wanted him!"

"But what did you want?" I asked. "Why did you want it, really?"

James turned and braced himself on the railing, his head down. A few drops of rain splattered on the back of his neck, which looked vulnerable above the collar of his denim jacket. "I don't know what you want me to say."

"Just tell me the truth."

We were at a standoff, both furious. I drew in breath after breath of stormy air, but it did nothing but left me feeling like I was suffocating. James stood up to face me. Rain slipped down his face and dripped from his chin.

"I should have told you I was still seeing him," he said, finally. "But hell, Anne, it's not like I was fucking him or anything. We just drank a few beers every once in a while. We shot some pool. We're friends, you know. It's what we do."

"So why didn't you just tell me, then? Why let me think he was gone?"

"You never talked about him. I thought you didn't want to. You never asked me if I saw him."

"I didn't know I had to ask," I said.

James gave me a helpless look. "I thought you didn't want to know."

I couldn't be surprised he might have thought such a thing. It seemed he knew me better than I'd thought he did. "I didn't ask him to leave."

He stopped. Stared. "What?"

"I didn't ask him to leave," I said. "I wanted him to stay. I asked him to stay."

James shook his head. He put a hand on the doorframe. More rain slapped us. "But you said—"

"I wanted you to think it was me that ended it. But it was him. He left. I wanted him to stay, but he left, anyway. But that doesn't really matter, does it? Because you should have told me you were seeing him."

"Yeah, because you've been nothing but balls-up honest with me the past few months," he said. "You should've told me that you were still on the shots, Anne. It might've made a big difference."

The second the words came out of his mouth, he clamped his lips shut. It was too late. I swiped water from my eyes, certain I wanted to see every nuance of his expression when he answered my question.

"What kind of difference?"

"Never mind. Forget it. It's done. We both fucked up."

"James," I said, and my voice was a warrior's voice, one without mercy. "If you knew I was on birth control and couldn't get pregnant, would you have changed the rules?"

He pushed me away with his hands, pushing at air, not touching me. I didn't move. Rain made tracks down my spine.

"Would you have said he could fuck me?"

"I don't want to talk about this anymore."

"James! Would you have let him fuck me if you'd known?"

"I don't know!" he shouted. "How do I know you never did? I know you did things when I wasn't around! How do I know you weren't fucking him every day?"

"Because we love you!" I cried. The wind came up and whipped away my words. "Because you said it was the one thing we couldn't do, and we both love you too much to hurt you like that! Why do you think he left? Why do you think I let him? Because we love you, both of us, and I love him, too, and it's nothing but the biggest mess I've ever known!"

It was a mess, but I had chosen it. I couldn't look at him anymore. I fled, down the deck and across the yard. I slipped on the wet grass and went down on my knee for a moment before I got up and ran to the sand and the water eating at it. Lightning lit the sky. Thunder, far away but coming closer, rumbled.

I waded into the lake. Water too frigid for August lapped

at my knees. I bent and splashed it on my face, trying to wash away the tears.

I thought of my dad, threatening to fill his pockets with rocks and wade out into the lake. As a child the threat had frightened me to the point of nightmares. I'd imagined my dad, hair floating like seaweed, face nibbled away by the fish, pockets bulging with stones. Sometimes it hadn't been my father, but me. As an adult I'd recognized it for the melodramatic, manipulative play for attention it was, but I still dreamed of the weight of stones holding me beneath the water.

Of how it would feel to drown.

"Anne!" The wind whipped James's voice away from me, but I still heard it.

I didn't turn. He shouted again. I lifted my face to the rain pouring down over me. Cold water from above and cold water from below.

"Anne! Get out of there!"

Lightning. Thunder. I wasn't in danger of drowning, not in knee-high water, but it was foolish to be standing outside during an electrical storm. I turned to look at him, silhouetted against the house.

I had never loved James desperately. Never without reserve. Afraid of losing him, I'd never let myself get lost in him.

He jumped off the deck, ran across the yard, down to our small strip of beach. Water splashed around me, and I winced, though my face was already wet. He grabbed me.

"Get out of there! What are you doing? Are you crazy?"

"No," I said, but because I wasn't shouting he couldn't hear me over the sound of the rain and thunder.

James pulled me toward the shore. "C'mon, let's get inside!"

I moved, but slowly, my feet numb. Everything felt numb. I stumbled, and the lake lapped at me like a friendly dog. James hauled me upright just as another blue-white flash lit the sky. Thunder rattled the ground within seconds. Electricity crackled in the air all around us. My teeth hummed. My tongue tasted like I'd licked a battery.

James yanked me upright and we stumbled out of the water. The sand, wet and cold, grated against my bare toes. The grass was slicker. More lightning lit the world around us. Though I was soaking wet, it felt like every hair on my body rose, straining toward the sky. The thunder was so loud my ears rang, and even after it faded it left the sound of the rain muted.

We made it into the house to the accompaniment of another round of thunder and lightning. James slammed the door behind us. We dripped in silence, staring at each other.

I wrapped my arms around myself to combat the chill. My teeth struggled to chatter. I gave up trying to stop them. The sound was loud.

The power went off, then flickered back. A second later it went off and didn't come back on. The next flash of lightning lit the kitchen, but neither of us had moved.

There are so few times any longer when we are fully in the dark. Even on nights without the moon, the light from the microwave or alarm clock is enough to give our eyes something to open to. Now there was nothing. The familiar landscape of my house had become a minefield, ready to stub toes and snag elbows.

I heard the slide of a drawer opening. James had found our flashlight, the one that recharged by winding a small handle and never needed batteries. I flung up a hand against the glare, which rivaled the lightning outside.

"Let's get dried off." He reached for my hand. "Follow me."

In our bedroom the patter of rain on the roof sounded louder than it had in the kitchen. It was just as dark, though, and James settled the flashlight on the dresser to illuminate the room. I lit a candle on the dresser. The scent of lilac began filling the space between us.

I pulled my shirt off and tossed it into a soggy pile, followed by my shorts and underwear. Naked, I actually felt warmer. My teeth stopped chattering. My nipples pebbled, but the gooseflesh that had humped my arms receded. I found some towels in the bathroom and used one, tossing the other to James.

I rubbed my hair as dry as I could make it, then finger-combed it. It would need a healthy dose of conditioner before I could do more than that. I liked the way it felt hanging down over my shoulders and tickling my back. I wrapped the towel around my body, tucking it under my armpit. It provided only scant coverage, hanging to just below the fluff of my pubic curls, but the plush material felt good on my skin.

"Are you going to leave me?"

The words came from behind me. I wished they'd been

said in the dark, so there could be no way I'd be able to see his face. I didn't want to turn, but when he said my name I had to.

"Are you?" he asked.

"Should I?"

"If you don't love me anymore. Yes."

"Oh, James," I said, my voice more tender than I'd imagined I could be. "I still love you."

He let out a low, strangled sob and went to his knees in front of me. He pressed his face to my stomach. I touched his hair, lightly.

"I'm sorry," he murmured. "For all of it. Everything. Please forgive me, Anne."

I'd never seen James cry. His shoulders heaved, and he grasped me around the thighs with such force I feared I might lose my balance. He wept like it hurt him. It probably did.

I couldn't stand towering over him this way. I pushed him back, but gently, and knelt in front of him. I pulled him close, and we embraced. His face fit just right against the side of my neck. I smelled rain on him, and the tang of the storm, and underneath it the same solid, clean scent that was uniquely his. He held me so tightly I couldn't breathe, but only for a moment before his grip eased. We stayed like that as the storm continued to rage outside.

"I love you." His face against mine was hot and moist. "God, I love you so much I don't know what I'd do without you. Please don't leave me, Anne. Please tell me what I can do to make all of this better."

I sat back to save my aching knees. He took my hands,

lacing our fingers snugly so I couldn't pull too far away. I didn't want to pull away, but I wanted to put some distance between us.

"I'm not going to leave you, James."

I couldn't imagine leaving him. I'd spent a lot of time anticipating that one day our love would fade, our marriage end, but I'd never been able to imagine what life would be like if that happened. I couldn't think of a life without James in it.

"If you want me to stop seeing him, I will." His thumbs passed back and forth over the backs of my hands. "Or…if you want him to come back."

That option made me shiver. "No."

James sighed, his head drooping so shadows hid his face for a moment. "He told me the same thing you did. That you ended it."

"I should have."

"Do you love him?" He looked into my eyes like he was ready for the answer, no matter what it was. "Would you rather be with him than me?"

I looked around our bedroom, smelling of lilac and thunderstorms and lit by flickering golden light as well as the harsh bright glare of the flashlight. I looked at our bed, our dresser, the desk that had once belonged to his grandmother. This was my house and home. The life we'd made for ourselves. It was perhaps not a perfect life, but it was a damned good one.

"I don't think so, James."

His laugh sounded more like a groan than a chuckle "You don't think so? You're not sure?"

I replied without quite answering. "I'm not the same person with him that I am with you."

He let go of my hands. I reached to take them back. I lifted each to my lips, kissing the familiar fingers. I pressed one to my cheek.

"I love you," I told him. "And all of this, our life, is everything I wished to have but wasn't sure I could keep. I never felt like that with Alex, James. I always knew that what we shared wouldn't last. He never belonged to me. Not the way you do."

It was a time for tears, but I didn't weep. I kissed him, instead, and held him close to me. Outside, the storm passed.

Inside, it had passed, too.

Chapter 19

*I*t was time for all the pieces to fall miraculously into place. For Evelyn to declare she'd been wrong after all and beg my forgiveness. For my father to give up drinking and melodrama. For my mother and sisters to fix their lives. For Alex to disappear forever, and James and I to live happily ever after with our white picket fence, our dog and two point five children.

Of course, none of that happened.

Something did change, though, inside myself. I stopped believing I could somehow fix it all. I didn't have to be the one to make it all better. I didn't have to be in charge. And somehow, they all managed.

The summer that had seemed so long and bright with possibility just four months ago had passed into fall. Too early for the trees to begin changing, the weather turned cool and cloudy. My yard and its lack of landscaping mocked me as a constant reminder of all the plans I'd failed to complete. I compensated by buying bags of bulbs and a special new tool designed to pull out plugs of earth just the right size for them. I bought gardening gloves, too, and special soil additives, and a watering can and a sun hat that tied beneath my chin but hung forgotten on the back of the kitchen door.

The significance of my efforts wasn't lost on me. We'd spent the summer rooting things up, James and I. Now was the time to see if we could make things grow.

"I got a call from Mary." Claire handed me another daffodil bulb. Six months along, her belly and breasts rounded like melons, she refused to bend over to help me plant but was perfectly satisfied to sit in the cool fall sunshine and watch me work. Or assist, she called it, which was to comment on my choices and hand me an occasional bulb.

I'd also had a call from Mary. No surprise, considering how attached she was to her cell phone. I made a noncommittal noise and concentrating on raking up another patch of earth with my garden trident.

"She's fine," said Claire, like I couldn't guess. "She said school's great so far."

"That's good." I swiped a hand across my forehead. The air might be cool but the work wasn't made easier for it. "How's Betts?"

"Fine. They're going to her house for Thanksgiving this year. Can't wait to see how that goes over."

"Thanksgiving." I sat back on my heels. "I think I'll cook this year. Want to come here?"

Claire rubbed a hand over her stomach. "You're not going to the Kinneys'?"

"No."

"You inviting them here?"

"I don't think so. No." I smiled.

"Then I'm here, baby. Last thing I need is the third degree from Mrs. Kinney about what I plan to do about the baby."

I reached for my bottle of water and took a long swig. "What *do* you plan to do about the baby?"

Claire took her time answering. "I'm keeping him."

I knew that already. It wasn't exactly what I'd meant to ask. "What do Mom and Dad say?"

"Mom says whatever Dad says, and he won't talk to me about it."

I smiled. "Figures."

She shrugged. "Patricia said I can stay as long as I have to, even after the baby's born."

"Saying it's easy," I said. "How are you getting along?"

She grinned. "Fine. Since she kicked Sean out, she's actually been way less uptight. That money from Alex really eased the way."

I could tell she was baiting the hook, but I chose not to take it. "Good."

"And I have the job with Alterna. They have on-site childcare. I'm only three credits from finishing my degree, and they'll do tuition reimbursement so long as I'm with them for at least a year."

"A year's a long time, Claire. Can you make that sort of commitment?" I teased.

She laughed and gave me the finger. "I'm not marrying the job, Anne."

I worked a while longer, until my back and knees ached. My fingers ached, too, from gripping the tools. I groaned and stretched until my joints popped and cracked. I stood, surveying the work I'd done.

"It looks good." Claire gave me two thumbs-up. "It'll be really pretty in the spring."

It was hard to see beauty in the patches of bare earth. I had difficulty envisioning how the dry, papery bulbs I'd planted would bloom into clusters like the pictures on the mesh bags that had contained them. I was glad I had my sister there to show me.

We both looked up at the crunch of tires on the gravel. I was expecting James, but the blue car pulling into the drive didn't look familiar. At least not to me.

"It's Dean!"

I'd seen Claire show enthusiasm for movies or rock stars or television programs. I'd never seen her look the way she did about the young man stepping out of the car in my driveway. Her entire face lit. I noticed something else, too, how she put her hands on her belly, almost by reflex.

She turned to me. "Umm...do you mind if I don't stay for dinner? I didn't think he'd be off work this early."

I gave her a raised eyebrow. "Dean?"

She actually blushed, something I'd never seen her do. Ever. "He's a friend."

"Uh-huh."

He strode toward us, hands in his pockets. Tall and lean, with sandy hair and a spray of freckles I could see across his nose as he got closer, Dean was not the sort of emo goth boy Claire usually favored. Then again, I supposed the principal of a local school wouldn't have fit her profile, either.

"Claire," Dean said, a tinge of the South in his voice. "I finished early. Thought I'd see if you wanted to come to dinner with me, after all."

He looked at me, then held out his hand. "Hi. I'm Dean."

He had a firm, warm handshake I returned. "Anne. Claire's sister."

She rolled her eyes. "Duh, Anne, like I didn't tell him that already when I told him where I'd be and how to get here."

Dean had a nice smile, the sort that crinkled up his eyes at the corners. He was looking at my sister like she was something precious. I liked him right away.

"Claire was going to stay for dinner here," I said, making mischief. "You're welcome to join us."

They answered at the same time, him with a "Sure," and her with a "No, thanks." They stopped and looked at each other, spoke again with the response the other had given. We all laughed.

"Relax," I told her. "I won't embarrass you. I promise. And I'll keep James in line, too."

The truth was, I didn't want to eat dinner alone with my husband. Having a buffer made it easier to deal with the strain between us. Left to ourselves, we'd been tending to long stretches of quiet that weren't angry…just sad. I wasn't sure what was going to happen to us. We didn't feel over. The problem was, we didn't feel much of anything else, either.

Claire looked hesitant. I'd met some of her previous dates, even a boyfriend or two, but though she'd often bragged or overshared about her extravagant love life, she'd kept most of it hidden. We had teased her a lot about being embarrassed by us, her sisters, when we knew it was probably half-true.

"I wouldn't mind," Dean said.

I wondered how long she'd been seeing him, and what sort of man would begin dating a pregnant woman. "It's lasagna, Claire. And garlic bread."

She groaned, a hand on her stomach. "That's right. Bribe me. My sister makes the best damn lasagna, Dean. And garlic bread to die for."

"It's my one talent," I told him.

He smiled at us both. "Sounds like it's a plan, then, doesn't it?"

Claire chewed her lower lip for a moment, then nodded. "Sure. Okay. But no asking Anne about stories from when I was a kid and no sharing old photo albums, you got it?"

Neither of us looked threatened, even though she'd put on a tough face. Dean made an *X* with his fingers on his chest. "Cross my heart."

"Anne?" She stabbed a finger at me.

"Don't look at me," I said, innocent. "I don't even have any embarrassing stories about you. Well, if you don't count the time you—"

"Anne!"

"Relax, l'il sissy," I said. "Your secrets are safe with me."

She started to give me the finger, but with a glance at Dean turned it into the shaking of her fist. Interesting, that.

I dusted off my hands. "I'm going to grab a quick shower. You guys can help yourselves to something to drink and the TV, if you want."

I made the shower longer than quick. Standing under the hot water felt so good I didn't want to get out. It pounded away at the knots in my shoulders and back and covered up the sounds from outside until all I could hear was the pounding of water all around me. By the time I'd finished, steam had turned the bathroom into a cloud-bank.

"Hey."

James's low greeting startled me so much as I came out of the bathroom that I jumped and whacked my elbow on the doorframe. I clutched my towel around me. He must have just arrived home, because he hadn't yet even changed his clothes.

"Hi," I said.

We stared at each other for a moment before I broke my gaze to search in my drawer for some underwear. James stripped out of his clothes and tossed them into the laundry basket. I watched him as I stepped into my panties and pulled them up, then hooked my bra.

The summer hadn't changed him much. He was leaner, harder, a little more bronzed on his arms from his work on the construction sites. He was still the same man I'd made love to with such passion only a few months ago. He moved the same, and smelled the same, and spoke the same. We were both the same, yet different. Once, I'd stared at him sleeping as my heart tumbled in my chest with wonder at how lucky I was to have him. Now I watched him stripping and felt the same twisting sensation, the rolling dip of the first hill on the roller coaster.

He caught me looking. "Anne?"

I shook myself a little and turned to find a pair of jeans and a T-shirt. "Are you going to take a shower? Dinner'll be ready in about five minutes."

"Yeah, I need one."

I felt his eyes on me as I tugged the jeans over my hips and buttoned them. "Did you see Claire and her friend?"

"Yeah. Dean. He seems nice."

"Yes." I found a T-shirt, soft and faded, that wasn't mine. My fingers passed it by and found another.

"Is he her boyfriend?"

I pulled on the T-shirt and looked at James, still so comfortable in his nudity. "I don't know."

He smiled. "Are you going to ask her?"

"Not with him around, no. I promised not to embarrass her. And that you wouldn't, either."

"Okay, okay." He held up his hands as he backed into the bathroom. "I'll behave."

"Good. Or else you'll be in trouble."

He paused, eyes gleaming. "Ooh. What'll you do, give me a spanking?"

"You wish." I smiled and tossed my damp towel at him. "Hang this up."

He bowed. "Your wish is my command."

"Wouldn't that be nice?" I said before I realized how it would sound.

James straightened, towel shielding him. "Anne…"

"The oven's pinging." I flashed him a smile meant to ease his mind but which probably didn't, and ducked out of the room.

I'd put the lasagna on warm and now only needed to

finish toasting the bread and tossing the salad, two tasks
with which Claire and Dean were willing to help. I set the
table and poured iced tea. By the time James had come
out of the shower, dinner was ready.

It was a nice meal. Dean proved to be well-spoken and
funny. He and Claire had an interesting dynamic. She was
softer around him, but not like she was trying to change
her personality. More like he brought out another side of
it. He and James hit it off, talking about sports and tools
and things about which Claire and I had no opinions. I was
content not to talk much, anyway.

Although I'd convinced her to stay for dinner, I couldn't
manage to get my sister to agree to stay to watch a movie.
Her response to my offer was a typical rolling of the eyes.
She plunked the lasagna pan into the hot soapy water and
dried her hands before stepping away.

"As if," she said. "Dean's taking me to the movies."

"Oh, a real date?" I looked into the den, where James
was showing Dean some sort of sports memorabilia. "Look
at that. James. Dean. James Dean."

And I was thinking of Alex again.

"Good one, Anne." Claire patted my shoulder. "Very
clever."

I nodded and turned my attention to the sink full of dirty
dishes. "What can I say? I'm a pundit."

The patting of my shoulder turned into a one-armed
hug. "You okay?"

"Sure. Fine." I smiled at her. "Always am, aren't I?"

She blew a raspberry at me. "You're a shitty liar."

"How long have you known him? Dean?"

She chewed her lower lip again, a mannerism that reminded me of Mary. "A couple years."

I was so surprised I could only stare at her. "What?"

She looked guilty, another unusual expression for her. "You heard me."

"But...you didn't..."

"Date him? No." Her smile turned a little secretive as she looked at him. "It never worked out until now."

"Is it working out now?" I had to ask. She wasn't just my younger sister, she was my baby sister.

"I think so. Yeah." She looked over at him again, and her gaze softened. "Yeah."

"Good for you. And he doesn't care about the baby?"

"Actually, he does care about the baby, Anne," Claire said wryly. "Which is a pretty important thing to care about, don't you think?"

"Yes. Smartass."

"I'm not marrying him or anything. Don't get your hopes up just yet."

"It's just nice to see you with someone who makes you happy, that's all, Claire." I'd have hugged her, but soap-suds covered my hands.

Claire looked toward the den, at the two men so deep in conversation. She looked back at me. "I wish I could say the same about you."

I nodded after a moment. "I'll be fine. We'll be fine. It's just a rough patch, that's all."

She leaned in. "Might it have something to do with a certain someone?"

It was my turn to roll my eyes. "What do you think?"

"I think," she said seriously, "you're going to have to find a way to let him go. Or else you'll both stay miserable."

I reached for a dishtowel and dried my hands. "I know. Believe me, I do. And it would be easy to blame this all on him, Claire, but it's not all about him."

"You know Alex told Pats he wouldn't charge her interest and she only has to pay him back a hundred bucks a month until she can do more."

"Did he? That was generous. Is that supposed to help me?"

She shook her head. "No. I'm just saying...that day I came over and you two were in the kitchen?"

I wasn't sure I wanted to talk about that day. "Yes?"

"I never saw you look that way at anyone before, that's all."

I'd thought I'd been careful not to look at him at all. "And?"

She shrugged, looked again toward James, then back to me. "It was nice to see you with someone who made you happy, that's all."

I managed a small, slightly bitter smile. "Déjà vu."

"Yeah," she said with a laugh. "I'm fucking with the matrix."

"He's gone," I answered in a low voice. "It's better this way. It's just going to take time, that's all. Things happen sometimes that don't turn out the way you intend them to."

Claire patted her belly. "Tell me about it."

The men looked like they were finishing their fascinating discussion about baseball or whatever. I lifted my chin and took a deep breath. "Have a good time at the movies."

"We will." She looked at James and Dean, who were still talking as they turned toward the kitchen. "Think about what I said, Anne."

"Find a way to let him go. Yeah, I know. It shouldn't be so hard, Claire, since he's already gone."

"Anne," my sister said with another pat on my shoulder, "you assumed when I said *him* I meant Alex."

I was quiet after my sister left with her new beau. James put on some soft music and began to clear the table. I concentrated on washing the lasagna pan, which didn't need to be returned to a gleaming state of near-newness in order to be clean, but which I scrubbed fiercely anyway.

Let him go. Let one of them go. Knowing it and doing it, two separate accomplishments. Let one man go. The question had to be, which one?

James brought the baking sheet from the garlic bread to the sink and slid it into the water. He put his arms around me. His breath caressed my neck, and a moment later his mouth brushed my skin. I leaned back against him, my eyes closed.

We stayed that way for a minute, saying nothing. The songs playing through the stereo weren't favorites, but they were slow and gentle. We swayed a little. James put his hands on my hips and turned me, soapy hands and all. We danced there in the kitchen, saying nothing. Perhaps having nothing to say.

The phone rang. We both looked at it, but neither of us moved to answer it. The machine picked up after two rings.

And he spoke.

"Hey...it's me. I just wanted to tell you that I'm finished here in Sandusky. The folks from Cleveland came through with the deal. I'm going to be overseeing their corporate offices in Tokyo. So I'm heading back out of the country. Just thought I'd let you know. Both of you. And I wanted to say..."

There was a long, long moment of silence in which James and I stayed frozen in place, listening.

"I wanted to say thanks for the summer," Alex said.

I thought there would be more. My mind insisted there must be more than that, the casual dismissal of our summer together. Something more important in his farewell than the one he left, but the call clicked off with nothing further.

I opened my mouth to say something, but the words lodged in my throat like barbs. All that came out was a small hiss of air. I looked up at James, who was looking at the phone.

He let go of me and went to the counter where the answering machine sat, its blinking light refusing to allow us to pretend we hadn't received a message. I knew he was going to pick up the phone and return Alex's call. I knew it in my gut, the way I knew the color of my eyes or how it felt to stub my toe against the dresser on my way to the bathroom in the dark. I knew it without a doubt.

James pushed the button on the machine. Alex's voice started speaking again. James pushed another button.

He deleted the message.

He turned to me. "Let's go to bed," he said, and so we did.

* * *

I'd never been to the Hotel Breakers before. I'd never needed to stay in the Point's oldest hotel, though I'd often passed by its white-painted grandeur while walking along the beach.

It had an old-style elegance about it, with a beautiful open rotunda and access to the beach. It was a hotel with history. The park was still open on weekends, and outside the roar and screams of the riders on coasters filtered through air crisp with autumn, but inside the hotel it was very quiet. Serene.

Alex opened the door after my first knock. He couldn't have been expecting me, but he didn't look startled to find me. He didn't step aside at first to let me in. When he did, it was with a begrudging sigh that might have been meant to make me feel guilty but failed.

The sound of the door closing behind me was very loud, and very final. If there was a chance of my walking away, it ended with the click of the lock. I had to close my eyes for only one moment, took only one deep breath. When I opened them, he was still there. I'd been half-afraid I was dreaming.

"Does Jamie know you're here?"

"Yes."

"He does?" He mustn't have been expecting a positive answer.

Alex ran a hand over his hair then down to cup the back of his neck. He wore a pink shirt, unbuttoned, and familiar jeans. Bare feet. I wanted to get on my knees and kiss each of his toes. I didn't move.

"Fuck," he muttered, without looking at me.

"Exactly."

This made him look up, sharp and fast, with eyes like a fox. His hand came away from his neck and fell open at his side like he wanted to grab something but wasn't certain what. His mouth parted, but he said nothing. He just looked at me with those gray eyes.

"I have to know something, Alex." My fingers went to the buttons at my throat and eased them open, one by one. "Do you want to fuck me?"

He said nothing, not even when I shrugged out of my shirt and tossed it to the floor. Not when I put my fingers to the zipper and button of my long denim skirt and eased it over my hips. I stood before him in my bra and panties, not the sexy lingerie one might expect of a woman about to seduce a man but simple, soft cotton.

He burned me with his gaze, but I didn't cower or back away from it. I held open my arms. "Do you?"

He grabbed me, hard, a roughness I'd anticipated but which nevertheless caused me to gasp. "Is that why you're here?"

I didn't struggle in his grip, though his fingers pinched my upper arms. "Yes. It is."

He drew me closer. I hadn't forgotten what it was like to be in his arms. Every piece of him fit every piece of me, no fumbling, no awkwardness.

"Jamie's my best friend," he whispered in my ear.

His conscience might have issues with this, but his cock had no such qualms. It pressed me through the denim. I remembered the feeling of him in my hands and against my body. In my mouth. I shivered at the memory of his taste.

"He's my husband," I whispered back.

His hair had grown out a little, the fringes of it over his ears a ticklish touch against my skin. We stayed that way, both of us breathing hard, cheek to cheek. He eased his touch on my arms, setting me loose. I didn't move away.

He groaned, pulling away to let his gaze travel over my face. He focused on my lips, first. Then my eyes. "Why, Anne? Why now?"

"Because I want to," I answered simply. "Because you're going away."

When he didn't answer, I pushed his shirt off his shoulders. Down his arms, past each wrist, over his hands. When his chest was bare I slid my palms over his skin. His nipples pebbled under my touch and gooseflesh humped his skin. I leaned forward, my arms around his waist, and put my cheek against him, over his heart.

"Because I have to let you go," I said at last. "You have to go."

He put his arms around me and held me tight against him. His fingers traced the jut of my shoulder blades. "I'm going. It's better this way."

"It's not," I whispered. "But that's okay."

I looked up, then put my hands on his face to draw him down to me. I kissed him, slowly and without mercy, giving him no chance to pull away. His hands tightened on my waist at first, then relaxed. Our mouths opened. Tongues met. I breathed him in.

The bed was only a few short steps away, but we took

our time getting there. I opened his zipper and reached inside, found his heat. I stroked him, no easy task inside his jeans. He broke our kiss to put his forehead on mine, his eyes closed.

"Anne," he said. Nothing else. I waited for there to be more, and when there wasn't I smiled and hooked my fingers in his waistband and pulled his jeans down all the way. I knelt before him and helped him step out of them.

He was naked and I was not, but I was the one on my knees. His cock rose, hard, and my hands and mouth found him without effort. He groaned again, louder. His fingers twisted in my hair as he pushed into my mouth. I slid my hand down his shaft, then weighed his balls with my palm.

There are few times when we know with absolute certainty we are going to do something for the last time. Life has a way of moving in circles, bringing us back to places we didn't expect and taking us away from those we do. There are too many times we don't pay close enough attention, and moments are lost in our assumption we'll have another chance.

I was not going to lose this moment with Alex. This was not an exploration of his body; I knew it already. I was paying attention. This would be the first and last time. I didn't want to lose a single detail.

His fists curled in my hair, tugging. I left my worship of his prick to sit back on my heels. He looked down at me, one of his hands moving to cup my jaw. His eyes gleamed. His mouth glistened from my kisses. He passed his hand over my cheek, then over the mass of curls. I closed my

eyes briefly at that caress. When I opened them, he held
out a hand for me to take. I stood.

Alex led me to the bed, pausing first to pull the com-
forter all the way down. The sheets beneath were white
and cool. The bed, soft. He laid me down with firm but
gentle hands, and covered me with his body while he
kissed me.

The thin barrier of my panties meant that every time
he rubbed against me, the friction on my clit doubled. I
opened my thighs and hooked my legs over his calves,
pressing his body harder against mine. Our kisses got
harder, too. Hungrier. We ate each other and made a meal
of our passion.

His mouth moved down my throat. He bit my shoulder.
I arched, crying out, and he licked me there. His weight
pinned me, but I didn't feel trapped. I wanted to be there,
beneath him. Around him.

Alex nuzzled my collarbone, nibbled the tender flesh
of my breast above the edge of my bra, used his teeth to
pull down my strap. He pushed his hands under me to
unhook it. When it came free he slid it over my arms and
threw it away without watching where it landed. His eyes
on mine, he cupped my breasts. When his thumbs passed
over my nipples, tight with longing, I let out a sound that
would have been embarrassing under any other circumstances.

"I know how to touch you," he said.

"Yes. You do."

He smiled with one corner of his mouth. "I want to hear
you make that sound again."

He didn't have to work too hard for it. I gave him what he wanted and was glad to do it. He replaced his hands with his mouth, sucking gently first on one nipple and then the other. His hands found other places to rest. A hip. A thigh. My belly. Under a knee. We rolled with each other, finding positions that pleased us.

Though we weren't covering new ground, and though this time we knew the end would be different, we didn't rush. Every touch, every kiss, every stroke and lick and suck each had its moment.

Alex was paying attention, too.

At last he lay on top of me, his prick rubbing my clit with every small half thrust. We were panting, hearts pounding. We'd pushed each other to the edge again and again, each time drawing back at the last possible moment before we spilled the other into climax.

Even pleasure can hurt if it's unrelenting. Every nerve in my body ached and sizzled with tension. Each kiss and touch sent shudders through me. The universe had become Alex's mouth and hands and cock.

He moved. I opened for him. He slid against me, the head of his erection slick from my wetness. He stopped, licking his mouth and taking a deep breath. His arms trembled as he held himself up. I shifted, tilting my hips to ease his way.

He pushed inside me one inch at a time instead of one full thrust. We were looking into each other's eyes when he'd seated himself all the way. I saw myself reflected there.

It wasn't fair how fast I came. I felt cheated. My body

betrayed me by responding too quickly to the pressure of his pubic bone on my clit and the thrust of him inside me. His mouth captured every cry I made. I unraveled from the pleasure, and his kisses wove me back together so I could come apart again.

I didn't count the number of times I came. It might have been once or a dozen times, so sensitized had I become to Alex moving within me. We made love forever, which didn't seem long enough but was all the time we had.

He slowed at the end, taking twice as long with each push and pull, in and out. He licked my mouth. Our bodies glued to each other. I wrapped my legs and arms around him, keeping him as close to me as I could. If I could have melded our bodies into one, I'd have done it just then, when pleasure filled me again and he shuddered with his own climax.

We came together at the end, in one of those times when everything works out right and nothing could ever be wrong. It was magic, ecstatic, electric.

Perfect.

After, we lay side by side in the big hotel bed and stared at the ceiling. Our hands linked at our sides. From outside I heard the rattle and clank of the roller-coaster train reaching the top of the hill, the moment of silence, and the rush and roar and screams of its descent.

It couldn't last forever. It wasn't meant to. So at last I rolled onto my side to face him. I let myself drink in the lines and curves of his face.

There were things we could have said, but it was enough

for me to kiss him one last time. I didn't ask permission to use his shower, just did anyway. I rinsed him off my body.

He hadn't moved when I came out of the bathroom wrapped in a towel. I dried myself and found my clothes. I put them on. Alex watched me without saying anything. I was glad for his silence. It made leaving easier.

Dressed, I pulled my fingers through my curls and used my reflection in his mirror to pull it into a semblance of order. I pulled powder, mascara and lipstick from my purse and gave myself the face of someone else. I smoothed my clothes. I stepped away.

I looked at him, and he hadn't moved.

"Goodbye, Alex," I said at last. "I hope you'll be happy."

He didn't answer. I wanted him to say goodbye. Say something. But he was a rugged rascal even at the end. He gave me a half nod and a half smile and left me wondering if I had risked everything for a few hours of useless lust. If that's all it had ever been. If I'd made a mistake in going there.

"Anne," he said when my hand reached the doorknob.

I stopped but didn't turn.

"When I said Jamie was the only one who'd ever made me understand how it could be to love someone..."

I turned and looked at him for the very last time.

"...he wasn't the only one."

I have only one regret about that day, and it's that my last vision of Alex was blurred by tears.

I closed the door behind me and stood in the hall outside as I caught my breath. Then I straightened my back and wiped my face. The beach outside was bigger and cleaner than the one by my house, but the water was the same. Cold and choppy, it darkened my skirt up to my knees. I'd gone to say goodbye, and I had done that. I had gone to let him go, and I'd done that, too. It was not a happy ending of the sort in fairy tales, but it was the only one we had.

"Be happy," I whispered to the water.

Perfection is too high a goal to strive for. Sometimes working hard brings more satisfaction in the end. We appreciate what we've almost lost more than what we've never doubted. James waited for me at home. I had a life there with him. With our children, if we had them. It was not a perfect life, but it would be a good one, if we both worked hard to make it so. My husband waited for me, and I would go to him in time.

For that moment, just then, I stood in the water with the wind blowing in my face, and I no longer feared I'd drown.